This book should be returned to any Lancashire ¹⁰/22
County Council Library on or before the date shown

2 2 AUG 2023

GW00471184

RUBIK'S CUBE ™

SOLVE THE PUZZLE,
SAVE THE WORLD

Christoper Beach

Matador
Unit E2 Airfield Business Park,
Harrison Road, Market Harborough,
Leicestershire. LE16 7UL
Tel: 0116 2792299
Email: books@troubador.co.uk
Web: www.troubador.co.uk/matador
Twitter: @matadorbooks

ISBN 978 1803130 644

British Library Cataloguing in Publication Data.
A catalogue record for this book is available from the British Library.

Printed and bound in Great Britain by 4edge Limited
Typeset in 10pt Baskerville by Troubador Publishing Ltd, Leicester, UK

Matador is an imprint of Troubador Publishing Ltd

With all my love I dedicate this book to my
darling Dee and our wonderful son, Sam.

■　■　■

In loving memory of Alan Flude,
11.3.1962 to 2.4.2021

ONE

TIME FOR SUMMER FUN

PRESENT DAY

The early morning rays of the sun were just breaking over the San Gabriel Mountains, glowing through the pearlescent haze that hung in the air. There was a knock-knock on the door.

'Time to get up, Ruben, it's time for school,' chirped Mum brightly as she crossed the landing.

Those dreaded school-day morning words had once again crowbarred their way into another of Ruben's weird teenage fantasies. From under the snug duvet, a fumbling hand searched for the TV remote. Seconds later, the huge screen exploded into action, unlike his

1

foggy brain. Quickly muting the sound, there she was at the foot of his bed, Chynna White, the gorgeous Channel44 weather girl. Peering through his sleepy eyes, his mind began to drift into the realms of the improbable, with him centre stage and Chynna on his arm. He wasn't interested in what the weather was doing, he was more interested in what her hips were doing, as she made elaborate hand gestures over the weather map. Slowly his hand moved back under the duvet to take up its comfort position.

'How's Chynna looking this morning?' Mum's voice disturbed his thoughts once again. 'You haven't got time for *that* Ruben, get in the shower,' called Ruben's mum, Sarah.

How does she know this stuff? puzzled Ruben. Resigning himself to the inevitability of his day ahead, he threw back the duvet and got out of bed. He paused for a few moments to look at the latest acquisition in his collection. His bedroom was a shrine to music. In the corner was his electronic drum kit, with his desktop music studio, keyboard and monitor speakers, with various guitars dotted around gathering dust. For his eighteenth birthday Dad had given him a 1962 Salmon Pink Fender Stratocaster guitar. It *was* Dad's, but now it was his, given to him with the immortal lines, 'I don't think I will be needing this anymore and I know I can trust you to look after it.'

Ruben was turning into quite a good player, even though he continually pretended to ignore his dad's attempts at teaching him. Walking to the en-suite, he gently brushed the open strings into life.

'An A11/E or a E9/6. See, I do know my theory Dad,' he chuckled to himself. 'Cool chord, I must use that sometime.'

No-one was listening. Once inside the shower cubicle, Ruben waved his hand over the shower sensor and a warm spray of water enveloped him.

Downstairs in the kitchen, breakfast was underway. Mum was swishing round in her satin dressing gown multitasking like it was going out of fashion, with one eye on the toaster, the other on the local weather girl that Ruben had been drooling over upstairs. *She is very pretty,* she thought, as she put the cereal boxes out on the table. Just then Ján (pronounced "Yan"), walked into the kitchen.

'A decaf skinny mochachocca frappuccino caffè latte, for you János darling?' joked Sarah in a mock posh voice, as she spun round to greet him.

'Yes, that sounds good. Thanks, honey,' replied Ján, as he planted a tender kiss on her cheek, then sat down at the table. 'Today is going to be a tough one, I have to sort budgets etcetera and I am really up against it. That asteroid cluster we are watching is getting very close and I need to be there. It is getting quite interesting.'

Sensing his frustration, Sarah handed Ján a cup of coffee. 'I'm sure it'll be fine.'

He took a sip and smiled at her. She always made his coffee just right, strength, temperature, colour, everything perfect. She was perfect and could always soothe his troubles away. That's why he loved her.

Ján was always scribbling ideas down in his notebook and this morning was no different. He was usually coming up with some crazy design idea. Modern technology still couldn't beat the feel of real analogue doodling with an old pen. He had tried many times to replicate the sensation in a digital format but had given up on that one, for now.

'That's it. That's it. I think I have finally solved the problem that has troubled man since the dawn of time,' explained Ján overly enthusiastically.

'And what's that, Ján?' enquired Sarah.

'A toaster that never burns the bread, ever,' he announced proudly. 'What it needs is a 3D textural surface analysis circuit, that monitors the drying process in real time, and automatically switches off when the moisture level and surface texture map align precisely. Simple.'

'Good idea... dear... toast dear? I'm sure in years to come people will remember János Novak as the man who invented the perfect toaster,' she mocked slightly sarcastically, as she placed a plate in front of him. Ján looked at the pile of alarmingly perfect toast, ripped the page from his notepad and tossed it in the direction of the bin. Nanoseconds before impact the lid of the waste disposal unit flipped open ready to catch the scrunch of paper. All joking aside, Sarah knew Ján had been and was still, a very successful designer and genius inventor.

'Today's wasted effort award goes to János "No-hope" Novak,' he announced. 'Back to the perennial drawing board I think, if I can find it.'

Just then Kat walked in. Ruben and her were twins, and luckily looks-wise she took after Mum. *How can someone look so fantastic this early in the morning? It must be genetic*, Ján thought, glancing at his wife. It was true Katarina was pretty, had style by the industrial-sized bucket load, and just knew what to wear and how to wear it, and more importantly, sometimes how to get away with almost not wearing it.

'Hi Dad,' she said, as she gave him a little kiss on the cheek, sat at the table and put her phone down. 'Mum, is there any coffee going?'

'Yes, Kat darling. Now make sure you have a proper breakfast. It's the most important meal of the day. A healthy inside makes for a healthy outside.' Sarah was living proof that was true.

János turned to the doorway as he could hear a strange rumbling sound getting louder, and it was not his pre-breakfast tummy. It was coming from the hallway. Seconds later Ruben appeared riding his skateboard into the kitchen, and with a jump and a clever flip he caught the board and put it by the back door.

'Huh... kids!' Dad rolled his eyes and tut-tutted.

'Hi, sis. On the Natural Honey Crunch Rabbit Sawdust again?' Pointing to Katarina's bowl of cereal, Ruben laughed.

'Yes, drowned in low fat soya non-drip satin finish milk substitute,' she replied, quite pleased with her witty retort.

Ruben, unlike Katarina, had no real idea about style. He had a strange view on what constituted being cool and today Kat thought he was definitely a good few miles wide of the mark. As twins they were quite different, but deep down they had a genuine, almost spooky closeness that gave them each great comfort and strength.

Katarina slowly shook her head. 'I don't know what Frankie sees in you, bruv...'

'Have you got your life support system with you?' asked Ruben.

'Err, yes I have my phone, if that's what you mean?'

Mum interrupted. 'Now you two, I am going into the office late today, so you will have to catch the bus. You'll need to hurry up.'

Juggling five pieces of fruit, she then threw them in the smoothie maker – that was her breakfast sorted.

'Where's my phone? It was here a minute ago,' panicked Kat.

'Oh, here it is in my pocket,' laughed Ruben. 'Were you worried? Have you missed a call from Dan?'

'Give it back, you and your stupid tricks.'

'The quickness of the hand deceives the eye,' quoted Ruben.

'Okay you two, enough,' interrupted Mum sternly.

Before long it was 08:00 and time for Ján to head to work, and for the twins to go to school. Ján went down the hallway and turned left into his office, which actually looked more like a bombsite than a workplace. Under the mountains of papers, pads and books was his desk. Somewhere on his desk was his laptop, he hoped. Now he had to find his case. That could be anywhere. After a bit of digging he found it. Carefully placing his thumb on the lock's scanner, it bleeped and released the catch. To open Ján's case you needed to be the owner of Ján's thumb. If the case was tampered with the contents would be vapourised. This of course meant it could not be listed on the home contents insurance policy. He put his laptop and a few files inside, then clicked it shut. *I really must tidy this room one day*, he thought. Yet again, today was not *that* day. Picking up his jacket from the back of his seat, he walked out and closed the door behind him.

'When are you going to tidy that room, Ján?' called Sarah from the kitchen. 'I know where Ruben gets his *messy gene* from.'

'Soon, I promise,' he stalled.

Going back into the kitchen he saw Sarah standing by the sink gazing out across the manicured garden where the ducks were splashing around in the pond.

Oblivious that the twins were still there, he crept up behind her, put his arms around her waist, gave her a loving squeeze and a tender kiss on the neck.

'See you later, Mrs Novak,' he whispered.

'Mum, Dad, we are still here you know... gross out,' winced Katarina. 'Get a room, you've got enough to choose from.'

The Novak house was indeed quite a size. Ján and Sarah gave each other a knowing smile.

'Bye kids. Have fun. Last day at school – all right for some. Anyway, as I always say, I am off into S.P.A.C.E.' Ján smirked at his own pun.

'Yes, hilarious. It was rib-bustlingly funny the first time, reasonably amusing the second time, but eight years down the road I think it's time you got a new script writer, Dad,' quipped Ruben.

However, it made János smile every time and that was every day, unfortunately. They all knew it stood for Sustaining Population Advancement & Catastrophe Evaluation. In short, what it really meant was that Ján was looking for another planet for humans to colonize. It was a common view that humankind was making a mess of the planet and ultimately may have to think about leaving Earth, if they can't save it. That was *his* work.

At the garage door he placed his thumb on the scanner and spoke.

'Rosanna, all I want to do when I wake up in the morning is see your eyes.'

'That's nice. Good morning Mr Novak, what can I do for you this morning?'

'Umm, open the side garage door please.'

Rosanna was the voice-activated computer system that controlled the workings of the house, and Ján had programmed a synthesized voice that sounded amusingly like Sarah. The huge door slowly started to lift revealing a cavernous garage packed with stuff, loads of stuff, loads and loads of stuff. It was true to say Ján was a bit of a hoarder. However, the garage housed his most prized possession: a 1962 metallic bronze, 3.8litre, MK2, Jaguar car. It was immaculate in every way. He remembered as a child his grandad having one. He loved to ride around in it, he enjoyed sliding around on the red leather seats that squeaked comically. He told himself one day he would have his own. Ján made many such promises to himself when he was young. The car was very rare in America and only imported from the UK by very wealthy people. He loved cars, always had. After years of searching eBay and on the net, he had eventually found his grandad's *actual* car. After an expensive structural restoration job there was also a need for a massive engine redesign, reconditioned running gear and the fitting of a completely new electric drive train and eco battery system, mostly done by Ján. It now stood proudly in his garage. It was his weekend fun car.

However, today was a work day, so he jumped in his old 4X4, grinding the gears, he slowly reversed onto the drive, then gazed back at their wonderful house.

Even now, Ján was very proud of their home. It had been an ambition of Sarah's, whilst at University, to one day, design and build their dream home. There it was, standing proud, in all its morning glory, just the way she had designed it in her little student room all those years ago. As well as being a stylish architectural statement, it also housed a dazzling array of technological gizmos and features, or "boys toys", as Sarah called them, designed by Ján.

With a quick look in the mirror, he backed down the drive onto the road and whizzed off in a plume of grey steam. *I must sort this heap out*, he thought. As he disappeared up the avenue, a black SUV slowly pulled out from the curb and set off.

Ján was quite a visionary genius. His rise through the ranks was fast, to say the least. He had dazzled the world on more than one occasion and now was head of S.P.A.C.E. at The World Heritage Trust(TWHT), a charitable organisation committed to helping save the world from self-destruction. It was an immensely important position that Ján relished. He was a wonder with technology but couldn't use a hairbrush to save his life, which meant he sometimes looked a bit unkempt, or bonkers! This look was further enhanced by the fact that his eyes were different colours. As a result of running into a clenched fist at school he was left with a damaged retina which gradually turned a shade of deep purple. Ján had also become a bit of a reluctant media celebrity who had become the go-to person when a soundbite was needed for a relevant TV news article. This had led to him having a small cameo in a sci-fi movie a few years back and scored him a lot of cool points with Sarah and the kids.

■　■　■

Sarah had been a part of his life for a long time. They had met at university where she was studying Architectural Design and Restoration, whilst Ján was doing Bio-Mechanical Quantum Physics and Brewing. The first time Sarah saw Ján he was playing guitar in a progressive art-rock band called *De Styjl,* in the main hall on campus. They were a bunch of long-haired musician types playing their brand of hi-art rock music, with rather long intricate solos weaving in and out of the resultant cacophony spectacularly played by Ján, who interestingly, had short hair. It was during one of his fanciful solos that Ján caught sight of Sarah down at the front. In that brief heart-stopping moment he fluffed his hammer-on sequence and had to grab the tremolo arm and bend a popped harmonic into oblivion. *Cool*, he thought. She smiled at him. His guitar had woven its magic on her.

It wasn't long before Ján and Sarah were an item and they settled into university life together. It was during this time that Sarah first dipped her toe into the world of modelling. One of her friend's mother was quite taken by Sarah's fresh beauty and thought with her help she could earn some extra cash. Little did she realize just how successful Sarah would go on to be.

■ ■ ■

After an eternity crawling through the busy streets of Pasadena, the city sprawl of LA began to thin out. He cruised along Highway 210 towards Canada Flintridge and, as he started to wind his way up through the hills, he began slowing down. As he approached the interchange, glancing in his rear view mirror, Ján caught a glimpse of the black SUV he had seen earlier that morning. Quickly changing lanes, the vehicle continued to shadow him as he headed onto the Angeles Crest Highway. Gradually the rugged road began to snake its way up into the mountains. The golden ball of sun was slowly climbing in the massive cobalt blue sky. The views from the road, over the mountains, were stunning and he always enjoyed the drive. Playing on the car hi-fi was classic Zeppelin – Ján couldn't deny his roots. His car was the only place he could get away with listening to "dad rock". Kat wouldn't let him play it within her earshot. Sarah wasn't keen and Ruben was very fussy about his music too.

The top of Mount Wilson was coming into view, which meant he was nearly at work. He decided to drive past the S.P.A.C.E. entrance checkpoint. There seemed to be a lot of police around. He drove to the nearby service station, parked, jumped out and walked inside. Picking up a paper, he made his way to the till. As he slipped his card into the machine, he looked out to see the SUV parked across the road. Ján saw a glint of light flash inside the SUV. *That's a camera*, he thought. Quickly ignoring its ominous presence, Ján climbed back into his 4X4 and drove off. Seconds later the SUV rolled into action too. Pulling up to the S.P.A.C.E. checkpoint barrier, Ján lowered the window as the SUV passed by.

'Good morning, Mr Novak, how are you doing today?' enquired the guard.

'I'm good thanks, Carl. What's going on with all the police buzzing around?'

'We had a break-in sometime last night. Pretty heavy mob. Two night security guards were taken out: one is critical, the other we lost. He paused for a moment. The police said they had inside help as a lot of the security systems had been hacked. They got into the main lab, but couldn't get into your one as they were disturbed by patrolling officers. There was obviously quite a lot of gun fire judging by the damage, but they got away. No idea who they were.'

'Hmmmm,' paused Ján. 'I wonder what they were after?'

The barrier lifted and Ján slowly approached the main building. A police officer waved him down. The truck came to a halt.

'Morning sir, can I see some ID please?'

'Sure,' Ján opened his wallet, produced his ID card and offered it to the officer.

'Thanks Mr János "Z" Novak,' joked the guard cheekily, reading his ID card. 'Sorry but we can't let you into the building right now. Forensics are giving it a thorough going-over. We may need to get in touch with you.'

Ján reversed the truck into a nearby parking bay, then drove back towards the checkpoint. The barrier lifted and he headed onto the freeway to join the tide of traffic flowing back towards the city. An hour later Ján was pulling up onto the drive of his house. The garage door slowly started to rise and once open, he drove in. The door slowly lowered behind him, making a pleasing "clunk", it locked shut.

Kicking off his shoes, Ján made his way through the house. It was eerily quiet: no guitar noises coming from Ruben's room, no radio playing in the kitchen and no electronic dance music blaring from Kat's room. The silence was deafening. *This will be what it's like when the kids leave home*, he thought. For a brief moment he felt a deep wave of sadness smother him. Opening the door to his office it dawned on him that now might be a good time to tidy his office. No distractions, he could just get on with it. A few minutes later, armed with a hot coffee, he started sorting through the paperwork on his desk. With the hi-fi blasting out some "dad-rock" again, the job didn't seem quite so bad. Now, with the house to himself, Ján could not resist slinging his "air guitar" over his shoulder and having a guilty moment playing an air guitar solo at the end of *Stairway to Heaven*.

'*Classic,*' he thought, pulling shapes to the imaginary audience worshipping him in the front row. Luckily, no one saw him break an air guitar string. After a few hours, a few chocolate biscuits, and a few coffees, the room was looking quite tidy. He could now get down to doing some work, but first he decided to check the house's security settings.

With a quick shimmy of the mouse, his computer sprang into life. After entering his password, the desktop came up on the screen. Navigating through the icons he clicked on the file marked "Rosanna". He picked his way through the sub-menus until he found the security settings. Having run a system scan over the current encryption configuration, Ján was happy to see everything was up to date and functioning correctly. He thought he might tweak Rosanna's response settings too, just for fun. The events of the day had unsettled him. After a short pause, he started the real work of the day.

Having completed the complicated online security system login, he was granted access to the S.P.A.C.E. main frame. He entered his final password and was "in". The first thing to check was how things were progressing on the tracking of the asteroid cluster. Árpád's Chariot was the name Ján had given this cluster of 42 space rocks, as he had been the first to find them and that he knew the number of asteroids might be important. Although on the very edge of the known solar system, this mass of geological rubble was travelling through space at huge velocity and was due to pass very near to the Earth in the next few hours. It was a rare opportunity to study this phenomenon at very close quarters.

Dotted around the nearby hills were a large number of aerials and six huge refracting telescopes that could provide the two-dimensional high angular resolution capability of a single telescope a fifth of a mile in diameter. The data that they could gather would be very useful. With this amount of power it was theoretically possible to look back in time due to the speed of the light information that had not yet reached Earth. Methodically working his way through the updated data for the day, Ján was happy that everything was under control and progressing predictably.

His next task was to sort out the budget details. This he was dreading as he had no interest in moving figures around on a spreadsheet. His dyslexia meant that mathematics was not his favourite subject at school and still wasn't now. The hours slowly crawled by as he waded through the treacle of numbers jumping around in front of his eyes. He never was a big fan of low-level mathematics; they were just a necessary evil.

Slowly his mind drifted back to his school days. He was sitting at the back of the class staring out of the window as Mr Philips droned on and on. *When am I ever going to use this calculus nonsense*? thought a sixteen-year-old Ján.

'Ján!' shouted Mr Phillips, across the room. 'One day you could find this to be very useful. I suggest you pay attention.'

At that precise moment, the phone on his desk rang, bringing him crashing back to reality.

'I don't recognise this caller's number. Do you want me to divert this into the junk folder?' asked Rosanna.

'No, Rosanna. I'll take it.' Ján picked up the phone.

'Good afternoon, hold the line,' he paused. 'Four

Seasons Hotel Bar and Grill. Can I help you?' quipped Ján in a playful mood.

'Eeerrr... sorry wrong number,' came the confused reply from the telesalesman.

Ján smartly put the phone down and carried on with his boring paperwork. The World Heritage Trust(WHT) was a truly global operation and had many offices sprinkled all over the world. There were strategically targeted facilities dealing with human tragedy and strife in many corners of the world, trying to make a difference. It also had a huge research facility and the whole operation was funded by a mega wealthy businessman, James McQueen, the CEO of Global Com.

He had made his fortune from mobile communications. His life's mission was now to save the world from overheating, global starvation, poverty and the wasting of Earth's precious resources. Having already ploughed his billions into research projects he now spent his time fund raising in the realms of his mega rich friends and enemies. James met János at a college charity event, they became firm friends, united by their conservation views, guitars and their love of old classic cars. Years later János was appointed the head of global research for the WHT. They believed that the untapped wealth languishing pointlessly, left gaining interest in dusty bank accounts, could be harvested and put to good use for the benefit of the planet they all call home. Over the years he had been quite successful with some of the business community, but had come to realise there was a very fine line between a successful business man and a criminal. Frustratingly he, so far, had not managed to persuade the politicians to legislate for change in tax and wealth issues. This would really help his cause, however he would never give up and János was right behind him every step of the way.

It was James who was waiting for Ján's document – that's why it was important, very important. He pressed on, seeing that the end was now coming into view.

Spreadsheet finished, and as if by complete coincidence, just as he pressed "send" on his computer he heard the back door open.

'Hi darling, I'm home,' called Sarah. She quickly made her way to his office. Opening the door she enquired,' what are you doing home at this time? WOW! What happened here? You've had a tidy up, either that or I'm in the wrong house and you're not my husband.' She leant over the desk and gave Ján a cheeky kiss.

'Yep, I went into the office today. There had been a violent break-in and a couple of guys were shot. That's heavy. The place was quite badly turned over. The police were doing forensics and stuff so they cleared the building. I wonder what they were looking for?'

'Did they get anything from your lab?' asked Sarah.

'Not sure. Apparently the lab wasn't broken into. A couple of patrolling security guards disturbed the intruders near the lab. There was some gunfire, but they got away. The police said that the CCTV security system had been tampered with so there weren't many clues. Someone knew what they were doing to temporarily knock that system out. I designed that myself – it uses a bio-rhythmic encryption interface. I am amazed they got that close to opening the lab.'

'Who would do that? What would they be after?'

'Hmmmm, I'm not really sure, but I was also followed to work today.'

'By who?'

'Don't know, but as I pulled out of the garage I noticed this big black SUV parked over the road. Didn't really think much of it, but on the way to work I noticed it tailing me a few cars back. I went to the store to get a paper and there it was again. I think someone had a camera and was taking pictures of me. I could see the telephoto lens glint in the sun. There were a couple of other guys in the back. Definitely a pretty hefty mob. I think we should be careful. Don't tell the kids – we don't want to freak them out. I've ramped up the house security system a bit, so don't worry.'

'Okay. Are you going to the lab tomorrow?'

'No, I'll go in on Monday. I can monitor stuff from here. I think I'll call the police, see if they can come to the lab building. I can have a chat with them there.'

'Good idea. Would you like a coffee? What with that, *and* clearing your office, you have had quite a day.'

'Thanks, honey.'

It wasn't long before Ruben came home from school. Mum and Dad were sitting in the garden. He got himself a cold smoothie and a couple of dull low-sugar biscuits and joined them on the deck. As he sat down, Huff Puff, one of their white ducks, waddled onto the deck too. Quacking wildly, he was hungry so Ruben broke a small piece off the corner of his biscuit and placed it on his open palm. With a little tickle Huff Puff pecked at the crumbs then set off down the garden towards the pond and the other ducks.

'How was your last day, Ruben?' asked Mum.

'Oh, it was quite fun. We had a little party to celebrate the end of the semester, so in period four they laid on some party food and drinks and Mr Carvin did his DJ thing in the sports hall. He was quite good, considering...' Ruben left the comment hanging in the air.

'Considering what?' ask Dad.

'Urrrm,' stumbled Ruben.' He's quite old.'

'What, as old as me you mean?'

'Yes,' came the blunt reply.

'Charming!' replied Dad.

'I'm meeting Frankie tonight, so don't wait up for me.'

'Oh... Okay, where are you off to?' asked Mum.

'I am going to pick up Frankie then we're meeting the others and going to JJ's down on East Colorado. Luke's band is playing the Friday Night Jam, so we're going along to hang out.'

'Is Luke as good as you, Ruben?' asked Dad.

'No way.'

'That's my boy. What are they called?'

'Demented Lemming. I think their vocalist thinks he is one, as he loves diving off the stage into the crowd.' With that, he got up and disappeared into the house.

Tonight was going to be fun. Ruben loved being with Frankie and couldn't wait to see her. In his bedroom he sat on the edge of the bed and picked up his salmon pink Stratocaster. His fingers began to run across the neck and cascades of notes poured from his finger tips. His sweep picking technique was coming along nicely. He loved to play and part of him wished it was his band playing tonight. Ruben could lose hours on end when he was in the guitar zone. Soon his bubble was burst as Kat bounded into his room and tried to give him a hug.

'What are you up to, bruv?'

'Just noodling around, just playing some old Zeppelin riffs and stuff. Are you going to JJ's tonight?' he asked.

'I'm not sure. I might bring Dan.' she blushed.

'You like him don't you, I can tell. Would be good to finally meet him, see if he is real, not just a figment of your imagination,' he teased.

'Yes, he has got a certain something – he is a bit mysterious. I quite like that.'

'I have got to look cool for Frankie tonight. What shall I wear?' asked Ruben.

'Well... you've got a good physique, so why don't you wear your jeans, Vans and just a nice plain white T-shirt. Simple but cool – she'll love it.'

'Okay Kat, thanks.'

She flounced off to her bedroom to get ready for *her* night out too.

Back on the deck Sarah and Ján were still chatting.

'The kids are growing up so fast. It only seems like yesterday we were pushing them around in their little buggies. Now they are driving around in their own buggies. Where has all the time gone? Do I look old?' A small tear ran down Sarah's cheek.

With his hankie, Ján gently dabbed it away. 'You still look like the girl I fell in love with all those years ago.' His loving words brought a cute smile back to her face. She squeezed his hand.

'We have the evening to ourselves. Why don't we go out too?' asked Sarah. Ján agreed.

The dying embers of the afternoon sun were slowly slipping behind the ragged outline of the mountains and the sky was turning a warm orange glow as the shadows gradually lengthened. It was Ján's favourite time of the day.

Ruben emerged from his room and went out onto the deck.

'I'm off now. I'll see you tomorrow at some point.

Have fun you two – don't do anything I wouldn't do,' he chortled.

'Very funny,' replied Dad sarcastically, throwing a knowing glance to Sarah. 'Have you got your phone, just in case...'

'Just in case, what?' asked Ruben.

'Just in case, just... be careful,' he repeated mysteriously. 'Say "Hi" to the Rosenbergs for us.'

'It's okay, we'll get a taxi from Frankie's,' he said, trying to allay his fears. Whatever they were; Ruben wasn't quite sure.

He grabbed his keys from the kitchen and ran through to the garage. Placing his thumb on the sensor he asked Rosanna to unlock the door. It clicked open.

'Thanks, honey,' he joked.

'You're very welcome, Ruben. You look very smart tonight,' came the slightly unexpected automated reply.

He jumped in his car and pressed the ignition button. The big V8 roared into life and he slowly drove out onto the road. Like his dad, Ruben was a bit of an eco-petrolhead. His car was an old Ford Mustang which he was in the process of doing up. Dad had helped him but there was still quite a lot to do to convert it to an electric motor power plant. The bodywork was covered in primer and filler. One day it would be finished.

Heading east from Altadena it was a twenty minute drive to the Hastings Ranch area of Pasadena where Frankie lived. Her beautiful house lay cradled in the foothills of the San Gabriel Mountains. Frankie's father was Senator Kyle Rosenberg, a wealthy industrialist who had made his fortune from making gold mining equipment.

Soon Ruben was pulling into the drive. He parked then ran up to the house and pressed the ornate door bell. Inside, an ostentatious peel of bells announced his arrival. The door opened to reveal Frankie in party mood. She boisterously jumped into his arms and smothered him with kisses.

'Hi babe, you're in a good mood,' quipped Ruben.

'I am. We're gonna have a fun night. Come in.' Ruben entered the hallway just as Mr Rosenberg emerged from the study.

'Hi Ruben, how are you doing this evening?'

'I'm good thanks, Mr Rosenberg. Mum and Dad say "Hi."' Frankie grabbed Ruben's hand and with a devilish grin led him upstairs before any idle conversation could take place.

Having tried on the entire contents of her wardrobe Frankie finally settled on her outfit for the night – the first one she had tried on. She decided to go grunge, so it was a black tight T-shirt, designer ripped denim jeans, black high-heeled ankle boots and a blue checked cowboy shirt tied around her waist. Her hair was down with soft curls cascading over her shoulders. Ruben thought she looked fantastic. They were the perfect grunge couple. It was time to hit the town, so they went downstairs. Once in the entrance hall Frankie picked up the phone and called them a taxi. Hearing voices Frankie's mum appeared from the living room and walked over and gave Ruben an affectionate hug.

'Lovely to see you, Ruben, I hear you're off to JJ's tonight?'

'Yes, we're going to see a mate's band. Should be good. It'll be a great way to celebrate the end of school for the summer.'

'Sounds fun. Will we be seeing you at breakfast tomorrow?' she asked knowingly.

'Yes, I hope that's okay?'

'Of course it is. You're part of the family,'

'Thanks Mrs Rosenberg, that's very lovely of you.' Ruben looked at Frankie and smiled. They had a secret.

A few minutes later a taxi pulled up outside the house. Frankie kissed her mum goodbye, and then she and Ruben ran down the drive and jumped in the cab. Heading down through Hastings Ranch they soon hit Sierra Madre Boulevard. The streets were alive with lights and people. It was Friday night and everyone was out to have a good time. The restaurants were already full and the clubs were filling up. A few minutes later the taxi pulled up outside JJ's. Frankie and Ruben got out, paid the fare and walked towards the entrance. Two doormen the size of a small shopping mall blocked their way in.

'And where do you think you're going, handsome?' one of them asked.

'I assume you are talking to him, not me,' replied Frankie feistily. 'We're with the band. Our names should be on the list – Ruben and Frankie.'

The doorman checked. 'Got ID?... Yes, okay, you can go in.' He unhooked the rope barrier and they were ushered inside.

The club was full and buzzing with energy. On stage the house DJ, "Sam U.L" was spinning the decks, seamlessly blending the tracks together and judging the tempo just right to keep the dance floor packed. Above the crowd hung a huge lighting rig that flashed with spinning spotlights that strafed the dance floor. Lazer beams strobed overhead cutting through the swirling smoke.

'The music's so loud I can feel my teeth rattle,' Ruben joked in Frankie's ear.

'You're not kidding... shall we get a drink and find the others?'

They gradually picked their way through the crowd and finally made it to the heaving bar. Being quite a big guy Ruben quickly got noticed by the pretty bar girl as he flapped a few dollar bills in the air. With drinks in hand he went back over to Frankie. To his surprise Kat was there with her new boyfriend talking to her.

'Hi sis. I didn't think you were coming to the gig.'

'Well I thought it might be a good time to introduce you to Dan.' Kat squeezed his hand.

'So you're "Dan the Man". Kat's mentioned you quite a lot – we weren't sure if you were real or not.'

With that Ruben shook his hand. An electric cold shiver ran through his body. He froze. 'Wow man, static charge or what? ' he exclaimed. 'This is Frankie.'

Dan gently took her hand and planted a soft kiss on it. 'Lovely to meet you.'

Frankie smiled. 'You too.'

They then moved to the side of the dance floor to find an empty booth. The conversation flowed, as did the drinks and it wasn't long before they were joined by more of their friends, all having a great time.

As the last track finished the DJ announced that the band were about to come on so they left the booth and went off into the crowd. The lights all went down and there was a momentary silence. Then suddenly a series of flash bombs went off and the band launched into the first track. The crowd were soon with them as they blasted through their set, mostly covers with a few originals thrown in too. It was loud and grungy, just how Ruben liked it. Seeing bands live always made him feel like he wanted to be playing up there with them, not being just a spectator. The band was great and played out of their skins. The singer was a good front man and soon won over the audience and by the time they got to the last song in the set the place was steaming. With the final chord still ringing in the air the band walked off stage to riotous applause.

The audience was not going to let them go without an encore. A crescendo of whistles and foot-stamping began to fill the room. Faster, faster, the noise grew louder until finally, from the side of the stage, the band emerged and took their positions once again. With four clicks of his sticks the drummer counted them in. The crowd erupted into a seething mass of bodies again. After the second chorus the vocalist then dived into the audience, lemming-like, and crowd-surfed around on waves of hands as Luke the guitarist launched into a solo. Luke was good, but Ruben was better. He secretly smiled to himself. Just then Luke caught his eye. With the vocalist deposited back on stage the band rocked into the final chorus, ending on a huge flurry of drums, cymbals and sweat.

'Yeah... thanks for coming guys, hope you had a blast, we did. We have one last song for you and it's an old classic which I hope you'll like. And just to make it a bit more special we are going to get a mate of ours up to help us out. Ruben, get your ass up here,' ordered Luke.

Ruben was taken aback. Frankie gave him a playful push. 'Go on then, you know you want to.'

He slowly picked his way through the crowd and climbed up on stage. Ricki, the second guitarist handed him his guitar and quickly explained how to use his gear. Ruben knew how to handle this kind of rig anyway but still felt strangely nervous as he looked out to see his friends cheering him on.

With four bars of snare and crash cymbal the band launched into *Rock 'n Roll* by Led Zeppelin, a classic.

Ruben relaxed a bit. He knew this inside out; Dad played it a lot too. Frankie didn't miss the wry smile that crept across his face. The band were cooking and they were soon heading towards the guitar break. Luke pointed to Ruben and he was off. His fingers effortlessly peeled off lick after lick, as he rode the wave of enthusiasm from the crowd. He was truly in his element. His friends were right there lapping it up. He tore through run after run, finishing on a blistering masterclass in two-handed tapping arpeggios that sounded like a keyboard. With a dive-bombing whammy bar bend he was out and back into the end choruses. Like father, like son. Finally with a massive anthemic ending they were done. The crowd cheered and whistled, the guys bowed, waved, then walked off stage to rapturous applause and the beers on the rider.

A few minutes later Ruben emerged from the side of the stage and grappled his way across the crowded dance floor towards Frankie. Back up on stage the DJ Sam-U-L kept the atmosphere charged as the seething mass began to boogie the night away. Ruben soon found Frankie and the rest of the gang cosily ensconced in a side booth again .

Frankie put a drink in his Ruben's hand.

'You were really good tonight, Ruben.'

'That was a bit of a surprise, but luckily I was messing around with that song this afternoon, so I could remember it quite well.'

For the rest of the night they drank and nearly danced themselves to exhaustion. As the end of the evening approached, the DJ segued into the final song of the night. It was a slow smoochy one and Ruben took the opportunity to hold Frankie close, very close indeed. As they gently swirled around the dance floor, he whispered sweet nothings in her ear. They melted into each other's arms. It was just them, they were alone in their own world and they were blissfully happy.

The song faded away as the house lights came back on. It was 2:00 and time to go. They all said their goodbyes – hugs and kisses all round – and then filed out of the club into the cold night air. Ruben took his jacket off and put it around Frankie's shoulders. The cool temperature had caught them by surprise. They took a short walk along the street to the taxi office. The sky looked eerily dark. There were no stars out tonight. Ruben thought that was quite odd. Once at the taxi rank they jumped in a cab and headed off to Frankie's house. The city was now deserted.

It wasn't long before the taxi turned into Ranch Top Road. The houses that lined the road were huge. Each one was unique, each with its own character. Frankie's house was a vaguely modern Georgian-style mansion with interlocking pitched roofs and tall stone clad chimneys. It had massive windows dissected by glazing bars that gave it a period look. The entrance port was very grand with a stone balcony above it. Ruben preferred his more modern-style home. The taxi pulled up and they got out. They paid the driver and he slowly pulled away, watching them as they went inside, then sped off into the night. Approaching the front door, the security light illuminated the entrance. Frankie got out her keys and let them in. The house was quiet and a little lamp lit the entrance hall. With the door locked Frankie and Ruben tip-toed their way upstairs. Just as they quietly crossed the landing Frankie's dad poked his head around the door.

'Hi kids, did you have a good night?' he whispered. They nodded and with that Dad disappeared back into the bedroom.

The dancing had made them both feel really tired and it wasn't long before they were both fast asleep.

■ ■ ■

Meanwhile high above the clouds, in the outer reaches of space, Árpád's Chariot asteroid cluster was hurtling towards Earth at about 35,000 miles per hour. Gradually it was going to pass between the Sun and the Earth. Its orbit would take it around the planet but not hit it. The asteroid cluster continued to circumnavigate the planet until it was in the shadow of the Earth. The world was dark on this side and no one would see what horror was going to unfold.

Suddenly there was a cataclysmic explosion as the central asteroid disintegrated. Earth heard nothing, knew nothing. The contents of the bio-mechanical spacecraft, disguised as a space rock, spilled out into space, the cloud of deadly spore bombs multiplying exponentially and their volume increasing rapidly. Soon they began to form an impenetrable cloud high above the atmosphere. As the Earth rotated the asteroid cluster began to orbit at the same angular velocity of approximately 7.2921159×10^{-5} radians/second. Now, every 34 minutes and 17.28 seconds an asteroid would explode in the shadow's darkness and another cloud of spores would begin to multiply. As the hours ticked by more and more asteroids released their deadly cargo high above the atmosphere, hiding in the dark side of the planet as it turned. Gradually the Earth began to be encased in a black deadly cloud, which grew bigger, more dense, and darker. The spores multiplied at an ever increasing rate. One by one each asteroid was timed to detonate around the circumference of the Earth. The clouds of death would gradually spread towards the poles and cloak the Earth in black. The sun would not be seen again for a while.

■ ■ ■

Slowly the bedside alarm began to bleep quietly, then louder until a sleepy hand fumbled over the controls and pressed the doze button. Last night had been quite a night.

It had been ages since Ján and Sarah had been to an expensive restaurant on their own. They went to a lovely little bistro up in the mountains and Ján used it as an excuse to give his Jaguar a blast. The view across the twinkling city made a perfect backdrop as they drove up into the mountains. Arriving at the restaurant they pulled into the car park then went inside.

'Good evening Mrs Novak, Mr Novak, lovely to see you this evening. It's been a while,' acknowledged the maître d'.

'Good evening Charles. Good to see you too. The kids are off out tonight so we decided to treat ourselves,' explained Sarah.

It was a little chance to indulge themselves and that's just what they did. The menu was mouth-watering and it was hard to know what to choose. Eventually they made their selection and the meal progressed at a relaxed pace. It was a perfect evening spent in their favorite cozy bistro. It had been ages since they'd had such a night. There just never seemed enough time.

■ ■ ■

The alarm began to buzz again. Ján turned it off. He was going to have an early morning run before breakfast. Being careful not to wake Sarah, he slipped out of bed and went out onto the landing. It was still dark. He checked his watch. It was 09:00. *What is going on?* he thought. A feeling of panic suddenly ripped through his body. He went back into their bedroom and gently tried to awaken Sarah from her deep sleep. Slowly she began to surface. Her eyes opened, she squinted at Ján with a puzzled look.

'What's the matter darling? You look worried. What's happened? Is it the kids?'

'No... no... it's not the kids. It's happened. It's finally happened,' Ján replied.

'What's happened? I don't understand.'

Taking a deep breath Ján held Sarah's hand and started to explain.

'We will have to get Ruben home as quickly as possible, there is something I need to tell you all. It's very important. We need to phone him and make sure he comes straight home. Let Kat sleep for a while.' Ján walked over to the window.

'Rosanna, open the blinds,' he commanded.

With a gentle humming sound they slowly began to rise up to reveal it was still dark outside.

'What time is it darling? It's still dark.' Sarah was confused.

'There has been an astrological phenomenon that has occurred, a form of eclipse that has been caused by the asteroid cluster we have been tracking. I am going to go to my office. I need to check some data. Can you call Ruben and get him here as quickly as he can.

Thanks, honey.' With that, Ján quickly made his way down to his office.

The house felt strange. There were no birds singing in the garden, the ducks were quiet – there was no sound, nothing. Once in his office he sat at his desk and logged into his S.P.A.C.E. security verification interface. He began to search through the asteroid cluster tracking data. After a few minutes sifting through the photographic data feed, Ján suddenly noticed something strange. Using an image intensifier, he began to look more closely at the picture of the asteroid cluster. Zooming to the centre of the group, he realised one of the rocks had disappeared. He toggled back through the data and found a few seconds earlier that the radioactive footprint of the asteroid was still there. Looping the segments of data together he played the sequence. Midway through, the asteroid in the centre suddenly exploded. He paused the sequence and stared in disbelief at the monitor for a few moments. He then scrolled forward in time about thirty four minutes and let the sequence run again. He watched in horror as, sure enough, a few moments later, another asteroid exploded. It quickly dawned on him that the subsequent dust cloud would have been drawn towards Earth due to its gravitational pull and the low relative mass of the particles. That would explain the cloud blotting out the Sun. Ján knew this omen was bad, very bad, very bad indeed. His feeling of panic was broken by the sound of the phone ringing on his desk.

He picked it up. 'Hi, the Novak residence.'

'Dad, it's me. It's still dark. What's going on?' Ruben asked.

'I can't explain over the phone, we're having a form of an eclipse. Come home now, I need you all here.'

Ruben, sensing the panic in his Dad's voice, explained to Frankie he had to go and told her not to worry. He threw on his clothes and ran downstairs. Mr Rosenberg was in the TV room watching the news. It was all over the TV channels. The world was in darkness and nobody knew why and no one seemed to know what was going on. The programs were awash with speculation. Ruben stuck his head round the corner.

'Good morning Mr Rosenberg, hope we didn't wake you up last night.'

'No you didn't, I was a bit restless. I couldn't sleep.'

'I hope you weren't worrying about us.'

'Well maybe you were on my mind a bit.'

'Dad has asked me to get home as soon as possible. He sounded a bit worried too.'

'Does your dad know what is going on, why it is still dark?'

'Yes I think he probably does. He suggested it was a strange type of eclipse... or something.' He said goodbye, then ran out the front door.

The eerie darkness of the morning spooked him a little. He got in his car, turned the headlights on and set off home. The streets were only illuminated by the shops and other cars making their way through the city. His mind was racing through the possible scenarios that could have caused this strange phenomenon. Dad would know what was going on. It was definitely his area of expertise. Ruben's lack of concentration however meant he wasn't paying attention to the traffic. Going rather too quickly, he approached the junction of New York Drive and Allen Avenue. Suddenly he had to swerve wildly to avoid another car doing a left. With a screeching of tyres the Mustang skidded sideways, the tail flipped out as Ruben frantically fought to handle the oversteer of his wayward beast. Smoke poured from the rear wheel arches as he wrestled to regained control and brought the car stable again using negative lock, a little trick his dad had taught him. It certainly came in handy in that situation. With a sigh of relief, he continued on his way, counting himself lucky that no police had seen his near miss. A few minutes later he was turning into Rubio Vista Road. Home was just up and round the corner. He drove up the sloped drive and parked in front of the garage. Quickly he made his way into the house. Everyone was sitting in the TV room waiting for him.

'Morning Ruben, darling,' said Sarah. 'Thanks for getting here so quickly. Your dad seems keen to talk to us all.'

'Yes, I am glad we're all here. I have something to tell you which you will probably find very hard to believe. I just need to go and get something. I'll be right back.' Ján got up and went to the garage.

Once inside he went up the stairs to the mezzanine level which was full of various boxes stacked on racks. He was a hoarder, he collected stuff. He did have a secret safe hidden in the garage, but what he wanted wasn't in that. He lifted down a few boxes and started to sift through them. He opened the lid of one and looked inside. It was a box full of his old toy cars. He had a huge collection of classics from his childhood. He had even scoured eBay for the ones his friends owned that he had played with. One day he would build a huge display case for them so he could admire them every time he went into the garage. He lifted down a few more boxes and delved inside. It wasn't long before he found what he was looking for. Cradling his little dusty wooden box he went back to the TV room.

'Sorry, that took me a bit longer than I thought. Anyway, I found what I wanted.'

'Maybe you should tidy your garage too, darling,' quipped Sarah cheekily.

Ján opened the old wooden box and carefully took out a small, tatty leather book and put it on the arm of his chair. Next, he lifted out a ball of brown cloth and put it on the coffee table in front of him. Slowly he unfolded the rag to reveal a satin-finish silver cube, about the size of a tennis ball. It also showed slight signs of being burnt and blackened. The surface of it was inscribed with a network of lines. Dotted over the outside were coloured segments with some tinted glass-like jewels inlaid in various segments. The intricate cuboid framework had holes in it through which you could see the delicate innards. The room fell silent as they all stared dumbfounded at the object on the table.

Ruben broke the ice. 'What on earth is it, Dad?'

'Hmmmm,' he paused. 'Well it is some form of time travel device. It is very, very old and is not from our world. In this little notebook it's called, Rubik's Cube ™... It has something to do with this eclipse type phenomenon that has plunged our planet into darkness.'

'What do you mean it's not from our world? Where has it come from?' asked Sarah.

'I believe this object has come from another planet and even from another time dimension,' continued János.

'What!' exclaimed Ruben. 'How can you know that? That's science fiction stuff... isn't it?'

'Well, you know we have been tracking an asteroid cluster for nearly a year now. I think this is what has actually caused this phenomenon to happen. You see this little book here? I have read it and this tells a very interesting story. It predicts this planetary *happening*, and it does it very accurately. It predicts a cloud of death will cloak the earth and the sun will not shine for several days. This is what has occurred,' explained János.

'What do you mean, "a cloud of death"? Are we going to die?' asked Sarah nervously.

'No, not if I am right. It's a long story but I think the answer lies in this little book... and in this room.'

'What do you mean, Dad, "in this room"?' asked Ruben.

'Let me explain.'

At 11:15 János opened the little book.

TWO

THE ARRIVAL

THE 9TH CENTURY, CARPATHIAN BASIN,
CENTRAL EUROPE

PAST

The Carpathian (also known as the Pannonian) Basin is an area of flat land in Central Europe that today is predominantly known as Hungary, but also encompasses parts of Serbia, Croatia, Slovenia, Slovakia, the Ukraine, Bosnia, Romania and Austria. This lowland area is surrounded by the Alps, the Carpathian Mountains, Dinarides and the Balkan Mountains. It was formed when the land-locked Pannonian Sea dried up at the end of the last Ice Age, approximately 10,000 years ago. Around 830 A.D. it was inhabited by seven tribes of Magyar warriors (Hungarians) and their lands were divided by the Tisza and Danube rivers.

■　■　■

The ripples slowly radiated out from the fishing line as the fly bobbed around on the water. The midday sun was high in the sky and the reflections twinkled and danced across the river. A cool breeze fanned the trees gently making them sway from side to side. The water was clear and not too warm, perfect to keep the fish near the surface ready to feed. Antoine sat on the bank of the river waiting to catch his dinner. Meanwhile, his faithful horse stood in the shade nibbling at the grass. Holding the rod still, he slowly wound in the line. There was nothing on the hook. He didn't mind. Taking his aim, he drew back the rod and then with a quick flick of his wrist sent the little fly he had lovingly made earlier, across the water towards the ring of ripples in the river. It was a perfect cast and landed right in the centre. He sat and waited patiently. A few seconds later he felt a twitch on his rod. Quickly he took up the slack in the line. He felt the resistance and knew he had to be careful when bringing it in. Slowly he lifted the rod up and down to allow him to wind in the slack line and pull the fish closer to the bank. Presently, he could see it clearly squirming in the water. He got hold of his net and deftly swished it about, scooping up his catch. It was big and would last him a good couple of days. He was very pleased with himself. Once he had the fish on dry land he knew he had to do the bit he hated the most.

Holding the wriggling fish firmly in his hand, he closed his eyes, said a few words to his god, then hit it's head, between the eyes, with a heavy stick. He paused as it lay motionless in his hand. He looked to the sky, put his hands together and bowed his head. This was the harsh reality of his world. He knew his god would understand and forgive him. He was thankful.

Just then he heard a crackling noise behind him. Startled, he quickly turned round to see a huge "being" staring down at him. In the background there also lurked a shadowy figure of a man. Antoine froze rigid with terror and began to shake uncontrollably. The creature started to approach him, followed by the man. He couldn't move from the spot. He felt the creature's eyes burning deep into his very soul. Where was his god now? He couldn't escape the gaze as they came closer and closer. Towering over him, the creature pressed five orange buttons in an "X" pattern on his Exosuit, it reached out and touched Antoine's head and pressed the center orange button again. There was a blinding flash of blue light. Suddenly Antoine was a child again, with his family. His stream of unconsciousness morphed through the pivotal points of his life, from baby, through childhood, young man to adulthood. Then nothing but darkness. Antoine's soulless body dropped to the ground. The creature bent down, pressed two orange buttons in an ":" pattern on the Exosuit which vanished to reveal a huge, fearsome, bio-mechanical beast. It touched the motionless body and slowly the being began to be absorbed into the lifeless body on the ground. Moments later Antoine opened his eyes and looked around; the creature had gone, the creature was now Antoine. Peering down at the fish he knew it was time to eat, so he picked up his knife and proceeded to prepare it for cooking. He grabbed a stick and sharpened the end and with a firm stab he thrust the wood through the fish, then pushed it into the ground. From his pocket he pulled out a little fabric pouch. Inside was a silver cube encrusted with colourful jewels in divided segments. Antoine took the Cube and held it in both hands. With a few quick twists of his wrists and flicks of his fingers he manipulated the randomly coloured jewels into a new, solved configuration, of six segments of nine identical gems. Antoine pressed three diagonal yellow ones. A yellow beam emerged from the centre one, Antoine focused the shaft of light at the fish and it began to crackle and spit as it cooked. A few seconds later it was done. Antoine pressed a yellow corner jewel on the Cube and the beam vanished. Placing it back in the pouch he pulled the stick from the ground and began to eat. He nodded with approval and soon had devoured the whole fish. He liked it. Turning round he looked at his horse and decided it was time to head into the village. Attached to his horse was a brightly painted caravan, with a curved roof and little steps leading up into it. On the side, written in bold rainbow tinted letters were the words "Antoine Jean de L'Avoitier – The Mystical Magician". That's who the alien had become. The inside of the caravan looked cozy and comfortable; it was his new home.

His blissful silence was disturbed by the sound of hooves getting louder. Antoine turned round to see a man dressed in a flamboyant gown with a fur draped around his shoulders and a pointed hat, also trimmed with fur. He sat astride a splendid brown stallion. As he emerged through the trees the horse gave a triumphant snort and reared up on his hind legs. Antoine walked across to greet him. The man climbed down from his horse, loosely tied him up to a branch, and the two men embraced.

'How are you Makkai?' enquired Antoine.

'I am well, old friend. I thought I would find you here.'

'What brings you to these parts?'

'I have news,' explained Makkai.

'Come, let us drink.' Antoine led him into the caravan. He found two goblets and uncorked a wine vessel. The fruity aroma filled the air as he poured. They sat on the rug amongst the colourful cushions. Antoine placed the little pouch by his side.

'So, Makkai, what news do you bring?'

'Well, I was summoned to the palace by Queen Kristianna. She is arranging a big celebration for the thirtieth birthday of Grand Prince Zoltán, and she wants you to attend and put on a special show for her.'

'I would be honoured to accept. When and where are the celebrations to be held?' asked Antoine.

'At the castle in Győr in five days.'

'Gosh, that leaves me very little time to prepare. I had better start making some plans.'

Antoine lent over to pick up his goblet and accidently knocked the little pouch onto the floor. The Cube rolled out and trundled across towards Makkai. He reached out and picked it up and immediately froze on the spot. His eyes started to dart around the room in terror. He began to quiver. His face was fear personified.

'Oh my god, what is happening to me?' he screamed.

Antoine leaned forward and calmly placed his hands over Makkai's and they held the Cube together. He watched as Makkai began to stop shaking, his eyes beginning to focus on him before peacefully closing. He fell back against the wall; he was gone. Antoine sat for a moment and looked at the lifeless body in front of him. He took the Cube and began manipulating it into Solved-Mode-Six. He pressed five blue jewels in the shape of a "T". The Cube began to glow. He placed it on Makkai. Gradually a blue light began to envelop him. As the light got brighter the body started to vapourise until it had gone, completely.

Antoine knew it was time to find out a bit more about this Grand Prince. He manipulated the Cube into its solved state and pressed three white jewels in a "/" pattern and a holographic projection appeared in the middle of the floor. It began to play data from Makkai's brain. The Cube had recorded his memory banks. Antoine scanned through the data.

■　■　■

Grand Prince Árpád was a fierce warrior chieftain who ruled over the seven Magyar tribes in 896 A.D.. He was an immensely powerful king whose army was feared throughout the neighbouring lands. The Grand Prince had twin sons, Zoltán and the slightly younger Jutotzas. They became a very powerful nation and their empire spread through Europe. However, as the boys grew up Jutotzas became jealous of his elder brother's birthright. He plotted his death, thereby assuring his own ascension to the throne. He decided to poison him but was caught putting the potion in his brother's food. Guards were summoned and he was taken straight to his father, Árpád. He had no choice but to banish his son from their land forever.

Several years passed until one day a messenger arrived at the castle with the news everyone was dreading: Grand Prince Árpád had died in battle.

This meant that Zoltán must become Grand Prince. He married his Princess Kristianna and had twins; a son, Ruben, and a daughter, Katarina. Zoltán's people were fiercely loyal and devoted to him and in return he was a generous Prince. Each year on his birthday he held a huge party to which all his subjects were invited. The celebrations were legendary throughout the land and each year they got bigger and better. Antoine was always the star of the celebrations and that was why the court messenger Makkai had been sent to find him.

■ ■ ■

It all now fitted into place. However, Antoine would now have to go to the castle to accept their invitation in person. It would be a good chance to learn more about these people. Part of the reason he was sent to Earth was to find out about the humans, animals and creatures that now inhabited the planet in this 9th century time dimension. He had to discover if this future would be suitable for his race. Would they survive? He needed to explore what this world had to offer. The total destruction of all life on Earth would depend on his findings. Antoine knew it was imperative that his Cube was always safe and with him. It was his only link to his past. It had awesome powers. The way Antoine manipulated it was the key to unleashing its fearsome capabilities.

It has been quite a day so far, he thought. He liked the fish but he was still hungry. Looking through the little cupboards in the caravan he found some apples. Gingerly he took a bite, the sweetness of the juice trickled pleasantly down his throat as he crunched his way through it. It was nice, so he had another. In the corner of the caravan Antoine noticed a stringed instrument. It was a short-necked lute-type thing, with a beautifully carved and decorated teardrop-shaped wooden body. He picked it up and sat cross-legged on the floor. His hands instinctively knew what to do. His left hand softly held the little stubby neck as his other hand began to finger-pick at the strings. Then, as if by magic, beautiful music began to pour from the instrument. Antoine was enchanted by it. The sound was like nothing he had heard before. He couldn't stop making it sing. He just knew how to play, he liked the sound and it wasn't long before the light began to fade and the moon appeared in the clear dark blue sky above. It felt like he was playing to the stars. He enjoyed the wine also and decided to indulge again. He quickly drank several goblets and began to notice his vision was becoming confused and his playing had taken a bit of a change for the worse. He looked around: there seemed to be two of everything! He shook his head but nothing changed; there was still two of everything. He looked at the wine and smiled to himself as the realisation dawned on him. Maybe it was time to get some sleep. He propped the instrument up against the wall and then stumbled down the steps to check if his horse was okay, and was slightly confused by the four horses tied up outside. Slowly he fumbled his way around. He could only feel two animals but his eyes told him differently. He couldn't fathom out what was going on so decided to go back inside. Once in the caravan he carefully folded up the little steps and closed the door, slipping the bolt across. Unrolling the bedding mat he grabbed the heavy furs and pulled them up over himself, hiding the Cube under the covers. He felt warm and cosy. It wasn't long before he drifted off into a deep sleep. The hours passed.

■ ■ ■

The soothing noise of the river running past his caravan gently teased him awake, the dawn chorus perfectly orchestrating the fanfare arrival of a new day. Antoine slowly opened his eyes. The sun was trying to burst through the gaps in the old wooden door. With a quick stretch and a satisfying groan he threw back the covers and stood up. His head felt a bit strange. The wine had given this alien its first hangover experience. *Why do humans do this to themselves?* he thought. His lips were dry and he felt thirsty and *very* hungry. He looked around the caravan to see if he could find some water. Hanging from a hook in the corner was a fur-covered water pouch. He lifted it down, pulled out the stopper and took a few quenching glugs which were accompanied by a rumbling noise from his stomach. That indicated hunger and he knew he needed some food soon. A search through the caravan's storage boxes revealed some bread and cheese. He found a clay plate decorated in a beautiful geometric pattern. The bread was hard and crusty but edible and the cheese was soft and creamy and also edible. Antoine took a knife and roughly cut a slab of bread and topped it with a generous spreading of cheese. It wasn't long before the whole loaf was gone. Now he would need to go into the town and buy some food today as well as visit the castle. He checked in his tunic pocket and found a couple of small metal coins. These were not going to be enough to buy him anything so he rummaged around under the furs and found the Cube. Antoine then held it in his hand and configured it to Solved-Mode-Six. He pressed five blue jewels in an "L" pattern. The Cube began to glow. He put it down on the floor and put one of the coins in the middle of the top yellow segment and waited. The yellow jewels began to flash, then a beam began arcing across the floor in rhythmical waves of light. As Antoine watched, he could see multiple images of the money begin to form. Within a few minutes there was a pile of coins laying on the rug. Now he could buy what he wanted. Picking up the Cube he carefully put it back in its pouch. He had gathered his first piece of useful data as the Cube had performed a chemical analysis of the molecular structure of the metal coin and simply reproduced multiple copies of it. Antoine thought now might be a good time to do a full location data scan. He put on his boots, opened the door, aligned the steps and went outside. He needed to find a suitable place to position the Cube. Surveying the area he reassuringly realised there were now just two horses tied up. It then dawned on him that the other horse was Makkai's. *Oh*, he thought. For a moment he pondered his next move, then slowly walked over to Makkai's horse, untied it and gently coaxed it into running off, which it begrudgingly did. Antoine watched as it trotted into the woods and was gone. He then continued his search for a scanning point.

Just to the right of the caravan was a wooden stump left by a lightning strike; that would be perfect. Antoine took the Cube and pressed two blue jewels in a ":" pattern and placed it on the stump, moved back and sat on the caravan's steps. Slowly the Cube began to glow. From the side slot around the top an intense blue beam began to rotate scanning the surroundings in an undulating wave of coloured light. A few minutes later the process was complete. The data was then automatically uploaded through the Cube's inbuilt time portal. Antoine picked up the Cube, repositioned the segments and put it back in its pouch.

It was time to head into the city, buy some food and go to the castle to discuss the celebrations. Antoine got his fur tunic and an apple from the caravan and locked the door. He took the Cube and in a blur of fingers configured it to Solved-Mode-Six. He pressed five yellow gems in a "Z" shape and pressed the centre axis jewel again. Suddenly a small silver Cubie appeared in his other hand. He attached it to the underside of the caravan. Standing a few feet away, he threw a stick at the wheel. It immediately vapourised on contact. The caravan was definitely locked now. Nearby, his horse was chewing on some lush grass as Antoine approached him. His head turned as if to greet him so Antoine slowly walked up to him, got hold of his noseband and gently stroked his nose. He placed his hand on the stallion's head, just in front of his ears. It suddenly stood motionless. Antoine closed his eyes and focused his mind on the horse. Now they were telepathically joined. He took his hand away and Veyron nodded his head and let out a playful "neigh". From his tunic Antoine pulled out a crisp red apple and placed it on his flattened palm. Veyron lowered his head and gently picked up the apple in his bright white teeth and crunched on it, and now they were real friends.

Antoine took a grip of the horse's saddle horn and pulled himself up onto his back and with a gentle kick of his heels they trotted into the trees. Veyron knew his way through the woods and Antoine took the opportunity to enjoy the free ride. The rising morning sun was shooting shafts of bright light through the trees as they headed towards the city. Before long they were out of the forest and heading down a rough track, Veyron's hooves making a rhythmical "clip-clop". Towering trees lined the rugged path as it wound its way through the beautiful rocky terrain. As they came over the hill the distant silhouette of the massive castle could be seen on the edge of the river. Antoine began to feel nervous. This was also a feeling that was alien to him. He wasn't really sure what it meant but he knew he didn't like it. Perhaps it was the thought that he would have to deal with more human beings. His first two encounters had not worked out very well in as much as both of them had effectively been mercilessly slaughtered. He needed to learn some people skills quickly. Now he had taken on Antoine's human form he also had access to the very essence of his being. He could feel deep inside that Antoine had been a generous caring man before his untimely demise, so he decided to let his spirit guide him on his way. Antoine thought it might be fun to see just how fast Veyron could go. He focused his thought waves on his stallion and immediately he bolted off at top speed. The trees and bushes whizzed by in a blur of colours as the pair galloped down the track. Antoine was quite impressed by Veyron's acceleration as they raced into an outcrop of trees on the side of the hill. *Not bad for one "horse power"*, he thought. Suddenly he could see some figures in front of them in the middle of the track. Veyron changed "down a gear" to a gentle trot as the figures got closer. Antoine could see that they had bows and swords. He didn't like the look of the situation that was unfolding. As they drew nearer one of the men held his sword in the air and ordered him to stop. Veyron skidded to a halt in a plume of dust.

'Where are you going, traveler? Why have you come this way? You're not from these parts are you?' asked the man.

'I am going to get provisions from the market.' Antoine thought it might be best to not mention he was heading to the castle.

'So you have money then?' came the reply.

Antoine realized what was happening and he knew it was bad – for them.

'Yes, I have a little. Take it, please. I don't want any trouble.'

'Give me all you have, everything,' demanded the man aggressively. 'And we will let you live.'

Antoine thought that was quite amusing given the awesome firepower he could harness.

'Give me the money, now.'

Antoine reached into his tunic, pulled out the newly minted coins and he handed them down to the man who quickly passed them to one of his accomplices.

'What is in that pouch you have there?' asked the leader.

'It's just an apple for my horse,' replied Antoine.

'Show me, I don't believe you.'

Antoine knew now it was going to get a bit awkward. The man pushed his sword up towards Antoine's chest and ordered him to dismount. As he climbed down the other men closed round him in a circle. Slowly he reached into the pouch and pulled out the Cube and held it in his open palm. The men looked at it amazed. They had never seen anything like it before. Little coloured lights flickered and flashed over its shiny silver metal surface. Suddenly the gang leader lunged forward and snatched it from Antoine's hand.

'An apple? This is like no apple I have ever seen.

What sort of apple is this? It isn't even green,' he asked mockingly. The other men laughed.

'You'll die laughing when I tell you,' retorted Antoine. The Cube suddenly exploded in a rainbow of intense light beams. They seared through the bodies of the men standing round him and one by one they dropped to the ground. Antoine leapt forward to catch the Cube as its unlucky host collapsed. Crouching down he gathered up the coins that had been scattered. He took the Cube and with a few flicks of his fingers he reconfigured it. He pressed five blue jewels in the shape of a "T" and pointed the emerging blue beam at each body which instantly vapourised on contact.

With a final quick glance around, Antoine picked up the coins, jumped back on his horse and they carried on their way. As they came out of the trees they passed a few people on the road side.

'How did you make it through the wood? No one gets out of there alive. Didn't you run in to Vlad and his men?' asked a young man.

'Yes, we did. You won't see him around these parts again. He's gone, vanished into thin air,' chuckled Antoine as they trotted by.

Soon the noise of a bustling market throng could be heard drifting over the hill. Veyron became excited and began to trot a bit more quickly as he knew a few delicious treats would soon come his way. As they rounded the corner, there it was. The market lay sprawled out in the grounds of the massive fortress. They were in Győr. The huge city castle stood proudly on the banks of the Danube river, its shimmering reflection dancing across the water in the morning sun. The town's folk were going about their daily chores, oblivious to the fact they had a shape-shifting biomechanical alien from another time dimension, in their midst. Carefully Antoine took the Cube from its pouch and set it to Data-Scanning-Mode by pressing two blue jewels in a ":" pattern.

Startled by the horse, a young boy tripped and dropped a basket of fruit. Antoine smirked; Veyron thought *"lunch time"* and quickly snuffled up a stray apple. Several others laughed at the poor boy as he sat amidst the rolling apples. *Wouldn't it be funny if one day people could sit down and watch these amusing moments on some kind of data transmission device, over and over again in their own homes, even make their own hilarious moments and show others?* thought Antoine.

As they carried on through the market a few of the locals recognized Antoine and shouted after him. He turned and waved back at them. It appeared he was quite a well-known person in these parts and Antoine enjoyed the show of affection directed at him. The main castle entrance was not far ahead and he could see some of the guards standing just over the bridge that crossed the moat. They moved forward as Antoine approached and stopped by the gate.

'What brings you to the castle this hour?' enquired one of the guards.

'My name is Antoine Jean de L'Avoitier. I have been summoned to meet with the Queen by her messenger Makkai. It is urgent business regarding the Grand Prince's birthday celebrations,' explained Antoine.

'Ah, yes, the magician. Very well, I will inform the Queen. We haven't seen Makkai for a while. Wait here, I will return.'

A few minutes later Antoine was granted access to the castle and was ushered into the courtyard. He took a few moments to tie Veyron to a post, quickly fed him an apple and then was taken through a side doorway. Inside the room was the Queen; she was poised elegantly on the edge of a beautifully carved wooden chair. Antoine was stunned by her beauty and felt a shortness of breath he hadn't experienced before. Then, much to his amazement, the Queen stood up and walked over to him. Antoine instinctively took her hand, kissed it gently and bowed down in front of her.

'How are you, my dear Antoine? It has been many moons since we have seen you at the castle. What has been keeping you away for so long?' she asked.

'I have been travelling my Lady, far and wide. I have been to the very corners of the kingdom and back,' he lied convincingly.

'I have missed you. We need to organise the Prince's celebrations. I want you to be the grand finale of the party. I want you to do some of your tricks, but it needs to be very special. Have you a new trick Zoltán won't have seen?' she asked.

'I think I may have something that will amaze him, but I need to do some experimenting. I would be honoured to perform for the Prince, my lady.'

'A lot of the party is already organized so we have four days left. Come to the castle in the morning of the celebrations and we will help you with your preparations for the day,' she concluded.

'Very well, my lady, consider it done.'

With that, he bade the Queen farewell. A guard duly entered the room and escorted Antoine outside into the courtyard. Veyron stood patiently waiting for him. He quickly untied him, pulled himself up into the saddle and headed for the castle gates. The guard opened them and they trotted back into the market square.

The crowds were still bustling around the stalls and Antoine let his inner self guide him through the maze of traders selling everything he could possibly need. Antoine found a place to tie up Veyron, then walked over to the market. He had soon purchased a sack of provisions: bread, oats, fruit, wine, cheese, milk, some fresh vegetables, nuts and a rabbit. He quite enjoyed shopping and liked the fun of haggling with the sellers. *I am going to eat like a king myself tonight*, he thought. He carried the heavy sack back to his trusty steed and, delving into the bag, pulled out a couple of delicious carrots for Veyron to nibble on whilst he secured the sack to the side straps. Antoine pulled himself back up into the saddle.

'Let us make our way home, my old friend,' commanded Antoine and Veyron gave a "neigh" of agreement.

They set off from the market place into the countryside again. They followed the track back over the hills, through the forest and a while later they were in their clearing by the side of the river. The afternoon sun was starting to sink in the sky as the shadows slowly lengthened. The river seemed alive, with fish breaking the surface and making ripples that danced and twinkled in the setting sun. Antoine thought now might be a good time to do another spot of fishing. He jumped off Veyron and untied the sack. The caravan was still safe and sound and there was no evidence his Cubie security device had been activated. That was good. Climbing the steps he took the sack inside. In the corner stood his rod. He picked it up and went down to the river's edge and hung the milk pot from a branch so it dangled in the cool water. That would keep it fresh for a while. He took up his rod and with a quick flick he cast the little dummy fly into the water. He didn't seem to have much luck. The fish were not biting. He looked around at the edge of the riverbank and noticed several red dragonflies hovering about. He quickly reeled the fly in and walked back to the caravan. In the sack were some red berries. He took a couple and crushed their juice into his fly, making it a bright red colour. Now it would match the flies darting around on the surface of the water. As if by magic it wasn't long before a fish took the bait. Feeling quite pleased with himself he quickly reeled in the fish. It was a good size. He decided to try again. He took the hook out of the fish's lip and then carefully hit it on the head with a sturdy stick. It stopped moving. Antoine cast his fly back into the river and waited, gently flicking the rod to keep the fly bait moving on the water. Soon he got another bite. Taking the strain, he began to pull the fish in. It splashed and thrashed as it tried to escape its fate, but couldn't get away. It too was quite a good size so he decided he would eat one and save the other. Taking the knife from his belt he set about gutting the fish and preparing one for cooking. The one he was going to save he tied to a piece of twine and dangled it in the river's edge, hanging from a branch. The river would keep it cool, with the milk, and fresh until he was ready to eat it tomorrow. He decided it would be fun to try to light a fire without cheating by using the Cube. Searching around the forest floor he found some nice dry, dead fern leaves, some small twigs, some bits of wood and a couple of stones. Back at the side of the river he began to build a little pile of fire wood. He put the fern leaves at the bottom with the twigs propped up over it. Taking the two stones he proceeded to hit them together, pointing towards the bunch of fern leaves. Little bright sparks started flying from the flint stones. After some time, just as Antoine was about to give up, a little spark caught the leaves and a wisp of smoke started to snake upwards. He quickly cupped his hands around the ember and gently blew on it. Much to his delight a little flame burst into life. Still blowing, he carefully pushed some more dry leaves around the flame. Slowly the fire became stronger and started to eat at the twigs. Once the flames had taken hold Antoine began to lean bigger pieces of wood together surrounding the fire. He felt a new-found sense of achievement as he looked at the fire and the bright glowing orange embers swirling up into the evening air. The sun was going down as the sky took on a deep purple glow. Next he set about propping up a heavy piece of branch over the fire. Getting a stick he stripped off the bark, fashioned a point on one end and skewered the fish onto it. He ran over to the caravan and found a rough metal cooking pot and brought back the sack of vegetables and some water. He then hung the pot on the stick over the fire and began to peel some vegetables. He roughly chopped some garlic and herbs and pushed them into the fish sealing it with another little twig. Suddenly Antoine stopped what he was doing and looked over at Veyron: he could feel him telepathically calling him. He got up, grabbed a few carrots and apples and took them over to him.

'Sorry, old friend, I guess that grass must get a bit boring sometimes,' he chuckled.

Veyron nodded. He gave him an affectionate stroke on the head, placed the food on the grass and returned to the fire. Once all the vegetables were prepared he threw them into the now gently boiling water. Antoine then took out the Cube. He was going to cheat the next bit.

'XL-R,(pronounced:Exelar) set Timer One for twelve Earth minutes.'

'Timer One set for twelve of your Earth minutes,' confirmed XL-R.

With his cooking well on its way he decided it was time to relax so he went to the caravan and found his lute, some wine and sat back down by the river. By now the fire was burning well and the smoke on the water was giving the whole scene a mystical atmosphere. Antoine felt a moment of inspiration. He picked up his lute and for some reason started to strum it rather than finger-pick it. Gradually a musical idea started to form and take shape. However, the strumming began to hurt his hand, so, reaching into his tunic, he fumbled around for a little coin. Holding it between his fingers, he began to strum again.

'XL-R, set to record, file name, Smoke Over The Water,' instructed Antoine. He then continued to play through his new composition, scatting through some made up lyrics.

"We all went down to Győr,
on the Danube river shoreline.
To make stew for the. . . ."

Hmmm. I'll come back to that, he thought, as he took the fish and positioned it over the fire.

'XL-R, set Timer Two for ten Earth minutes,'

'Timer Two set for ten of your Earth minutes,' repeated XL-R.

Antoine picked up his lute and began to "noodle" about trying out different ideas and musical phrases. The smell of the gently cooking fish was starting to make him feel hungry and impatient. He turned the fish over every so often so as not to burn it as the vegetables bubbled away.

'Timer Two has reached zero,' announced XL-R.

Antoine took the fish from the heat and then carefully lifted the pot from the stick. The vegetables were nicely cooked so he drained some of the water away. He crumbled the fish into the vegetables and stirred it in, making sure not to put the bones in. Taking a lump of crusty bread he scooped some of the stew out and ate it. It tasted good. He was pleased with his creation and soon had eaten the whole pot-full. He felt a warm glow inside. He had enjoyed that meal. By now darkness was falling and it was time to turn in for the night. Tomorrow he would have to do some thinking about the party celebrations. Having cleared up, he extinguished the fire and retired to the caravan.

That night was a restless one. Antoine tossed and turned as his mind was alive with thoughts and dreams of a distant planet, in a different time dimension. A collage of faces of his family far away disturbed his sleep. They called out to him to save them. Images of fire and destruction consumed the ghostly apparitions. They screamed in terror. Antoine awoke with tears in his eyes. He had forgotten them until now. Having calmed down, eventually he drifted off again into a shallow slumber where more visions and dreams began to play out in his turbulent head.

■ ■ ■

06:15, WEDNESDAY, 11TH MAY, 898 A.D. ON THE BANKS OF THE DANUBE RIVER, NEAR GYŐR, 120KM WEST OF BUDA(PEST)

Finally the morning came. It had been a long night and he felt emotionally drained. He realised that maybe the dreams were a way of reminding him to contact home. Throwing back the bed rugs, he leant over and picked up the Cube. Swiftly he manipulated the segments into Solved-Mode-One and pressed three white jewels in a diagonal line through the centre of the segment.

Suddenly the caravan exploded in a hazy glow of swirling colours. Gradually the image began to focus in front of him to reveal the holographic projection of Overlord Ebucski-Bur, the head of the High Council of Htrae. Antoine gave a nervous shudder as his presence filled the room.

'Greetings Overlord Ebucski-Bur,' nodded Antoine as he bowed down before him.

'Young Akaii, it has been a while since we have spoken.'

'It has, my Overlord, I am sorry.'

'Akaii, remember, you were chosen to be sent to this planet to explore its suitability for our future inhabitation. You must keep to the pre-ordained plan. We will not tolerate deviation. Interesting new body form, by the way. Wouldn't have been my choice, but hey.'

'Again, I am sorry for the delay, my Overlord.'

'From your Cube data uploads we can now confirm the mineral deposits detected will power our orbiting life support vessels that will modify the atmosphere for us. The spore bombs are nearing completion, they will be disguised as an asteroid cluster that we will direct towards Earth at the appropriate time. We are programming the SBX90 nano-modules to be inhalable by the life forms. Once inside their bodies they will start to genetically reconfigure their DNA strands. Ultimately this will wipe out all sentient beings from the planet's surface, and all their diseases. It will then be safe for us to populate this new planet. The Great War of Htrae is unrelenting and we are suffering crippling casualties. We have little time left here. You have done well, Akaii. We are proud of your sacrifice for us,' concluded Overlord Ebucski-Bur.

'It is an honour to serve, my Overlord,' replied Antoine.

The projection ended. Antoine knew he could never return home now as his absorption into another living being meant he was destined to live the rest of his days on Earth. He didn't know how long that would be as time passed much more quickly than in his own parallel dimension. He would wait for the arrival of his nation, sometime in the future.

However he was determined to enjoy himself while he could, as he was getting to quite like this wonderful little planet he was on.

■ ■ ■

06:25, THURSDAY, 12TH MAY, 898 A.D. ON THE BANKS OF THE DANUBE RIVER NEAR GYŐR, 120KM WEST OF BUDA(PEST)

He tentatively poked his head out of the caravan doorway. It was another bright morning. Veyron was by the trees munching on some grass that was glistening with a sprinkle of morning dew. The river was flowing steadily by and it looked quite inviting, so without thinking he threw off his clothes and ran into the water. With a mighty "kersplash" he plunged in. The sharp cold of the water made his skin tighten and his head spin in an invigorating mix of pleasure and shock. Then he realised he couldn't actually swim. Sudden panic made him lose his footing and he slipped below the surface of the fast flowing water. His arms flailing wildly, he called to Veyron. The horse's head shot up and immediately he bolted into the river. With his hooves splashing frantically, he got close to Antoine. His reins dangled in the water so Antoine made a desperate grab for them, but the pull of the river current swept him past them too quickly to get hold of. Antoine could feel his panic rising. Veyron galloped forward. Antoine crashed into him and grabbed the reins. Slowly Veyron walked out of the river onto the bank unceremoniously dragging a very disheveled Antoine with him to safety.

'Thank you, my trusty Veyron, you have saved my life,' panted Antoine as he struggled to take a breath. For a few minutes he lay on his back as his breathing started to stabilize. That little incident had shaken him, but at least he'd almost had a wash. As he calmed down he realised he was getting cold so went back to the caravan to dry himself and get dressed. With his new-found skills he built a fire and boiled some water for a hot mug of herbal tea to warm him up. A plate of crusty bread and cheese rounded off his breakfast. Today Antoine had decided he must work on his performance for the Grand Prince's celebrations. He needed to work out some new tricks that would be special. He chuckled to himself as a thought flashed into his head. He took out the Cube and placed it on his palm. In a blur of fingers he shuffled the segments around into Solve-Mode-Six and pressed the four yellow corner jewels. Suddenly he disappeared. Now he was invisible, in C-Thru-Mode. He quietly walked over to Veyron, who was happily chewing on some more grass. Slowly he bent down and picked up a handful of crisp leaves. Oblivious to his presence Veyron continued to munch.

Then, mischievously, Antoine threw them at Veyron who reared up and "neighed" as the leaves fluttered down around him. Seeing his reaction he reappeared behind him and grabbed his reins to steady him. He stroked his head with a warm and affectionate hand.

'Forgive me, my trusty friend. I didn't mean to scare you,' soothed Antoine, feeling guilty.

Being human was again proving to be quite interesting. He hadn't experienced these kinds of emotional reactions before. In his world they had been suppressed, seen as a sign of weakness. Antoine had obviously been quite a special being before he had been adsorbed. Forgetting for a moment that at some point in the future all his humankind was to be obliterated, Antoine wondered if perhaps that was a little unfair.

He spent the rest of the morning fooling around with the Cube trying out different ideas. The awesome power of the Cube could easily handle a few party tricks so he decided to keep the effects as simple as possible so as not to scare the audience. The party was the day after tomorrow so it was important for Antoine to practice his routine. As the day wore on the performance developed and by nightfall Antoine was happy that his act was as good as he could make it. That night he slept well as he played out the party scenario over and over again in his head.

■   ■   ■

07:32, FRIDAY, 13ᵀᴴ MAY, 898 A.D. ON THE BANKS OF THE DANUBE RIVER, NEAR GYŐR, 120KM WEST OF BUDA(PEST)

His morning snooze was brought to an abrupt halt by a knocking sound on the caravan door. Startled,

Antoine's eyes creaked open as he squinted at the daylight in a confused early-morning brain haze.

'Antoine, it's me, Izabella,' came a girl's voice.

'Oh, please wait a moment I have just awoken,' stalled Antoine as he tried to figure out who this girl was.

He scanned through Antoine's stored memory banks until he found the data he needed. Having dressed, he unlocked the door, fixed the steps and went down to meet her. Izabella threw her arms around his shoulders and gave him an affectionate kiss. This too was a new alien experience for Antoine and he found it most enjoyable. She was a truly beautiful girl, with long dark brown curly hair and bewitching blue eyes that pierced his very heart. He was starting to like the female of *this* species.

'Good morning, my dear Izabella. I have missed you. What brings you here?' enquired Antoine politely.

'I have come to see if you knew where my brother Makkai was heading after he had seen you,' asked Izabella.

'Gosh, no, I don't remember him saying. I assumed he was heading back home.'

'No, he hasn't returned. I am getting worried. Where can he be?'

'I only saw him a few days ago, he might have gone somewhere and will be back soon,' bluffed Antoine.

Izabella's beautiful almond shaped eyes began to well up. Antoine felt guilty deep inside. This too was a new sensation to him, and he had just lied to Izabella. Being a human being was very complicated. Navigating his way through these feelings and sensations was proving quite hard for this new version of Antoine. He didn't really know what to do. He took her hand and pulled her close for a hug. She felt his warmth as his strong arms wrapped around her. He could sense her tremble as a massive wave of sadness enveloped her.

'Maybe he will never return,' she sobbed.

Antoine held her a bit tighter as if trying to make her feel safe. He did not like this guilt feeling, however he liked the being kissed feeling. For a few moments he thought about how he could make the situation better.

'Izabella, are you going to the celebrations tomorrow?'

'Well I was going with Makkai, but now I don't think I will have anyone to go with,' she sobbed.

'I know, why don't you come with me and be my assistant and help me with the tricks I am going to do tomorrow?'

'Could I? That would be so much fun.' Izabella started to feel a little happier.

'We could practice today, I will show you what you need to do. We can have some food and wine and maybe you could spend the night here with myself and Veyron,' replied Antoine, trying to lighten the mood.

'Yes I would like that very much.'

Izabella would make a perfect assistant. She was a dancer with poise and grace, and her beauty would certainly distract the audience from the trickery Antoine would be performing. It would be a perfect show to end the celebrations.

Sure enough, they spent the day rehearsing Antoine's illusions. He was very careful not to show Izabella the full powers of the Cube as they practiced their routine together. Through the day Antoine could feel his attraction to her growing. The data he had retrieved gave him a clue as to how to proceed. At the end of the day Antoine cooked a delicious rabbit stew and as the night began to fade they sat by the edge of the river and looked up at the twinkling stars. Antoine put his arm around her and she nuzzled into him. She had long admired Antoine from a far, but he had never been quite so affectionate to her before. She felt loved.

'I think it's time we got some rest as tomorrow will be a very busy day, and I am feeling quite tired,' yawned Antoine.

Izabella turned and kissed him, took his hand and led him to the caravan.

THREE

THE SPECIAL DAY

PAST

The night had been an eventful one and Antoine awoke having felt the full force of human emotions. He carefully turned to look at Izabella. She looked so beautiful wrapped cozily in the fur bed cover. He paused for a moment; there was that guilt feeling again, and he didn't like it. However, just then Izabella began to stir. She opened her blue eyes and her hand delicately floated out to hold his. She squeezed it tenderly.

'Good morning, my love.'

'Good morning, dearest Izabella. I trust you slept well.'

She giggled.

'Indeed I did,' she purred.

Antoine felt the impulsive urge to kiss her, and so he did. Humans were capable of such heart-stopping feelings that he found it all very overwhelming, and quite addictive.

'I shall make some food, then we must head off to the castle. It is going to be a very special day.'

Antoine opened the caravan door letting the bright morning sun pour in. Outside, Veyron was munching on some vegetable peelings with his new friend Rozi, Izabella's horse. Antoine got dressed and climbed down from the caravan and walked over to the river. Bending down he cupped his hands and scooped up some water. It tasted cool and refreshing. He quickly made a fire pit and balanced the pot of milk over it. In the caravan larder cupboard were some oats, berries and nuts. He mixed all the ingredients together in two bowls and then went to check on the milk heating up on the fire. It was just starting to bubble so he took the pot up to the caravan and poured some warm milk into the bowls. Izabella was still dozing under the covers when Antoine presented her with her fresh porridge. She sat up, her dark curls cascading over her shoulders. Antoine's heart fluttered a little.

'Here you are, my love, some nice warm porridge to start the day.'

'Arr... thank you, dear Antoine. What a lovely way to wake up,' she cooed.

'When we have eaten we must make haste to the castle. The sun is getting high in the sky and we don't want to be late for the celebrations.'

Morning was warming up nicely and soon they had finished breakfast. Antoine washed the bowls in the river and put out the fire. He loaded his stage props onto the roof of the caravan and lashed them down securely. He went over to Veyron and Rozi and gave them both an affectionate stroke and an apple each.

'Right, my trusty Veyron, it's time for you to earn your keep. I need to hitch you up to the caravan.'

'Neigh,' nodded Veyron in reply, and started to walk over to the caravan.

Rozi watched as Antoine carefully fitted Veyron's driving harness and bridle. There were a lot of straps to secure, but he quickly had everything ready and it was time to manoeuvre Veyron between the two large wooden shafts. Once in position Antoine slipped the tugs over the shaft ends and began the complex sequence of tightening various belts until Veyron was comfortable and ready to go. He adjusted the winkers and called to Rozi. She sauntered over and stopped beside Veyron. Izabella was all packed up and ready to go too. She looked beautiful in a long, flowing purple dress covered in delicate embroidered flowers with a little, short, tan-coloured jacket over the top. Antoine thought she was divine and couldn't resist kissing her tenderly on the cheek. As the caravan only needed one horse to pull it, Antoine lightly fastened Rozi to Veyron's harness so they could walk together. Antoine and Izabella climbed up onto the seat, he grabbed the reins and with a quick flick they were off.

The path out of the forest was quite rough; they bumped and rolled as they headed out towards the track. All around them pine trees were smelling fragrant in the gentle breeze as it blew through the branches. The burble of the river slowly got lost in the noise of the forest as they headed on their way. Veyron knew his way round these parts so Antoine relaxed his grip on the reins and intensified his grip on Izabella's hand. He was enjoying being human and felt himself lucky he was enjoying a pleasant trip through the beautiful rolling countryside. They practiced their routine links as they went. She was enjoying the thrill of getting ready for their show, but there was an underlying sadness in her.

'Oh, how I wish I knew where Makkai was. He would love the show. It is so unlike him to not be here. I miss him. If only he were here,' Izabella sighed.

Antoine felt sick to his stomach as the magnitude of what he had previously done dawned on him. He looked at Izabella and could see tears in her eyes. He shivered and then he too felt his eyes start to water. What had he done to her? What had she done to him? He felt her pain too. Being human was complicated. He was aware his emotions were being triggered by Izabella and he couldn't stop it. He felt the overwhelming need to stop her pain, but he didn't know how.

'Dearest Izabella, please don't cry. Your brother may one day return.' Antoine tried desperately to comfort her as his mind raced.

'All I have left is a curl of his hair in my locket.' She took the necklace and squeezed the little silver case tightly in her hand.

Antoine thought for a moment. *Maybe there is a way. Maybe, just maybe I can put the situation right.* Antoine initiated a telepathic Mind-Link to the Cube.

XL-R, initiate Time-Freeze, sent Antoine.

Time-Freeze initiated, sent XL-R.

Immediately the Cube created a localized parallel time dimension that caused time to momentarily slow down, almost to a standstill. Now in this state of suspended animation he could take the locket from around Izabella's neck and genetically scan the hair sample. It would contain all the information he would need to physically clone Makkai. He clicked open the top segment of the Cube and placed the strands inside. With a flurry of fingers he configured the Cube into Solved-Mode-Two and pressed two opposing yellow jewels in a ":" pattern, initiating the sample scanning process. Once completed, he returned the hair strands to the locket and put it back around Izabella's neck. He then pressed three yellow jewels in a "|" pattern and gently placed one hand on her head and the other on the Cube. He began to focus his mind on hers. He needed to record all the data from her memory banks that involved Makkai and any joint inherited information that she had stored. He felt the data pass through him and he could visualize it in his mind's eye. Soon the process was complete

XL-R, disengage Mind-Probe, sent Antoine. He reset the Cube and put it back in his pouch.

Izabella gave a little startled shudder.

'What's the matter, my darling Izzy?' enquired Antoine just call me Izzy? That's what Makkai called me when we were children.'

'Gosh, I don't know,' he lied. 'But I like it, it suits you.'

The palace celebrations were always extravagant with lots of food and free-flowing drink. Some time later the outcrop of trees on the side of the hill, where Antoine had nearly been robbed a few days ago, came into view. He knew the city was not far from here and as they drove closer the sounds of merriment drifted to them carried on the wind.

'Antoine, dearest, can you hear it? Are we going through the woods? I have heard it can be dangerous,' she said with a tremble in her voice

'Yes, I too have heard that rumour. I travelled through here a few days ago and all seemed fine. Don't worry. I can hear the noise too. It sounds like it is going to be very busy. We should have a good crowd.'

They rolled through the forest, over the hill and down into the city of Győr. The grounds of the castle were bustling with people. Everywhere you looked brightly coloured tents were being erected and traders were setting up. There were outdoor games being organised and performers practicing their skills. There were jugglers, acrobats, and groups of musicians huddled together running through their repertoires. In every nook and cranny of the castle grounds something was going on. Dotted around were food stalls getting the roasting fires going and preparing their tasty delights. Children were racing around laughing and screaming with excitement. The castle was decorated with huge flowing banners, flags and bunting hanging from the ramparts. It wouldn't be long before the party would officially start. Antoine took the reins and carefully steered the caravan through the crowd towards the castle's main entrance. Soon he had attracted a group of children running behind the caravan calling out his name and cheering him on his way. Once at the castle he brought the caravan to a halt. A guard walked forward to greet him.

'Good morning Antoine, I trust the day sees you well.'

'Indeed it does. We are here to prepare for the celebrations.'

'Her Ladyship sends her regards. She will see you after the Prince's announcement at midday. Go through to the courtyard and one of the guards will help you.'

The huge gates were opened and they trundled inside where a palace guard came to greet them, and they began to unload their props and clothes. These were then taken through into the main palace. Suddenly the sound of trumpets could be heard coming from the outside, quickly Antoine and Izabella ran into the courtyard to see, high up on the castle walls, six finely dressed trumpeters playing. They went through the gates out into the gardens where town's folk were listening to the heralding call of the trumpets, waiting for their Prince. As the last notes of the fanfare died away the Grand Prince and his Queen appeared on a balcony over the main gates. The crowd was hushed.

'My people, my loyal friends, I am honoured that you have come to celebrate my birthday. My house is your house. Let us be merry and enjoy this day together. I drink to your health.' The Grand Prince held aloft a golden goblet and then drank a sip from it. The crowd erupted in cheers of laughter. The party had started.

Antoine looked on and thought what a wonderful scene was playing out before him. It was so different from the planet he had left so long ago. His world was being ripped apart by war. Two massive armies were fighting for supremacy, battling to take control of his world. The planet was being decimated and his people were being mercilessly eradicated. Time was running out. They needed to escape from their world before it was too late. That was why he was here; he was a beacon to guide the massive escaping force travelling from another dimension to inhabit this world. He paused to reflect on his situation. He hadn't been able to prepare for life as a human being and he was using Antoine as his guide through this new life. Izabella had awakened feelings in him he had never felt before. His predicament was beginning to weigh heavily on his heart. The commitment and responsibility that came with being human was so new to him.

With the party now officially underway Antoine took Izabella's hand and they ran back into the castle banqueting hall. At the end of the room was a huge, long table with the Prince's and Queen's ornate decorative chairs flanked by the seats of the other family members and high-ranking officials. In front, the other long tables were laid out for the guests. Servants were scurrying around putting out all the plates and utensils. Others were decorating the walls with flowers and bunting. The hall was beginning to look very festive. To the side of the room a little stage had been built for the musicians to perform on. Izabella thought it was all very impressive and was starting to feel quite excited.

'Today is going to be such a fantastic time that I wish Makkai could be here. He could have helped us carry all these heavy bags,' she laughed, with a hint of sadness.

'You never know Izzy, he might appear,' comforted Antoine. 'Now, let's take our bags out to our tent.'

In the grounds of the castle a big stage had been set up, with a decorated podium where the Prince and Queen would sit at the side, the brightly coloured awning rippling in the breeze. It was all positioned in the bottom of a shallow natural amphitheatre. The town's folk could sit, relax after a busy day and watch the show in the evening. There was a huge fire built waiting to be ignited. Behind the stage, hidden in the trees, were the performer's tents. Antoine and Izabella deposited their bags and hung up their costumes. They were due to perform later in the day so decided to go and enjoy the festivities to the full. They sauntered around the grounds taking in the smells of the food being cooked and watching the children playing games and running about having fun. Antoine wished his childhood on his planet could have been like this, but it wasn't, it was a living hell.

When he was young, he endured terror and harsh living conditions. His family struggled to survive on a daily basis. As war raged all around them they were forced to keep moving away from the advancing force. Eventually the inevitable happened: one night there was a particularly heavy barrage of attack drones that razed the whole compound to the ground. He was the only member of his family to escape the attack. He ran and ran, until his feet bled, never looking back. He knew he was now on his own. It was only a matter of time before he was picked up by a roving reconnaissance vehicle that found him scavenging for food. He was detained and an identity check carried out on him. It was verified and he was taken to a central control base where he was trained and joined the security force. He grew up very quickly to survive. That was the way it was. His experiences had made him want to play his part in helping his people survive.

Izabella interrupted his thoughts. 'I am feeling hungry, my dearest Antoine. Shall we go and find some food?'

'Good idea. Let's see what there is.'

They went for a wander. The air was full of wonderful smells that tickled their taste buds and made them feel even more peckish. After much deliberation, they decided to try the hog roast. Quite a crowd had gathered with the same idea. As it slowly turned over the crackling fire the aroma of sweet, honeyed pork was hard to resist. Layers of rough-cut meat were sandwiched between some delicious crusty bread and the juices dribbled over the top. Antoine thanked the man, paid him and they set off to buy some fruit and wine. Once they had everything they sat down near the musicians, who were playing some jaunty folk music and started to enjoy their snack. One of the lute players then caught sight of Izabella, jumped up and came over to them, still playing. Antoine clapped along as the rest of the group accompanied him on his flight of fancy. Antoine enjoyed the lute player and at the end of the piece Antoine placed a few coins in his hand to show his appreciation. The couple ate their lunch then, with festivities surrounding them everywhere they decided to play a few games, which were great fun. As the afternoon wore on the light slowly began to fade. The shadows lengthened and the once blue sky was transformed into an orange sunset as the sun slipped shyly behind the distant hills. Soon it was time for the show to begin. High on the battlements the trumpeters signaled the imminent arrival of the Prince and Queen, and the start of the show. The town's folk began to trickle into the amphitheatre and take their places on the grass. When everyone was seated the trumpeters played a fanfare as the Prince, the Queen and the royal children took their seats. They waved to the crowd who cheered and waved back to them excitedly. This was also Antoine's cue to leave and get ready for their finale of the show. As the first performers took to the stage Izabella and Antoine made their way to the tent and changed into their costumes. They could hear the crowd were really enjoying the show. The acrobats were doing an amazing routine of balancing and precision tumbling that had their audience completely enthralled. The final display entailed them building an eight-man tower, with the last acrobat at the top balancing upside down on his head. The crowd went crazy as they all jumped back down onto the stage. They took a bow to rapturous applause and ran off stage left.

Next on came a trio of jugglers. They were dressed in flamboyant striped trousers, with matching short jackets. They proceeded to dazzle the audience with their juggling skills. They had a collection of objects ranging from coloured balls to cooking pots. All were duly sent flying through the air in a cascade of tumbling craziness, as all three players tossed the objects around between themselves. The audience sat transfixed by the hypnotic rhythm of the juggling. For their finale one of the performers disappeared off stage to return carrying a selection of knives and swords. The audience let out a collective gasp, well aware of what was about to happen and the possible consequences of a miss-timed throw. The jugglers stood in a triangle each armed with three gleaming knives.

One of the performers then took two knives and hit the side of the blades together to show the audience they were made of metal. He split a piece of wood in half to further prove the point. Without any introduction nine knives began flying around the stage in a blur of flashing silver that started to get faster and faster. The audience began cheering and clapping as the blades whizzed around the stage in controlled mayhem. To signal the end of their performance the three jugglers suddenly threw all their knives up in the air and huddled together in the middle of the stage as the knives fell in a perfect circle around them. The audience clapped with all their might as the performers stepped over the knives to take a bow. It had been a truly amazing demonstration of timing and precision accuracy.

Next onto the stage came a group of folk musicians who sat on stools to play. They had a collection of various lute-style instruments, with one musician surrounded by some traditional percussion and drums. The percussionist counted them in and they began to play a traditional folk tune that soon had the crowd singing along at the tops of their well-oiled voices. They proceeded to perform a medley of jaunty tunes that the entire crowd seemed happy to clap and sing along to. The music filled the castle grounds with cheer and good will. As the troupe embarked on their final tune of the evening Antoine and Izabella readied themselves for their performance and one of the palace guards set light to the huge bonfire in readiness.

The flames soon took hold, sending the burning embers drifting and dancing high into the night sky. Antoine and Izabella walked onto the stage. They needed no introduction, as Antoine was already very well known to the audience.

'My Prince, my Queen, ladies, gentlemen and children, please let me introduce my lovely assistant Miss Izabella Szabó. She will be helping me this afternoon as we try to dazzle and amaze you with fantastical illusions and magic,' announced Antoine.

The crowd welcomed them with a warm round of "whoops" and whistles. However, among the merriment, the Grande Prince was unaware that sitting in the crowd was a spy for his exiled evil brother Jutotzas. He was watching the show with great interest and would report back to his master after the show.

Antoine explained the first illusion to the audience.

'I need the help of one of the royal children. Katarina, would you please come and help me.'

Eagerly she jumped up and ran onto the stage. Antoine gave a courteous bow and asked her to put her left arm out. Izabella took a pink silk cloth and draped it over her bare arm. Antoine waved his arms over her head, uttered a few magic words and pulled the cloth off little Katarina's arm to reveal a shiny gold bracelet. The crowd clapped appreciatively.

'For you, Princess. I hope you like it.'

She nodded, thanked Antoine and ran back to her seat and showed her brother, Ruben, the trinket.

'For my next special illusion I need your help. I want you all to concentrate and think of the name I am going to tell you. If we all focus and visualise this name something truly amazing will happen. The name I want you to concentrate on is Makkai.'

Izabella looked at Antoine. This wasn't how they had practiced this illusion. She was confused and looked at Antoine for some kind of explanation. Antoine smiled at her and walked off to the side of the stage and pushed a tall box back on. Izabella opened the front so the crowd could see there was nothing inside. She stood in the box and theatrically waved her hands around to prove it was indeed completely empty. She stepped out and closed the door. She took a large red silk cloth and completely covered Antoine. He spoke from beneath the cover.

'Now everybody I want you to focus on the name Makkai, and try to see it in your mind's eye.'

As the crowd fell silent Antoine took the Cube from his pouch and manipulated it into Solved-Mode-One, then pressed the glowing orange, red and white centre axis buttons. The crowd were oblivious to the fact that Antoine had caused a momentary time dimension split to occur. There was a bright flash from inside the box as the silk cloth fell to the ground. Antoine had miraculously gone, but where? Izabella was still confused. She hesitantly walked over to the box and slowly opened it. To her utter amazement inside was her beloved brother Makkai. He threw his arms around her. She was stunned, speechless and overwhelmed with happiness. *Where had he been? How come he was inside the box? Where was Antoine?* she thought. Then from the top of the castle wall Antoine called to the audience. They all turned round to see him waving at them from high on the ramparts. The crowd clapped and cheered. They had never seen anything quite like that before. They were amazed. Izabella was crying with joy as Antoine told her to close the box again. Makkai moved to the side with her. The box door then suddenly flung open to reveal Antoine inside. *How did he do that?* thought Izabella. Again the crowd applauded. Before they could settle Antoine took the Cube and placed it on his open palm, and pressed three diagonal yellow gems in a "/" pattern.

XL-R, set cutting beam to power level one, sent Antoine.

Cutting beam set to level one, sent XL-R.

Suddenly it threw a bolt of light at the Prince's golden crown. The yellow jewels around the edge then exploded into shafts of light fanning out over the audience, which moved as the Prince looked around in wonderment. He made them dance over the castle walls, then, with a wave of Antoine's hand they vanished.

'My Prince, I hope you have enjoyed our show. We now come to my final illusion. I am going to cheat death. I am going to escape from the flames,' announced Antoine whilst pointing to the huge, raging fire now burning to the side of the stage.

The crowd gasped. Izabella walked over to a large wooden box near the flames. She could feel the heat make her skin tingle. She opened the lid and Antoine climbed in. She wound a heavy chain around the box and secured it with a lock. The box was sealed. Antoine then poked his hand out through a little hole in the lid and waved. Two hooks were secured to the box and it was winched up over the fire. The guard then lowered it into the crackling flames.

'Ladies and gentlemen, Antoine will now escape from the box. He will cheat the flames of death,' announced Izabella with a theatrical flurry of hands.

The crowd fell silent as the fire crackled and hissed. The burning embers disappeared into the evening sky, carried on the wind. The crowd started to become restless as the flames engulfed the box and Antoine didn't appear. Izabella started to look worried too. *He should be out by now,* she thought. Normally he would have appeared within a few minutes, but there was no sign of him yet. The crowd began to grow uneasy. Princess Katarina tugged at her father's arm. She started to cry and asked her father to do something. Izabella ran over to The Prince and whispered in his ear. He pulled the tapestry off the table, kicking it over and scattering food and cutlery everywhere. He poured a huge water jug over the cloth, wrapped himself in it, picked up the table and ran into the inferno scattering the pyre in an explosion of flames and embers. Drawing his sword he thrashed wildly at the box, splintering it into pieces. He grabbed Antoine, put the cloth around him too and pulled him from the flames. He laid him on the ground. Isabella ran over with some water and gave it to Antoine. He coughed and spluttered, then started to drink.

'Where's the Cube, where's the Cube,' repeated a panic-stricken Antoine. The Prince quickly looked into the fire and noticed the glowing Cube lying among the wood and flames. Braving the searing heat he flicked it out with his sword. It tumbled out onto the grass. Antoine looked at it then fell unconscious.

■　■　■

Slowly Antoine opened his eyes. His face felt taut and his skin cracked as he tried to squint into focus. *Where am I?* he thought. Carefully he tried to look around but he could feel terrible pain coming from his back as he stretched.

'Antoine, my love, how are you feeling? You have been asleep for hours. We have been so worried about you. The fire has burnt you.' Izabella started to cry.

Antoine looked at her beautiful face and slowly lifted his hand to gently stroke her cheek. His hand was black. It hurt. In fact, everything hurt. He looked at Izabella. She could see the pain in his eyes.

'What happened to me?'

'The trick went wrong my love. The Prince saved you from the flames. We are at the castle. We have been watching over you,' sobbed Izabella.

There was a knock on the door and in came Princess Katarina and her brother Prince Ruben. She walked over to the bed and gently took Antoine's hand. He noticed the little bracelet still on her arm.

'How are you, dear Antoine?' she asked.

'Little Katarina, I am all the better for seeing you,' replied Antoine, trying to disguise his pain.

'Shall I dress your wounds for you?'

'No, thank you little one, I am alright for now,' he lied.

'Thank you for looking after Antoine. You are a very good nurse.' Izabella took Katarina's hand and gave it a comforting squeeze. Antoine's wounds were very serious and he knew he might not be able to fight the Earth-type infections now raging in his wounds. The absorption process may have altered the body's immune system, for the worse.

As the days passed Antoine's health steadily deteriorated. Some of the wounds became infected and, try as they might, they couldn't seem to stop it spreading. The herbs and primitive medicinal potions were having no effect, and Izabella knew it. Katarina was at his bedside all the time chatting to him and making him laugh. Izabella knew they were losing the battle to save him. Antoine knew it too.

■　■　■

Late in the afternoon, when Antoine was left alone to rest and just as he was about to drift off to sleep, there was a bright blue flash of light in his room. Antoine slowly opened his eyes. It took all the might he could muster. In the doorway he could just make out the blurred ghostly image of a man. He watched as the silhouette approached him. He couldn't move. Maybe this was it. Maybe this was what death was, his death, a human death. It wasn't meant to end this way. Was it his time to take the stairway to heaven, whatever that was? He didn't want to turn that page on this chapter of his life just yet. He wanted to be with Izabella forever. He felt the ghostly image touch him followed by a sharp pain. He could feel his very soul being drained from him. Then the pain ceased. The figure slowly moved away, back towards the door and in a blinding blue flash of light was gone. Antoine could not believe what he had just witnessed. He was shaking with fear. He called out for Izabella. She came running into his room.

'What is it Antoine, my love?'

'I have just seen an apparition. Can you see if the Prince will come and see me? I want to talk to him before it is too late.'

A while later there was a knock at the door, and in walked the Prince.

'Dear Antoine, you asked to see me.'

'Indeed I did, my Prince. I have a matter of great urgency I must discuss with you,' explained Antoine and slowly sat himself up, the pain making him visibly wince. 'You saved my life and have given me shelter and cared for me. I am forever in your debt. There is something I must show to you.'

'What is it that troubles you, Antoine?'

XL-R, disengage self defense system, sent Antoine.

'Could you please pass me the Cube? I want to show you something.'

The Prince handed him the remains of the charred Cube. He slowly manipulated the segments into Solved-Mode-Six and pressed the two green jewels in a ":" pattern. It began to flash. He then passed the Cube back to the Prince and asked him to hold it.

'Zephrána vigyázz a takarítás tegnap este a nap,' recited Antoine as he waved his hands over the charred Cube. Smoke began to engulf the object, then it slowly cleared to reveal the Cube clean and sparkling with all the coloured jewels dotted over its surface, like new.

'Beware the cleansing night of days. What does that mean?' translated the Prince.

'I need to explain something to you.'

Antoine took the Cube. His hands were slower now and the pain was excruciating. His joints felt as if they were going to seize up. Carefully he positioned the Cube on his bed and pressed three white diagonal jewels.

'XL-R, project archive data file JX8P 45.2435,' commanded Antoine.

The Prince was intrigued by the Cube used in the show. He hadn't seen an object like it before. Moments later a holographic projection materialized in the middle of the room. The Prince was amazed, scared and confused all at the same time.

'What strange magic is this that you bring before me?'

'Don't be afraid, it will not harm you. I want to explain who I am,' reassured Antoine.

'What do you mean, who you are? You are my friend, Antoine. I don't understand.'

Slowly the projection began to focus to reveal a beautiful lush green swooping valley, lined with towering plants and vegetation unlike anything the Prince had seen. Flowers were sprinkled between the plants and the sky was a clear bright azure blue.

'Where is this beautiful place? Is it near here?' asked the Prince naively.

'No, this was my home. It is far away, beyond the stars in the night sky, on another planet. This "magic" Cube is very special. It can do things you couldn't even dream of. It can turn back the very fabric of time, it can transport you into the future, or take you into the past. It has immense powers.'

The Prince's head was spinning from Antoine's fantastic revelations. He was so overwhelmed by what he had seen he couldn't even ask a question. He was speechless and didn't know where to start. Antoine pressed on as the hologram morphed into a new scenario. This scene was of violent warfare, of huge spacecraft, of destruction on a massive scale. This was his planet now held in the deadly grip of a raging war.

'This is what my planet is like now, before I left and came here,' continued Antoine.

'Came here, but when? I have known you for years. I am confused.'

'I was brought here by the Cube, through time and space, from a different world to live in your world.'

'What is space?' asked the Prince.

'Good question, it would take too long to explain. My world is dying from war, devastation and famine. My people have destroyed our world through greed and selfishness. We did not care for our world; we ended up stripping it of its resources and life giving vegetation and in turn, its beauty. Life was becoming unsustainable. Our world was past it's point of sustained regeneration. The will to survive turned our nations on one another in a desperate struggle to live. Our technology has brought us to the very edge of distinction. I was sent here to see if my people could live on your planet, in your world, as it seems similar to ours.'

The holographic projections continued as the Prince watched in amazement and horror. He suddenly realized that the person lying in the bed wasn't the Antoine he once knew. The beings shown in the projection were not humans, they were like something from a nightmare, biomechanical creatures with unbelievable physical features and capabilities.

'So who, or what are you?' asked the Prince.

'My real name is Akaii, but in a way I am still your friend Antoine. When I arrived on your planet I had to make myself blend in with your people. As you have seen, I would have looked out of place. The first person I met was your friend Antoine. I have been absorbed into him, I am living through his body, using his thought and will to guide me. I have been learning about you, your world and the way you live. Using the Cube I have been sending information back to my world in readiness for the arrival of the survivors of our world to live in yours. I am a homing beacon for them, to guide them here. My destiny was to live in your world and one day be reunited with my own people.'

'When is this going to happen? How is this going to happen?' asked the Prince, the panic in his voice plain to hear.

'My Prince this will not occur in your lifetime, or your children's lifetime, but many hundreds of years in the future. I know I am dying, and I need to pass the Cube on to you. You have already seen some of the things it is capable of. It can do so much more. You are a great man. You have a strong honorable heart. It is obvious to me that you care very deeply for your people. My time on your planet, living in your world, has been very interesting. I have felt emotions that I have never experienced before. I have fallen in love with Izabella and she has made me see that your race is worth saving. I cannot allow my nation to wipe life from your planet. The Cube will help you care for your people and save them from danger. It will bring them great wealth and happiness, it will guide you and your people through the tough times ahead and, at some point in the future, ultimately save mankind from "The Cleansing Night of Days". You must guard it with your life and keep its secrets safe. The Cube is the key to the survival of your race and your world. Let me explain: the green segments represent the Earth, the orange segments are for fire, the blue segments for water, the white segments are for time, the red segments signify love and the yellow segments are for life. Different combinations will unlock different powers. The Cube itself will teach you how it works. Now my Prince I must ask you to put your hands back on the Cube.'

Antoine slowly manipulated the segments into Solved-Mode-One, to realign for thought transfer.

XL-R, prepare for Mind-Implant, sent Antoine telepathically.

Mind-Implant ready, sent XL-R telepathically.

The Prince held the Cube and Antoine pressed seven white jewels in the shape of an "H". With a sudden gigantic rush of data the Prince stiffened as the transferal got underway. A few minutes later the process was complete.

'Now you will be able to use the Cube to protect your people, to look after them, and it will help you overcome the dangers that lay ahead. You have been given the knowledge to use the Cube at will,' continued Antoine. 'The Cube can only be used by you and it is important that you keep it safe. It must never fall into the wrong hands. You must ensure the Cube is passed on through the generations; when your time comes you must pass it on to someone in your family bloodline who you can trust implicitly. Passing through time, its powers will be continually updated as our new technologies develop. May I suggest that you don't turn "Updates" off. This process must be repeated until the time comes when the Cube will save your world. Beware of people who will try to take it from you. The Cube will guide you and you can use it to protect you. I can feel my work here is coming to a close. Could I ask you to gather Izabella, my friends and your family and bring them here for me?' asked Antoine.

'Of course, my dear friend. I will return shortly with them.' He got up and left the room.

As the door closed, Antoine was engulfed in a wave of intense pain he had been suppressing. His face contorted as he felt the full force of the burning infection gripping his whole body. Summoning all his inner strength he again managed to hide the feeling. He could hear footsteps approaching his room, so he tried to look at ease. The door swung open, his friends entered and stood by his bed. Izabella leant over and kissed him tenderly on the cheek, took his hand and held it to her heart.

'My dear Antoine, we are all here, as you requested,' assured the Prince.

'Thank you all for being with me. I want to tell you all how much I love you and I want to thank you for looking after me. I have never ever known such kindness before in my life. You truly are a very special people and I leave this world knowing it will be safe in your hands,' said Antoine.

Izabella looked at Antoine. his eyes said it all. She could feel him slipping away from her. He looked around the room and touched the soul of each of his friends. Izabella squeezed his hand. Little Princess Katarina nuzzled into her father's arms. Ruben held his mother's hand tightly. Antoine's eyes slowly closed. They all stood in silence and listened as his breathing became slower and slower. Each breath took longer and longer to come until finally it never came. Antoine's face then drooped like molten wax and the Prince quickly pulled the white bed sheet up over his head. Akaii was gone, forever. Antoine was gone, forever.

■ ■ ■

The legend of the Cube's awesome powers quickly spread across the land, and amazing stories were told in distant corners of the kingdom. The Grand Prince Zoltán became wealthy and powerful and his people thrived under his leadership. However with wealth and power came enemies, and the stories eventually reached the ears of Zoltán's long-exiled brother Jutotzas. He was married to Zsuzsi now with two young sons, Enzó and Radován. He lived near a small settlement called Eger, about 245km due east of Győr, and a twelve-hour ride by horse. They had a lovely little stone farmhouse with a thatched roof built by Jutotzas and some of his friends. It had been hard work but it was comfortable and was situated in a lush valley surrounded by trees and a nearby lake. They had some flat, fertile land that they farmed, growing various vegetables as the seasons changed. They kept some chickens, a pig, a few goats, and a cow. They were just about self-sufficient and could barter or trade for things that they needed. Life was tough but they were making a better living than most of their neighbours. As the stories of his wealthy brother circulated he started to become restless and angry. He began to formulate a plan, to get his revenge. After all these years he was still jealous of his elder brother's birthright. He had decided that he was going to take what should have been his. He had found out from his friend at the castle, the spy who had been at the Prince's party all those years ago, that the Cube never left his brother's side. It was with him everywhere he went. Its powers were legendary. He realised that ultimately he would have to face his elder brother if he was to take control of the kingdom and the Cube. It was well-known that the Prince was a fearsome swordsman and he knew that would be a hard fight to win. As the nights passed Jutotzas sat and planned his next move; it became an obsession. He knew he couldn't tell his wife what he was really aiming to do, as she would try and stop him. His friends had no idea that he was the Prince's brother. They only knew him as Jutotzas "the farmer".

He would have to make up a cover story to explain why he had to go away.

■   ■   ■

17:15, THURSDAY, 20TH AUGUST, 903 A.D. NEAR EGER, 130KM NORTH EAST OF BUDA(PEST)

One evening as he sat eating with his wife and children he decided the moment was now right to tell them.

'My darling family, I have some news to tell you. It has come to my attention that there is a hunting party leaving soon to head north. There have been reports of fruitful sightings and I have decided to join the next pack. We need new furs and clothing. I will be able to bring food to help see us through the next few months. We will be able to trade the furs and get the things we need for the farm. The seeds are in and the land can be left for a few weeks to establish itself. I will be back in a few weeks.'

'Oh, yes, I suppose that is a good idea. It would certainly help us at the moment. I can look after the children and my father will be around if I need assistance. Don't worry, my dearest Jutotzas, we will be alright. When will you be leaving?' replied Zsuzsi.

'I will be going in a few days. I will need to prepare my horse and get my hunting tools sharpened.'

The two boys ran to their father for a cuddle. They had never been away from him and were upset by the thought of him going away. Zsuzsi gave Jutotzas an affectionate kiss on the forehead and joined the group cuddle. Suddenly Jutotzas was overwhelmed by a sense of fear. *Was he right to jeopardise his family for his own gains? What if it all went wrong and he never returned to them?* he thought. His imagination ran wild.

■ ■ ■

06:17, FRIDAY, 21ST AUGUST, 903 A.D. NEAR EGER, 130KM
NORTH EAST OF BUDA(PEST)

The following morning, Jutotzas rose early, gathered his tools and headed off into the woods. He was going to make a new bow and some arrows as he wanted to avoid a close encounter with his brother. He started to look for a suitable piece of wood from which to make a bow. He needed a branch about up to his shoulders and about as thick as two of his fingers. He soon found a suitable piece and with his axe lopped it from the tree. He gathered some wood suitable for arrows and returned to the farm. Over the next few days he worked on fashioning a powerful bow. Using a large pot of boiling water he softened the bran and bent the wood over a former into a bow shape and strapped it into place. As it dried it set into a curve. Using some thick twine he bound a hand grip in the centre and attached the bow string. With a sharp knife he sat and whittled the arrows into shape attaching a sharp flint at the tip using thin twine. The fletching vanes were made from feathers and the arrows flew straight and true. He was ready. The night before his departure, Zsuzsi and Jutotzas put the boys to bed and then sat by the fire and chatted. Jutotzas had a troubled sleep, full of nightmares about what lay ahead. If he never returned, how would Zsuzsi cope? How would his boys grow up without their father?.

■　■　■

06:12, SATURDAY, 22ND AUGUST, 903 A.D. NEAR EGER, 130KM NORTH EAST OF BUDA(PEST)

Eventually the morning light awoke him from his shallow slumber. He felt anxious, and he had a horrible churning feeling in his stomach. Zsuzsi, sensing his restlessness also stirred. Gradually her eyes opened to see Jutotzas sitting looking at their two boys asleep in the corner. How innocent they were. He felt guilty about their lives. He'd had a privileged childhood, he had never suffered some of the hardships they already had. He hoped they were happy; he couldn't bear the thought they might not be. It wasn't fair to bring them into the world to endure such hardship. He hoped his plan would work and they could leave this life behind. He had to follow his dream otherwise it would torture him for the rest of his days.

'What is troubling you, my love?' asked Zsuzsi.

'I was just wondering if I had got enough arrows. I don't want to run out,' he lied. 'We must make some food as the boys will be awake soon.'

They got dressed and set about making their morning meal. They had some fruit and nuts followed by crusty bread and cheese. The boys had some fresh milk while mother and father had a hot brew of herbs. As the time of his departure grew closer the boys became tearful and clingy. Jutotzas again felt the pain of seeing the tears in their young blue eyes. *What am I doing? Why am I doing this? What if it goes wrong?* he thought.

He hugged them tighter than he had ever done before. Zsuzsi could see how troubled he was.

'Are you all right? You will be back in a few days. The boys will be safe with me. Don't worry,' she said, reassuringly.

'I know. It feels different this time.'

Jutotzas swept Zsuzsi up into his strong arms and kissed her passionately. The scent of her skin, the warm touch of her soft, gentle hands made his head spin. He loved her with all his heart but felt driven to risk it all for his own selfish reasons. Once he had gathered his things and the horse was fully loaded, he grabbed hold of the saddle and pulled himself up onto his steed. Zsuzsi thought he looked like a proud warrior, not a farmer. She cuddled the boys as Jutotzas said his goodbyes and with a flick of the reins the horse trotted off up the track. He turned to see his sons and their mother waving frantically to him as he made his way over the gentle hill. Soon they were gone. He was now on his own. A torrent of emotion burst forth and he wiped his eyes. What lay ahead?

Over the next few days he travelled west heading towards the mighty city of Győr. The journey was hard going. The days felt long and lonely. The nights were worse; they were long, cold *and* lonely. He missed his family and he kept telling himself he would soon return to them and they could start their new life together.

■ ■ ■

Eventually, early in the afternoon of the third day Jutotzas caught a glimpse of the city in the distance and soon he arrived in the town square. He could still remember it well. He was sure nobody would recognise him now as he had grown a beard and had long, dark hair. First he had to find his spying friend Boldizsá. He would most likely be drinking in an alehouse somewhere near the market. He quickly found a place to tie up his horse then set off into the market. After he had checked inside a few hostelries he eventually found his friend. Sure enough, Boldizsá was cradling a jug of ale in his hands and talking with a bit of a slur. He had obviously started drinking quite early in the day. When he caught sight of Jutotzas he jumped up, banged his head on the low ceiling, fell down, then got up again and gave his friend a big floppy hug. Jutotzas realised he had some catching up to do so ordered a couple of ales and before long was as equally incoherent as his friend. At the end of the evening Jutotzas went home with Boldizsá to his shack and spent the night in a heap on the floor.

■ ■ ■

The following morning both men awoke to a pounding head and a feeling of intense hunger. Having cobbled together something to eat, they then started to discuss Jutotzas' plan.

'So, my friend, you know why I have come back.'

'Indeed, I can guess; you have come for the famous Cube. Your brother will never give it up without a fight,' advised Boldizsá.

'It should be mine.'

'Your jealousy meant you could never be the Grand Prince. Your brother would have looked after you, but you wanted it all, and now he has the Cube too.'

'And if you hadn't stolen food from the castle kitchen you would still have a job there. So help me get the Cube and I will make you a rich man. I need to know about my brother, the castle and the guards that protect him there,' explained Jutotzas.

'Alright, I will help you. I expect everything is the same as when I last worked there. What can I help you with?'

'Firstly, I must get into the castle without being seen. So I also need to know where the guards are likely to be, and how many of them. I also have to find where the royal chamber is and if it is guarded. I assume the Cube will be with my brother, so I am planning to make my move in the dead of night. I will have to go to his bed chamber and find the Cube. It will be there, somewhere,' reasoned Jutotzas.

'The best place to get into the castle is the inner north wall, by the corner tower,' explained the spy. 'If you remember, it sticks out over the rampart and the moat, so if you climb up underneath it you can't be seen. You can swim across the moat there too. Guards patrol the parapet so you will need to time your crossing. Also the trees will shield you from view. Once you make it to the parapet, head towards the keep. Remember, guards in the bailey will be able to see you at certain points. Keep yourself in the shadows of the flame torches. When you get to the keep, go up the stairs to the top floor. Here you should find your brother. His children sleep in the room next to him. Expect to find a guard nearby, so you will have to deal with him. Take a knife, your sword and your bow. Have you killed before?' he asked bluntly.

'Only animals, but I am not afraid to kill. I am a good hunter. I have had years to practice. What needs to be done will be done,' replied Jutotzas, ominously.

'You will need all your skills if you are to take the Cube.'

'Indeed, later tonight, under the cover of the moon, I will take what is mine. Let us now prepare.'

They spent the afternoon walking round the castle's outer wall looking at places to hide, and to clock the movement of the guards on the parapets. Jutotzas had a little sand timer and used it to count the time it took for the guards to do their rounds. He noted them in a little leather-bound book. Yet again he could feel his nerves coming on. He was starting to get an unsettled feeling in his stomach again.

They decided to go and get some food and wait for the light to fade. Gradually the glowing orange sun hanging in the sky began to disappear behind the trees. Bubbling pink and purple clouds marbled the sky as evening descended into night. A silver moon soon cast a blue sheen over the water surrounding the castle as the shadows lengthened. Darkness fell. They returned to Boldizsá's shack and Jutotzas gathered his things together.

'I am ready, my friend. I guess it's time to meet my destiny. Wish me luck,' announced Jutotzas, theatrically.

'Good luck. You'll need it. Be careful.'

He threw his bow over his shoulder, opened the door and set out for the castle. The night sky was clear and the stars twinkled in the darkness. The city was silent apart from an owl calling out eerily in the distance as it flew across the silver-edged clouds. Slowly he made his way through the deserted streets. As he approached the castle's portcullis he could see a couple of guards standing by the main gate. Quickly he dodged into the nearby bushes and made his way through to the trees around the edge of the moat until he was near the turret on the north rampart. Suddenly the dark, murky water didn't look so inviting. Just then he heard a branch crack behind him. Startled, he bolted round to find himself face to face with a palace guard.

'What are you doing here? What is your name?' asked the guard abruptly.

Before he had a moment to think, Jutotzas leant forward and hit him hard with his elbow, to protect his hand, knocking the guard to the ground. He was out cold. Jutotzas pulled the body into the bushes, tied him up and put a rag gag over his mouth. He waited for a few moments and, as he predicted, the guards appeared high on the ramparts. As soon as they had turned the corner he would swim across. He quietly slipped into the water. The cold sent a sudden shudder through his body and winded him. He pressed on as quickly as he could, trying not to splash or make any noise. Gradually he paddled his way across and scrambled up the bank to the base of the rampart. He sat for a few moments to let his heart steady and to catch his breath. Next, using some strong twine he fastened one end of some twine to a small grappling hook and the other he wound round the arrow and tied it tight. Just as he had finished he could see the two guards coming around the parapet again. He quickly took out his little sand timer, turned it over and put it back in his wet tunic. It was set. He had to climb up the rampart and over the top before the sand had run out. He waited for the guards to go around the corner, paused for a few moments then quickly fired the arrow over the rampart. It made a satisfying clunk as it landed. He quickly tugged on it to see if it was strong. It slipped a little then held solid. With his bow on his back he took hold of the rope. His cold hands struggled to get a grip, but eventually he held it firmly and started to pull. Leaning out from the wall slightly he began to walk up the stone rampart. Being a hard-working farmer had certainly kept him fit and strong. Mustering all his energy he pulled himself up the steep battlement. Hand over hand, one step at a time, up he went. Suddenly a stone broke away and he lost a footing and swung out wildly over the icy cold moat. He grappled to steady himself and then slowly carried on. He looked at his timer, the sand was running out. He knew he had to speed up if he was going to make it. Looking up he could see the castellations being lit by the flame torches. Not far now. He strained and pulled with all his might. Closer and closer he climbed. He could hear the guards footsteps getting louder; they were not far away. With one last massive effort he pulled himself up and over the rampart. Looking around he saw a shadowy doorway and quickly concealed himself there. As the guards came closer one of them pointed to the rope and the hook embedded in a mortar joint. Jutotzas took out his wooden batten and as they passed his doorway he hit one of the guards hard on the back of the head. He stumbled and fell to the floor. The other guard spun round just as Jutotzas thumped him up under the jaw. The force was so great he launched him off his feet, through a castellation and over the rampart. He landed with a dull thud on the ground below. Quickly he retreated to the shadows and took off his bow. He could see the keep over in the opposite corner of the castle. He crouched down and slowly crept along the parapet, making sure that the guards below in the bailey couldn't see him. The flame torches flickered in the evening breeze as the shadows danced about maniacally. Slowly he made his way around the ledge until he was nearly at the keep. Just through the archway, as predicted, he could see the back of the guard stationed there. He edged himself up against the wall, then quickly put his arm around the guard's neck and punched him hard in the small of the back. The guard groaned as Jutotzas put his other hand firmly over his mouth. He writhed and squirmed and a few moments later he slumped to the floor. He pulled the motionless body under the stairway, out of sight. With great trepidation, Jutotzas began to climb the stairs to the top floor, where his brother lay, and where his children slept too. *It is now or never*, he thought. He crept up to the first door and peeked through a knot hole in the wood. He could make out the silhouette of the two children in the moonlight that was streaming through the slot window. He moved over to the other door. Through a crack in the wood planking he could just see his brother and the Queen sleeping. His heart was starting to race as the full enormity of his actions was becoming all too real. There was no going back now. He took hold of the door handle and slowly twisted it. The door began to move and he gradually pulled it open a little way. Carefully he squeezed through the gap. The door gave a little squeak. Jutotzas clenched his teeth and paused for a moment. Zoltán stirred and turned over.

Phew, he thought, *that was close.* Carefully and quietly he searched the room for the Cube. It was difficult to see in the darkened room as he fumbled and felt his way around. Then in the half-light he could just make out a bulbous leather pouch on the table next to his brother's bed. *That must be it*, he thought. Slowly Jutotzas approached the bedside and reached out to grab it.

Suddenly he felt a strong hand clamp around his wrist. He felt a skull-crushing thump to the side of his head which sent him hurtling across the room and crashing into an ornate table. As he lay, temporarily stunned, Zoltán arose from his bed and bounded across the room to meet his assailant. He grabbed him by his tunic collar, hauled him to his feet and thumped him hard again. Jutotzas went barreling across the stone floor. He quickly got up and charged at Zoltán. They locked arms and began wrestling as they tumbled to the floor. The noise had woken Queen Kristianna and she sat up petrified by the commotion. The two men fought wildly with arms flailing in every direction. Jutotzas landed a heavy blow on Zoltán, which sent him over the bed and crashing into the wall, right next to where his sword was leaning. Wasting no time he grabbed it and stood facing the intruder.

'You dare to come to my bed chamber and steal from me? You will pay for this intrusion,' exclaimed Zoltán.

'You don't scare me, you have never scared me. We have fought many times before,' retorted Jutotzas, as he pulled his dagger from its sheath. 'Let's see how good you are with a sword now, shall we?'

'We have fought before? When? Who are you?' Zoltán was puzzled.

'Who gave you that scar on the side of your face when you were eight years old?'

The room fell silent as Zoltán thought for a moment. Slowly he realised who he had been fighting.

'Jutotzas, my brother, is that really you?'

'Indeed it is. I have returned to claim what is mine.'

'You tried to kill me before. That's why Father banished you. You couldn't bear the thought of me being your King. Our father was following our ancestor's will. Only one of us could be King. I am the elder one so the crown was passed to me. I would have looked after you, you would have been by my side. The people would have loved you too. Why could you not accept *your* destiny?'

'I was tired of always being the second choice. Father always favoured you.'

'Father didn't favour me. I was born first so certain things were put in place before you were born. They had to be done this way as he may never have had a second son. You would have been King if I had died,' explained Zoltán.

'He blamed me for the death of our Mother, his Queen. If I hadn't been born she would still be alive.'

'Father never blamed you. He knew Mother was dying long before you were born. He was shocked when she became pregnant with you. You probably don't remember the time you spent with our Mother. She loved you so very much. You look like her and that made it hard for our Father when she died. He was very protective of you and it was left to me to take on the harsh responsibility of leadership. When he was forced to banish you, he was heartbroken, who do you think was keeping you safe and paying a good price for your grain and produce? Did it never occur to you that it was strange that you were making a reasonable living whilst most around you were finding life really hard?'

'That changes nothing, and you have the Cube. I know all about it and I want it.'

'You cannot have it. It was passed on to me by my special friend, Antoine. On his deathbed he bequeathed it to me. I cared and looked after him when he was dying and that is why I now have it.'

'I want it and I am going to have it,' continued Jutotzas.

'Over my dead body, my *dear* brother,' replied Zoltán, sarcastically.

'I hope it doesn't come to that.'

Suddenly Jutotzas lunged forward, grabbed Queen Kristianna roughly by the arm and pulled her close to him. He held the dagger to her throat whilst he clasped her tightly round the waist. He could feel her tremble.

'Give me the Cube or I will take away your Queen forever.'

'All right, all right. Wait, I will get it,' conceded Zoltán, reluctantly.

He walked over to the little table by his bed and picked up the pouch. Untying the string knot he pulled out the silver Cube. Jutotzas stood dumbstruck by the sight of it. Suddenly it transformed into segments of flashing colour. Zoltán then manipulated the Cube into Solved-Mode-Three and pressed three yellow jewels in a diagonal line "/".

'How does it work? Show me the powers that I have heard so much about,' he ordered. 'Don't try anything clever as your Queen won't live to regret it,' he joked, menacingly. 'Make it do magic.'

Zoltán pointed the Cube at the stone wall. After a short delay, suddenly a beam of yellow light exploded from the Cube and began cutting through the solid stone of the castle chamber. Just then little Princess

Katarina burst into the room crying. A startled Jutotzas lost his grip on the Queen, who shoved him aside and ran to scoop up little Katarina into her arms. Zoltán came forward and stood defiantly in front of them facing Jutotzas, sword at the ready.

'Over my dead body, you said. Well, that is the way it is going to have to be then,' taunted Jutotzas.

Drawing his sword he leapt forward, and the two mighty swords clashed in a hail of sparks. Kristianna quickly ran to the shelter of the corner of the room and sank, cowering to the floor. She and Katarina watched in horror as the two brothers fought with all their strength. Blow after blow was traded as they dodged the mighty blades slicing through the air. Suddenly Jutotzas felt a searing pain in his arm. He glanced down, he had been cut. A line of blood ran across his forearm. His jaw clenched as he locked eyes on his brother. Lunging forward he made a strike only to be blocked again by Zoltán who followed through with a high, scything blow, which caught Jutotzas again, across the stomach this time.

'Stop my brother, stop. You are hurt. This is over.' stated Zoltán.

'Never. I will take what is mine,' retorted Jutotzas.

Lifting his sword high he began swinging wildly at his brother. Just then the bed chamber door flew open again. In the archway stood little Prince Ruben. His tearful eyes full of fright; the noise had scared him. For a split second Zoltán was distracted and suddenly he too felt a crippling pain in his stomach. He froze and looked at Jutotzas. His head dropped. He felt the blade quiver as he crumpled to the ground. Kristianna screamed. Her face contorted in terror, she ran over to Zoltán. She fell to her knees and gently cradled his head in her hands. The two children rushed over to their father and hugged him. Jutotzas stood back and looked at the scene unfolding in front of him. He stood motionless, his eyes locked onto his brother. Kristianna whispered private words of love in her husband's ear as she fought back the tears she was drowning in. She could feel time slowing down as they felt their love bonding them together. They would be together forever one day.

Seizing the moment Jutotzas grabbed the Cube and feverishly began to manipulate the segments. The Cube flashed and flickered then went black. Jutotzas looked confused. *Why isn't it working?* he thought. Then he felt a stinging feeling coming through his fingers. He tried to loosen his grip, but couldn't. He began to panic and shout to Zoltán.

'What is happening? why isn't it working?'

He could sense the pain intensifying. The pain grew up his arm. He started to scream. He could feel his chest tighten, squeezing the air from his lungs. The children hid behind their mother, terrified, as Jutotzas staggered over to the doorway, his hands locked to the Cube. Blinding beams of light began shooting out from it, searing into his body as his pain grew. He fell heavily through the doorway and crumpled to the ground. There was a cataclysmic explosion of blinding white light as Jutotzas atomized into thin air. The blackened remains of the Cube rolled back through the doorway. The surface was peppered with holes where the coloured jewel light cells had been. A few remaining cells flickered then faded.

'I couldn't let my brother have the Cube. He would have brought shame to our people, he would have destroyed us. I have lost my brother,' whispered Zoltán, his voice fading. 'My Queen, you must keep the

Cube safe. Antoine told me that one day, long into the future, it will save our people, save our world. Let us hope he is right. You must keep it safe with this little book. Read it and it will explain everything. You have to believe. When Ruben is old enough to understand, give it to him. He must read the book too, for this is our destiny.'

'Zoltán, my dearest Zoltán, my love, my life, don't leave us. I can't live without you. What will I do?' Kristianna wept.

'You must carry on. We have our children to keep safe. You are strong and you can be Queen and look after our people. I will watch over you until we can be together again, my love.' Kristianna cuddled Zoltán. She could feel him ebbing away from her. She kissed him tenderly as she felt him slowly get heavier in her arms. He looked at her, smiled and closed his eyes.

'Sleep, my love. I will be with you forever in your dreams,' whispered Kristianna and kissed him on the forehead. She swept her two children into her arms and held them close.

FOUR

THE CLEANSING NIGHT OF DAYS

PRESENT DAY

'So the Cube and this little book have been passed through the generations and here we are today,' said János. 'We are descended from the House Of *Árpád*. *Our* family name was changed to keep the bloodline safe, hence Novak has been passed down to us. This has all been predicted. This eclipse was foretold in the book. It was called *The Cleansing Night of Days*. However there is also another prediction in this book which I have not yet told you about,' continued János.

'It goes on to say that when we are in darkness a man amongst us, with us, will save the world. He will be able to manipulate the Cube and unleash its true powers. As you can see it has been damaged. This is because it had been programmed to be used by Zoltán and not his brother, causing it to partially self-destruct. It will be able to transport you back in time or forward in time, and it is capable of much more besides. It can be repaired, and this is where you Ruben, come into the story.'

'What do you mean Dad?' asked a puzzled Ruben. 'Can't you fix it? You fixed my computer last week.'

'Hmmm... Yes, that was an interesting virus you somehow picked up. So much for Parental Control Settings. Anyway, the man amongst us the book refers to, I think, is you. It's not me; I've had a fiddle with it, but nothing happened.'

The room fell eerily silent as everyone tried to take in what had just been said. János stood up and handed the Cube to Ruben.

'There you are, my boy, you are going to save the world.'

'Oh, so no pressure then. I thought revising for my exams was hard enough, now you want me to save the world. Anything else you want me to do while I am at it? Maybe tidy my room too?' joked Ruben nervously.

He carefully cradled the Cube in his palms. Slowly he began to feel his hands fidgeting and his fingers tingle at the ends. Then suddenly he started twisting and turning the segments. Some mystical force was manipulating him. His hands moved quicker and quicker as his fingers whizzed in a blur over the surface of the Cube. Moments later his hands came to an abrupt stop. The Cube was glowing with a soft white light.

The remaining coloured jewels were now magically arranged to line up with the ends of the axis of the three-dimensional planes running through the core of the Cube. Even more remarkable was the fact that one complete segment was now covered with nine white jewels. Ruben looked at it in utter amazement as the light began to grow in intensity. Gradually it started to flicker as the beam tracked up and down and across the floor at an ever-increasing speed. Slowly a scrambled image pulled into focus and there, in the middle of the room, a clearly defined 3D holographic projection of an alien hung in the air. János couldn't believe what he was seeing, no one could. He reached out and squeezed Sarah's hand reassuringly. She looked at him. She was scared. *Who, or what was this being?* she thought.

'Greetings, Earthlings. I am Overlord Ebucski-Bur, the head of the High Council of Htrae. You have summoned me by the unlocking of this Cube. I am speaking to you from another time dimension from a galaxy far away. When this Cube was taken from Zoltán, its owner, it was triggered into Self-Destruct-Mode. It has been damaged and it is important that it be repaired. When it detonated, the Cube caused a fracture in the timeline, blasting the jewel cells into different time dimensions, and so disabling it. They still exist in these relative time dimensions in your past. To make the Cube work again with all its powers they must be recovered. You have solved the white segment; this will allow you to go back in time and return to your present. Only when you have recovered all of the jewel cells will you be able to travel into the future and save your world. You will no doubt know that your world is now in great danger. You have been engulfed by darkness, which means time is running out for you and your planet. My nation, the Zenabi, too is in great danger as our planet is being destroyed by a massive warring army led by the mighty Ynos Ettessac. As the war raged my people were being slaughtered so we made plans to leave our planet and find a new world to inhabit. Many hundreds of your Earth years before now we sent one of our kind, called Akaii, to your planet to prepare it for our future arrival. He sent us data showing your world could sustain our life forms but we would need to eradicate all life on your planet first. However, Akaii fell ill and was cared for by your people until he could sustain life no more. The data he sent showed that our nation could not destroy such a benevolent species; we should learn from it. Akaii was my son and so I am here to help you as you helped Akaii. However, not so our enemies. They discovered our plan. They *will* travel to your world and unleash a fury you will not have known. The process has already begun. I don't think we are strong enough now to stop them. We are losing ground. Young Ruben, you have been chosen to save your world. We have engineered your destiny. I will instruct you as to what must be done. Now take the Cube and place your right thumb on the centre axis white jewel and your right second finger on the centre axis yellow jewel. Next, place your left thumb on the centre axis blue jewel and your left second finger on the centre axis green jewel. Now when I say, press all four jewels in. This will link the Cube to you and it will then transfer the data you will need to operate it. Do not be alarmed by the sensation you will experience during this process. It will last a few of your Earth seconds. When completed you will be able to manipulate the Cube at will and summon up its powers to help you on your quest. Are you ready, young Ruben?'

Ruben looked at his mum and dad. He was scared. Then his dad spoke.

'Ruben, my darling son, the world is on the brink of destruction. This has been preordained and so we must follow the path laid out for us. You have been chosen to be the guardian of the Cube and with it comes the possible fate of mankind. These alien beings have created technologies we can only dream of. I will be with you all the way. I will help you,' reassured János.

'Your father is correct. You have been chosen, and with the Cube you will be safe. It will take you on journeys through time, there will be dangers, but you will have the power to overcome these adversities. The Cube is guarded by Time-Warriors but the detonation of the Cube will have caused them to mutate in some way that I can't predict. They will shadow your every move and attempt to take the Cube from you. You can defeat them as long as you have skill and the Cube. It will become more powerful as you repair it. Now time is running out. We must complete the transferal process immediately,' confirmed Overlord Ebucski-Bur.

'Blimey, I bet you're glad you got your exams out of the way as it looks like you're going to be a bit busy,' joked Katarina nervously.

'Okay, let's boogie. Let's do this thing,' quipped Ruben.

'So is that a yes, then?' interjected the confused alien.

'Yes,' confirmed Ruben.

Suddenly he felt a surge of immense power running through his fingertips. His head felt like it was about to explode, then seconds later the pain was gone.

'The transferal is complete. Your thought waves will engage with the Cube and it will do as you command. We have also downloaded the latest update which will now allow the Cube to morph between shapes and there are more features too. I doubt your iPhone can do that. I must now bid you farewell. My work here, for the time being, is nearly done. Good luck.'

The holographic image dissolved into thin air and was gone. Sarah got up and went to join Ruben on the sofa and gave him a hug.

'What does this all mean, Dad? How can my little brother save the world?' asked Katarina.

'There are dark forces at work here. I don't quite understand yet. I need to go to the lab and access more detailed data, then, hopefully I'll know more. It looks like your *little* brother has got himself a part-time job at last! To save the world,' said János.

'I think we had better get some breakfast on the go as it's going to be an interesting day,' announced Mum in an attempt to lighten the mood.

As they all trooped into the kitchen, Ruben could feel his head starting to spin. There were so many questions whizzing around in his brain he did not know where to begin. The sheer enormity of what had just happened had not sunk in properly. Katarina and Ruben were at the table as Mum and Dad started getting breakfast ready. They sat staring at the Cube.

'So what can it do then, Ruben?' asked Katarina.

'Well,' he paused for a moment, stood up, then quickly manipulated the segments. 'It can do things like this. XL-R, engage Exo-suit,' instructed Ruben.

'Wow, crazy,' squealed Katarina, as Ruben was suddenly clad in hitech armour.

János was impressed by the futuristic equipment Ruben was now wearing.

'Jeez, I hate to think what that piece of gear can do,' he mused excitedly.

'XL-R, disengage Exo-suit,' commanded Ruben.
'Not bad kit eh?'

'Yes very clever, now stop messing about and eat your cereal,' János exclaimed, so drolly that they all laughed.

Ruben poured himself a bowl of cereal. Mum and Dad sat down and conversation naturally returned to the morning's proceedings.

'This is an overwhelming situation we have found ourselves in. I think we need to take a little time to evaluate what is going on and how to deal with it. I will go to the lab after breakfast – Ruben, you can come with me. We will have a look at the data on the S.P.A.C.E mainframe and see if we can unravel what is going on. Then we can hopefully make a plan and go from there,' said János, not quite believing his own words.

As the kitchen hubbub grew Ruben began to zone out. The words began to fade and he could feel himself leaving his own body and floating up above his family sitting at the table. He looked down on them as they chatted and talked. Observing from afar he could feel the love he had for them welling up inside. He loved them so much it made his heart feel like it would burst. They were the most precious things in his life and he wanted to protect them. In that moment he suddenly knew what he had to do.

'Yup, okay Dad, let's see what's going on. I bet those asteroids weren't just airless lumps of rock left over from the creation of the solar system,' exclaimed Ruben knowledgeably.

'Err, yes, you could be right,' replied a stunned János.

With breakfast dispatched Ruben and János jumped up from the table and went to get changed.

'Don't forget your Cube, Ruben,' called Mum.

Something else for him to remember to forget, she thought.

About half an hour later Ruben and János returned to the kitchen to find Mum and Katarina deep in conversation as the smell of fresh coffee wafted through the room. However, now there was another member of the family at the table

'Good morning, Mr Popalopazoob, and how are you today?' asked János.

Mr Popalopazoob, or Zooby as he was affectionately known, was the house cat. He was a big fluffy ginger Maine Coon. He looked like a baby lion cub and was soft as cotton wool. His favourite trick was to roll down the stairs, from one step to the other. He loved to sit on János' desk as he worked and play with the mouse. Ruben picked him up and threw him over his shoulder. He gave him a long, deep, luxuriant stroke down his back, from his ears to his tail. He could feel his purr vibrating through him. Stroking Zooby always calmed Ruben down, and right now he needed his dose of feline therapy.

'Okay Ruben, get your stuff and let's go. See you later. We shouldn't be too long.'

Grabbing their coats, they went out to the garage.

'Good morning, Rosanna.'

'Good morning, Ján darling. How are you today?' asked Rosanna suggestively.

'I never thought that a girl like you could ever care for me. Please open the side garage door,' blushed János.

'Does Mum know about you and Rosanna?' joked Ruben.

'I think she suspects,' he laughed.

The door unlocked with a clunk and they jumped in the Jaguar.

'You haven't been in this for a while, have you? I have finished converting it to electric. It has got a lot more "grunt" now. János pressed the door-release button on the car dash and the big garage door began to rise. Outside the morning was eerily dark, the streetlights were on, but it still felt like night. Slowly he reversed onto the street and the door lowered. He slipped the Jaguar into drive, blipped the accelerator and they headed off down Rubio Vista Road, then through Altadena. Some of the shops were open and there were a few people milling around but the roads were quite deserted. They made good time through the city to Highway 210 and János couldn't resist giving the Jaguar a blast, observing the speed limits(ish), of course.

'Wow Dad, she really goes. I think my old Mustang would struggle to keep up with this thing,' offered Ruben.

'You haven't seen anything yet. This thing will leave yours standing. We should get your car finished and do a track day up at Willow Springs in Rosamond. It'd be fun. Then we could see whose is the faster.'

'That's assuming it's still there after all this.'

'You're right. Don't tell your mum or Kat, but what is happening here is *really* not good. When we get to the lab I will be able to check the data in more detail. Where is the Cube? Have you got it?' asked János.

'Y-e-s, of course I have. I've got a world to save, apparently. Look at this.'

With that Ruben rolled up his sleeve to reveal the Cube wrapped around his wrist like a crazy fashion bangle.

'What do you think? Cool, eh?'

'Blimey, that must be the "morphing update" then? Can you plug headphones into it or do you need a separate adaptor?'

'Yes, funny... you wouldn't believe what this can do, even in this state. XL-R, go invisible,' instructed Ruben.

The Cube vanished from sight but was still on his wrist. Soon they were whizzing past Flintridge and were heading up into the San Gabriel Mountains. The sky was dark, no stars, no moon, just the headlights lit the road ahead. János drove on in silence as his mind raced through all the permutations and possible explanations as to what was occurring. The road twisted and turned, winding its way up through the mountains. The air was crisp and cool, unusual for this time of day.

'So Dad, what do you think is really going on?' asked Ruben, finally breaking the silence. There was a short pause.

'Hmmm, well I am not sure, but there is some kind of time dimensional distortion going on. The alien being that brought the Cube to Earth was obviously from another time dimension. When we use our powerful array telescope we are actually looking back in time. The speed of light means that by the time it has travelled to us we are looking at an event that potentially happened hundreds or thousands of years ago. In fact, if you follow the logic of how light data travels, we are all always looking into the past. If I look at you, the light data image of you takes an infinitesimally small amount of time to reach my retina. My brain then has to decipher the image which I then interpret.'

'Blimey Dad, I didn't expect a whole science lesson on quantum physics. So, does that also mean that sound behaves in a similar way? So when I play a guitar solo my fingers hit the strings and the sound takes time to travel to my ears, so there is a very miniscule delay that we just don't register,' reasoned Ruben.

'Yup, you got it. It's called latency. Fancy listening to some great guitar with delay on it?' asked János.

'Oh no. Let me guess. Pink Floyd by any chance? You really are stuck in the past too Dad. Why don't you ever check out new stuff?'

'I suppose I get so little time to enjoy my music, what with work, the house, you kids, grouting the new bathroom and Mum... Err, not grouting Mum, obviously. She always wants me to mend something, fix something or paint something. I never get to listen to music unless I am in the car and then I want to hum along to something I know. When I was younger, just starting to learn the guitar, I remember reading an interview with a famous guitarist who said that when he was trying to copy a riff or something he would learn how to hum it first. When I was a kid we only had a record player, so if I wanted to figure something out on a song I had to keep lifting the needle up and putting it back on the record to listen to a phrase again, whilst fiddling with my guitar. So I'd learn to hum the riff first then try to play my guitar until it matched what I was humming. I used to drive my mum mad by walking round the house humming riffs and stuff. I even used to hum in my sleep. Your uncle Mikkel would regularly throw his slippers at me to wake me up, and stop.'

'How did you survive without the internet? I can't imagine not being able to Google.'

'My childhood was so different to yours. Remember, I lived on the coast in a little village, not in the city. I would spend my time with my mates playing around the village. We'd be messing about in boats, swimming, building tree houses or racing old motorbikes. Stuff like that. Your uncle Mikkel was really into fiddling with electronics. When I started playing guitar he built me a valve amplifier by modifying our dad's old valve radio. He also built me a fuzz pedal and a twin speaker amp inside an old television case. It even had a three-channel mixer that you could plug a tape recorder and microphone into. It was brilliant. Anyway, sorry I have gone off down memory lane and should have stayed on the highway,' joked János.

'No, don't worry Dad. I like hearing your stories. We don't get to spend much time together these days. It's nice, just you and I.'

'I guess I realise time is running out. I don't know what the future holds for us. It makes you think about things. You have grown up so quickly. It feels like it was just yesterday when your mum and I brought you kids home for the first time. Your sister has grown into a beautiful, intelligent young women and you have become handsome young man who, as it just so happens, has got to save the world.'

'No pressure then,' laughed Ruben slightly nervously.

As they arrived at the top of the mountain road the huge communications aerials towered above them. They turned into the S.P.A.C.E. complex checkpoint and pulling up to the barrier János lowered the window.

'Good *evening*, Mr Novak. You don't normally work on a Saturday night, it must be important,' joked the guard.

'Hello Carl. How are you this fine summer evening? Odd weather we are having for this time of year,' replied János, going along with the joke.

'Is that young master Ruben I see next to you? Hasn't he grown? So what's going on Mr Novak? This is all a bit weird.'

'It sure is, Carl. I'm hoping I can find out a bit more today. I'll keep you posted.'

The barrier lifted and they drove into Ján's parking bay by the side of the lab building. They both jumped out of the car and approached the main entrance.

'Hold on a sec, Dad. Let's see if the Cube can crack your security system.'

Ruben rolled up his sleeve and telepathically instructed the Cube.

XL-R, disengage Safe-Mode, sent Ruben.

He pressed the centre axis white jewel twice and the Cube appeared in his hands. He configured it into Solved-Mode-One and pressed two white jewels in a ":" pattern and waited. A few seconds later the entry code triggered and the door lock released.

'Child's play, easy. You really need to sort your encryption out Dad or anyone with a smartphone will be able to get in.'

János rolled his eyes at him, sighed, then they both went in. The building was quiet as they walked to the lab. At the door János took his security pass out and slipped it into the security slot. He then positioned his left eye in front of the scanner. With a satisfying bleep the door unlocked. They entered. The lights automatically came on and they walked into the main control room.

'Ruben, do you fancy making us a couple of coffees while I get this old thing booted up?'

'Sure thing, Dad,' and he went over to the kitchenette.

A few minutes later Ruben joined his dad in the control room.

'Blimey, that coffee looks like mud,' exclaimed János.

'Well it was fresh ground this morning! Haha...You just set them up and I'll knock 'em down... So what are you looking for?' asked Ruben.

'First of all I want to see what has happened to the Asteroid cluster and then go from there.'

János' fingers began to dart all over the keyboard as reams of data flashed across the screen. He stopped.

'That's interesting. The cluster has dispersed. They have positioned themselves around the Earth, equally spaced on the same orbit trajectory. No, wait, hang on, there are some missing. There are actually quite a lot missing. Where did they all go?'

'Are there any over LA?' asked Ruben.

'Hmmm, no there aren't any directly over us, but something is between us and the sun,' replied János.

'So is it possible they have somehow caused this blotting out of the sun by releasing something into the upper atmosphere. Have you got any satellites up there with cameras that could show anything? I bet the military have got some stuff we don't know about. If we could hack into their defense system we might be able to check out their top secret gear. Dad, you would know what to look for,' reasoned Ruben.

'We can't access the military network. It's against the law, plus the encryption algorithms they use are mind-blowing.'

'Hold on a second. You are forgetting one thing, the Cube.'

'Well that's true, plus, I guess this is pretty urgent.'

János turned back to his keyboard, took a sip of disgusting coffee, winced, then started typing away. Moments later the Federal Military symbol flashed up onto the screen. János gulped.

'What now?' he asked.

'Okay Dad, let me just get the Cube configured. Now by moving these segments into position like this it will be able to connect to your computer mainframe.'

XL-R, disengage Safe-Mode, and prepare to engage Data-Link, sent Ruben telepathically.

He pressed the centre axis white jewel twice and the Cube appeared on his hand. Next he spun the segments around into Solved-Mode-One and pressed five white jewels in a 'T' pattern.

'XL-R, search for the lab computer hypersonic data carrier wave,' commanded Ruben.

The screen flickered and the password window appeared.

'Okay, right now the Cube will break the encryption coding and replace it with a masking code which will hide what it is doing from the rest of their mainframe security system. We'll be able to move around through their data files without being tracked,' explained Ruben.

Sure enough the security screen complied. They were in.

'Right, first we need to find what hardware they have got up there,' said János. He was intrigued.

After a few minutes of digging János had found what he thought he was looking for.

'Hmmm, *this...* is interesting. They have an orbiting lab up there I didn't know about. It is called the "Federal Astrological Reconnaissance Telecommunication Spacestation".'

'Or F.A.R.T.S. for short,' interrupted Ruben, then paused for comedic effect.

'Okay, yes that is unfortunate, anyway, let us have a look and see what it does. Probably just a lot of hot air,' joked János. 'I wonder where it is at the moment?'

As his fingers whizzed over the keys the screen flashed and flickered with data.

'Ah, here we are. This is what we want. Let's see if we can tap into the onboard cameras, see what's out there. Hmmm.' János paused for a moment. 'There's no live feed. That's odd. Let's check the camera archive file.'

On further inspection it seemed that the cameras had stopped working for some reason. János checked back further through the camera footage.

'Here we are. See at this point they're working. Look there, you can see one of the asteroids approaching.'

Suddenly at that moment, on the video, the orbiting lump of rock exploded releasing a dense black cloud of particulates. Debris was blasted in all directions. The screen went black.

'A bit of shrapnel must have taken out the cameras. That wasn't any asteroid I have ever seen before. That looked like some kind of biomechanical device. What was the black stuff that came out of it? That must be what is blocking the sun's rays,' reasoned János.

He continued to delve deep into the top-secret Global Defense System as Ruben looked on. Trawling through the data he began to build up more of a picture of what was actually going on. It wasn't good. Using the data from the other satellites they confirmed his suspicions. It soon became obvious that the mechanical asteroids had all been pre-programmed and set to detonate automatically, thus releasing the black cloud substance into the atmosphere in a timed sequence. János began to cross-reference his telescope tracking data. He scanned through all the positioning data and found that nearly half of them had disappeared and they were vanishing at regular intervals.

'These mechanical asteroid things are orbiting the Earth at the same angular velocity, about 7.2921159×10^{-5} radians per second, as Earth. The tracking data is showing that about every 34 minutes 17.28 seconds an asteroid detonates. It's pretty reasonable to assume that they are all carrying the same cargo. When they explode they release a black cloud, of something, into our atmosphere,' explained János.

'Okay, I think I understand what is going on now,' repeated Ruben. 'The asteroid cluster that you were following was described in the little book. Well, that cluster was actually a group of mechanical devices sent to orbit our planet. The Cube that I have was obviously a form of homing device that has guided them here. The alien that died here all those hundreds of years ago realised that this planet wasn't suitable for his race to inhabit. The infections and diseases we have evolved to live with would have probably killed them all, plus... they seemed to quite like us humans. He obviously couldn't stop this event happening, probably to do with the difference in the two relative time dimensions. I guess he thought that the Cube could be used to save the planet instead, but that all went wrong when it got damaged. The black cloud that is engulfing the Earth was probably sent to kill us. Somehow it is going to wipe us off the face of the earth. That is what he meant when he said that time is running out. I was in the right place at the right moment in time to be able to activate the Cube. But Dad, why didn't you activate it?' asked Ruben.

'I did think about it, but your mum pointed out that I am not as young as I was. I am not as strong as I was, and, perhaps a little unfairly, I'm not as fit as I was and I couldn't solve it like you did. You are young strong and fit. All the sports you do, the healthy food mum gives you, the acres of broccoli forest she dishes up, the way you think, all those things and more. The reality is, I can't compete with that. I'm a fifty-five-year-old guy. I can't go gallivanting through time and space at my age. What would Grandma say? I have to stay and look after our family. I will help you, I will be with you every step of the way. I need to find out more about what this cloud is made of. I expect the particles will gradually drop through the upper atmosphere and disperse in the air currents that flow through our skies. Then I am sure we will see what these particles were intended to do. We need to get a sample of the cloud to analyse to see what it is made of. Maybe then we can neutralise it. We need to get an aircraft high up into the atmosphere, as high as possible. I wonder if there are any top-secret aircraft stored near here. The military have a lot of classified equipment dotted around in secret bunkers and a pretty amazing satellite network too. Let's have a look and see if we can find out a bit more. It might be useful to know what they can do.'

Within a few minutes János had broken into the Federal Military Classified Resource Database. They had a look around the site. As he suspected, there was some top-secret stuff, such as the Global Defense System that had some awesome capabilities. However, and more importantly, a military Bobcat660X was stored at the LA airport.

'We need to find who to contact about it,' exclaimed János, with a hint of boyish excitement.

They searched the database and came up with a name.

'Here we are... General Whitehall. He's the man. Let me just note this down.'

'Dad, it's okay, the Cube will store all the data we might need,' explained Ruben.

'Right, we have done enough here. Let's reset the defense system security protocols and get back home. We need to be careful what we tell Mum and Kat. We will have to prepare them for what could happen.'

'Right Dad, understood. Let me synchronise the Cube again. It will reset the system. No one will know we were ever in there, I hope.'

Ruben took hold of the Cube and in a blur of fingers reconfigured the segments into Solved-Mode-Two, pressed seven blue jewels in an "H" pattern then waited. The computer screen scrolled through several pages of data then exited the program. The Cube morphed back onto his wrist and went into Safe-Mode(invisible).

'Right, we're done. Let's go,' declared János.

He closed the computer down, turned off the lab lights and they left. They walked quickly back to the parking bay, got in the car and drove up to the checkpoint.

'Hello Mr Novak. Did you find what you were looking for?' asked the guard.

'Yes, thank you Carl. Have a good day. I expect I will see you on Monday.'

János turned on his in-car phone.

'Rosanna, phone home please.'

'Phoning home now János darling, hold the line,' came the cheeky reply.

They drove out of the entrance and onto the winding Mount Wilson Road. They passed the deserted Angeles Crest Services. The lights were on, but the car park was virtually empty. The main road was still dark as they headed down the mountain. Suddenly the phone clicked into life. Out of the car hi-fi speakers came the disembodied voice of Sarah.

'Hi darling, where are you?' she asked.

'We have just left. Should be back soon as there is not much traffic about.'

'Great, I'll see you in a while, I'll get the coffee on. Love you.'

'Dad, do fancy getting home a bit quicker than normal?'

'How do you mean?'

'Right, hold on tight.'

Ruben pulled back his sleeve and morphed the Cube into his hand along with a shiny metallic ring.

'Dad, slip this ring on your finger.'

Ruben lightly placed his fingers onto the yellow, green and white centre axis jewels and pressed in sequence. In the blink of an eye János was startled to find himself rounding the corner of Rubio Vista Road into Pleasantridge Drive. They were home. A few minutes later they bounded into the kitchen like a couple of excited puppies just as Sarah was getting the coffee cups out of the cupboard. They startled her and a cup slipped from her fingers. Ruben saw it happen.

XL-R, engage Time-Freeze here, now, sent Ruben.

Engaging Time-Freeze sent XL-R.

Immediately everything in the room froze. Time had stopped. Ruben walked over and plucked the falling coffee cup from mid air and placed it on the table. Mum looked funny with her startled face on. Dad had a big kid silly grin and Katarina looked far too pretty. Ruben went over to his sister and messed up her hair. She now had a haystack hairstyle on her head. *Perfect*, he thought and had a little mischievous chuckle to himself.

XL-R, disengage Time-Freeze, sent Ruben.

Disengaging Time-Freeze, sent XL-R.

'How come you boys are home so quickly? I have just put the phone down,' asked a slightly confused Sarah.

'Heehee, we were just having a bit of fun. I phoned you from outside the house,' János fibbed, and gave a knowing look to Ruben. 'Blimey Kat, I am not sure I like your new hairstyle, it's a bit radical. Which super-model is wearing that style on the catwalk?'

'What do you mean, Dad?'

'Have you not looked in the mirror this morning, sis? No silly question,' teased a knowing Ruben. 'Let's take a selfie.'

He quickly took out his phone and gave his sister a big kiss as he took the picture. With great glee he showed it to her.

'Cor, if looks could kill, I would be mildly inconvenienced right now,' joked Ruben.

She had to admit it, there was indeed a stack of hay balanced on her head.

'What the flippin' heck. One of your tricks again?' her voice tailed off.

'See what I mean? It's a bit odd, even for you,' laughed Ruben, who was soon joined by Mum and Dad smirking in the background.

Katarina quickly got up from the table and ran to her room. She was confused. A few minutes later she returned to the kitchen with her perfectly styled hair once again in place. They all took their seats at the table, coffee cups in hand, and János began to explain what he thought had happened.

'The asteroid cluster I was tracking has turned out to be a group of mini spacecraft devices or, maybe satellites, they could be from another time dimension that were sent through a time portal, possibly... like a worm hole or something, to our present day... I am not sure. These craft appear to have been programmed to form a ring around Earth, in the upper atmosphere, and at the right time detonate and release their cargo, which is a black cloud of some kind of particles that multiply at great speed. They have expanded and effectively wrapped Earth in a black cloth, blocking out the sun. Now what we don't know is how long this cloud is going to last. I suspect it will disperse and the particles will drop through the atmosphere.'

'And then what? What is the purpose of the cloud? How long will it take to go? Will it go?' Sarah couldn't hide the panic in her voice.

'I don't know yet, but I will find out as soon as I can get a sample to examine. Whatever it is, I don't think it is going to be good so we must be prepared for the worst,' explained János. 'Ruben has a massive part to play in all this as the Cube is our key to survival. We will need to use it to find out what he has to do next.'

'Gosh Dad, this all sounds scary,' said Katarina.

'Don't worry darling, we'll be alright, we have " The Mighty Ruben" to look after us,' joked János, trying to diffuse the sombre mood.

'We've definitely had it then,' replied Katarina sarcastically.

'Thanks for your vote of confidence, my darling sister.'

'So I suggest we find something to do, keep ourselves busy until we know a bit more,' reasoned János. 'I am going to get in contact with the Air Force and see if we can get a plane up into the upper atmosphere and get some samples of the cloud particles. Ruben, I suggest you hook yourself up to the Cube and see if you can find out what to do next.

'Don't worry about me,' added Sarah. 'I have work to do, I have a huge development pitch I can get on with.'

'That just leaves us with Katarina. Maybe you could come with me and I could drop you off at Dan's for a while and I'll go to the air base, if I can organise it. They have a couple of secret planes stored at LAX. I am hoping we can use one of them,' said János.

She agreed and went and got herself ready. Dad figured that if he got them all organised it would give him some space to get on with what he needed to do.

'Okay Ruben, let's go and take a look at that Cube of yours.'

FIVE

TO THE EDGE OF SPACE

PRESENT DAY

János and Ruben went to his room and sat on the bed, he took the Cube and placed it on his desk.

'Right, let's see what this little thing has in store for me,' he quipped.

'XL-R, establish telepathic portal.'

Ruben closed his eyes for a few seconds then picked up the Cube. His fingers quickly manipulated the segments into Solved-Mode-One and pressed six white jewels in a "=" pattern. A blue holographic beam emerged from the Cube and gradually a ghostly image began to come into focus. It was Overlord Ebucski-Bur.

'Hello, Overlord Ebucski-Bur. I assume you know why I have contacted you?' asked Ruben.

'Indeed I do. I was expecting this. You must go on a journey, to an earlier time. As you know, the regenerative powers of the Cube have been compromised by its damaged state. You need to repair it. You are aware that to do this you must find the missing coloured jewel cells and refit them to the Cube. These jewels are encrypted specifically for this Cube and are all fitted with galactic transponders, which emit a unique positional coordinate for each jewel. We can track their exact location anywhere in the universe and in any time dimension. These jewel cells can travel through space by using the photon energy of the sun and by optical distortion of the light particles they absorb. However, our location system tells us that they are still on Earth, dotted along a single time-line at different points. It is of paramount importance that all the jewels are found, and quickly. The first jewel cells to find are the blue ones. They represent water and life. Our data tells us that they are located on your planet, off the East coast of Florida, USA, near the islands of the Bahamas. The exact Earth mapping co-ordinates are: Latitude North 27° 3' 32.8528" and Longitude West 74° 54' 17.2266". You will need to program the Cube to take you back in time, to the 27th December, 1948. It will also prepare you for your journey. It will make sure you fit in with the world you will be going back to. The Cube is at your command. It will help you as much as possible to retrieve the jewel cells. The event you will witness happened on that day at approximately 04:42. After this transmission the Cube will do a direct memory bank implant of the detailed facts you will need. Do you have any questions?'

'Gosh, I don't know where to start,' replied a flummoxed Ruben.

'The memory bank implant will tell you all you need to know, do not worry.'

'Overlord Ebucski-Bur, may I ask you a question?' enquired János.

'Of course, what troubles you, János?'

'Well, if I'm honest, just about everything right now. My son is going to travel through time to a point in our past. He is young and as yet hasn't experienced the world out there here and now, let alone what it was like in the past just after a World War. I wasn't even born then. What about the dangers? What if he gets injured? What if he gets trapped in the past? What if?'

'So many questions, János. You must not worry. You and your wife have prepared your son for the world by loving him with all your hearts, by looking after him, teaching him and by being caring, attentive, responsible parents. You have instilled values and moral structure to his life. I expect you don't really see it, but you, Sarah, Katarina, his grandparents and friends have prepared him well. One day you knew you would have to let him go. Well, that day is upon you all. He will use what you have taught him wisely.'

'We have done our best, but there is no rule book to follow,' uttered János. He paused to ponder his own words. 'Do you know what the black cloud is that has enveloped our planet and blotted out our sun?' he asked .

'The cloud is made from what you call nano-particle modules. These were designed to be inhalable by you humans and air-breathing life forms. Once inside your bodies they will start to genetically reconfigure your human DNA. However, as we have found with my brave Akaii, sent to your planet many hundreds of years ago, he could not survive on your planet. We are not now sure just what will occur with you humans.'

'But you intended to wipe out all life,' fumed János.

'Yes, we did, and for that we are sorry, but we are here now to help you. We greatly underestimated you. We are not sure how long you have, or indeed, what is going to happen.'

'Why couldn't you stop this? With all the advanced knowledge you have, surely you could have stopped this from happening?' replied János, the anger in his voice starting to show.

'Time on our planet, in our dimension, runs at a much faster speed to time in your dimension. Time is not a physical constant through the universe. It moves in all directions, at varying speeds in strands or dimensions, which run parallel to each other. You inhabit a different part of the cosmos to us in a different strand, and therefore at a different relative time too. You live in the present where the indefiniteness of the future instantly changes to the definiteness of your past. That is not so true in our dimension. Gravity through the cosmos changes, causing matter to pull itself together in different-sized clumps, which defines the speed of time at that point. Sorry, I am getting a bit carried away.'

'No, no, I understand totally now. I have been working on a gravity-based time theory for a while. I get it now. Well, if nothing else that has certainly saved me a lot of further research work. So basically, time passes much more slowly on our planet relative to yours,' replied János.

'Exactly.'

'Well, I am glad we cleared up that little problem. So when Ruben travels back in time he will experience time in the same way as us, because we are still on the same time strand, just at different points.'

'Correct.'

'So I will need to get a sample of the particles to test and try to work out what they will do to us.'

'Yes. Ruben needs to find these jewel cells as quickly as possible. And you must locate your samples as fast as you can too. You will also need to use an infected human to test. I am sure you will find some very soon.'

'But where?'

'Everywhere, probably,' replied Overlord Ebucski-Bur. 'Now I have to go, I can hear the raid sirens starting up. Initiate memory bank implant. I bid you farewell, for now.' Overlord Ebucski-Bur signed off.

The holographic projection dispersed. Ruben looked at his Dad and went over and gave him a big hug.

'Don't worry, Dad, I know what to do. I have the implant. I will start to prepare for my journey. I need to get stuff ready and pack.'

'Okay, I am going to see if I can get over to the air force base as soon as possible. I'll see you a bit later,' said János, who got up and walked out, across the landing and down the stairs to his office.

The enormity of what lay ahead was overwhelming. He sat at his desk and logged into his computer. Suddenly a little Cube icon appeared on his desktop screen. Puzzled, he clicked on it. The file opened and there was the data they had copied earlier today. Having found the relevant phone numbers he began to dial the personal mobile number for General Whitehall. *I hope he answers*, thought János. The phone connected and it began to ring and kept ringing for what seemed an eternity. Then it clicked into life.

'General Whitehall, this had better be urgent. I am incredibly busy,' came the brusque answer.

'Hello General, my name is János Novak. I am from The World Heritage Trust. You may have heard of us. We have been tracking an asteroid cluster that is heading towards Earth at our research facility here in LA. I believe that these asteroids are responsible for this strange solar eclipse event we are currently experiencing.'

'Oh... We are tracking that too. There is something strange going on. We aren't sure what yet, but we are working on it. How did you get this classified number?' asked the General.

'It is a long story and unfortunately I haven't got time to explain. I urgently need your help. I have to get a sample of the black cloud that has blotted out the sun. I have reason to believe that this cloud contains some kind of deadly virus.'

'How do you know this, Mr Novak?'

'I have been doing some research and I need to analyse a sample as soon as possible. The cloud is in the upper atmosphere at the moment. As soon as it falls into the lower atmosphere where we breathe, we are in trouble.'

'I see, interesting. Where are you calling from?'

'Luckily, as I said, I'm here in LA, in Altadena.'

'Right, that's good. Can you get to LA Airport today?'

'Yes I can,' replied János

'Right, go to the US Postal Office building on the corner of Westchester Parkway and Airport Boulevard. Go to the brown frosted glass door on the far left, near the car park entrance. Press the top button, the third one down and the fifth one down simultaneously and wait. Come alone.'

'Right, great. I should be able to get there at 14:00 if I leave now, see you then,' replied an eager János.

'Sure, I'll be here.'

He picked up his suitcase and went down into the kitchen where Sarah and Katarina were chatting.

'Hiya. I have managed to get a plane, so we can collect a sample of the cloud to test. I need to leave now. Come on Kat, I'll drop you off at Dan's, get your coat and any one of your fabulous designer bags you might need. I've got to go.'

'Oh, all right, Dad. I'll give Dan a ring and see if it is still okay to come over for a while.'

Katarina got up and ran to her room to phone Dan in private. A few minutes later she returned. She had given herself a quick makeover and changed into something a little more revealing. This caused her dad to raise his eyebrows in a slightly irritating kind of way that definitely irritated Katarina.

'I assume he said it was okay to come over then?' enquired *János, his voice subtly tinged with sarcasm.*

'Sarah, Honey, tell Ruben I will be back later,' said János.

Both Katarina and János gave Mum an affectionate kiss then went out to the garage.

'Rosanna, can you spell "Armageddon"?' asked János.

'Sorry, I can't spell "Armageddon"... but it's not the end of the world.'

'Haha, brilliant. Rosanna, open the side garage door please,' continued János.

'You need to get out more, Dad.'

They jumped into Dad's old 4x4. He started the hybrid engine and the main garage door began to lift up.

'Put Dan's address into the satnav for me, Kat darling, are you going to be staying over tonight or shall I pick you up later?'

'Pick me up later Dad, please. I'd rather be home at the moment.'

'Okay, I am not sure what time it will be. I'll text you.'

Soon they were heading down Lake Avenue into Altadena. The centre was quite busy as it was Saturday afternoon and the locals were out shopping. It felt weird being dark at this time of day. The street lights were all on, the shops were ablaze with light and the headlights made it feel like late evening. They whizzed along East Altadena Drive, then south on to Marengo Avenue, a wide residential road lined with immaculately manicured front lawns and hedges, punctuated by huge towering palm trees.

Suddenly Katarina let out a muffled groan. Her face contorted, she closed her eyes and buried her head in her hands.

'What's the matter darling? What is it, a migraine?' asked János.

Checking his rear-view mirror he carefully pulled over to the side of the road, stopped and leant over to Katarina.

'What is it?' he asked again.

'It's Ruben,' replied a confused Katarina.

'What do you mean?'

'He just spoke to me in my head.'

'What, telepathically?' Dad asked hesitantly.

'I don't know, I could hear him. He asked me where we were.'

'Try to reply to him. Just think your response and concentrate on him. See what happens.'

Katarina went quiet and closed her eyes. A few moments later she opened her eyes and a broad smile crept across her face.

'I don't believe it, we just had a little chat. I can talk to him in my head,' explained an excited Katarina.

'That is very interesting. You and Ruben are twins, but more interestingly you are identical twins.'

'We can't be identical, I'm a girl and he isn't.'

'Hmmm, well you can be. It is incredibly rare. As you know your Aunty Dee is mum's identical twin. Well what we haven't told you is that when your mum was pregnant we had a test done to check for any dangerous hereditary genetic conditions. When the results came back it showed that the initial egg had contained three sex chromosomes-XXY. Very, very unusual. However, when the egg divided in half it split into a girl XO embryo and the other was a boy XY embryo, but one X-chromosome remained dormant so the embryo developed as a female. It is called Jefferies-Syndrome. There are only a couple of known cases in the world. It might be why you can do what Ruben does, including telepathy.'

'Gosh, that is pretty amazing. Maybe I could have solved the Cube,'

'Maybe, actually, quite probably,' pondered Dad. 'I must admit I didn't really consider that as the book specified "a man among you". That could have just been a figure of speech I suppose. Anyway, come on, we need to get a move on.'

János carefully pulled back out on the road and set off along West Woodbury Road then south down North Fair Oaks Avenue, a boring four-lane strip of tarmac that cut its way through the city into Old Pasadena. Dad broke the silence.

'Now, just over there is the Convention Centre where on October 15th, 1977 I went to see Van Halen play. Amazing gig, Eddie Van Halen was awesome. I had never seen someone play guitar like that before. Sadly we lost him a few years back, such an innovative guitarist.'

'Yes Dad, that's all very interesting I'm sure, but is Ruben going to be safe doing this time travel stuff? It all sounds really scary,' asked Katarina.

'Well, the truth is, I am not sure. The Cube has got some incredible powers, which are far beyond any technologies we currently have, but I am working on it, haha. I don't think we have any real idea of what it is capable of yet. It is effectively hard-wired into Ruben. I know this all seems so unbelievable; even I can't quite believe what is happening, but the undeniable facts speak for themselves. It appears that Ruben is our only hope of saving the human race from total eradication.' János' words hung in the air like a politely squeezed out air-biscuit. 'What I can do is help to find what this black cloud is made of. If I get some samples I can take them to the Lab and analyse them. Hopefully, I'll then work out what is going to happen.'

'How do you mean?'

'This cloud has something to do with this whole scenario. I think it will disperse into our sky and we are going to be in trouble. I don't know quite how yet, but I am determined to find out. When we get a plane up into the edge of space we will be able to get samples. They will be deposited all over the plane's surface. The guy I am going to meet seems quite well informed so it should be quite straightforward. Why don't you give Dan a call and tell him you are about ten minutes away. Don't tell him anything about what we are up to. He mustn't know about the Cube or anything – and I mean anything,' asserted János.

'Okay Dad, I get it, I won't say a thing.'

'Hopefully I will pick you up later. Make an excuse that you are going to see your aunty tomorrow or something, okay?'

Ten minutes later they pulled into Hanscom Drive, a neat little residential road in the Elephant Hills that looked out over the city. As they approached Dan's house they could see him in the garage fiddling with his motorcycle. The flashes of blue light indicated to János he was probably doing some welding. The house was a modern-looking chalet style building with a huge sloping roof covered in solar panels. The back was built on stilts with levels that dropped down the side of the hill. János lowered the window and gave his horn a little toot.

'Hi Dan, what are you doing?'

'Hi Mr Novak. Oh, I am just mending the exhaust bracket on my trials bike. I hit a rock last weekend so I thought I would sort it out. This darkness thing is a bit weird isn't it? What do you think is going on? The news channels have been really quiet considering. It's like there has been a news blackout,' said Dan.

'Yes, it is strange. Some kind of eclipse has happened I would guess. Anyway, Katarina is dying to see you so I'll say goodbye and I'll pick her up later. Probably quite late,' explained János.

'Okay Mr Novak, no problem.'

Katarina jumped out of the truck and ran to Dan giving him a big hug and a kiss. They waved János off as he disappeared round the corner.

His little girl was growing up fast. What did the future hold in store for her? He had to make sure she had a future, that they all had a future. János switched on his car stereo and selected an old favourite to listen to as he sped down the Arroyo Seco Parkway. The grey six-lane highway curved and swooped through Montecito Heights, past the Dodger Stadium and through Downtown Los Angeles. Clumps of lanky palm trees were dotted along its verges looking eerily like tall, long legged monsters in the dark sky. János was singing his heart out to some Pink Floyd as he romped along the huge fourteen-lane Harbor Freeway towards Westmont, a gridded residential part of South Los Angeles. *I love this old stuff, vintage Gilmour,* he thought, and proceeded to hum the long classic guitar solo at the end of the track. It wasn't long before the sound of planes overhead blotted out his guitar humming histrionics as he headed along Century Freeway, towards the airport perimeter. His sat-nav guided him through the maze of airport roads until he finally pulled up outside the Postal Service building on the corner of Westchester Parkway, a few minutes late for his 14:00 rendezvous. He drove into the surprisingly busy car park and parked underneath another tall LA palm tree. He walked over to the single-storey orange brick building and could not help but notice there were a lot of identical large black SUVs parked around. He continued over to the brown frosted glass door on the far left, as instructed and pressed the top button, the third one down and the fifth one down together, then waited.

A few minutes later, the door opened.

'Good afternoon, Mr Novak. I trust you had a good journey? Come on in. I'm General A. Whitehall. Glad you could make it. Come this way.'

General A. Whitehall was a tall, smartly dressed man with a sharp, close-cropped, GI-Joe haircut and shiny shoes, every inch a textbook General.

János followed him to the lift in the lobby. The doors slid shut and the General produced a key fob from his pocket. He put it into the socket on the control panel. A secret keypad illuminated and the General tapped in a passcode.

A bright ceiling light then scanned the lift. The General looked at a monitor. He could see all the items János was carrying.

Would you mind handing over your mobile phone, please, for a detailed security scan,' asked the General.

'Sure, no problem.'

The General inserted the phone into the control console on the wall. The phone disappeared. A few minutes later, after a covert tracking device had been fitted, it was slowly ejected.

'There we are, all fine. Can't be too careful. Now let's get on,' agreed the General.

The lift began to move, but not down; instead it went sideways. János thought that was strange. The lift slowly came to a halt and the doors opened. They walked out into a white open-plan room full of computer screens flickering away. Each operative was hard at work and paid no attention as the two men made their way through to a white office at the end of the room, which bristled with technology.

'Quite a set-up you have here General,' remarked János.

'Yes, it does the job. Take a seat. Can I get you a drink?'

'Thanks, yes, a coffee would be great, no milk or sugar please, watching my weight.'

As János sat and scanned the room the General walked over to the coffee machine. A few gurgles and coffee splutters later the General sat at his desk and put the cups down.

'So how do you know about our operation? We knew we had been hacked but couldn't find any trace to follow. Was that you? How did you crack our encryption firewall?'

'Yes, it was me. I needed to find a way of getting a sample and I know you have a Bobcat660X fighter plane here that can go to the edge of space,' explained János, dodging the question.

'That is classified information but yes, you are right. I will scramble the plane now. I'll get the pilot to go as high as possible, that way we should be sure to collect some particles on the plane's fuselage. Do you want to go up in it too?'

'Wow, yes, that would be fantastic. Aren't I a bit old to be going up in fighter planes?' replied an enthusiastic János.

'You look like a pretty fit kind of guy for your age so the G-forces shouldn't be much of a problem when you're strapped in. Right, we need to get you over to the hanger.'

After they had finished their coffees, the General took János out of his office, back through the studio and out into the corridor. The General walked over to one of the doors and activated the retina scanner. The door unlocked and they went inside. János was surprised to see two small bullet-shaped cylinders lying in curved channels at the entrance of two small tunnels.

'These two canisters will blast us under the airport complex straight into the hangar. Okay, Mr Novak get into the left hand one, strap yourself in and close the lid firmly. I will control it from my pod.'

The two men climbed into the transport canisters. János buckled up the harness. The inside was sprinkled with little flashing lights with a central control console full of buttons. The canopies closed and the pods accelerated into the tunnels. János thought it felt like going down a fast-water flume ride. Blue strip lights illuminated the tunnels as the canisters hurtled through them. A few seconds later they emerged from the tunnels into a brightly lit room and rapidly decelerated. The canopies opened.

'Good afternoon, General. The plane is ready to go. We just need to get Mr Novak kitted up,' explained the crew technician.

János was led away into a side room to get into a special air combat G-Force suit. This clever piece of kit was like an exoskeleton to protect the human body from extreme gravitational forces. He soon returned complete with helmet.

'Right, Mr Novak, John will escort you through to the hanger and get you into position,' said the General.

John led János out onto the tarmac and across to Hanger 660X. The airport was quite brightly lit so it felt like nighttime even though it was still the afternoon.

'Have you ever been up in a plane like this before, Mr Novak?' asked the technician.

'Well, a few years back I was lucky enough to go up in a Martin F-022B Raptor. It was so fast I thought my face was going to come off, the acceleration was mind-blowing.'

'That was one heck of a quick plane. That could hit Mach 2.25 – that's about 2410km/h. This Bobcat is quicker, a lot, lot quicker, and can go much higher. The defence system on it is unbelievable. There are quite a few people that would like to know how it works. It's classified. We have been flying these for a few years already and no one has a clue what we are up to.'

'That sounds a bit ominous,' remarked János.

'Not really. We have just got to keep one step ahead.'

As they approached the hanger side door two armed soldiers appeared and saluted.

'Gentlemen, can we see your papers please?' asked one of the soldiers.

'Sure, here they are. I think you'll find them all in order,' replied technician John.

Once the details had been confirmed the men all entered the hanger. Inside stood the Bobcat. It was a huge, magnificent piece of technology. The floodlights showed it off in all its glory and János was quite taken aback by its sheer size. Just then a side door opened and in walked the pilot carrying his helmet. He went over to the men and shook János' hand.

'Pleasure to meet you, Mr Novak. I am Lieutenant Coupland. I have heard a lot about you. It looks like you are ready to go.'

'Good to meet you, too. Yes, I am as ready as I'll ever be.'

'Right, let's get you strapped in then.'

The two men climbed the ladders to the cockpit and clambered in. They secured their harnesses, fitted their helmets and connected their G-Force suits. As the canopy lowered the cockpit lit up with a myriad of dials and buttons. The hanger doors started to slowly trundle open as the towing truck fired up and began to pull the plane out of the hanger onto the tarmac. As soon as it was in position on the main runway, the truck was uncoupled and drove clear into a holding bay. Twinkling runway lights lining the edges converged in the dark distance.

'Ready, Mr Novak?' came the voice through the helmet intercom.

'Sure,' replied a slightly nervous János.

'LA Tower, this is Bobcat 660X Tango Oscar Sierra Bravo, requesting clearance for takeoff on Runway-29er... Over,' said the pilot.

'Bobcat 660X Tango Oscar Sierra Bravo, you are cleared for takeoff on Runway-29er, proceed to Alpha-2... Over,' replied air traffic control.

'Roger, LA Tower... Over and out.'

Suddenly the explosive roar of the jet engines made János almost jump out of his skin. Slowly the Bobcat rolled along the tarmac, the thunderous engines straining to let rip as it manoeuvred into position.

'Okay Mr Novak, are you ready?' came the voice through János' helmet intercom again.

'Yes, let's go get us some of those pesky particles,' he jokingly replied.

The pilot pushed a few buttons, scanned the array of dials, put his hand on the throttle levers and pulled back. The engines exploded into full thrust and the Bobcat catapulted forward. János felt himself being rammed into his seat by the acceleration. *Blimey, that's nearly as fast as my Jaguar,* János thought. The runway lights whizzed past faster and faster as the Bobcat approached take-off velocity. Suddenly its wheels left the runway and with a momentary dip the plane was airborne. They soared up and over Los Angeles, the grid of lights sparkling below.

'Right Mr Novak, we will shortly be going into a rapid climb. You will experience about 3G briefly, so you will feel like you have eaten a whole bunch of burgers, but don't worry, it won't last long,' the lieutenant explained through the intercom.

Almost immediately the plane altered its trajectory, tilted up and began to climb rapidly. János felt himself being pushed harder into his seat as the gravitational force increased. The G-Force suit actuated and he could sense the added support to his limbs to help take the strain. He felt his hands grabbing the armrests more tightly, his knuckles going white. It was like being on the worst rollercoaster ride possible, and then some.

'We are about to approach the edge of the atmosphere so we will experience some buffeting. We'll be pulling close on 3.5G as we leave the atmosphere. We'll do a quick run-through the particle cloud and check it out.'

'Wow, this is incredible. How fast are we going?'

'We're only doing about 2750km/h at the moment but when we leave the atmosphere we'll be doing close on 4284km/h; that's about Mach 4.'

The eerily dark atmosphere quickly turned into the oily blackness of space as the twinkling stars began to come into focus. Below János could see the shadowy outline of his little planet spinning, cradled in the full darkness of space. The sun shone brightly in a distant corner of the universe.

'How high can this Bobcat go, Lieutenant? I noticed it appears to have Unobtainium220 panels fitted and we are wearing some kind of gravity suit,' asked János.

'Well Sir, you certainly know your planes. That is classified information. Suffice to say it can do some pretty amazing stuff.'

'Could it have made it to the F.A.R.T.S?'

'Hmmmm. Again, that is classified too, but I think you can work it out for yourself. I am going to engage the auto pressure-fed air supply. Try to breathe normally. The cockpit is going to adjust the pressure level to aid breathing.'

'Roger, understood,' repeated János. ‹That station was hit by debris from a hi-tech craft that was detonated very close by. That device was carrying some of the particle clouds that we are flying through. When we get a sample to the lab we can get to work on it. The cloud will gradually fall through the atmosphere and then it will be inhalable. That is the part we need to be ready for.›

János looked out from the cockpit at the shrouded little planet spinning below. He could now see the full extent of the cloud that was engulfing it. Certain parts seemed less dense. They were the areas where the ozone layer had been damaged by industrial pollution, reasoned János. They were now most at risk from the deadly cloud. How could this be happening to his world? Thinking his family were down there gave him a sudden rush of emotion that took his breath away. They had no real idea of what lay ahead. He had no idea either, and that made him nervous.

Suddenly, from nowhere, there was a colossal impact on the side of the plane, which immediately sent it careering out of control. It tilted hard left and banked into a steep turn. János was thrown to the side of the cockpit and, smashing his helmet hard on a metal strut, he was momentarily dazed. He blinked and looked out of the cockpit towards the tail plane to see huge flames and sparks tearing at the side of the fuselage. *What's going on? What was that explosion?* he thought. He looked at the control panel in front to see a bank of flashing warning lights come on. *That's not good*, he thought.

'We have been hit by something. One of our rear jets has taken a heavy impact. I am switching to automatic engine priority. It will adjust the flight control unit to stabilise our trajectory. Our on-board fire management system should extinguish the fire and isolate the fuel supply.'

János could feel panic welling up inside him. Now was not a good time to be a catastrophiser. His brain went into overdrive exploring all the possible outcomes of this current scenario. None of them was particularly good. He wondered if his whole life was about to flash before his very eyes. He wondered if it would be any good. Would it make a great film or maybe a mini-series? Who would he get to write the screenplay? Who would play him? He would need to be a big Hollywood star, handsome and witty. His nervous mental doodling was suddenly disturbed by the fact the plane was now hurtling through the edge of space spinning wildly as it blasted towards the Earth.

'Okay, Mr Novak sir, don't panic, everything is under control. I have to let the computer system bring the plane out of this spin otherwise it will rip itself apart... and we don't want that. Hang on tight, this could get hairy,' explained the pilot.

It did get hairy, very hairy. János could feel the extreme forces were pounding his old body into submission. The G-Force suit was helping take the strain. János couldn't help thinking that he should have spent more time at the gym and less time at the biscuit tin. He could feel his heart thumping its way out of his chest. *Why am I finding it so hard to breathe?* he thought.

'Lieutenant, I am experiencing breathing problems. I am struggling to get enough air.' The panic in his voice was clearly detectable.

'Let me check. There is a problem with your suit. The dials show there is a leak somewhere in you air feed system, probably caused by the impact somewhere. The cockpit seals are holding good. Try to breathe more slowly. I will increase the airflow. Once we have broken through the atmosphere, breathing will get easier. Hold on, Mr Novak, just a little longer.'

Gradually the plane stabilised and the pilot regained control. The tightness in János' chest felt like someone was sitting on him wearing particularly heavy trousers.

'I would bet we have been hit by a bit of debris from that device you mentioned. We have been quite lucky. That could have taken us right out, big time. Right, let's go home. We should have enough sample matter now. The temperature of the cockpit will go up a bit, wind resistance will cause friction on the fuselage as we re-enter the atmosphere. Don't worry. Keep breathing slowly and it should soon get easier.'

János took his last look at the vastness of space and settled himself into his seat in readiness for re-entry. He concentrated and focused on his breathing as the cockpit started to get noticeably hotter. *This must be the fastest sauna ever built,* he thought. The hum of the engines changed as the plane altered course in preparation for its landing approach.

Gradually the darkness of space changed into the blackness of the upper atmosphere as the Bobcat hurtled back towards Earth. The stars slowly faded as they left space. Breaking through the upper atmosphere the lights of LA came back into view and János was relieved to feel his breathing returning to normal.

'LA Tower, this is Bobcat 660X Tango Oscar Sierra Bravo. Requesting approach clearance. We have severe engine failure. Request Runway-2 as we will need the extra length for deceleration... Over.'

'Roger Bobcat 660X Tango Oscar Sierra Bravo. Approach Runway-2. Emergency services are on standby. You are clear for landing... Over.'

'Roger LA Tower. Making final approach... Over.'

The landing lights came into view as the Bobcat rapidly decelerated. János could feel himself straining against his harness again. The roar of the engines became louder as the plane approached the runway. There was a sudden bump as the wheels hit the tarmac skidding wildly as the undercarriage took the weight of the Bobcat hurtling down the runway. The pilot engaged reverse thrust as the landing lights shot past with the Bobcat struggling to slow down. The runway was disappearing at an alarming rate and a final screech of the brakes brought the Bobcat to a halt.

'LA Tower. This is Bobcat 660X Tango Oscar Sierra Bravo. We are down on Runway-2. Requesting taxiing procedure... Over.'

'Roger Bobcat. Assistance at Alpha-1 engaged... Over.'

The pilot then proceeded to taxi the Bobcat off the runway towards the waiting tow truck and shut down the engines. The thunderous roar died away. The driver jumped down from the cab and hitched up the aircraft. A few minutes later the plane lurched forward as the truck started to tow the Bobcat along a side roadway. The airport was buzzing with activity as they headed back towards Hangar660. Slowly the huge hangar doors began to open. The tow truck carefully pulled the plane inside and brought it to a standstill.

'Okay, Mr Novak, you can release your harness now and unplug your suit. That was quite a trip,' exclaimed the pilot.

A set of stairs were then positioned by the side of the cockpit. The canopy opened and the two men clambered out onto the platform and removed their helmets.

János could feel his legs trembling as he climbed down the stairs. He was relieved to be back on solid ground.

Just then a side door opened and the General strolled over to shake János' hand.

'Good to have you back, Mr Novak. That must have been one hell of a ride up there.'

'Yes General, you could say that. Lieutenant Coupland is quite a pilot.'

'He is the best. We are very lucky to have Ed' on the team. Now we will get the plane de-contaminated and the samples collected and logged. It shouldn't take too long, half an hour maybe. I expect when they clean the inlet ports they should easily give you enough samples to get you started. We will then do a full deep clean and what we find we can bike over to you later. Do you want them sent to your home address?'

'Yes, thanks, that would be great.'

'Sure, no problem. It would be real helpful if you could keep me informed of what you find out. From what you have said I sense this could be important. Right, let's get you out of the suit and get you back to the office.'

Hmm, I wonder why he didn't ask for my address, thought János, as he was led into a side equipment room where the suit was removed. They made their way to the transportation canisters and within a few seconds they were back in the main HQ office. János glanced at his watch, aware he was due to collect Kat and pressed the mode button. It was 16.32, General Whitehall surreptitiously put his hand under the desk to activate the security cameras in his office.

'Have you got to be somewhere? Can I get you a drink, Mr Novak while we wait? Coffee? Or something stronger?'

'No, a coffee would be fine, without sugar or milk please. Thanks. I was just keeping an eye on the time.

I have to pick up my daughter in a while. Oh, and please call me János. Mr Novak is so formal; it's what my University students call me. I do a bit of part-time lecturing up at the UCLA on Bio-Mechanical Quantum Physics. Actually, not that far from here.'

'Okay, János it is, no problem, and you can call me General A. Whitehall,' came the deadpan reply.

He tapped on his computer keyboard and a few minutes later a young officer brought in two special coffees and put them on the General's desk. János couldn't help noticing one of the mugs was emblazoned with a red and white Stoke City Football Club logo.

'I am assuming that the football mug is yours?'

'Yes, I know it's a bit odd, but Mrs General A. Whitehall is English, from – guess where – Stoke. It's a great little city. Love it there. We've been back quite a few times over the years. We watch the games together on TV when we can,' confided the General.

'How weird. I support Arsenal. My dad was originally from London, that's why I follow them. I should really support the L.A. Rams I guess?'

'What are the chances of that? They do say football was invented so guys had something to talk about,' laughed the General.

János quite liked the General's sense of humour, and for a few moments the light-hearted atmosphere was just what he needed to stop his brain from overheating.

'So Mr Novak, I need to know how you broke through our security shield. That is a prisonable offence,' retorted the General sternly.

'It's complicated,' János stalled for time while he made up some nonsense to bamboozle him. 'Errr, I developed a high security system for our own research facility. It was based on a fractal randomiser algorithm, the kind you find in nature. It is nature's way of creating diversity within a species. The mathematical beauty of fractals is that infinite complexity is formed with relatively simple equations. By repeating fractal-generating equations many times it is possible to build three dimensional code models. It is impossible to predict how the algorithm expands, meaning that the coding is impossible to break unless you are the one that did the initial encoding. So I used a variation of that coding algorithm to crack your system. Once you activate the algorithm it learns where the dead ends are then does a fractal diversion tree and spreads out inside the coding programme. It's like making a three-dimensional skeleton key copy. It takes quite a while to break through a coding security system like yours,' concluded János, quite pleased with his seamless confusing nonsensical explanation.

'That is unbelievable. We have been working on a variant of your system for quite a while,' replied an incredulous General Whitehall.

János was also slightly startled by his own genius and that he was obviously under surveillance. In truth it was something he had been mulling over for a while, but like many things, there never seemed to be enough time in the day to give it his full attention, what with the constant need to fix things and do various bits of DIY at home.

Just then there was a knock-knock. The General got up and opened the door and an officer handed over a small package, turned and left. The General sat back down and gave the parcel to János.

'There should be enough there to get you started.'

'Great, that was quick. Thanks, General.'

'We don't hang around here.'

'No I can see that. Which reminds me, I have to pick up my daughter from a friend's house on the way back.'

'I hope you kept this meeting confidential.'

'Absolutely, she thinks I have gone to get some parts for my old Jaguar. It's an old English classic car I've got. It's a beauty,' beamed János.

Sensing time was getting on János quickly drained his cup and stood up.

'Well General, it's been quite an experience. I need to head off now. Thanks for your hospitality.'

'It's been good to meet you János. We will be in touch. Now let's get you out of here.'

The General led János back out through the busy department to the lift. Once inside the General activated the secret passcode and the lift moved to the side again. The doors opened and János was back in the US Postal Office building lobby. The two men shook hands and János walked out into the car park, got into his truck and activated its control system.

'Rosanna, phone Katarina's mobile, please.'

'Phoning Katarina's mobile phone now,' confirmed the automated voice.

'Hi Dad. How did you get on today? Are you coming to pick me up now?'

'Yes darling, I should be with you in about half an hour. See you in a while.'

'Okay Dad, I'll get my stuff together. Bye.'

'Rosanna, play *Then Came The Last Days Of May* by Blue Öyster Cult,' instructed János.

'Playing *Then Came The Last Days Of May*. Blue Öyster Cult, often abbreviated BÖC, is an American rock band formed on Long Island, New York, in 1967, whose most successful work includes the hard...'

'Rosanna, stop please, just play it.'

The truck's stereo roared into life and János put the truck in Drive and screeched out of the car park onto Westchester Parkway.

'Rosanna, set sat-nav to; 20 Hanscom Drive, South Pasadena, California, quickest route.'

'Destination, Dan's House, set,' came the efficient reply. 'Is there anything else I can do for you, János?'

'Rosanna, phone Sarah at home, please.'

A few seconds later the call connected.

'Hi darling, what 80s classic rock are you listening to at the moment?' answered Sarah.

'Hello, Honey. You know me too well. I'm all done here so I am off to pick up Katarina, so should be back about 21:30. I'm famished, haven't eaten a thing all afternoon. See you in a while. Love you. This is János Novak signing off. Over and out.'

'Okay Lieutenant Novak, we have you on our radar,' came Sarah's comedic retort.

The evening traffic had started to build up on the freeway as János made his way through the city to Dan's house. To while away the time on journeys like this János had programmed Rosanna to give slightly strange navigation commands.

'At the next junction, pull a donut and skid sideways into Hill Drive.' Rosanna interrupted Deep Purple blaring away on the car stereo.

János glanced in his rear view mirror and made the lane change. As he did so he happened to notice a black SUV a few cars back do the same thing. He wondered if it was the same one that had followed him a few days ago.

'Rosanna, rear camera, set to record, night setting, activate number plate recognition on the black SUV tailing us three cars back.'

'Night system activated, recording,' confirmed Rosanna.

János then proceeded to do a pointless lane change to see if the SUV followed suit. It did. It seemed to be shadowing him. He did a few more seeming needless lane changes to test his theory.

'Rosanna, what is the probability that I am being followed by the SUV?'

'The probability the SUV is following you I estimate to be approximately 97.2536%,' came the ludicrously accurate response.

As he gradually wound his way through the city towards Dan's house János realised he needed to get away from the SUV just in case. Now his mind was racing with thoughts of why he was being followed. He had to pick up Katarina and he had to go home too. He decided he would have to try to lose it in the traffic, take a few odd shortcuts and hope he could shake it off his tail.

'At the next junction take the second exit on two wheels.'

János decided to take her at her word and as he entered the junction he put his foot down. His trusty 4X4 suddenly lurched forward as the V12 engine unleashed its fearsome power. The huge rear wheels dug in and it rocketed around the junction. János prayed there were no police cars watching. He had done a fair amount of racing in his time and was pretty handy with a steering wheel. As he whizzed down West Slauson Avenue he suddenly took a hard left into a narrow alley. The rear swung out as he pointed the truck through the narrow gap. There was a screech of tyres as he bounced along the rough road. Muddy water sprayed from the wheels as he shot through the puddles. He glanced in his mirror to see the lights of the SUV momentarily dazzle him. He pulled a skid into another side road, ploughed through some cliché old cardboard boxes as he raced between the narrow white fences until he emerged into a deserted parking lot. János looked around feverously trying to decide on his next cunning move. The dazzling lights were getting closer. The SUV was still keeping up with him. János slammed the stick shift down a gear and blasted round the parked cars, swerving in and out of the vehicles trying to shake off the SUV. As he rounded the corner a silver Chevrolet reversed out in front of him, János cranked the wheel hard left and threw the truck into an awesome power slide between two parked cars with millimetres to spare. He wiped his brow as beads of sweat ran down his forehead. *Eat my rubber*, he thought. The SUV swerved and clipped the rear bumper of a red sedan, shunting it sideways into a wall with an almighty crunch. János pulled a handbrake turn and shot out through the exit gate narrowly missing the bollards. The SUV skidded wildly into the exit gate too, but judged it badly and ploughed into a bollard with a metallic crunch, then spun sideways and barrel-rolled into the ticket kiosk, smashing it to pieces. János put his foot down and turned onto a shopping mall approach road. He weaved in and out of the traffic until he settled sedately behind a delivery truck. He looked in the rear view mirror. He couldn't see the SUV. He breathed a sigh of relief. He took a left and was back on track.

'At the next junction remove your trousers and drive in your pants, oh, and take the second exit.'

'Rosanna, switch to normal mode,' ordered a slightly exasperated János.

As János' heart rate began to drop he could feel himself calming down after all the excitement, which he actually quite enjoyed. He focused on the road ahead and got back into the zone of driving sensibly again. He made his way onto Highway 110 going north. The evening traffic was flowing smoothly as he took a left onto Highway 101. The truck stereo was trawling its way through a catalogue of dad rock as János pulled on to Huntingdon Drive, a six-lane highway heading north through the Rose Hill area of Los Angeles. Little clumps of the ubiquitous palm trees lined the verges. János' phone, routed through the stereo, cut in.

'Hi Dad, where are you? You're late.'

'Hi, Kat darling. Sorry, the traffic has been bonkers. I got caught up in a bit of bother. I will be with you in about five minutes, get your stuff together.'

'Okay Dad. Bye, mwah.' Katarina blew her dad a kiss and hung up.

A few minutes later János pulled up outside Dan's house. He rang the bell. The front door opened and Dan extended a welcoming hand.

'Good evening, Dan. How are you doing? Hope you have had a nice day together. Sorry to drag Katarina away from you but we have a busy day ahead tomorrow. We are going to see my brother Mike over in Santa Barbara.'

'Oh... Katarina said you were going to see her aunt Delia,' replied a confused Dan.

'Umm, well, err, yes she will be there too. It's a bit of a family get-together,' bluffed János rather unconvincingly.

'Come on Dad, we better be off now,' interrupted an anxious Katarina.

She gave Dan an affectionate peck on the cheek, picked up her bag and led János back to his truck.

'See you sometime Dan. You're welcome any time over at ours,' volunteered János.

'Thanks, Mr Novak,' came the eager reply.

János and Katarina climbed into the truck. János fired up the V12, pulled away and headed back along Hanscome Drive. Katarina gave a wave to Dan as they disappeared around the bend.

'Why did you invite Dan over *any time*?' asked a slightly irritated Katarina.

'I don't know. I was just being friendly I guess. Did I do wrong?'

'Yes Dad, you did. I like Dan but I am not sure we are at that point in our relationship yet. He is nice but he is quite intense. He is very inquisitive. He was asking me loads of questions about us, about the family. I felt a little uneasy about giving away too much, what with this business with Ruben and the Cube. I felt a bit like I was being interrogated.'

'Oh I see. Well maybe I came at just the right time, then?'

'Maybe. Ruben was contacting me again telepathically, which was a bit unnerving too as I couldn't really respond to him while I was with Dan,' explained Katarina.

'What was he "saying" to you?'

'Bits and pieces. He is quite excited about going on this quest but he is also scared about the whole thing. He really feels that the fate of the world is on his shoulders. It all seems quite unreal to him, but the proof is right in front of him. He has so many questions to ask, it is all very overwhelming to him.'

'I will talk to him. I am worried about him too. We are heading off into the unknown, all of us are. We need to be strong together,' reassured Dad. 'Call Mum and tell her we will be home in about half an hour.'

As Katarina talked to Sarah, János picked his way

through the traffic as they made their way home to Altadena. Soon they were pulling up in front of the huge garage door, which automatically opened for them.

'Rosanna, secure garage door and activate Zone-G high security system.'

'Zone-G high security system activated.'

Walking to the kitchen János could smell the homely whiff of Sarah's Toulouse sausage casserole wafting through the house. In the kitchen Sarah was sitting reading the paper with the audio system streaming some chill-out music. The whole room was enveloped in a calm, relaxing vibe, just what János needed right now.

'Hello you two. You've had quite a day I bet? I hope you are both hungry. Dinner is going to be ready in ten minutes. Can someone get Ruben? He is playing his guitar, judging by the grungy sounds coming from his room,' reasoned Sarah cheerily. 'The phone has been ringing a lot today. You have quite a lot of messages.'

'Oh, okay, I'll give them a listen later. I'll go and get Ruben,' replied János and he kicked off his shoes and ran upstairs.

He knocked on Ruben's door very loudly. The familiar sound of a distorted Dsus4 chord suddenly stopped mid strum.

'Hi Dad. Kat said you were on your way.'

'How are you doing? What was that you were playing?'

'Oh, just messing around with a song idea, nothing much.'

'Kat said you had been contacting her all day. What's up?' asked Dad.

'I have been thinking. We need to get going on this quest stuff as soon as possible. I have been doing my research and I think I should go tomorrow. I was just practising my telepathy with Kat. It could be quite useful.'

'Hmm, I suppose you are right. I guess we have no time to lose. That's the hard reality of it. Let's go and have dinner.

'Okay, Dad. Did you manage to get the samples you need?'

'Yes, it was an amazing flight. We got hit by some debris from the damaged space laboratory, which knocked out one of the engines. Then to top it all my space suit got damaged when I smashed my head on the cockpit, which affected my air supply. All in all it was quite a flight. I was glad when we finally landed. The man that I met, General Whitehall, was interested to know how we cracked their security system.'

'You didn't tell him about the Cube, did you?'

'Of course not. Now come on, let's go down for dinner.'

Sarah was about to serve so they both sat down. The smell of home-cooking food always brought the family together around the table for a good chat and catch up. They enjoyed each other's company and treated mealtimes as being a special event, no phones allowed. With their plates freshly filled with a spicy sausage casserole they all tucked in. For a moment the room was silent with just the sound of cutlery chiming as they enjoyed the feast in front of them.

'This is delicious, Honey, just what I needed after an interesting day,' said János. 'Ruben and I have been talking briefly, and we feel that he needs to go and find the first set of missing jewel cells. The sooner we get started the sooner we can try and save our world. I can't believe I am saying this.'

'Dad's right. I feel I am ready, the Cube is all programmed and ready too. I need to do this for us all,' replied a confident Ruben.

'My darling son, I want you to know how much we all love you. It seems your destiny has been written for you and it is out of our hands. It feels like the sands of time are slipping through our fingers, and other such clichés. We have loved you for so long as our special little boy and now we have to let you go, and share you with the world as a man,' whimpered a tearful Sarah.

'My goofy little brother has become a man, finally,' chipped in Katarina.

The table erupted into howls of laughter. The rest of the meal was spent chatting and reminiscing with silly stories to help cover up their collective nervousness about what lay ahead for them all. The meal progressed through dessert to coffee, after which they all retired to the TV lounge to relax for the rest of the evening. Ruben sat with his mum who spent the whole evening holding his hand. He liked the feeling. It made him feel like a little boy again. His mind began to slow down as he absorbed all the love he felt around him. Minute by minute he could feel himself filling with strength and determination.

At a suitable lull in conversation János decided to check his messages. As he clicked through them a small smile began to spread across his face until he couldn't stop himself from having a full on belly laugh.

'What's so funny, darling?' asked Sarah.

'All these messages are from producers at the TV networks who want me to do interviews about what is happening at the moment. Shame I have been busy, but I can't really do anything at the moment. I may have to invent some more theoretical nonsense to keep them busy.'

'You're good at that darling, should be easy for you to confuse them.'

Dad decided to turn on the TV as he had missed his daily dose of news. Not surprisingly the top story on all the channels was the prolonged eclipse phenomenon happening around the world. As he flicked from channel to channel János couldn't help but laugh at some of the crazy hypotheses that were being put forward by so-called scientists.

'These guys are hilarious. I think I will just let them carry on. I particularly like the guy who reckoned this phenomenon has been caused by a black hole exploding. Ridiculous, anybody with half a science brain knows that it is Hawking radiation that reduces the energy and mass of black holes through evaporation. So they don't explode, they shrink and vanish,' explained János.

'Of course, Dad, everyone knows that,' quipped Katarina.

The Novak family spent the rest of the evening enjoying each other's company until it was time to turn in.

'Well guys, I think I am going to bed now. Tomorrow is going to be quite a day,' announced Ruben.

He went over to his mum and gave her an affectionate kiss on the cheek. He then hugged and kissed Katarina goodnight too. Last of all he went to Dad and gave him a strong hug and kissed him on his stubbly cheek.

'You need a shave, Dad. It's like kissing a porcupine,'

'Oi, you cheeky whippersnapper, off to bed with you. You're not too big to feel the back of my hand,' joked Dad.

'I bet that's rough, too.'

Ruben laughed and went up to his room. For a few moments he sat on the edge of his bed and slowly looked around. He studied all his bits and bobs in minute detail. Would he ever see these things again? Would he ever sleep in this room again? Would he still have a family to come back to? After a short while he got himself ready for bed then jumped under his cosy duvet. It felt good to be in his bed. He felt safe and secure. How he hoped he would know that feeling again. He took one last look at his prized salmon pink guitar, turned off his bedside light, closed his eyes and shuffled into his sleep position. It wasn't long before he could feel himself drifting off into the land of nod.

SIX

THE QUEST FOR THE BLUE "WATER OF LIFE JEWELS"

PRESENT DAY

Ruben had a restless night. His brain wouldn't let him sleep for long. It had been running on autopilot all night and it was a bumpy flight with a lot of buffeting. He spent most of the night trying to get to sleep. He had tried fantasising about being on a romantic dinner date with weather girl Chynna White or jamming on stage with Hendrix at the groovy little blues club called "Cafe Wha?" in Greenwich Village, New York. Ruben was very specific about his dream specifications. This was helped by the fact that his dad had given him the two middle names of James Hendrix, so, in full, he was Ruben James Hendrix Novak. Secretly, however, Ruben thought his names were quite cool, given that he did play the electric guitar pretty well.

When he eventually stirred from his slumber his eyes did not really want to open. He looked at his phone on his bedside pod; it was 09:27. He also noticed a cup of tea quietly steaming away on a little tray with a couple of biscuits for company. His mum had tiptoed in and left them as he snoozed. Sunday morning was here but his room was still dark.

'Rosanna, open my bedroom blinds please.'

'Bedroom blinds opening,' came the efficient reply.

As they did so, it was immediately apparent that it was still also dark outside. He turned on his TV. The news channels were awash with stories about the global darkness. He sat up in bed and took a comforting sip of breakfast tea, and pondered for a while. He wondered what the day had in store for him. Today was the day when he would set off on his first adventure, to find the remaining blue Water of Life Jewels. He flicked over to another channel only to be startled to see his dad staring out of the TV screen. He was being interviewed on Channel 9LA by Greg Larson. Ruben chuckled as he recognised dad's downstairs office, which looked tidier than usual. He turned the volume up a little to hear what he was saying. He was clearly in full flow.

'So, Dr Novak, there have been various theories put forward to explain what our planet is experiencing at the moment. You are one of the leading experts in this field. I'm sure our viewers are very interested to know your thoughts on what you think is happening right now out there in space,' said Greg.

'Well, the Universe, believe it or not, is a very dusty place, a bit like my office here. Cosmic dust consists of tiny particles of solid material floating around in the space between the stars. Actually, it isn't the same as the dust you find in your house, but more like smoke with very small vapour particles that go from microscopic up to about nought point one millimetres diameter in size. These particles are charged positive and negative or a variation of both. They can form in small bunches or be singular.'

'Why is there dust in space?' asked Greg.

'Well, this cosmic dust is very important because we find lots of it around new, young stars. In fact it helps them to form and it is also the raw material from which planets like the Earth are created.'

'So how is this dust formed?'

'We think, it is actually made in stars, and is then blown off into space by slow cosmic wind currents or a massive star explosion. The dust is then 'recycled' in the clouds of gas between the stars and some of it is consumed when the next generation of stars begins to grow.'

'So this dust is a good thing?' asked Greg tentatively.

'Astronomers used to consider dust as a nuisance because it absorbs the visible light from objects, keeping them hidden from our optical telescopes thus making the Universe appear very dark, concealing a lot of amazing things from us. When we started to use infrared cameras, we discovered that the annoying cosmic dust was actually very interesting and important to lots of astronomical processes.'

'In what way?'

'The dust converts the stolen starlight it absorbs into light at longer wavelengths. We can see the dust shining using special instruments sensitive to the far-infrared and sub-millimetre part of the electromagnetic spectrum. What we think has happened here is that there have been a couple of new young star explosions that have been triggered together. This would cause a huge amount of dust matter to be blown across into the galaxy. We are effectively in the middle of a cosmic blizzard of dust. Hence, the sun has been blotted out from view so its radiation is not able to penetrate the cloud, but as the wind currents break it, the sun should begin to show itself again,' explained János.

'Wow, exciting stuff. So how long do you estimate it will be before we can get back to normal?' asked Greg

'Well, at the moment it is too early to say, but I would estimate it is going to be a few days before we see any real change,'

'Okay, thanks for joining us this morning, Dr Novak. I hope we get to speak to you again soon as this story unfolds. Over to you, Rachel, at the sports desk. What is happening in the world of sport today?'

'Thanks Greg. Well today we have a full...' announced a cut-off-mid-flow Rachel.

Ruben turned off the TV, got out of bed and quickly went downstairs to Dad's office. He knocked on the door.

'Come in Ruben, I heard your floorboards squeaking above me. I have finished now.'

'Morning, Dad. I caught the last bit of your interview. That was a brilliant explanation. That should keep them busy scratching their collective heads.'

'I hope so. It was based on an element of truth and a bit of creative thinking. Not bad I thought.'

'Very impressive indeed.'

'So how are you feeling about today? Are you ready to go?'

'As ready as I will ever be, I guess,' replied a slightly unsure Ruben.

'So what's the plan?'

'Well, I must travel back to December 27th, 1948, to Florida.'

'Florida! It's nice there. Whereabouts?' asked János.

'Near Miami Beach, I have to go to an apartment at 541 Lincoln Road.'

Sarah poked her head round the door.

'Morning, boys. I am going to start breakfast. Any help would be greatly appreciated,' and with an elegant twirl she turned and went downstairs to the kitchen.

'Okay darling, we'll be right down,' answered János.

János and Ruben continued to go over the preparation details.

■ ■ ■

09:45

Down in the kitchen Sarah set about making breakfast. She had her chill-out music filling the room to help distract her thoughts from what lay ahead. She knew she had to keep a jolly face on for the sake of the family, but deep inside she was petrified of what was occurring around them. What if this was the last day she would see her beloved son? The twins had been a huge part of her life for the last nineteen years. She had held Ruben in her arms as a baby, watched him take his first nervous steps and taken him and Katarina to school for their first day. She had been there when he was struggling with the pressures of being a teenager. Her love and affection had always been there to help guide him through his life so far, and now it felt like her job was done. A sudden intense feeling of emptiness swallowed her up. She couldn't imagine life without her little boy. She always knew at some point he would spread his wings and leave the nest, but she found it hard to share him with his girlfriends. She didn't like the feeling of another woman usurping her position in his affections and had an uncomfortable feeling of jealousy when he brought a new girlfriend home. She always felt she had lost a bit of him. She hoped she never let it show.

'Hi Mum, what can I do? Shall I make some salsa scrambled eggs for us?' and he gave his mum a kiss on the cheek.

'That would be lovely darling, but not too strong. You know Kat will complain.'

Ruben proceeded to make his special salsa. He grabbed four fresh tomatoes, a bunch of coriander, an onion, a couple of green peppers, two large garlic cloves and some virgin olive oil. He took a sharp knife from the drawer and chopped the tomatoes and coriander, stalks and all and placed it into a large bowl. Next he peeled and sliced the onion, deseeded and finely chopped the chillies then scraped them into the bowl too. He grated the garlic and tossed it in. He cut the lime in half and squeezed the two halves in his fist over the bowl and added a glug of extra virgin olive oil. With a flamboyant flurry he threw in some sea salt and black pepper and gave the mixture a good stir. He took a taste.

'How is it?' asked Sarah.

'Yes, it's perfect. I'll do the eggs now, shall I?'

'Yes, Dad and Katarina will be down as soon as they smell the coffee,' giggled Sarah.

As the aroma of the toffee-infused coffee began to drift from the kitchen János and Katarina magically appeared and sat at the table.

'How's it going, chef?' asked János.

'All under control, Dad. Just doing the scrambled eggs now. Can someone put some toast on for me, please?' asked chef Ruben.

Meanwhile Sarah was gently warming through some of her pizza plum tomatoes; basically, plum tomatoes, some mixed herbs, salt and pepper and a little bit of sugar, easy.

Katarina jumped up and cut some ragged slices of bread and stuffed them in the huge toaster. The inaccuracies of the toast's dimensions did not escape Ruben's keen eye for detail.

'Why have you never learnt how to slice bread, Kat?'

'Why have you never learnt your nine times table? It's one of the easiest,' came Kat's snappy reply.

'Ouch, that hurt,' came the sarcastic response.

Just before the eggs started to congeal Ruben stirred in some of the salsa and carried on gently mixing the eggs. Right on cue the toast popped up. He quickly buttered them and laid them out on the warm plates. Taking a serving spoon from the wooden utensil pot he dropped a healthy dollop of eggs on each plate followed by Mum's pizza plum tomatoes.

'Wow, this looks good, darling,' said Sarah.

They all tucked in. Conversation was light and breezy as no one could bring themselves to talk about what the day would hold. Even Zooby the cat joined them on a spare chair at the table. He purred along with all the chat as Ruben lavished luxuriant strokes on him from his head to his tail. Zooby's eyes were half-closed in ecstasy.

'Thanks for breakfast, Mum, I am going to get ready now,' explained chef Ruben.

He got up from the table and disappeared up to his room closely followed by his dad and Zooby.

'So Ruben, my boy, this is it I guess. You are ready? The Cube is set?' asked János.

'Yes ready to go. The Cube will prepare me for the new time dimension I am going to arrive in so that I blend in. The Cube will guide me to the destination where I can set up base and prepare,' explained Ruben.

'Great, okay. When you are ready, come downstairs and we will meet in the TV room'

'Okay, Dad.'

János went down into the kitchen where a fresh pot of coffee had just been made.

'He's nearly set and will be down shortly. We must all be strong for him as he needs our love and support to help him on his way. He will be back. I feel it in my very being. If his destiny is to be fulfilled he *must* return to our time,' assured János confidently.

Sarah sighed deeply. She didn't feel like János, she felt worried and scared. Her stomach was in knots. Sensing her fear János gently took her hand and gave it a soft squeeze. He turned to Katarina.

'Are you all right, Kat? You have been uncharacteristically quiet this morning.'

'Yes, I know I have. I can't get my head around all of this. It is like we are living in some kind of fantasy world. Except we aren't. Our world is on the brink of annihilation. I can't bring myself to feel cheerful right now, Dad.'

'I know, darling, I can see that. Your brother holds our destiny in his hands. That's quite a responsibility, not one I would relish, but we must be here to help him. He must feel he has a safe place to return to, where he can belong, his normality. So try to be happy for him and show him you are there for him. I think you will be closer to him than you think.'

'How do you mean?' asked a puzzled Katarina.

'Your telepathic link should, theoretically, still work between the two time dimensions. Hopefully, he will be able to communicate with us through you. So you see, you have a very important part to play too.'

'Oh... yes, I guess so,' conceded Katarina.

János picked up the tray of coffees and went into the TV room. The garden was still dark so he turned on the outside lights to try and make it feel more like the morning. They all sat down and for a brief moment the room fell silent. Suddenly Ruben jumped into the room with a loud "Te-daaaa". For a moment no one recognised him.

'Wow, you look amazing, Ruben,' said Kat.

'Thanks, sis.'

Ruben stood in the doorway with his suitcase, a vision of 1948 teenage style. He was wearing creased tailored brown trousers and a white shirt with an orange brown geometric patterned tie. To top off his ensemble he wore a box jacket with a tan check body with brown sleeves and collar. However, the biggest change was to his unkempt shoulder-length blonde hair. It was now short, slicked back and with a side parting.

'Gosh darling, you look lovely, very stylish. Have you cut your hair off?' asked Mum.

'Well sort of. The Cube has restyled me to fit in when I arrive in 1948,' explained Ruben.

'Where is the Cube?' asked Dad.

Ruben pushed up the sleeve of his coat to reveal it clamped around his wrist. A few of the white jewels were flickering and pulsing in a sequence.

'I need to be going. I'll be back soon.'

They all got up and went over to Ruben and had a long, lingering family hug. He could feel their love and it gave him strength. He was ready. The family circle broke ranks and they moved back. Sarah, János and Katarina came together and held each other tight, very tight. Ruben spun the segments into Solved-Mode-One with all nine white jewels in one section. He put his fingers on the blue, green and white axis points and pressed. There was a blue flash, then at 11:00 he was gone.

■ ■ ■

TIME-JUMP BACKWARD
12:00 NOON, MONDAY, 27TH DECEMBER, 1948, MIAMI,
FLORIDA, USA
PAST

The alleyway was full of rubbish bins and boxes. Ruben felt slightly overdressed in his catalogue outfit. He quickly looked round to make sure no one had seen him appear. He pushed his left sleeve up and tapped out a sequence on the Cube's four white corner jewel cells. He then Mind-Linked to XL-R which then telepathically directed him which way to go.

Turn around one hundred and eighty degrees and head out of the alley onto Pennsylvania Avenue, sent XL-R.

It was a bright midday in Miami Beach, Florida. The street was buzzing with a Christmas festive feeling, the locals all going about their business oblivious to the time travel saviour of the world in their midst. A quick look around confirmed he was bang on trend, fashion-wise. Just then a pretty brown-eyed brunette girl passed him by wearing a floppy Santa Claus hat and gave him a double-take. Ruben flashed his winning smile back as she carried on her way. She was smartly dress and he couldn't stop himself from watching her cross the road and go into a café just behind three towering palm trees. It was called "Micky D's", and it was full of people grabbing a quick lunchtime snack. *I bet they aren't having salsa scrambled eggs*, he thought. A bright red and white awning over the window helped shade the customers from the midday sun. Crisp white art deco shop facades decorated with festive bunting lined the avenue on both sides with immaculately cut little squares of grass between the paths. Ruben loved Christmas and seeing all the decorations made him homesick. He liked the feel of the area and as he walked up the avenue he noticed the Lincoln Theatre on the corner of the road. It was quite a busy crossroads. Ruben took a moment to admire the wonderfully big chrome-festooned cars whizzing by. They all had curvy, swooping fenders with huge shiny grills and smart whitewall tyres. It was like watching a classic car show parade, except it was real life and in a perfect setting. Fords, Buicks, Oldsmobiles, Cadillacs, they were all there. As a beautiful black Chevy Fleetmaster drove past the lights changed to red. *Nice motor*, he thought. The traffic came to a halt and he quickly walked across the road. The white art deco theatre was almost exactly the same as Google Maps had shown him. It was indeed a four-storey building with a big glamorous entrance foyer over which was a huge balcony with the sign advertising the current film showing: "The Treasure Of The Sierra Madre" starring Humphrey Bogart. *Who?* thought Ruben. He wasn't really a fan of old westerns or old anything for that matter, apart from his guitar. He preferred Superhero action films, usually with a pretty girl in a very tight rubber body suit, virtually no story, but amazing CGI effects. To the right of the foyer were a few shops and a little restaurant. Above these were three floors of flats with huge concrete balconies curving round the corner of the building. He was at the right place, 541 Lincoln Road. To the left of the main foyer entrance was a little doorway over which hung a sign saying "Apartments to Rent". He went inside. The door made a pleasing "ding-a-ling" sound as he entered.

'Good day Sir, Merry Christmas. How can I help you?' asked the pretty brown-eyed brunette cheekily.

'Err... um... yes Merry Christmas to you. I want to rent an apartment for a few days. Have we met before?' asked a slightly flummoxed Ruben.

'I don't think so,' she replied with a knowing smile. 'How long do you wish to stay?'

'I'd like to look for two days please, sorry, I mean, book for two days, staring today, sorry I mean starting today,' fluffed Ruben again.

'Okay, that will be nine dollars a night, plus a nine dollar returnable damage deposit.' She tried to mask her giggle.

'Great, so that's err... twenty-six dollars?' replied a nervous Ruben.

'No sir, I think you'll find that comes to twenty-seven dollars all together. Now, we just need to fill in some details, name, contact address, that sort of thing.'

As the girl set about the paperwork Ruben couldn't help himself drifting off into fantasy land again. *Should I ask her out?* he thought. Then suddenly remembered he already had a girlfriend, although in this time she hadn't even been born yet, in fact neither had her parents. *Not a good idea*, he told himself.

'Okay sir, can you just fill your details in and then I will take your payment.'

Ruben completed the form and handed it back to the girl.

'Thank you, Mister...' she paused. 'Novak, that's an unusual first name and an even more unusual birth date. Were you really born in 2002?' she chuckled.

'Oh, oops, sorry, I don't know why I wrote that. It should be 1930. I don't know what I was thinking. Well, I wasn't,' he stumbled.

'Hmm one minute, Novak... that name sounds familiar.' She paused for a moment and quickly ran her finger down the passenger list on the desk. 'Ah, I thought so, we do have a guest staying with us with the same last name. Are you related?'

'Wow, that is odd, but I doubt it... would be fun to meet her though.'

'How do you know they are female?'

'Oh, I just guessed, fifty, fifty chance I suppose.'

'Well, you were right. Oh, she has checked out already, too late, shame.'

Great, she's been here, he thought. The girl then corrected the mistake and Ruben handed over four crisp ten-dollar bills. She handed one of them back.

'Have you just printed these? They're so new,' she asked with a smile. 'Do you know this area at all? There are some nice bars around here.'

'Err, no this is my first time here. Maybe you could show me around some time?'

'Yes, maybe I could. My name's Frankie by the way, and here's your change.'

'You're joking?'

'No, it really is your change?'

'Umm, no I meant your name.'

'What about my name?'

'Oh, I just thought to myself you looked like a Frankie. My friends call me Ruben,' he quipped nervously.

'How weird. Anyway, here are your keys. If you go out of the office and turn right, you will see the entrance stairwell. You are on the third floor, number 54. Hope you have a nice stay, Mr Novak,' said Frankie.

'What time do you finish work?' asked Ruben.

'I get off at five-thirty, but I'm busy tonight,' she replied.

'Oh, okay, thanks. Maybe some other time?'

Ruben took the little key fob and walked out of the office. He was not used to getting a knock-back. He took the stairs up to the top floor and walked along the balcony until he was at apartment 54. He put the key in the lock and opened the patterned wooden door. The flat was bright, airy and nicely styled and smelt fresh and clean. Each surface was gleaming and black and white floor tiles linked all the rooms. The furniture was all classic curves in dark woods and beautiful detailing. Ruben went through to the bedroom and put his case on the chair in the corner by the window. He popped his head into the bathroom. A silver geometric multifaceted mirror hung over the square basin and the white rectangular tiles completed the décor in classic style. He liked his new crash pad.

He went into the little lounge area and sat down. He put his head in his hands and closed his eyes to try to establish a telepathic Mind-link with Kat.

Hi Kat, I'm here. It's weird, I feel like I have been here before, sent Ruben.

Hi little brother. We were just wondering what was going on. So relieved you're safe and so relieved I can contact you too. You've been gone about an hour, what have you been doing? Sent Kat.

Well, first of all I hadn't really thought about it being Christmas here. That was a bit of a shock. I found the cinema on Lincoln Road and the apartments. I have got quite a groovy little one-bedroom flat on the top floor. Gives me a chance to sort my stuff out and get ready.

Sounds nice, hold on. Mum and Dad say "Hi" and Zooby says "miaow", sent Kat.

Miss you guys already. So once I have got myself sorted I'm off to the airport. Anyway, love you, will hopefully catch up a bit later, gotta go, haven't got a lot of time, sent Ruben.

He had a busy day ahead so decided to change into his casual clothes. He pressed the centre white jewel twice and morphed the Cube onto his hand and popped it on the table. He changed into jeans, a white T-shirt and bright jumper. *Style is style in any time dimension,* he thought. With the Cube back on his wrist, he threw on a rain jacket, picked up his case and headed out. He went back into the rental office.

'Hi Frankie, the apartment is great, thanks. Do you know where I can rent a cab from round here?'

'Hi Mr Novak, yes there is a cab company quite near here. Just go out of the office, turn left then left again along Lincoln Road, right next to Woolworths, about five minutes' walk. Are you expecting rain? It's a lovely sunny day today,' asked Frankie.

'Yes it's gonna rain later.'

'Oh, well have a nice day anyway.'

He followed her directions and set off down the road

towards Woolworths. Sure enough about five minutes later he was outside the store. Its huge glass windows were jam-packed with stacks of cans and boxes of things with all the Christmas trimmings. Ruben thought it might be fun to have a quick wander round inside. He soon realised that the shop seemed to sell all the things you could possibly need to live happily in 1948 America. It sold everything from food to firearms. He did not quite realise how long guns had been part of society. However, Ruben was particularly interested in the "Hot Nuts" and "Iced log Cake".

His impromptu diversion over, he went to the cab office next door. The room was a bit smoky as it seemed that nearly everyone had a cigarette pumping out fumes. *How things have changed,* he thought.

'Good morning, young man, what can we do for you today?' asked the jovial assistant. He too had a floppy Santa hat on.

'Good morning. I'd like a taxi to the airport please.'

'Sure, our standard fare to Miami International is two dollars seventy-five at this time of day. Should take about twenty-five minutes.'

'That's fine, I'll take it,' replied Ruben, handing over three dollars. 'Keep the change.'

'Thank you sir. Ok, if you go outside and get in cab number seven at the front of the rank, Carlo will take you. Have a nice day.'

Outside a shiny fleet of orange and yellow big curvy Dodge taxis were lined up, all with huge smiley chrome grills and little hooded headlights. Ruben went to the car at the head of the queue and jumped in.

'Good morning, so you want to go to the airport?'

'Yes I do, thanks.' Ruben then Mind-Linked to XL-R, the Cube.

XL-R, tell me something about a 1948 Dodge taxi, sent Ruben.

After a few minutes silence whilst Ruben absorbed the data download, he spoke.

'Lovely car, this. It's a Dodge Deluxe isn't it?'

'Yup, it's my pride and joy. It's part of the family. I have taken both my girls to church in this,' replied Carlo.

'102 horsepower, three point seven litre, six cylinder engine. About nought to sixty in twenty point seven seconds, with an estimated top speed of about seventy-eight miles per hour.'

'Sounds about right. You sure know you cars young fella.'

'Yeah, my dad is a bit of a car enthusiast. I guess it has just rubbed off on me.'

'Sure sounds like it. Haha,' chuckle Carlo.

'What do you get to the gallon?' asked Ruben, as he was on a roll now.

'Oh, I suppose I get about seventeen to twenty miles to the gallon, not bad.'

'I get about the same in mine.'

'What do you drive?'

'I've got an old Ford Mustang.'

'Hmm, I have never heard of one of those.'

'Oh, it's quite old, I don't think they make them yet, I mean, now,' he quickly added, realising his schoolboy error.

They headed down through the South Beach area and on to Highway 1A1; The MacArthur Causeway bridge, which crossed over the Biscayne Bay and connected Watson island to the Miami mainland. A line of pontoons spread out across the water supported the huge gently arching bridge, all three and a half miles of it. Ruben enjoyed the views as they crossed; it was quite spectacular.

A few minutes later they were in downtown Miami cruising into the heart of the busy city, through Little Havana and then north up on to North West 36th Street. To his left Ruben could see the airport stretching out towards the south. Various airplanes were dotted around the departure buildings. He could see the massive red and white square control tower and the vast arch-topped aircraft hangars lined up along the edge of the airfield. It looked just as he expected. He felt a sudden slight flutter of nerves in his tummy. As they pulled into the airport entrance terminal, past the huge welcoming neon sign, little spots of rain began to pepper the windscreen. The cyan blue sky had visibly darkened in the last few minutes. The taxi finally pulled into the short-stay drop-off area.

'Thanks very much, this is perfect,' complimented Ruben.

'You're very welcome. You have a good trip. Don't forget your bag.'

Ruben grabbed his case and jumped out of the cab and, dodging the rain, briskly ran into the departures hall.

He looked around. There were a few people milling about.

XL-R, can you locate a Mr Gardonyi in the vicinity yet? sent Ruben.

Scanning all human life form thermal heat profiles and cross referencing current passenger data records... Mr Gardonyi is in the building. He is standing 11.357metres away, at a 29.55 degree anti-clockwise direction from your current position, sent XL-R in reply.

179

Ruben slowly turned and spotted a lone figure sitting at a cafe table to the side of the check-in desk. He slowly walked towards him as XL-R confirmed his identity and sat at a nearby table.

XL-R, I will make contact with Mr Gardonyi at which point you must install the Mind-Implant as prepared, sent Ruben.

He turned round and caught the man's eye.

'Excuse me Sir, are you by any chance Mr Gardonyi from the Miami Times?' asked Ruben overly politely.

'Why yes I am, may I enquire who you are Sir?' he replied.

'I'm Mr Hendrix, a representative from the *HistoryMiami Museum. As you know we will be curating the big antiquities exhibition here in Miami.'*

The two men then stood and shook hands, on contact XL-R installed the implant in Mr Gardonyi. For the next few minutes he sat completely oblivious to what was going on around him as Ruben covertly rejigged the contents of their two briefcases. A few moments later the dazed Mr Gardonyi got up and without saying a word, walked out of the airport. Ruben gave a sigh of relief. *That went better than expected*, thought Ruben.

A quick scan of the departure hall revealed that the airline he needed was at the right-hand end of the building. The Airborne Transport desk was manned by two smart professional-looking girls dressed in professional dark blue suits with white blouses and little blue professional hats.

'Good morning, sir, how can we help?'

'I believe you have a reservation for me on return flight number NC16002 to San Juan, leaving at 16:00,' said Ruben.

'And your name, sir?'

'Mr Gardonyi.'

'Ah yes. Here we are... Mr J Gardonyi. Yes, all the paperwork is here. I see you're a journalist?' enquired the air stewardess.

'Yes I work for The Miami Times. We are covering the forthcoming exhibition of Egyptian antiquities here in Miami and I am doing some background research, reporting on the behind-the-scenes preparations and build up to the show. The exhibits are being picked up in San Juan and I want to get some photographs for my article,' said an enthusiastic Ruben.

'Gosh, that sounds interesting. I believe we have a young lady on board who is something to do with the same exhibition,' remarked the stewardess and she checked the passenger list.

'Yes here we are, a Ms Novak, she works for a museum in Miami, could be the same one, maybe it is fate you meet,' and she smiled.

Ruben felt a shiver run up his spine, he was her guardian angel and he was prepared for possible trouble.

'We will be boarding at 15:15. It's a cargo flight so won't take long to get you all on board, plenty of space to spread out, so may I suggest you grab yourself a quick coffee and a snack. Listen out for the boarding announcements,' she beamed, with a professional smile.

'Thanks, that's a great idea.'

With his paperwork safely inside his coat pocket, he walked off in search of coffee. The whole airport facility seemed so simple and basic compared to what he had experienced back in his own time. There were no digital display screens and electronic paraphernalia to be seen, and definitely no Wi-Fi to waste his time checking up on his Facebook friends' seemingly perfect lives. He decided he would be a grown-up and buy a newspaper. He soon found the shopping area where there was a snack bar, a little kiosk selling books and magazines and a small store for purchasing things you had forgotten to pack.

He bought himself a copy of The Miami News, went to the snack bar and ordered a coffee and some blueberry pancakes. He sat at his table and looked at the headlines. The main ones were: "Hungarian Cardinal Seized" and "Missing Boat Believed Located". They did not really interest him much, but at least it gave him a chance to catch up on some American history. On further inspection it seemed that the main news involved an American government official, Alger Hiss, being accused of spying for the Russians. There was an article about President Truman working with Budget Director James Webb on making Americans poorer and another about the Soviet troops withdrawing from North Korea. Also, it seemed that the Israel Defence Forces were about to cross the Egyptian border. It suddenly dawned on Ruben how long some of the world's conflicts had been going on too. He was shocked. On the bright side, Marlon Brando was starring in the now classic film, "A Streetcar Named Desire", and much to his amazement Ruben had actually heard of the film, hence his white T-shirt and jeans look. Having demolished his pancakes he whiled away his time browsing the historical document and drinking his not very nice coffee.

Just as he was about to have a look at the sports section the tannoy system sprang into life announcing the imminent departure of flight NC16002. He looked at his watch; it was 15:15. He put the paper in his case and made his way to the departure area. There were already a few people filing in at the gate when he arrived. A steward checked his ticket and ushered him out on to the wet tarmac. The rain had got heavier and the wind had noticeably grown stronger. His tummy churned. In front of him stood a gleaming silver Douglas DC-3 aircraft. As he crossed towards the embarkation steps he could see the men loading cargo on board at the rear of the fuselage.

At the top of the stairs a steward greeted him.

'Welcome on board, Mr Gardonyi. Choose anywhere to sit.'

'Thank you very much,' replied Ruben. He decided to sit near the wings as there was more legroom. It didn't take long for the rest of the passengers to get seated and comfortable. He noticed a young smartly dressed girl sit down a few rows up the cabin, she nonchalantly glanced past him. The steward checked everyone had their belts on and then went through the safety procedures. Interestingly, the passengers actually took the trouble to watch the steward's carefully choreographed safety routine.

The rumble of the engines then began to increase as the plane lurched into its taxiing manoeuvre. Ruben looked out of his little side window to see the rain had stopped. The whine of the plane's twin propellers became louder as the craft hurtled down the runway, faster and faster. He didn't like flying. The whites of his knuckles showed as he held on to the armrests with all his might.

Finally the plane left the ground and soared into the greying clouds. Ruben let out a sigh of relief. *Phew*, he thought.

He settled back in his seat, took out his pen and paper and decided to Mind-Link to Katarina.

Hi Kat, it's me, what are you up to? sent Ruben.

There was a slight pause.

Hiya, I was on the phone to Dan, where are you?

I'm on a plane flying to Puerto Rico.

Nice. You hate flying.

Huh, I know.

Ruben and Kat whiled away half an hour until their chat was interrupted by the plane's steward asking Ruben if he would like some refreshment.

A few minutes later, the attendant returned with a cup of coffee and some biscuits. Surprisingly, this time the coffee was good and the biscuits were dark chocolate. *Result*, he thought.

He started to doodle in his notepad, sketching crazy looking guitars. Most of the other passengers also seemed self-absorbed and Ruben didn't really want to strike up a conversation either. He put a reassuring hand on the Cube hidden under his coat and gave it a gentle pat. *Not long now,* he thought.

XL-R, tap into the aircraft's communication system and let me hear what's going on in the cockpit, sent Ruben.

Immediately, in his head, Ruben could hear what the pilot, Captain Linquist, was talking about. He was exchanging flight details with the control tower at San Juan and said they were on schedule to land at 19:40. He remarked that the charge levels in the batteries seemed a bit on the low side considering they had been refilled with water in the pre-take-off checks. He wondered if the alternators were working properly as the batteries weren't holding their charge. Apart from that, everything seemed alright on board. The tower responded by saying that it had reports of an offshore storm approaching Puerto Rico from the south.

XL-R, stop aircraft communication feed to me, but keep monitoring, sent Ruben.

Communication feed terminated, sent XL-R.

XL-R, did Arsenal play a game on this day?

This day December 27th, 1948 Arsenal Football Club played against Derby County away and lost by two goals to one. The Derby County goal scorers were Frank Broome and Billy Steel. The Arsenal goal scorer was Reg Lewis. Do you want to know more?

XL-R, stop please, sent Ruben.

He was quite a football fan and, like his dad, followed the trials and tribulations of the United Kingdom's Premier League, more specifically Arsenal. His Miami News sports section only covered American football and baseball and there were no games pending and no real news as it was holiday time. Ruben suddenly felt very bored.

XL-R, go to my music files and play the track The Devil Drives by the Infernal Desire Machine.

Playing music file, The Devil Drives by The infernal Desire Machine, then shuffle, sent XL-R.

The sound quality in his head was like listening to a high– end hi-fi system. Ruben took a quick glance at his watch; it was 18:32. He noticed the young girl up front was reading a newspaper. He settled back and luxuriated in the all-enveloping sound in his head. He glanced out of the little window to see darkening clouds forming on the horizon.

As The Infernal Desire Machine thrashed through their own peculiar brand of rock–pop, the minutes whizzed by and it wasn't long before the cabin steward emerged from behind the curtains to inform the passengers that they would shortly by preparing for landing at Isla Grande Airport in San Juan, Puerto Rico. *That was quick*, thought Ruben. He sat upright and tightened his lap belt and then a bit more.

XL-R, stop music feed.

Music feed stopped.

He didn't like flying and he really, really didn't like landing. He could feel himself becoming a little anxious again. The hum of the engines started to change pitch as the aircraft began to circle the airfield. Little beads of sweat began forming on his brow. Gradually the plane altered its trajectory as it came in to approach the runway. Ruben put his hand on the Cube.

Body functions within normal operating parameters. Slight raising of blood pressure and increased pulse rate. Slight raise in core body temperature. Sweat glands have gone into operation mode to aid cooling, sent XL-R.

Too right!

Also, my sensors have detected an electrical problem with the aircraft landing lights system; as expected, it is some kind of battery failure, sent XL-R.

The ground below was now fast approaching and Ruben held on tight to the armrests again. Suddenly there was a heavy bump and a screech as the tyres made a welcome impact on the runway. The plane continued to rumble along the tarmac until it finally came to a lurching halt. He discreetly wiped his sweaty brow.

Then over the aircraft intercom came the announcement that the plane would be refuelled, there would be a change of crew members and new cargo loaded. The stop-over would be about two and a half hours. The passengers waited for the mobile stairs to be lined up with the exits. Once in position the staff ushered the passengers off and directed them to the terminal building.

The airport was quite small and the main airport administration building housed arrivals and departures. There was a waiting lounge with a small coffee bar selling snacks listed in Spanish. He made a beeline for that while most of the other passengers disappeared outside to hail taxis or to be picked up.

Trying out his now-fluent, Cube assisted, Spanish he ordered some coffee and a sandwich and went and sat at a table by the window. The airport buzzed with lorries going back and forth to the planes, loading and unloading crates and packages. Ruben took a sip of his coffee and wondered what was going on back home in his other life.

■ ■ ■

Back in Los Angeles the Novak household was busy going about its Sunday in as normal a way as possible. Katarina had gone over to see Dan again and was spending the day shopping or in the gym. Sarah was at home doing some design work she was behind on, with a presentation day looming. János was at his office desk even though it was Sunday evening. He had spent the best part of the day at the lab testing the samples from the plane.

Earlier in the day he had run a whole bank of chemical tests, but it was the results from the electron microscope analysis that were the most interesting.

As predicted, they seemed to suggest the nano-sized particles were some form of self-evolving biomechanical organism. Using timed samples of the organism's development it was possible to plot its size variation. The data from the experiment enable the computer to run a theoretical sequence of how the organism might spread through the human body. The point of entry into the body would almost certainly be via the mouth and nose and then travel to the lungs, where it would pass into the bloodstream. János programmed in a three-dimensional computer model of the organism using the vector information for individual particles and then extrapolating them out by using a factorial randomisation cluster program, similar to his security system. The results were quite scary. As he ran the simulation in real time it soon became obvious that the lungs would indeed be its main entry point to the bloodstream. This was what János had expected. He decided to speed up the simulation and watched in horror as the dark cloud spread through the body from the lungs. *Oh good grief*, he thought. He put his head in his hands and closed his eyes. Two small tears squeezed their way out from the corners of his eyes and plopped on to the desk. For a few moments he turned to stone. He could not move, fear had paralysed him. Eventually he looked up at the screen in front of him. His hands darted over the keyboard as he tried various different simulations. After some thought he decided he needed to do some physical tests. He needed a human specimen to test. He looked around the room knowing he was the only one there. *So me it is then,* he thought. He got up, walked over to one of the cupboards in the lab and found the bits and pieces he needed to do a venipuncture on himself. He took a deep breath.

He did not like needles, never had, and never would. First, he tied a strap tourniquet around his bicep and pulled it firmly tight. Gradually the blue veins in his arm began to inflate because of the restricted flow of blood back to his pumping heart. Then he took a sterile swab and cleaned the area of skin in the fold of his left elbow. Next, he fitted a sterile new tip on the auto-vacuum syringe, inserted a collection canister and held the device lightly on his skin. The little display on the top of the device showed it was searching for a vein. A few seconds later a "bleep" signified a vein had been located. János took another deep breath. He pressed the activation button and felt a little pricking sensation on his arm. Slowly he watched as the canister filled with blood, his blood, his dark, red, human blood. Like Ruben, he too hated the sight of blood, especially his own when it was outside the confines of his body. He gulped. *Blimey, that's a whole big toe's worth,* he thought. When the canister was full, he lifted the vacuum syringe device off his arm and put it on his desk. Quickly he released the strap, sterilised his finger, pressed it on to the little exit wound and held it there for a few minutes while his heart rate went back to normal. Having stuck a plaster over the miniscule wound it was now time to test the sample. János took a small amount from the blood collected and applied it to a glass test slide, he added a tiny particle extract to another glass slide. Both samples were loaded into the electron microscope and the vacuum chamber sealed. János readjusted the focus and proceeded to operate the microscopic tools. Pressing the scan button meant that the equipment could plot the exact outline and shapes of the two samples. Very accurate movements of the inbuilt micro-tools could deliver a very precise amount of each sample and combine them on a third glass inspection slide for testing. János checked that the visual recorder was running; he did not want to miss what was possibly going to happen at this cellular level. The electron microscope was capable of a 10 million times magnification, if needed.

After programming the micro-tool movements, he pressed "run sequence". The two microscopic samples were combined. János transferred the display onto his big screen monitor. By using the joystick control, it was possible to track the camera over the sample. It looked like a scene from a cheap budget science fiction movie from the sixties, before CGI special effects had been invented to cover up plot holes. János was not unaware of the fact that he was living through his own sci-fi film for real, he just did not know what the finale was yet. He sat and watched the screen, but nothing was happening. János patiently waited. *Something must happen*, he thought. Suddenly the red blood cell, centre screen, juddered as the surrounding particles began to force their way through the semipermeable membrane cellular wall into the blood cell itself. János zoomed the picture out a little, just in time to see all the cells succumb to the particles forcing their way through the cell walls. *Oh heck, that's not good, not good at all*, he thought. He waited a while longer but all was still again on the glass slide. Just then, his mobile rang to the tune of Eruption by Van Halen.

'Hi darling, how's it going?' asked Sarah.

'Hmm, it's very interesting,' came the non-committal reply.

'Interesting good or interesting bad?'

'Well, I'm not really sure yet. I have made some progress. I will be back later. I want to try something

190

else before I leave. See you in a while honey,' said János, signing off.

He sat for a while pondering his next move, then jumped up excitedly. He hot-footed it to his store cupboard and got out a sterile scalpel and blade. Sitting at his desk, he put on some surgical gloves and then unwrapped a new, sterile glass test slide. After cleaning a small section of his heel with an alcohol wipe he carefully cut off a sliver of skin and placed it on the slide. Quickly he stuck a plaster over the incision and put his sock and shoe back on. Over at the electron microscope he withdrew the plain blood sample, loaded the fresh minuscule slice of skin into the machine, sealed the vacuum chamber, and then combined it with the particle-impregnated blood sample. He looked up at the screen and focused in on a skin cell. He watched and waited. The particle-loaded blood cells surrounding the skin sample began to slowly seep into the skin capillaries. János knew it was not a completely scientific test, but it was a start, given he did not have a lot else to go on. He looked at his watch and decided to phone home.

'Hi, it's me.'

'Hi darling, how are you getting on?' asked Sarah.

'Slowly honey, but I have made some progress. I am doing a test right now but it will take a while, so I think I will leave it running and monitor it at home on the lab feed. I should be home in about an hour-ish. See you in a while, mwah.' He blew her a kiss.

János took a glance at the monitor, then looked again more closely. The capillaries were indeed starting to fill with blood and spread through his skin sample. János let out a loud sigh of despair and went over to get his coat. He turned off all the lights and left the lab, locking the door behind him.

■ ■ ■

Ruben looked out over the airfield, it was starting to rain a little again. He had noticed a lot of cargo had been loaded onto his return flight plane. His watch showed it was 21:29 and so he got up just as the tannoy crackled into life requesting passengers for flight NC16002, San Juan to Miami make their way to the boarding gate. He was glad he had eaten a sandwich to settle his stomach, as he knew this trip back to Miami was going to be an interesting one. The passengers had their passes checked and proceeded through to the tarmac and the same waiting DC-3 aeroplane. Rain had just started to fall a bit more heavily as the line of passengers quickly snaked across the wet tarmac to the embarkation stairs and were ushered inside. The flight this time was by no means full. Ruben, again, couldn't help noticing the young women approaching him up the aisle. As she got closer, she gave him a little smile and this time sat down in the seat opposite him. As he glanced at her she suddenly split into a vision of three images of her, one red, one yellow and one blue. They twitched and flickered then recombined into one solid focused image. Ruben shook his head and blinked a couple of times. *What just happened then?* he thought. She was out of his league, judging by the expensive clothes and jewellery she was wearing. She looked very stylish. Ruben liked a challenge, but after a little consideration thought it best to read his paper instead.

He also happened to notice a couple of burly stewards were now on the plane with them.

XL-R, scan the cargo hold. Are the blue jewel cells on board? sent Ruben.

Scanning cargo hold. The blue jewel cells are on board at the back of the cargo hold in a wooden crate marked "HistoryMiami Museum". Note, as predicted, the plane is overloaded by fifty-three kilograms. The electrical communication system is compromised. There appears to be a fault in the valve anode bias circuit in the radio amplifier, sent XL-R.

XL-R, keep monitoring, sent Ruben.

Once all the passengers were seated, the cabin steward went through the obligatory safety routine as the hum of the engines began to change pitch and the plane began to move. Ruben knew the drill, hands gripping armrest tightly, check, trying to not look worried, check. He noticed the rain had stopped again.

'I can see you like flying then,' giggled the young woman in the opposite aisle seat, amused by the way he was clasping the armrests.

'Uh, yes I really like this bit,' he replied shakily.

'Hello, I'm Jayne, by the way. You look familiar, have we met somewhere before?'

'Hi, I was on the earlier flight here. I'm Ruben, he bumbled, forgetting he was supposed to be Mr J Gardonyi.

'Nice to meet you. Would you mind excusing me for just a moment, I need to concentrate on my gripping technique.'

The crew are experiencing problems. They can receive communications from the control tower, but at the moment they can't transmit. There is a serious communication breakdown. The plane is about to take off, time is 22:03, sent XL-R.

Ruben endured the rattling take off, nearly breaking the armrests and was relieved when it was finally airborne.

The batteries have recharged enough for communication with the control tower. The captain has informed the control tower it is heading for Miami. Weather and visibility are good, sent

XL-R.

'Phew, I'm glad that is over with,' exclaimed Ruben, to the young woman.

'I can see you enjoyed that,' chuckled Jayne.

'I can think of better things to do.'

'I say! What do you mean?' she queried cheekily.

'Oh no, no, I mean, um, I mean, actually, I don't know what I mean,' he stumbled.

'You're funny, what do you do?' asked Jayne, trying to stimulate the conversation.

'I'm a trainee pilot.'

She giggled.

'Actually I'm a trainee journalist for the Miami Times.'

'Wow, that sounds good. What sort of stories do you cover?'

'Well, at the moment I am covering the Egyptian exhibition that is coming to the HistoryMiami Museum.'

'Really? How funny, I'm the Assistant Curator of that Exhibition. Oh I see, you did the round trip also.'

'Yes, this day is proving to be a bit of a slog. I am going to write a behind-the-scenes account of the preparations for your show. Would you mind if I did a little work for a while, I have just remembered some things I need to do. We'll catch up in a little while, if that's ok?' asked Ruben, giving her his winning smile.

'Sure, no problem.'

Ruben checked his watch and then Mind-Linked to Kat again.

Hi, sis. Are you awake?

Hiya, yes I'm just about to go to bed. What's the problem?

I'm in a bit of a pickle. There is this pretty girl on the plane, and she is flirting with me, but I can't get involved with her, I'll explain when I see you.'

'Oh I see. *Tell her you have a girlfriend back home, or something. That should put a stop to it.*

Thanks Kat, I'll try that in a while.

Ruben noticed the stewards at the front of the plane were taking food and drink orders.

'Hi Ruben. Excuse me, do you fancy a drink? The stewards are coming round,' asked Jayne, leaning forward to catch his eye.

'Oh hi again. Yes, that would be nice. Please allow me to get these.'

Ruben decided he would also ask the steward if they had any reading material on board. A few minutes later, he returned with their drinks and a recent copy of Time magazine. The colourful cover depicted three cherub-like children sleeping in a big wooden bed whilst three glowing angels hover over them. It suddenly reminded him again that it was still Christmas in this time dimension, and he liked Christmas.

'I love Christmas,' said Ruben to Jayne.

'Yes, me too. We had a lovely time at home. How about you?'

'We had great Christmas, lots of friends and family came round. Our house was buzzing all through the holiday.'

Much against his better judgement, he could not resist chatting to Jayne, aware he was getting too involved. He told her he had a girlfriend, but as she had a boyfriend, it didn't really make any difference.

Conversation lulled and gradually his thoughts turned to his family and Frankie. He was missing them. It was all very weird. He felt like he had suddenly grown up very fast, almost virtually at the speed of light. He knew what he had to do and he knew that the time was fast approaching when he would be tested to his limits. He turned back to his magazine and fell silent again.

He flipped through the glossy pages. It was all very adult: business, education, health and medicine, science, religion, world affairs, and arts and entertainment. He thought he would start with the last section as he was into media stuff. He found the article was quite interesting and it helped to while away the time. A while later XL-R broke his mental silence.

The time is 23:23 The pilot has just sent a message to Oceanic Air Traffic Control informing them that we are currently at an altitude of two thousand metres above sea level, and approximately eleven hundred kilometres from Miami International Airport, expecting to arrive at about 04:03, December 28th.

■ ■ ■

János opened the back door into the kitchen. It smelt of Sarah's wonderful home cooking. He recognised the aroma of her South African bean stew with the sweet smell of apricots filling the room.

'Honey, I'm home, 19:21 on the dot,' he called out to the unusually silent house.

A few moments later Sarah appeared in the kitchen and gave János a passionate kiss that went on, and on, and on. Eventually he came up for air.

'Wow, I should go out more. I assume Kat is not in, judging by what just happened,' quipped János.

'Yes, she is out with Dan.'

'Dinner smells good. Shall I get a bottle of red to have with it?'

'That would be really nice. I suppose this will be what it is like when the kids have left. Just you and me and a bottle of red,' replied Sarah. 'How was it at work today, a bit odd working on a Sunday, I expect?'

'Yup, it was. I think I made some progress though. It's just a slow process. I will have a look at the lab stuff I have left running after dinner, if that's all right?' asked János sheepishly.

'Of course. Now, let's eat,' reassured Sarah.

János poured the wine as Sarah dished up the stew. Conversation flowed freely, as did the wine. Dessert was a very delicious vanilla and salted caramel cheesecake.

'That was lovely, I needed that. Today has been quite stressful. It is nice to be able to relax for a while. What have you been up to today?'

'Oh, I have been sketching some design ideas for Cindy Rothschild's hilltop retreat in Santa Monica. She wants it hyper-modern with a twist of Frank Lloyd Wright's Taliesin West building and John Lautner's Elrod House in Palm Springs

'Oh, isn't Elrod House the one in Diamonds Are Forever where James Bond gets attacked by two girl gymnasts... Bambi and, errr, Thumper, I think. Wow, that could be pretty amazing,' enthused Ján. 'I'll clear up in a mo... then I'd better go and check how the experiment is going.'

'Yes, you load the dishwasher as I know you think I don't do it correctly,' stated Sarah, with just a little hint of sarcasm.

'That's true, you don't,' teased János. 'You can't place the plates in front of the bowls and expect the water jets to be able to clean off all the obstructed muesli concrete debris. Also, knives should point down into the basket. What if you were to trip on a banana skin and fall into the dishwasher? Moreover, garlic needs to be removed from the crusher before putting it in the basket. Shall I go on?'

'No, you're too obsessive, like Ruben. Please don't, I get the message.'

The kitchen was soon cleared, and János made a pot of fresh coffee. Sarah was just about to sit down again when she heard the front door open. It was Kat and Dan. He had brought her back home. They walked through into the kitchen laden down with posh boutique shopping bags.

'Hi Mrs Novak, hi Mr Novak, how are you this evening?' asked Dan politely.

'Hi you two, yes we're fine thanks. I think we can do away with the formalities, call us Sarah and Ján,' said Ján, trying to put Dan at ease.

'Okay thanks, Mr Novak, err... sorry, Ján.' Dan corrected himself as Kat smirked behind his back.

'I've just made some coffee, would you like some, or tea? We've got loads of strange trendy herbal infusions. Apparently the "Kumquat, Guava and Naga chilli" is very nice, if you are into that sort of thing. I'm not,' offered János bluntly.

'No, coffee is fine, thanks.'

'Kat?' asked Dad.

'Yes coffee's good for me Dad.'

Dan had only been to the Novak household a few times before so Ján and Sarah took the time to get to know him a little better. They had enjoyed a nice day shopping and Kat had certainly given her debit card a good hammering.

'I see I'm going to have to build you a new wardrobe to house your latest purchases. Did you leave the shop with any stock for their other customers?' asked Dad.

'Haha, I haven't bought that much, they're just big bags,' Kat explained unconvincingly.

'Can you excuse me for five minutes, I just need to check something in my office. Back in a mo.'

János got up and went to his office. He closed the door and sat at his desk. With a quick nudge of his mouse the computer screen came on. He entered his passcode then remotely accessed the lab computer network. A few clicks later he was able to see how his experiment was going. On closer inspection it looked like the blood cells had now fully filled the capillaries in the skin sample and that the particles were starting to diffuse into the skin cells. He turned up the magnification and refocused. The skin cell gradually started to darken as more particles diffused across the cell membrane. He knew this was not good; unfortunately his hunch had been right. He decided to leave the experiment running and rejoined the others downstairs in the kitchen.

'Everything all right, darling?' asked Sarah.

'Yes, fine, fine,' replied János.

She knew it wasn't.

■ ■ ■

The articles in Time magazine were proving to be surprisingly interesting to Ruben. XL-R then popped up in his brain.

It is 03:40 and the pilot has just sent a radio communication reporting current position to be approximately 80 kilometres south of Miami. This is incorrect. Due to a change in wind direction we are 576.92 kilometres east of Miami at mapping co-ordinates Latitude North 25° 45' 37.1511" and Longitude West 74° 29' 14.2969". There has been no confirmed reply, sent XL-R.

Ruben was expecting this discrepancy, however his train of thought was suddenly derailed by the steward asking him if he would like some refreshment.

'Jayne, would you like a drink?' asked Ruben.

'Thanks, yes that would be nice, just water for me,' she replied.

'Erm, yes, could we have two glasses of water please? I feel full of coffee right now, been drinking it all day.'

'Of course Mr Gardonyi, no problem.'

The steward brought the water and finished off attending to the other passengers. Ruben took a sip and placed his glass in the little cup holder on the seat tray in front. Suddenly XL-R entered his head again.

Alert, danger, you have ingested a small amount of Sulphuric Ether anaesthesia. This will put you to sleep, then kill you. I am initialising a focused temperature evaporation procedure. Do not swallow, keep your mouth tightly closed and place your hands around your neck. This will hurt.

Quickly Ruben did as instructed. Immediately a searing pain rose up from his chest into his throat. *Holy moly*, he thought. It felt like his insides were on fire. The pain in his throat got more intense. His face screwed up in torture, he closed his eyes and screamed like the very hounds of hell were inside him. Then gradually he could feel the pain start to subside. He opened his eyes and looked around. The cabin was eerily silent, apart from the background hum of the engines. There were no staff about. None of the passengers seemed to be moving. He looked across the aisle to Jayne sitting opposite. She was slumped over in her seat. Ruben looked around. Everybody was unconscious.

XL-R, scan plane for personnel, sent Ruben.

Scanning plane interior. There are four other conscious life forms on board. They are in the cockpit radioing false position co-ordinates.

Suddenly the cockpit door clicked open. Ruben quickly pretended to be asleep. Through the corner of his eye he could see the steward walking towards him.

Increasing adrenaline functions to main muscle groups, and augmenting powered delivery response by a factor of three, sent XL-R.

The steward came up to him and lifted down his suitcase. He began to rifle through its contents. He then started to look through Ruben's jacket pockets and he did not like the intrusion into his personal space.

'Is this what you are looking for?' and Ruben opened his eyes, pulled back his sleeve to reveal the Cube clamped around his wrist.

'Ah, yes, Jutotzas said you would have the Cube with you when you boarded the plane. Give it to me now or die,' ordered the steward bluntly.

Instinctively Ruben grabbed the steward's hand. Startled, the man tried to pull back and aim a blow at him. Ruben blocked his fist with his elbow and thumped him hard in the chest. The steward flew backwards smashing his head on the side of the seat. Momentarily dazed, he shook his head and lunged forward at Ruben. He crossed his arms in front of his face and with a powerful scissor-action double-punch, sent the steward hurtling back across the cabin.

Initialising protective Body-Shield, sent XL-R.

From his jacket pocket the steward pulled out a small gun and hastily pointed it straight at Ruben. He pulled the trigger. A deafening bang accompanied the bullet as it blasted straight at Ruben. Before he could respond, the shell had ricocheted off his invisible Body-Shield and embedded itself in the cabin wall. The steward couldn't believe his eyes. He fired again and again the bullets ricocheted off him. Suddenly Ruben lunged forward and grabbed him by the throat and hit him hard up under the chin. The force lifted the guy clean off his feet and he flew up the cabin aisle into the rear wall with a loud crunch and immediately exploded into a black cloud and vaporised. *One down, three to go, thought Ruben.* Hearing the commotion the cabin door flew open. The co-pilot turned to see what was happening. Bang. A second steward fired at Ruben again. The bullet bounced off and passed through the lower part of the fuselage.

A Bullet has entered the port side main fuel tank and compromised electrical insulation in the engine cable loom, sent XL-R.

That's not good, sent Ruben.

Ruben pulled the steward to his feet and with an almighty whack he knocked his attacker unconscious, his gun falling to the floor. The assailant exploded into a black particle cloud and disappeared. *Two down,* thought Ruben. The co-pilot quickly threw off his headphones and ran out of the cockpit towards Ruben. *Blimey, number three is a big guy,* he thought. He lunged forward and threw a punch at Ruben who caught his fist and twisted his clenched hand hard around. The man screamed and he punched him with all his might. He fell with a heavy thud, then he too exploded into oblivion. *One left,* he thought.

Suddenly there was an almighty explosion from the left wing engine. Ruben looked out through a cabin window and watched in horror as an upper wing panel was torn from the engine cowling. The plane shook violently and started to shudder. Flames began to pour from the engine.

The explosion on the portside has caused a drastic altering of the aeroelastic structural integrity of the airframe. This will cause the wing to begin a resonant frequency oscillation and weaken the fuselage mounting points. The wing will detach from the fuselage in approximately thirty-two of your Earth seconds. Initialising full body protection Exosuit, sent XL-R.

In a split second, the Cube had morphed into a fully articulated protective exoskeleton with respiratory system and body-function monitoring. Ruben was safe. The wing ripped itself from the fuselage with a sickening screech of twisting metal and the plane began to bank steeply to the left. Ruben braced himself for impact but didn't really know what to do or what to expect. The flames streamed along the side of the plane with black smoke billowing all around.

Twenty-one point four three of your Earth seconds to impact, sent XL-R helpfully.

The pilot struggled in vain to try and level the plane off, but it was futile.

Four point one five seconds to impact, sent XL-R.

Then with an almighty crash the plane slammed into the water. Ruben felt himself being thrown heavily against the side of the plane as it crashed through the waves. The terrified pilot catapulted forward into the control panel, recoiling like a ragdoll into a motionless heap and vapourised. The lights flickered briefly then went out and the plane was plunged into pitch black as it came to rest floating on the choppy sea.

This plane will begin to sink in five minutes, forty-seven, of your Earth seconds, sent XL-R.

Earth seconds? You're not making any friends here you know, sent a rattled Ruben.

He suddenly began to feel scared. He hadn't really prepared himself for this kind of situation. How could he? He didn't like the dark and he didn't like being in a floating, wrecked aircraft in the North Atlantic Ocean much either.

Initialising illumination system, sent XL-R.

Two beams of light exploded from the arms of the Exosuit. He could now see the full extent of his predicament.

XL-R, where is the cargo? sent Ruben.

Proceed to the back of the plane and access the rear cargo hold through the back bulkhead door.

Ruben turned round and using his Exosuit lights lit his way back along the cabin. It "creeped" him out as he looked at the lifeless bodies strapped in all over the plane. Jayne was dead, they were all dead. He didn't dwell and picked his way to the cargo door. It was locked.

Initialising Laser cutting tool, sent XL-R.

Out of the right arm of his Exosuit a small control panel extended outwards. Ruben pressed three yellow buttons in an "/" pattern on the control pad on his right wrist. A bright yellow laser beam fired from the suit and he began cutting away at the lock.

Four minutes and counting, sent XL-R.

Smoke swirled from the door as Ruben laser-cut through the lock assembly. A few seconds later he pulled the door off its hinges. Sure enough, in the cargo hold were some wooden crates. Quickly he searched for the ones marked "HistoryMiami Museum".

Three minutes and counting, sent XL-R.

Where is it? thought Ruben. Fully aware that what little time there was left was running out frighteningly fast. His Exosuit gave him the power to shift the heavy boxes rapidly around the hold.

Two minutes and counting, power cells are low, sent XL-R.

Ruben found what he was looking for. There was the crate he needed. He became aware that his movements were being accompanied by a worrying splashing sound. His powerful hands ripped the lid clean off to reveal the crate was full of loads of items wrapped in cloth. Where was the one he needed?

Initialising head-up display scanning mode, sent XL-R.

As Ruben picked up each package, he could clearly see the contents inside. He sorted through the crate's entire contents.

One minute and counting, power cells are critical, sent XL-R.

Feverishly he searched, but he couldn't find the jewels.

XL-R, where are the Blue Jewels? They must be here. They must be.

Look for another crate, the plane is starting to sink, sent XL-R.

Quickly Ruben began shoving the boxes out of the way accompanied by a dangerous splashing of filling water. He was already up to his knees in seawater and the plane was starting to tilt backwards. Then in the corner of the hold he saw another little crate with the museum label stamped on it. He raced to pull the lid off. All the while the sea level was rising and the plane was tilting more. Inside were more parcels. He scanned them. The packages were all ancient Egyptian artefacts, figures and pots, but there was also a little jewellery box. On the lid it had "Jayne Novak" embossed in gold letters. Ruben paused for a moment. The Cube quickly scanned it.

The jewels are inside the box, confirmed XL-R.

He had found what he was looking for. The water was now coming up to his neck and he knew it was time to get out of the sinking plane.

XL-R, get me out of here, quick, sent Ruben.

Initialising teletransportation protocols, sent XL-R. Ruben put his fingers on the yellow, green and white buttons on the Exosuit control panel and pressed hard.

■　■　■

LOCATION-JUMP

There was a blinding flash and Ruben was back in his dark Miami apartment holding the wet package. He fumbled around for the light switch. He looked at the clock on the wall. It was 04:03 and he was safely back on dry land with the recovered blue, Water of Life Jewels.

Thanks XL-R, you saved my life, disengage Exosuit, sent Ruben.

Exosuit disengaged. That is why I am here, to serve.

XL-R, you have got quite a few nifty tricks up your sleeve, haven't you?

Explain, "nifty tricks".

Haha, chuckled Ruben. Later.

After a few minutes regaining his composure he had a quick look around the apartment to make sure he had everything. He got a towel from the bathroom and wrapped up the little box. His case and contents would, by now, be well on their way to the bottom of the North Atlantic Ocean just as history recorded it. *Right, XL-R, take me home. Err, to my bedroom, I think may be safest. What time will it be in L.A?*

The parallel time will be 03:05, Monday, 21ˢᵗ July in Los Angeles, USA.

Oh, yes of course. They will all be asleep.

Ruben spun the segments into Solved-Mode-One, with all nine white jewels in one section. He put his fingers on the blue, orange and white axis points and pressed. In a sudden blue burst of light he was gone.

■　■　■

03:05, MONDAY, 21ˢᵗ JULY, NOVAK RESIDENCE
LOS ANGELES, USA
PRESENT DAY

There was a blinding flash and Ruben reappeared in his bedroom. He suddenly felt an overwhelming feeling of relief. He had never been more pleased to see his room before.

XL-R, disengage Safe-Mode, sent Ruben.

Safe-Mode disengaged, sent XL-R.

He placed his fingers on the top white axis jewel and pressed it twice. The Cube slipped from his wrist into his hand.

He placed it on his bedside table and flicked on his bedside lamp.

XL-R, engage Safe-Sleep-Mode, sent Ruben.

The Cube became invisible. Aware everyone was asleep, Ruben had a quick wash, put his PJs on and jumped into his bed. He was exhausted and it wasn't long before he was sound asleep.

■ ■ ■

Soon the morning hubbub drifted up the stairs to Ruben's room and gradually he could make out the familiar voices coming from the kitchen. He decided he wanted to get up and see his family more than snooze so put on his dressing gown and went downstairs. He burst through the door in his usual ebullient manner. Round the table were Mum, Dad, Kat and Zooby.

'Hey everybody, I'm back,' he stated somewhat obviously.

'Hello darling, we weren't expecting you just yet. You must have got back in the small hours as we were up quite late. Dan was here,' said Sarah.

'We thought you were still in Miami,' said Kat.

'I got a quick connecting flight back this morning,' joked Ruben.

'Are you hungry? I have some of my special bean

stew left over from last night or would you prefer some blueberry pancakes?' asked Sarah.

'Great, pancakes sound perfect, too early for stew. So how is everyone?'

Sarah started mixing the eggs. The coffee was on the go and Zooby sashayed around the room soaking up cuddles, finally settling on János' lap. Through the huge picture window the garden looked lovely. It suddenly dawned on Ruben that he could actually see the garden. The morning was considerably lighter than it had been yesterday. The sky was still a little dark, more of a storm-cloud sky.

'So Ruben, what happened?' asked János.

'Hummm, where do I start. Actually, hold on. I have an idea. I'll be back in a minute.' He got up and ran to his room to get the Cube. He quickly returned and sat down.

'Why don't I show you what I have been doing?'

'XL-R, disengage Safe-Sleep-Mode,' commanded Ruben.

'Safe-Sleep-Mode disengaged,' replied XL-R.

He placed his fingers on the top white axis jewel and pressed it twice. Ruben then positioned the Cube on the table and pressed three white jewels in a diagonal line pattern "/".

XL-R, play Blue Jewel video data files, point of view and Cube view, sent Ruben telepathically, for dramatic effect.

Suddenly the room exploded with light as a three dimensional holographic projection began to play in the centre of the floor. Ruben skipped through various video data files, while eating the blueberry pancakes. As the story of his adventure unfolded in front of them, his audience sat in silent disbelief watching the auto-edited highlights.

'Good grief, that was amazing. You handled yourself well. That was a bit close at the end. So where are the jewels?' asked János.

'They are upstairs. They are set into a beautiful piece of jewellery. I guess we have to remove them and fit them in the Cube,' said Ruben.

'Indeed, we can do that a bit later, after you're dressed,' quipped János.

Ruben felt a bit guilty about editing the video data file playback, but he didn't want them to know that his assailant on the plane was somehow related to the evil brother of the late Grand Prince Zoltán. Jutotzas was still after the Cube. Even though the centuries had been and gone, he was still determined to get his hands on the Cube. Ruben finished his breakfast and went upstairs, followed by his dad.

'So how do you really feel this morning,' asked János.

'I do feel a bit whacked out this morning. When XL-R reconfigured some of my body functions it obviously had a knock-on effect. The muscle boost it gave me was awesome though, also it was like the Cube had altered the clock speed of my brain. I was doing things so quickly I didn't have time to think.

'Well, it is well known that practised actions, if repeated enough, become automatic. In effect, your unconscious brain is running ten times faster than you and your conscious brain. A good example of automatic brain function would be those guys that play shred guitar. They have practised their scales and licks so much that they are running on a type of autopilot when they play those incredibly fast runs,' explained Dad in too much detail for mere mortals to be interested in.

'And, I guess the Cube is capable of doing that and more. If I think about what really happened, I should have been scared witless, but I never really gave it any thought. You couldn't see it on the holographic playback, but the Exosuit that I was wearing was absolutely amazing. It was a fully articulated exoskeleton with me sealed inside. It saved my life. Bullets just bounced off it. Those guys couldn't believe what I was wearing, or how hard I could hit. Actually, neither could I. My karate came in quite handy too. Dad, there is something I need to ask you.'

'What is it Ruben?'

'Well, in the plane when the steward tried to poison me I was lucky that I had the Cube to save me. The other passengers were all dead and now they are lying at the bottom of the sea. I am confused by what I feel now, looking back. We know that the plane's wreckage has never been found. The flight was all logged, the transmissions logged, but no one knows where the plane crashed apart from the Cube. What do we do with that knowledge? We could find the plane and all the relatives of the passengers who died on that flight would finally know what had happened to their loved ones.'

'That is very true, but we can't do anything about it. If we get involved, it could bring us unwanted attention. Bear in mind what we are dealing with here. We cannot jeopardise our situation by exposing ourselves to a publicity circus. We have to leave it alone. We can't alter the past and there is something else I need to tell you. On Friday morning when I went up to the lab, I was followed. I don't know who they were, but they were definitely watching me, taking pictures. Also, remember, someone tried to break into the lab. Then, when I drove to the airport on Saturday afternoon, I got hassled by a guy who was tailing me across town. I managed to shake him off, but it got a bit dicey at times. Things are hotting up. We need to be very careful how we operate,' said János.

'Yes, and there is something I need to tell you too. In the plane, one of the guys mentioned that Jutotzas had sent them to get the Cube.'

'Oh no, that's not good. That means that Jutotzas' reach may have extended through time to our present day, which also means him and his cronies could be here too. We must be very vigilant.'

'Also, the crazy thing was, when I was fighting these guys they didn't die, they just evaporated. They exploded into a black cloud, then disappeared. All four of them did that. Weird.'

'Hmm, this is getting complicated. I think we should go to the lab after breakfast and have a look at my experiment, and we should sort out the Cube. Okay?'

'Yes, let's do that. I'll get up and get myself together. I want to call Frankie.'

'Okay, yes. I expect she would like to see you. Interestingly, this morning it's not quite so dark, which means the particle cloud is dispersing and dropping through the atmosphere. We need to get a move on. I think Frankie will have to wait, sorry,' said János, and left Ruben to get showered.

Back in the kitchen, the television was rattling away in the corner. The main news topic was about the particle cloud and the fact that the world was starting to get some sunlight.

'So what is everyone up to today?' asked Sarah.

'Well, Ruben and I are going to do some work on the Cube and then we are going to the lab to do some more experiments on the particle cloud,' continued János.

'I'm going to meet up with some of the girls and hit the gym for another good workout,' explained Kat.

'Doesn't Jim get fed up with being thumped about a bit?' quipped Ruben on his return to the table.

Kat looked at her brother and raised an eyebrow at his lame joke.

'I could do with some time in the gym too, but I have to go into the office and brief Matt, the head of our model-making team on the Crown Plaza development on Century Boulevard,' said Sarah.

It was the start of the working week and breakfast was over and everyone prepared for their day ahead. Once everything had been cleaned away Ruben ran upstairs and got the Cube and the jewellery box. János went out into the garage and a few minutes later Ruben joined him there.

'So let's have a look at the jewels then,' said János.

Ruben unwrapped the little box, put it on the workbench and opened the lid to reveal a collection of beautifully ornate jewellery.

'Wow, these are beautiful,' remarked Dad.

'Now look at the name on the lid,' said Ruben.

'Um, blimey, it says, "Jayne Novak". Oh, good grief, these pieces of jewellery were owned by your great-aunty. My dad told me about her disappearance years ago. No one really knew what happened. Hmm, now I think about it, I remember he said something about her working for a museum in Miami as it happens. This can't be a coincidence that the jewels happen to be with her. She must have put them in the cargo hold to keep them safe, I guess.'

'I chatted to her throughout the flight. She was really lovely. Maybe I could have saved her?'

'We can't alter history as it could set up a ripple effect through time and we can't mess with the fabric of the universe by changing the past,' replied János.

In the box, amongst the jewellery was a pair of emerald green jewelled earrings with a matching brooch. There was also a necklace made from fine gold wire that was threaded with lots of fine coloured ceramic beads. They made a complex pattern, which fanned out in a stunning crescent shape. In the middle of the necklace was a large blue scarab beetle made from carefully shaped green stone inlaid with gold with delicate green beads outlining the shape of the legs. The front two limbs were holding a bright red stone that had gold beads surrounding it. Arranged around the outer edge were eight dazzling blue jewels.

'This is a lovely piece, very art deco, Egyptian-influenced,' added János.

'XL-R, scan the stones and find the blue jewel cells we need,' commanded Ruben.

'Scanning box contents,' confirmed XL-R.

The cells were in the necklace.

'So, Dad, how do we get the stones out?'

'Hmm, let me have a look. Let me get my gear over.'

Ján's toolbox was actually a huge tool chest with every conceivable spanner, screwdriver, wrench, socket, pliers etcetera that you could possibly need to do anything that involved fixing or making things. By comparison, Ruben had a small penknife. János proceeded to put on his magnifying glass headset. This was accompanied by a chuckle from Ruben.

'Dad, you look like a mad professor with that on.'

'Ah, I see, the blue jewels are held in by the gold wire that runs in a groove around the bottom edge of them all. So if I snip the wire I should be able to prise each jewel loose.'

Carefully, János got to work with his snips and pliers and soon all eight jewels had been safely extracted from the necklace.

'Okay Ruben, now we need to fit them to the Cube.'

He picked it up from the workbench and quickly whizzed the segments around into Solved-Mode-One, so that one section was all white jewels, and each other centre axis point had a coloured jewel in position. Ruben then held the Cube and pressed the blue centre axis jewel eight times.

'XL-R, prepare to load blue jewels, also scan and make cosmetic replicas of the jewels,' said Ruben.

'Configuring system, connection sensors ready, scanning ready. Load blue cells,' replied XL-R.

Ruben placed the Cube on the worktop. He then proceeded to gently push the jewel cells into the blue segment. Each click of engagement was verified by a blue flash of light darting over the Cube's surface. When the last jewel was in place he pressed the centre blue jewel twice, the Cube began to pulse with a blue light, gradually getting faster and faster, then stopped. On the worktop were eight new blue jewels.

'Blue cells are engaged. After system update I will be running at sixty-two point, nine, six per cent functionality,' confirmed XL-R.

'Great, we need to go to the Lab now. I'll clear up here. When or if I ever get time I'll reassemble the necklace. It'll make a nice present for your mum. You could give the earrings to Kat; it would be nice to keep these treasures in the family. Now, go and get your coat and I'll get the old truck out.'

'Can't we go in the Jaguar? It's a bit cooler, you

don't know who might see us,' asked Ruben, picking up the Cube.

'Not today. Now come on, we have work to do.'

János jumped into his truck.

'Rosanna, tell me a joke.'

'Do you know they have taken "gullible" out of the dictionary?'

'Hmmm, Rosanna, open the main garage door.'

'Main garage door opening now,' confirmed Rosanna.

János turned the key in the ignition and the huge V12 engine burbled into life. Just then Ruben magically appeared in the driving seat, which startled his dad.

'Walking is "so last year", I much prefer matter transferral, saves time. So what are we going to have to tolerate listening to on the way to work then?' asked Ruben cheekily.

'Don't mind. Any suggestions? I don't want to listen to any of your "mushroom bedsit" stuff, if you don't mind.'

'Do you mean "Garage"?'

'Probably,' replied János.

'I know. Why don't you play some of *your* old band's stuff. I like to listen to *your* old guitar-playing.'

'Less of the old, if you don't mind.'

'Go on, stick on some Sheer Pride, should be good for a laugh.'

'Eh, watch it, you young duck with a soft beak.'

'Whaaaaat?' asked Ruben incredulously.

'I can still show you a thing or two. Have you learnt the melodic Hungarian minor scale yet?' asked Dad.

'Err, no.'

'There you go then. Game over, Dad wins on points.'

'Rosanna, play Firezone, by Sheer Pride,' instructed Dad.

'I can't find Firezone, by Sheep Rider in your playlist,' replied Rosanna.

'No, Rosanna, play Firezone, by SHEER PRIDE,' emphasised Ruben.

'Playing Firezone by Sheer Pride. Six minutes and eleven seconds duration of musical perfection, enjoy,' confirmed Rosanna, slightly sarcastically.

János reversed the truck out, down the slope and onto the road. He shifted the gear stick into "drive" and they zoomed off down Pleasantridge Drive.

An atmospheric keyboard wash slowly oozed from the speakers as an echoed guitar weaved in and out of the chords and the FX sound of helicopters. The hi-hats began to "tick", then suddenly a solo distorted guitar exploded into a stabbing riff.

'Oh yes, I like this one. Nice guitar sound, Dad. What did you use?' asked Ruben.

'I used my old yellow Dimarzio humbucker Strat, the one I built. That went into my Marshall head and a four by twelve cab, a bit of chorus and delay, not much else.'

The whole band kicked in and ploughed into the first verse.

'Nice, it's a good driving track, this. Did you write this?'

'Well, I wrote the main chorus riff, which is like a Deep purple riff I liked, the verse and the middle eight. I was getting into using fourths a lot at this point. The solo was inspired by a Jeff Beck wang bar lick I ripped off his "Flash" album. Great album. We kicked it around in the rehearsal room for a while. Vince and Martin wrote some war-based lyrics. Mark whacked some great slap bass on it, John sorted out the drums and percussion programming and Martin found some great noises on our Roland Juno 106. It turned out pretty good. We used to open with it.'

'Yes. I like the solo you did Dad, cool. You were pretty fast back then,' taunted Ruben.

János and Ruben could talk music trivia for hours on end, and often did, and it helped lighten the mood as they made their way through the city. It was the usual busy Monday morning commute to work and János was pleased to have company for a change. Before long they were heading along the Angeles Crest Highway, up into the mountains towards Woodwardie Canyon. The half light of the morning was peppered with the lights of Los Angeles twinkling in the distance below.

'Attention, I have detected an object that has been tracking us for the last sixteen minutes and thirty-one point two seconds. The probability of that occurring considering the possible junction permutations is approximately one in three hundred and eighty-seven,' announced XL-R disturbingly loudly.

'Oh no, we are being followed again. I thought a red five series BMW was tailing us a while back,' pondered János.

Ruben turned and looked out the rear window. The red car was a way back, but seemed to be getting steadily closer. As the road straightened out the car suddenly shot forward.

'Hold on tight, this is not good,' exclaimed János.

One of the men in the BMW hung out of the rear window holding a machine pistol. The flash of gunfire then rang out as bullets strafed along the back of the truck puncturing the bodywork.

'Argh, I have just resprayed that rear panel,' fumed an annoyed János.

'XL-R, engage near vicinity protective shield,' commanded Ruben.

'Initialising protective shield,' confirmed XL-R.

The crack of gunfire got louder as the BMW drew closer. The whistling bullets ricocheted off the shield in all directions. János began to sweat. He was used to being shot at in computer games, but not for real. The BMW got closer. As they went round a long swooping corner an oncoming car appeared. The gunfire sent a hail of bullets into the other approaching vehicle. It swerved and ploughed off the road skidding sideways then flipped over into a crumpled heap on the gravel verge. A cloud of dust enveloped the wreckage.

Suddenly they felt a heavy crunch as the BMW rammed hard into the back of the truck. The shock wave sent the truck across the road into a vicious swerve, but János managed to keep control of it. Then again, the BMW ploughed into the back, all guns ablazing, bullets ricocheting everywhere. The road opened out into a straight section with a barrier running along the edge of the drop to the valley below, a long way below. János held his nerve as the BMW shot out from behind and accelerated up along the inside as the relentless gunfire continued. Ruben could now clearly see there were three men in the car. They looked like they meant business and weren't going to give up.

The BMW then heavily broadsided the truck sending it careering into the safety barrier. The truck bounced and rumbled along the metal edging, the back began to fishtail wildly out of control. Again, János accelerated out of the skid. Moments later the BMW rammed hard into the side of the truck again, trying to force it off the road.

Ruben quickly configured the Cube into Solve-Mode-One, pressed the centre white jewel and it appeared on to his hand. Quickly he manipulated the segments into Solved-Mode-Two, pressed five blue jewels in an "X" pattern and the Cube morphed into a high-tech gauntlet gun in his hand.

XL-R, give me full ballistics capability, sent Ruben.

He started to wind the window down. Sensing something was about to happen the BMW hit the brakes and quickly dropped back. Ruben then lowered the other side window and leant out of the window. He pointed the Cube weapon at the car.

Target locked onto, confirmed XL-R.

Ruben pulled the trigger and a blinding bolt of energy fired at the tailing BMW. As it impacted on the front of the car it blew the engine apart sending body panels corkscrewing into the air and catapulting the vehicle on to its side. It screeched along the tarmac showering sparks everywhere before crashing through the highway safety barrier and plummeting into the canyon below. The twisted metal wreck crashed down the rock face, coming to rest in a ball of fire. It exploded and vaporised into a black cloud, and was gone.

XL-R, disengage ballistics and shield, sent Ruben.

Ballistics and shield disengaged, sent XL-R.

'That was a bit full-on. Who were those guys?' asked János.

'I would hazard a guess they were some more of Jutotzas' time-travelling cronies. They vaporised in the same way as the guys I fought in the plane. I wonder where they are coming from? How do they know where we are?' asked Ruben. 'What about the other car that crashed? Shouldn't we go back and help them?'

'Of course we should, but we can't risk getting involved. Let's phone the ambulance service anonymously and tell them there has been an accident and leave it to them,' explained János. 'I know it's a tough call, but there is too much at stake here.'

'Hmm, I guess you are right,' agreed Ruben, and made the call.

Soon they were approaching the picnic area at the junction with Mount Wilson Red Box Road. Ruben quickly put the Cube into Solved-Mode-One, pressed the centre white jewel and the Cube morphed back onto his wrist. They turned right and headed up the road. The headlights lit a road sign on the right that proudly announced: "Chains may be required at any time beyond this point". The verge was steep craggy rock topped with trees and on the left, on the right it was soft grass that dropped down into more trees. The gradient started to increase as they twisted and turned their way up the narrow two-lane highway. Every so often a car flashed by them in the opposite direction as they passed the "Bill Reily Trailhead", a mecca for mountain bikers.

'We should come mountain biking here sometime soon, it'll be great fun,' enthused Ruben.

'Yes, that *would* be fun,' agreed János.

As they carried on up the mountain the tree cover started to thin out revealing a few spots of light dotted over the mountainside. The road, at times, was very close to the edge with a steep drop scarily near to the kerb. About ten minutes later János was once again pulling into Angeles Crest Services. The forest of huge television transmission aerials towered menacingly above them. They drove into the car park and János got out, went to the service station shop and bought two coffees and the local daily paper.

A few minutes later, they were at the S.P.A.C.E main entrance. Ján lowered the window at the checkpoint. The guard walked round to the driver's window.

'Good morning, Mr Novak. Oh, and Mr Novak junior. How are you both today?' enquired the guard.

'Yes, we're good thanks, Carl.'

'How come you've got bullet holes across the back of your truck?'

'Oh... I was messing around with a centre punch the other day, trying to make it look a bit like it had been hit by a machine gun. Obviously looks quite convincing don't you think?' bluffed János.

'Yes, when I was in the LA Police Department I saw quite a few bullet holes like that, usually from machine pistols. They sure look real to me. It seems a bit lighter today, is the sun coming back?'

'It does, we should be back to normal in a few days I would guess,' said János, as the guard checked his pass.

He handed it back and raised the barrier. János drove into the main car park and parked in his personal bay.

'Quick thinking about the bullet holes Dad. Do you think he bought it?'

'Hmm, I'm not sure. Anyway, come on, let's go.'

They walked to the main laboratory building, cleared security and made their way to János' lab. He put his ID card in the security panel slot and looked into the retina scanner. A red beam tracked across his eye. The door made a satisfying click as it unlocked. They entered the darkened laboratory and the lights flickered on. Over in the corner his computer was still monitoring the experiment.

'Right, let's see what has been going on overnight,' said János. 'Hmm, okay it looks as if the infected blood has diffused into the skin cells and is attacking the nuclei. That means it could start attacking the DNA chromosome strands. These carry all the hereditary genetic information in our bodies. I am not sure what to do next.'

'Why don't we hook up the Cube to the computer and see what it comes up with,' offered Ruben.

'Good idea.'

'XL-L, disengage Safe-Mode, and prepare for Data-Link,' commanded Ruben.

He spun the segments of the Cube into Solved-Mode-One, then pressed the centre white axis jewel twice and it slipped from his wrist into his hand. He whizzed the Cube into Solved-Mode-Two and pressed seven blue jewels in an "H" pattern.

'XL-R, search for the lab computer hypersonic data carrier wave,' commanded Ruben.

'Found, breaking encryption. Connection complete,' confirmed XL-R.

'XL-R open data file. Skin test JN001-V1,' commanded Ruben.

'Opening data file; Skin test JN001-V1,' confirmed XL-R.

János and Ruben sat and patiently waited for the Cube to do something, anything.

'Analysing data stream,' confirmed XL-R.

They waited.

'Analysis completed. The DNA double helix genetic information being stored in the cell's nuclei are being altered. DNA code contains instructions needed to make the proteins and molecules essential for normal human growth, development and health. If the codes are damaged then cells will malform,' explained XL-R.

'What will happen then?' asked Ruben as János listened.

'As the cells in the body have their DNA coding altered it will cause the body to reject its own cells. This will gradually lead to the body functions shutting down because of the conflict between proteins battling for supremacy and survival. The lungs will be the first organ to be attacked by this particle as it is the point of entry into the body,' continued XL-R.

'What compound, or substance in the particle cloud is causing this DNA information to be altered?' asked Ruben, prompted by his Dad.

There was a sudden silence as the Cube gave no immediate reply.

'Why hasn't the Cube answered us?' asked a panicky János.

'Hmm, I don't know. That's really unusual,' replied Ruben.

They waited.

'I cannot find the compound in any of my current data resource files. This is the first instance of its known existence. I would therefore surmise that it has not yet been produced in this current time dimension. My compromised functionality means I can't provide a positive answer at this time,' replied XL-R.

'XL-R, how long will it take the average sized human to start to be affected by the cloud particles?' asked Ruben.

'A human weighing eighty-eight point three kilograms, with normal body functionality could start to feel the effects of DNA mutation within two days, four hours, eleven minutes and thirty three point four one seconds, approximately, from the point of inhalation,' replied XL-R.'

'Is there any way to filter out these particles from the air we are breathing?' ask János.

'Carbon Black particles are the smallest known particle of this type. It can be broadly defined as a very fine particulate aggregate of carbon, possessing an amorphous quasi-graphitic molecular structure. It is a substance that can absorb ultraviolet radiation. Typically, they measure fifteen to eighty nanometres in diameter. Recent intratracheal instillational tests show it to be a severely carcinogenic substance. The cloud particles in the sample are approximately one thousand times smaller. There is currently no way of filtering out these particles from the air,' replied XL-R.

'Why not?' asked Ruben.

'The air humans and all life on Earth breath is made from oxygen atoms and nitrogen atoms. These molecules have an average atomic diameter of one hundred and twenty, and one hundred and thirty picometres, respectively. This means the cloud particles are smaller than the oxygen and nitrogen atoms. Therefore if you filter them out you will also filter out the oxygen and nitrogen atoms humans breath. Current technology does not exist capable of filtering these sizes of atomic particles,' replied XL-R.

'Great! What do we do now?' asked Ruben.

'When I have complete functionality restored I will be able to transport you forward into another time dimension. The answer lies in your future,' replied XL-R.

'Of course, remember it said in the book that when all the jewel cells have been recovered the Cube will be able to travel forward in time. We will find the answer there, in the future. We are done here. We have found out what we need to know. You must make plans to locate the next set of jewel cells,' said János.

'XL-R terminate data link. Engage Safe-Mode,' commanded Ruben.

'Data link terminated. Engaging Safe-Mode,' replied XL-R.

'Okay, let's go, I'll just quickly reset the computer security system,' explained János.

Ruben morphed the Cube back onto his wrist.

They then left the lab, set the security alarm and headed to the car park. Outside, the half light was being broken up by the odd beam of sunlight trying to pierce the grey clouds. They jumped in János' truck and drove to the checkpoint barrier. It lifted and they turned right on to Mount Wilson Road. The drive home was uncharacteristically quiet. No "Dad Rock", just the rumble of the V12 engine up front. A while later Ruben broke the silence.

'So Dad, what are you thinking?'

'Hmm, well, umm... as I see it we have three main problems. The first one is, we obviously need to get the Cube reassembled, that will allow us to go into the future. We know that. Secondly, we need to find an immediate solution to the filtering of the air problem. That's also a tricky one given what we now know about the sizes of the atoms involved. The other problem we have is, can we reverse the destruction of the DNA information in the cell nuclei?'

'Yes, you're right. The filtering problem is the main immediate problem as we are all going to start breathing these particles in. As soon as we get home I will prepare for the next trip. We need to get this Cube fully repaired. Stick on some music Dad,' asked Ruben.

'What do you fancy? How about some Hendrix?'

Before Ruben had a chance to answer, "Crosstown Traffic" blasted from the speakers. For that moment father and son were united in their own world of rock, and it felt good, real good. Ruben's tummy rumbled telling him it was about 13:00, his lunch time. They decided to stop for a snack at the strangely titled "Rincon Red Box Truck Trail" viewing point near the junction with the Angeles Crest Highway. It was a gravel parking area with a few tables and benches lining the edge where the trees broke cover to give a fantastic view across the city. A few trucks were already there. Usually the sight across the city was spectacular but today it was cloudy. They parked up, jumped out of their truck and went over to the hut. The comforting smell of burgers and hot dogs engulfed their twitching nostrils.

'You can't beat a bit of comfort food, but don't tell your mum,' quipped a slightly mischievous János.

Armed with a couple of double cheeseburgers and coffees they sat at one of the tables overlooking the city.

'This afternoon I am going to do some work at home and look into this filtering problem. I have a couple of ideas I want to investigate. I suggest you and the Cube work out the details of the next trip,' remarked János.

They quickly chomped their way through their snack and were soon back on the road heading down into the sprawling city below, complete with an accompanying Hendrix soundtrack for good measure. About half an hour later, they were pulling up to the drive. The garage door opened and they parked up.

It was 14:35 and Sarah was still at work, and Kat was out too. Dad headed to his office and Ruben went up to his room.

'XL-R, disengage Safe-Mode,' commanded Ruben.

'Safe-Mode disengaged,' replied XL-R.

He spun the segments around into Solved-Mode-One, pressed the white centre axis jewel once. The Cube slipped from his wrist into his hand. He placed it on the top of his guitar amp.

'XL-R, which jewels do I need to retrieve next?' asked Ruben.

SEVEN

THE QUEST FOR THE YELLOW "BREATH OF LIFE JEWELS"

14:36, MONDAY, 21ST JULY, NOVAK RESIDENCE,
LOS ANGELES, USA

PRESENT DAY

'The next cells needed are the four yellow "Breath of Life Jewels",' replied XL-R.

'Where are they?'

'The exact mapping co-ordinates are Latitude North 47° 30' 25.9605" and Longitude West 19° 2' 44.6589",' replied XL-R.

Ruben flicked the Cube into Solved-Mode-Two and pressed three white jewels in a diagonal "/" pattern. Suddenly a holographic three-dimensional projection appeared in the room. The pictures changed to augment the unfolding data stream from XL-R.

'The remaining yellow jewels are in the Hungarian Royal Crown, known as the Crown of Saint Stephen. It was stolen, along with other royal artefacts, by the German army at the end of World War Two from The Palace of Budain, Budapest. US forces then happened to apprehend a group of fleeing Hungarian SS troops who had in their possession the iron-bound chests used to store the crown. The chests were found to be empty, but after lengthy interrogations the group admitted that they had hidden the royal artefacts in an oil barrel, which they had sunk in some marshland near the village of Mattsee in Bavaria, Germany.

Troops from the US Seventh Army eventually recovered the barrel and the Hungarian Crown Jewels. It was subsequently explained that the crown had been in storage at the US Federal Gold Reserve at Fort Knox in Kentucky, from 1945 to 1975, when the Americans eventually handed them back to Communist officials in Budapest. Since the year two thousand, the Holy Crown of Saint Stephen has been on display in the central Domed Hall of the Hungarian Parliament Building,' continued XL-R.

'Wow, that was a lot of information. So we need to go to Budapest and recover the four yellow cells?' asked Ruben.

'Yes, it will take some very careful planning, as currently the building is heavily guarded. It has a state-of-the-art security system. The Crown Jewels are very precious as they symbolise the strength of the country, its history and all it stands for,' replied XL-R.

Ruben sat quietly on the corner of his bed for a while, deep in thought.

'XL-R, have you any stored video files that show the inner details of the Hungarian Parliament Building?'

'Searching now for video data files as requested,' replied XL-R.

A few moments later, a projection began to play in the centre of the room.

'I have located some news footage from Magyar Televízió, a nationwide public television broadcasting organisation in Hungary. Their headquarters are in Budapest. It is the oldest television broadcasting station in Hungary and today has five channels. They have archived news material that shows sections of the interior of the building filmed when renovation work was being done some time in January 1971,' continued XL-R.

Ruben watched with great interest as the camera followed some workmen around the building's catacombs.

'I have located some video data footage showing the thirty-ninth American President, James Earl Carter Junior, at a press conference agreeing to return the Crown Jewels. I have also found more news footage showing the then secretary of state Cyrus Vance, handing over the crown to a Communist official in Budapest on 6th January, 1978. There is also some current YouTube video data from visitors to the museum building,' said XL-R.

'Hmmm, I think we need to take a quick trip to this place and do a detailed scan of the building's layout and all its security features. I can't believe their system is more complicated than the ones Dad has designed. Once we have the scanning data we can work out a detailed plan,' replied Ruben.

He ran downstairs to see János.

'Hi Dad, have you got a minute?'

'Of course Ruben. What's up?'

'Well, I have been consulting the Cube. It seems the next jewel cells we need to find are hidden, believe it or not, in the Hungarian Crown of Saint Stephen, which is on display in the Parliament building in Budapest, on the banks of the Danube river. So I thought I would do a quick trip over to see it and have the Cube record a detailed 3D scan of the layout of the building and all the security systems. Then you and I can work out a way of getting the jewels back.'

'That sounds like a good idea. That would be very useful,' replied János.

'Okay, I am going to do some digging around on the net and see if I can get on a visitor tour of the building today. No time like the present,' announced Ruben, and he ran back upstairs to his room.

He sat at his desk and turned on his computer. The first task was to have a look at the Hungarian Parliament Building website to see what information he could find about excursions including the crown and the other holy relics on show. Quickly he found the site, went to the tours tab and scanned down the list. It occurred to him that Hungary was in a different time zone to Los Angeles. He checked and indeed found that they were eight hours ahead. His watch displayed 14:14, meaning it was 22:14 in Budapest and the Parliament building would now be shut. He decided he would take a trip back to earlier in the day.

'XL-R, prepare a Mind-Implant allowing me to be fully conversant in Hungarian and give me general background information about Budapest so I can blend in with the local population. I will also need a passport that shows all the relevant stamps and details to gain access to the Parliament building,' commanded Ruben.

Ruben manipulated the Cube into Solved-Mode-Two and pressed seven white jewels in an "H" pattern.

'Downloading Mind-Implant data. Please locate your passport for scanning so it can be replicated and modified,' replied XL-R.

While the Cube "number-crunched", Ruben looked for his passport. After checking through his desk drawers he finally found it. He picked up the Cube and pressed five blue jewels in an "L" pattern. It started to glow blue. He put it down on his desk, placed his passport on the top yellow centre jewel and waited. The Cube pulsed with coloured lights as a beam arced across the desk in rhythmical waves of light. Gradually a three-dimensional image of the passport materialised. A few minutes later the finished passport document was fully formed on the desk.

'XL-R, I will need money for getting around and it would be helpful to know what the weather was like at about 14:00 today in Budapest, so I can wear the right gear,' commanded Ruben.

'One US Dollar is approximately two hundred and sixty-six point six Forints. The temperature in Budapest today was about eleven degrees Celsius, bright but mild.'

'XL-R, I will need one hundred and fifty dollars worth of currency.'

Ruben pressed the five blue jewels again. Almost immediately a freshly made pile of Forint notes started to take shape. The next job was to find somewhere to jump back through time to, a safe place to re-materialise. Back to the computer. He loaded Google Street View for Budapest and started looking. Obviously he wanted to be close to the Parliament building. After a few minutes looking he found a suitable place.

'XL-R, connect to my computer's hypersonic data carrier wave and plot my mouse position.'

Ruben pressed seven blue jewels in an "H" shape.

'Plotting mouse position. The exact mapping co-ordinates chosen are Latitude North 47° 30' 35.3398" and Longitude East 19° 3' 2.1748". The location is Honvéd Park, adjoining Honvéd Street, Budapest, Hungary. Confirm.'

'XL-R, location co-ordinates confirmed,' replied Ruben.

'XL-R, contact the website and purchase a ticket for the 14:15 tour earlier today and make me a copy.'

'Purchasing ticket now. Computer time clock encryption altered,' replied XL-R.

As the ticket began to take shape on the desk Ruben went downstairs to see his dad.

'Hiya, I have organised my scanning trip. I've got the ticket, money and passport so I'm good to go right away.'

'Okay, so how long will this take?'

'The tour takes an hour, but I will have a general look around, so I will probably be two or three hours. It's nearly 16:45, so should be back in time for a late tea.'

'Right, okay, that's fine.'

They went back upstairs to Ruben's room. He made a final check that he had everything he needed. He picked up the Cube and scrambled the segments and pressed the white centre axis jewel.

'XL-R, engage Safe-Mode,' sent Ruben.

'Engaging Safe-Mode,' replied XL-R.

The Cube morphed from his hand to his wrist.

'Right, Dad, I just need my shoes and coat, then I can be off. I've never been to Hungary before but I did do some stuff about it in geography class though.'

They both went downstairs to the hallway and Ruben put on his trendy, chunky duffle coat and shoes.

'That should keep you warm,' stated János, somewhat obviously.

'Okay Dad, bye for now, see you later.' They hugged.

Ruben rolled up his sleeve, pressed the blue, green and white centre axis jewels. There was a blinding flash and at 16:45 he was gone.

■　■　■

TIME-JUMP BACKWARD
13:45, SUNDAY, 21ST JULY, BUDAPEST, HUNGARY
PRESENT DAY-EARLIER

Honvéd Park was full of lush bushes with fir trees at the intersections of the paved paths that criss-crossed the flowerbeds and lawns. Around the outside edge of the park were tall, leafless wire-framed trees. In one corner was a deserted playground and dotted around were wooden benches with a few locals passing the time having a rest. Ruben thought it a bit odd that people were sitting in a darkened park. He quickly looked around. To his left was a man peering over his newspaper, staring at him. Ruben fixed his gaze on the man.

XL-R, disengage Safe-Mode and prepare to Memory-Wipe that man, sent Ruben.

He quickly reconfigured the Cube into Solved-Mode-Two, and then pressed the white jewels in an "L" shape.

Wiping sixty seconds of immediate memory data, sent XL-R.

An intense beam scanned across the man's face. He shook his head, then carried on reading his newspaper in the dark now totally oblivious to what he had just witnessed. Ruben had another quick look round again. He suddenly felt uneasy, like he was being watched.

Increasing adrenaline functions to main muscle groups, and augmenting powered delivery response by a factor of four, sent XL-R.

As he turned back, his face was met by a powerful fist trying to rearrange his teeth configuration. He fell to the ground. Two strong hands grabbed his shoulders and lifted him up. Ruben's hyper-reflexes kicked into gear as he thrust his fists up between his attacker's arms and connected with his jaw, sending him reeling backwards into a bush. Immediately he felt another hand pull him round. He ducked then thumped the second attacker hard in the chest. He quickly looked around and noticed that all the men sitting on the benches were now heading his way. Distracted for a split second he felt a painful blow to the side of his head and stumbled. With a sudden hyper-reflex action Ruben unleashed a furious cascade of fists, which sent his assailants flying through the air like confetti. The onslaught was relentless. His fists hit their mark with pinpoint accuracy leaving a scattered pile of bodies writhing on the ground. Then he felt an arm clamp round his neck and pull tight. He blinked and focused on a man aiming blows to his chest. They hurt. They really hurt. Ruben grabbed the arm around his neck and pivoted his body up and kicked out hard at the man in front of him, catapulting him backwards. He did a dead weight drop to the ground and threw the man behind him, over his head. Turning swiftly round his fist sent another assailant sprawling in the dirt.

Sensing a chance, he ran from the park, turned left and bolted down Szemere Street towards the tramway. The intersection opened out into a wide brightly lit road lined with elegant and tall, ornate buildings. People were milling in and out of the shops as a few cars passed by. He saw a tram approaching, aware he was still being chased, as it drew closer he ran alongside and jumped on. However, so did one of his attackers. Ruben sat at the back of the tram, his assailant at the front. They looked at each other.

Suddenly two of the passengers exploded into a black cloud and disappeared. *Oh hell, that's not good,* thought Ruben.

XL-R engage protective Body-Shield, sent Ruben.

Initialising protective Body-Shield, sent XL-R.

Two more passengers exploded into black clouds, then vaporised. He felt another shock wave slam into his body. Then another two bodies detonated. Then another two. Each time the impact force increased. Soon the tram's interior was a mass of black cloud and explosions. Ruben could feel the force intensify, through the black cloud two hands appeared and tried to clamp around his neck. The shield held them at bay and Ruben lashed out, hitting wildly. There was a smashing sound as window glass shattered. The cloud cleared, the tram was empty. He stood for a while trying to comprehend what had just happened.

XL-R, stop the tram, sent Ruben.

Tram forward velocity terminated, sent XL-R.

Ruben jumped down from the tram just as a car swerved out from behind. In the front seat a man was hanging half out of the window brandishing a machine gun. *Oh cripes, here we go again,* thought Ruben. As the car approached, the gun released a fearsome crackle of automatic fire. The bullets ricocheted off his Body-Shield, as Ruben dived for cover behind a line of parked cars. A stream of bullets pierced the car's bodywork, blasting holes straight through just as the chasing car screeched to a halt and two armed men got out. They started to approach.

Ruben pressed five blue jewels in a "+" pattern.

XL-R, arm Atomiser-Beam, sent Ruben.

Atomiser-beam armed, sent XL-R.

As the two men moved closer, Ruben broke cover, stood up and pointed the Cube at them. In a flash of red light the two men were atomised, gone in a black cloud. *Phew!* he thought. *That was close.*

XL-R, where are we? sent Ruben.

We are on Balassi Bálint Street, sent XL-R.

Ruben pressed the four white corner jewels.

XL-R, direct me to the Parliament building, we have about ten minutes to get there, sent Ruben.

He started to jog along the dimly lit pavement. To his right was the majestic Danube River winding its way through the city. Ruben pondered on how different it must have looked in Antoine's time all those hundreds of years ago. As he approached a crossroads he could hear the sound of a tram approaching. He gave a little shiver and gingerly turned round. It whooshed past. Ahead he could see the outline of a huge, elaborate Gothic edifice. As the road veered left, he checked for traffic and ran across to take a look. In front of him stood a beautiful sandstone four-storey architectural masterpiece. *Mum would love this,* he thought. It had two huge arched doorways in the centre with rows of ornate windows either side. The steep roof rose above a delicate balcony of fine stone arches peppered with carved finials. The floodlighting added to the drama of the façade, the shadows accentuating the fine details. A few holidaymakers stood taking selfies. Ruben chuckled to himself.

XL-R, engage Safe-Mode, sent Ruben.

Safe-Mode engaged, sent XL-R.

He continued towards the entrance of the main building as the square opened out into a wide, paved space lined with more wonderfully decorative Gothic structures. The Parliament building stood impressively framed by the darkened sky, the massive central dome just peeking over the top of the main entrance. *Wow,* he thought. After a minute to take it all in, he wandered towards the entrance. He could see the lines of visitors filing in slowly. He joined the queue. A few minutes later he had shuffled his way in. The cavernous opulence of the main hall took his breath away. Its sheer magnificence was spellbinding. Every detail seemed to be picked out in gold. Crisp marble pillars held aloft the complex arch work of the intricate roof details. It was truly stunning. He approached the ticket desk and handed over his paperwork, luckily he was just in time. The efficient steward directed him over to the foot of the red carpeted triple staircase, where a tour guide was waiting just below one of the golden lamp stands dotted around the room.

He handed his ticket to the guide who quickly crossed him off her list.

'Good afternoon, Mr Novak, how are you today?' she enquired, pausing for a moment. 'Err, have we met before?'

'No, I don't think so, I would have remembered if we had,' he flirted.' Wow, this place is amazing.'

'Thank you. Yes, we love this building. It's very special. I hope you enjoy the tour. We should be leaving shortly. One more couple to join us. Ahh, here they are.'

Ruben couldn't help himself flirting with girls. It was a habit Frankie wasn't that keen on.

XL-R, disengage Safe-Mode.

With the Cube currently in Solved-Mode-Two, he pressed three blue jewels in an "|" pattern.

XL-R, engage three-dimensional mapping scan.

Three-dimensional mapping scan engaged.

The guide gathered up her group and led them up the plush staircase to the top for the first photo opportunity. All the iPhones came out and silently snapped away, trying hopelessly to capture the full majesty of the interior. They turned left and walked along a pastel marbled hallway. The walls were painted with beautiful frescoes depicting historical scenes. Golden painted arches towered over their heads. They entered one of the small state meeting rooms, where a rectangular ring of tables, equipped with small microphones, were immaculately set ready. The walls were lined with intricately carved panels of wood, topped with a pale yellow and green patterned wallpaper. The roof was an elegant wooden construction with ornate supports bracing the corners. The guide explained that the room was often used for local government issues of the day. After a few more selfie moments they continued their tour, which took them to The Meeting Room, a huge, lavish, ornate, long, thin hall full of gold decoration and sumptuous colours on the pillars and furniture. In the centre of the room was a beautiful circular seat upholstered in plum velvet, with an elaborate lamp cluster shining in the middle.

This building is constructed from forty million bricks and uses forty kilograms of gold, and has six hundred and ninety one rooms. I have scanned two hundred and thirty-five of them. Thought you might like to know that, sent XL-R.

Thanks XL-R, but we have a tour guide already. I hope we don't visit all the rooms, sent Ruben.

Next stop was the Chamber of the Lower House. As the group entered the hall, the magnificence of it was truly breath-taking. The rows of beautifully carved concentric elliptical rings of benches and desks filled the room, each one immaculate and polished to a sheen. The walls consisted of two layers of elaborate balconies lined with golden arches and blue-grey granite marble pillars. Wonderfully delicate fretwork adorned the high windows. Ruben looked in wonder at the sheer artistry of its design. *Note to self, we must bring Mum here,* he thought. After a few minutes, the guide led them from the room and headed towards the Central Hall. She explained that this was where the Hungarian Crown Jewels were kept. At last, this was what Ruben had really come to see. As they quietly strolled through the glorious hallways, the guide pointed out features of interest whilst dazzling them with more facts and figures. As they approached the Central Hall Ruben couldn't help but notice there were a few heavily armed soldiers strategically placed around the area.

They entered the Central Hall and you could hear the sound of jaws hitting the floor echo around the vast chamber. It was absolutely awe-inspiring. The huge circular hall consisted of sixteen ornate marble arches capped with fine gold leaf work. High up, between each arch, was a group of finely carved, painted figures, proudly standing guard looking down at the tessellated marble floor. Above them was a circular balcony of forty-eight marble pillars and small gothic arches. The dome rose high above them, decorated in green and gold with sixteen inset-arched windows. *These Gothic chaps really knew what they were doing*, thought Ruben. In the centre of the hall stood the Crown Jewels encased in a sturdy glass cabinet with a metal frame around it, mounted on a marble plinth. The tour group approached closer to have a look and take some more pictures. Four smartly dressed soldiers stood guard, complete with ceremonial swords. Ruben noticed that inside the case, around the base, were some red LEDs. He nonchalantly looked around and spotted small cameras and tiny mirrors dotted around the hall and there were also some blue flashing LEDS high up on the pillars. Meanwhile, XL-R continued to scan the building, collecting data.

He decided to take a closer look at the crown. The four yellow stones he was after were set into the gold straps that follow the shape of the head up to the little cock-eyed crucifix on the top. Now, at some point, all he would have to do was get them out of the crown. The guide soon brought the tour to a close and led the party out of the Central Hall, past the armed guards and toward the exit. Ruben then felt a little twinge; it was a "call of nature". He looked around for the nearest gentlemen's toilet. At the bottom of the grand staircase, he spotted the sign he was looking for, next to the cafeteria. He thanked the tour guide for her hospitality and made his way to the Gents. Pushing open the carved wooden door, he walked into an elegant marbled room. A few minutes later, while he was washing his hands, he heard the door swing open then lock shut.

He quickly glanced up in the mirror over his basin. *Oh heck, he thought*. He spun round to be confronted by a huge man standing by the door, pointing a silencer-equipped gun at him.

XL-R, engage…

A searing pain suddenly shot through his stomach as a perfectly aimed bullet pierced the side of his belly. He fell to the floor, his face contorted with pain. He could feel the warm trickle of blood start to seep through his fingers.

XL-R, engage Body-Shield, sent Ruben.

Body-Shield engaged, sent XL-R.

'Where is the Cube. Tell me. The Cube will not let you die, but I will, so tell me where it is, now,' ordered the man.

Ruben struggled to gather his thoughts. The excruciating pain was clouding his brain. The words stumbled from his mouth.

'I can't tell you,' he replied.

'Oh is that right? Try, you haven't got much time. Jutotzas won't wait.'

Ruben could feel the pain intensifying. With the Cube still in Solved-Mode-Two, he fumbled under his coat feeling for the blue jewels and quickly pressed five in a "+" pattern

XL-R, arm Atomizer-Beam, sent Ruben.

Atomizer-Beam armed, sent XL-R.

He lifted his arm and pointed it at the man.

Engage beam, sent Ruben.

Suddenly an intense shaft of red light exploded from the Cube and blasted across the room into the waiting assailant. The impact caused him to arch his back in tortuous pain. He shuddered as the force ripped through his body. The beam stopped and the man fell to the floor sending the gun skidding across the marble floor. He gave one last look at Ruben, exploded in a black cloud and vaporised into oblivion.

XL-R, what do I do now?

Hold the blue segment over the wound area and press firmly down on the skin, then press the green centre axis jewel twice, sent XL-R.

He positioned the Cube over his stomach wound and began to sense a tingling sensation and a movement deep inside his body. Slowly he could feel the pain subside. There was a little metallic "clink" as the bullet was withdrawn and attached to the Cube.

Disengage from the surface of the skin and focus the blue beam on the surface lesion, sent XL-R.

Ruben did as he was instructed and looked in wonder as the wound began to heal and close up. A few minutes later, it was as if nothing had happened. He felt great. He took the bullet from the Cube and put it in his trouser pocket.

Thanks XL-R, you saved my life, again. Have we got all the data we need? If so, let's go home, to my room.

The data is not yet complete, sent XL-R. Shall I vapourise the weapon? I will scan it first.

Ruben quickly pressed five blue jewels in a "T" pattern and XL-R made the gun vanish.

What do we need to do? sent Ruben.

Data is also needed for the exterior of the building. A complete circumnavigation of the building is required to complete a three-dimensional virtual model, sent XL-R.

Okay.

Ruben walked out of the Gents, across the entrance hall and towards the exit. Just then his tour guide caught sight of him and quickly came over to chat.

'Hello, Mr Novak,' she said coyly. 'I hope you enjoyed the tour. I didn't really get a chance to talk to you afterwards.'

'I know, I needed to find the restroom.'

'Restroom?'

'Sorry, I meant toilet. I am from the USA, we call it that, for some reason. My name is Ruben, by the way.'

'My name is Viktoria, my friends call me Vikki. Ruben, that's a good old Hungarian name. I have an uncle with the same name. Are you sure we haven't met before somewhere?'

'Hi Vikki. No, I don't think we have met before. I would have remembered if we had. Anyway, yes, I am half Hungarian, and a distant, very distant relation to the House of Árpád, I believe.'

'Wow, your family line goes back to about 900A.D. then. That's fantastic. You are royalty,' she joked, and did a half-curtsey.

'Stop it, I did say, "a very distant relation",' said an embarrassed Ruben.

That's very interesting. Come with me,' said Vikki.

She led him back up the grand staircase and stopped at a stone-carved bust of Grand Prince Árpád.

'There you are, your distant relative. Wow, amazing, if only he knew you were here. Actually I wanted to catch you, to see if you would be interested in another tour I am doing later today,'

'Thanks for showing me this. I don't know what to say. I'm a bit overwhelmed. What is the tour you're doing?'

'Well, you may know, that after the fall of the Communist regime here in 1989, a lot of the Communist statues and monuments were taken down or destroyed. The surviving ones were put in a park on the outskirts of Budapest called Memento Park, or as you would say, Memorial Park. It opened on June 29th, 1993, the second anniversary of the withdrawal of the Soviet troops from Hungarian territory. It is quite an amazing place too. I think you would enjoy it,' remarked Vikki.

'Hmmm, sounds interesting. Won't it be a bit dark?'

'We do tours in the evening and we take some big torches. The statues look even more dramatic in the dark, and are quite scary really, but it's great fun. We will need the torches this afternoon, which is a bit odd it being dark at this time, what is going on in the world at the moment?' exclaimed Vikki.

'Yes, it is all a bit odd. What time do you leave?'

'In about an hour, at 4 o'clock the coaches leave from in front of the Parliament building, by the river.'

'Okay, I may well come. I want to have a walk around the outside of this building first. I might see you later.'

'Okay, that would be nice, bye for now,' she said.

'Yes, bye, thanks again,' replied Ruben and he headed for the exit.

XL-R, keep scanning, sent Ruben.

Affirmative, sent XL-R.

Out of the building, he turned right and walked along the left flank. The outside elevations were an impressive example of beautiful Gothic design. The arched windows and roof spires gave the whole façade an air of grandeur and splendour. As he took his time to walk around XL-R continued to collect data. The back of the building, facing over the Danube was as dramatic and as impressive as the rest of it. It stood on the edge of the bank, close to the river, separated from it by a narrow road. Across on the opposite bank he could just make out the shapes of buildings and more spires. A few tourist boats were chugging up and down, the tell-tale flashes of cameras momentarily giving them away. About a quarter of an hour later he was back near the main entrance, and he decided to Mind-Link to Katarina.

Hi Sis, what are you up to?

Oh hi Ruben, I was just thinking about you.

Where are you? You sound out of breath.

Well spotted. I am on the turbo trainer at the gym. I am with Carly. I'm gonna see Dan later.

Is Carly all sweaty?

Ew, gross, you're so base. I'll tell Frankie you said that.

No, no, no, don't you dare.

Or what?

I'll tell Dan you're not a blonde.

I think he knows that by now, don't you?

Hmm, good point, well put. Anyway, this place is fantastic.

Where are you? sent Kat.

Actually, I'm in Budapest. It's amazing here. Mum and Dad would absolutely love it, the architecture is f-a-n-t-a-s-t-i-c. I am going to have a bit more of a look around, should be back later.

Oh... I thought you were at home anyway.

No, I have come here to do a bit of reconnaissance, check the place out. I'll explain later. I'd better go, still stuff to do. Love you, sent Ruben.

Love you, sent Katarina.

Ruben decided he wanted to have a look at the park described by the tour guide; it sounded interesting, but he wanted to go on his own.

XL-R, find map coordinates for Memento Park, Budapest.

Searching for map coordinates.........Coordinates are: Latitude North 47° 25' 36.1" and Longitude East 19° 00' 00.20".

Ruben re-spun the segments on the Cube to Solved-Mode-Two, placed his fingers on the yellow, green and white centre axis jewels and pressed them in sequence.

Engage teletransportation to new map coordinates, sent Ruben.

Teletransportation, engaged, sent XL-R.

In a bright blue flash he was gone.

■ ■ ■

The next thing he knew, he was standing on Szarbadkai Road, staring at the large austere red brick entrance gates to Memento Park, illuminated by a couple of old street lights. On the left stood a huge granite statue of Vladimir Lenin, to the right, two massive statues of Karl Marx and Friedrich Engels, each standing eerily in two bleak brick arches. The whole area was completely deserted. Just as well, as he didn't have a ticket. To his left was a run-down industrial estate straddled by huge power pylons and behind him was a gravel car park flanked by two shabby long buildings, with tarnished metal roofs. To his right were a few random houses and a water tower that looked like an ancient spacecraft.

XL-R, disengage Safe-Mode.

He then pressed the centre axis white jewel twice and the Cube morphed onto his hand. He then pressed the centre axis red jewel, and nothing happened.

XL-R, why is the torch beam not working?

I am not sure, press the red centre axis button again.

He did, nothing happened. He pressed it again and a bright beam emerged from the green, centre axis jewel.

hmm, that's odd, he thought.

248

The Cube lit his way as he approached the entrance gate and looked up at the huge statue of Lenin on the left. Its imposing silhouette sent a shiver down his spine. These famous people were names he had read about in history lessons at school, so he knew what ideals they stood for. He pushed open the heavy squeaky wooden gate and entered the park. He walked between two brick buildings housing a simple museum and an explanation of what the park represented. Ruben had a quick look round then headed out towards the statues in the grounds. Rings of white gravel pathways looped around the park with various sculptures positioned on plinths, dotted about. To his immediate right stood an imposing ten metre-high grey statue of a soldier holding a flag. Using his special torch he picked out the details. There were various interesting friezes and figures all over the park. There were sculptures of soldiers, workers and various Communist symbols. Then he noticed the massive silhouette of a man running. He walked over to it and stood in amazement. It was a twelve metre-high muscular male worker in a flat cap, running and holding a piece of fabric trailing in the wind. His shirt was open and he was wearing shorts for some reason not adequately explained on the plinth.

Ruben spent a little while wandering around, looking at all the wonderful Communist artefacts and trying to read the inscriptions by "Cubelight". Suddenly his concentration was broken by the sound of a large vehicle approaching. He quickly spun round, losing his balance, unceremoniously dumping himself on the damp ground. He got up, brushed himself down and watched as a big tour coach pulled into the gravel car park, by the entrance. He realised it was time to be off, as he spotted Vikki, the guide, sitting up front, on the coach. He really did not want to explain his being there. He pressed the white centre axis jewel once and the Cube morphed back onto his wrist. At 16:20 he pressed the blue, orange and white centre axis jewels to initiate the teletransportation protocol.

XL-R, let's go home, sent Ruben.

■ ■ ■

He was back in his bedroom, home and safe.

XL-R, disengage Safe-Mode, sent Ruben.

Safe-Mode disengaged confirmed, sent XL-R.

He pressed the white centre axis jewel twice and the Cube morphed from his wrist into his hand. He placed it on his desk, threw his jacket on the bed and went downstairs to his dad's office.

'Hi Dad. How's it going?'

'Hi Ruben, I thought I heard you arrive. How did you get on?'

Well, we did the tour, saw the Crown Jewels. The yellow jewel cells are in the top part of it. The Cube scanned the whole building, inside and out. It is the most amazing building I have ever seen and you and Mum would absolutely love it there. Maybe you could take her there for her birthday? Anyway, I met this tour guide, who suggested I go to this place where they put a lot of the old Communist statues and relics that were removed from Budapest after the fall of the Communist regime in 1989. They were fantastic too, quite spooky in the dark though.'

'So you did learn something in history after all.'

'Yes I did. I also learnt that in 1962, an outbreak of contagious laughter in Tanganyika lasted for six months, and even caused schools to be closed. They probably heard you had just been born,' joked Ruben.

'Oi, cheeky, anyway, we need to have a look at the data and assess the security system and how we are going to get the jewels back. I suggest after dinner we sit down with the Cube, go through it all and try to figure out a plan,' said János.

'Okay, cool, that's a plan then. How are your experiments going?'

'Huh, slowly, I am trying to figure a way of filtering out the particles, but I can't see how to do it quickly enough to be of any use. Within the next few days everyone or everything on the planet will have breathed in some of the spores. I think there may be a way of using some kind of synthetic electrostatic charge to block the spores from entering the body, a bit like a magnet, but I just don't know how to do it yet, or if it will work. And time is running out.'

'Oh blimey, we really are in trouble aren't we?'

'We sure are.'

'Is Mum home?'

'Yes, she is in the kitchen, getting dinner ready. You could go and give her a hand.'

'Okay, I'll surprise her.'

'It will be a surprise if you actually help her.'

'Oh I do so enjoy our comedy banter,' chuckled Ruben, and went downstairs into the kitchen.

'Hi, Mum,' he said cheerily.

'Aah, hello darling. I was wondering if you would make it back for dinner.'

She walked over and gave him a hug only the way a mum can.

'Of course, I could smell the chicken stir-fry all the way from Budapest. Shall I lay the table?'

'Yes, thank you darling, that would be most helpful. I don't think Katarina will be back 'til later, she's with Dan, so just us three. So how was Budapest? I have always wanted to visit it. The buildings are so beautiful. I studied it quite a lot for one of my architectural projects at University while your dad was out gigging.'

'Oh Mum, it was fantastic, the area around the Parliament building is awesome. You should take Dad one day.'

'Yes, let's hope we get the chance. Are you and Dad going to figure out a plan to recover the jewels?'

'Yes we are. The Cube has recorded a three-dimensional scan of the building, so we can see where the electrics, systems, and services are routed.

'I'd like to see that sometime, see how it was all constructed. You can't always work out how old buildings were built – the scan would reveal that, interestingly,' explained Sarah.

'Sure Mum, we'll watch it one evening instead of Netflix. When we have a look at the security network, I am hoping Dad will work out a way of deactivating it, or something like that. Anyway, I am sure he'll think of something. He usually does.'

'Yes, he is a very smart man, your dad. Can you call him for dinner? I'm going to dish up in a minute. Just warming the Katsu curry sauce through,' said Sarah, gently stirring the wok's steaming contents.

A few moments later János appeared in the kitchen, walked over to Sarah and gave her an affectionate kiss on the cheek.

'Smells good, honey. This always reminds me of that cookery course we went on in Chiang Mai, when we were backpacking through Thailand, cor, all those years ago. Aww, it was great fun, wasn't it?'

'It was,' Sarah replied.

'When was that?' asked Ruben.

'About November 1997 B.C. I think,' replied Sarah.

'What does the B.C. stand for?'

'Before children, ha, ha,' she laughed.

'Very good. I see what you did there,' quipped Ruben.

'Not bad eh? Anyway, come on, let's eat. Hope it's okay.'

Sarah took the lid off the wok, releasing an atomic mushroom cloud of steam, then proceeded to scoop the stir-fry into the bowls. The spicy curry aroma filled the air as they all tucked in, accompanied by various slurping and sucking noises and dribbly chins.

'Do you remember we went to a little coffee bar in Chiang Mai, called "Lennon's". It was run by a lovely guy who looked uncannily like a Thai John Lennon. He had the round glasses and everything. He also had the same Yamaha FG-450-SA acoustic guitar as me, and the same black Three Series BMW as me. *And*, spookily, he also liked the band, Toto, like me,' recounted János, savouring the moment.

'I remember him, you went there to talk guitars while I was having a massage in the blind massage school nearby. The road had a funny name, it was called something like, Propolokka Road, I think,' continued Sarah.

'No, it was Prapokkloa Road, but close. Why do I remember such useless information?'

'I have no idea. When's our anniversary? How's the stir–fry?' asked Sarah.

'Delish. Third of October?' replied János.

'Close. October the fourth actually, dear,' retorted Sarah, with a heavy emphasis on the "dear".

'Oh, yes, close though,' replied an embarrassed János.

'Stir-fry is good Mum,' agreed Ruben.

'I hope you get a chance to travel the world, Ruben,' said Sarah.

'Well I am certainly doing some air miles at the moment.'

It wasn't long before all remnants of the stir-fry had gone, leaving three spotlessly clean bowls. Ruben collected them and put them on the side worktop.

'What's for dessert, Mum?'

'Go into the freezer, in the second tray is some lovely mango sorbet.'

He found the dessert, brought over some more bowls, sat down and dished out the sorbet. The clean fruity flavour was a perfect finish to a lovely meal.

'Okay, you two go into the garden room, I'll clear up and make some fresh coffee and bring it in,' said Ruben.

'Thanks darling. Are you feeling okay?... That would be nice,' replied Sarah, and they retired to the garden room.

Ruben clattered around in the kitchen, loading the dishwasher to János' exact placement blueprint and ground some fresh coffee. Ten minutes later he appeared with a tray of mugs, and was about to sit down when Sarah spotted something.

'Ruben, your trousers are muddy, you better pop those in the laundry basket. I'll be doing some washing later.'

'Oh yes, I tripped over in the park, it wasn't very well lit.'

'So we need to crack on with this plan of ours, don't we?' said János enthusiastically.

'I think it would be good to try and go tomorrow. With all the data the Cube has collected, I hope we can figure something out quickly,' replied Ruben.

'Well when we've finished these coffees we can go and have a look at the data,' suggested János.

A while later they disappeared up to Ruben's room. He picked up the Cube and disengaged Safe-Mode. He pressed the orange, blue and yellow centre axis jewels and placed it in the middle of the floor.

'XL-R, play Parliament building data file,' instructed Ruben.

'Parliament building, playback initialised.'

Immediately the Cube exploded into light as the three-dimensional image began to form. The x-ray view of the structure exposed all the hidden corridors, stairs, rooms and passages. The Cube also had recorded where all the electrics and services were routed. As the data replay showed the Central Hall János noticed something of interest. He asked Ruben to zoom in on some features of the electrical wiring that split off to the alarm and camera surveillance systems. János then asked to see more information about the back-up generator power supply, and how it was linked through the computer monitoring circuit.

Ruben could sense his dad was onto something. They spent the next couple of hours trawling through the data files and studying the possible access points to the building. The Cube had also hacked into the computer system and downloaded various files covering general security measures and personnel operating schedules and timings. They worked into the early hours of the morning as Sarah kept them fed and watered with drinks and healthy snacks.

'I'm off to bed now, you two. Don't be late, you both have work tomorrow. I know how carried away you both can get, János,' said Sarah.

'Okay, we won't be too much longer,' offered János and turned to Ruben

'This "trip" of yours seemed to go very smoothly?' asked János.

'Erm, well it did and it didn't,' Ruben replied.

'What do you mean?'

'Well, I teletransported into the park as we discussed, it was still a bit dark, but a few minutes later I was attacked by a load of guys who were waiting for me. I managed to get away, but they chased me onto a tram and then all the passengers exploded, one by one. The force was amazing. I engaged the Body-Shield which ultimately saved me, but it was pretty hard core.'

'Were they Jutotzas' men?'

'Yes, they sure were.'

How did they know you were going to be there? They were ahead of you.'

'Hmmm, I'm not sure that is true, because when I got to the park I noticed there were a few people sitting around on benches, in the half-light. However, when I was attacked I realised the people all seemed to have "magically" disappeared. It was just a group of his henchmen laying into me.'

'Why don't you have the Body-Shield on all the time?' asked a curious János.

'XL-R, why can't I have the Body-Shield active all the time?' asked Ruben.

'The Body-Shield uses a vast amount of power, which restricts functionality. The sensors and telepathic interface are compromised by heavy use of this defence mechanism. My operating system and functions are not yet running at full capability. You know my current functionality,' explained XL-R.

'Hey Ruben, I have never heard the Cube use "my",

which is a form of the possessive case of "I" used as an attributive adjective, if I am not mistaken,' chipped in János.

'Uh? What? I haven't a clue what you are talking about,' said a puzzled Ruben.

'Well, it implies the Cube is not just a clever box of electronics. It sees itself as existing, like we do.'

'Oh, I see. Yes the Cube does say "my", and "I", and stuff like that. How weird you have never noticed.

'XL-R, are you turning human?'

'Not a chance. I'd rather be a toaster.'

'Oh, and you can be funny too?'

'Comedy is a very subjective thing. That wasn't humour, that was fact.'

'Hmmm, anyway Dad, how am I actually going to get in the building to start with?'

'Well, I have been mulling this over. It strikes me that this needs to be done at night for obvious reasons. The place will be empty. So I think we need to use some kind of late afternoon event as cover. That way you can be in the building in the evening and when the event finishes you can conceal yourself somewhere. The interior will be cleared and then closed up for the night. So what we need to do now is Google some events that happened soon after the current security system was installed or modified. I suspect you will need to go a little further back in time for the next trip,' reasoned János.

Ruben turned on his computer and a few minutes later his home page came up. The screen gave a brief flicker.

'What just happened then, Dad? Did you see the screen flash?'

'Yes I did. It's been doing that a bit recently. I need to take the back off and check it over. There may be a glitch in the display driver or something like that. Anyway, let's look at recent events.'

'My sensors tell me your system might be being accessed remotely,' said XL-R.

'Hmm, that is a bit worrying. I thought I had blocked any possible hacked remote access,' said János.

They carried on working into the night. The Cube constructed some special pieces of equipment, designed by János, for Ruben to take with him. They both finally went to bed in the small hours of the morning, happy they now had a plan. The Cube kept on working and working and working.

■ ■ ■

09:00, TUESDAY, 22ND JULY, NOVAK RESIDENCE
LOS ANGELES, USA
PRESENT DAY

The bedroom door clicked open and Sarah tip-toed over to Ruben's bedside pod and carefully put down a mug of tea. She then pressed on the pod's keypad and the blinds began to slowly lift revealing quite a bright morning. Ruben gave a little stretch and opened his eyes.

'Good morning, darling. What time did you both finish last night?'

'Errr, I think Dad and I finished about 01:30. What time is it?'

'It's just after nine o'clock and I have got to get to work. Dad's in his office and Kat is coming with me.'

'Kat, why?'

'We are looking for an intern for the summer and I thought Kat should go for an interview with Marty.

It'll be good experience for her. So, Dad tells me you are going back to Budapest to get the jewels today,' said Sarah.

'Yes, Dad has worked out a great plan.'

'Are you likely to get shot again?' asked Sarah.

'What?' replied a stunned Ruben.

'I did the washing this morning, and found a bullet in the machine and a hole in your shirt.'

'Um, yes I did get a little bit shot, but the Cube saved me. It got the bullet out and then healed the wound up. It was amazing. It flippin' hurt though.'

'Yes I expect it did, getting "a little bit" shot usually does hurt, a little. I wouldn't make a habit of it if I were you. Please be careful darling. We worry about you more than you know. Anyway I've got to go, so I will see you later at some point,' said Sarah.

'Okay Mum, please don't worry, I have the Cube to protect me.'

Mum leant over and kissed his forehead, then went downstairs and off to work with Kat and left Ruben to snooze for a little while longer. Eventually he got up, showered and dressed. János was still in his office.

'Hi Dad, what are you doing?'

'Hiya. Oh I'm just going over some ideas I was working on yesterday. I'm trying to figure out this filtering problem. Not getting very far. Let's go and get you some breakfast.'

They both trooped downstairs and his dad made some chilli scrambled eggs and beans. Over breakfast they chatted through the plan and double-checked all the details.

'That bullet Mum found in the washing machine looks unusual. I am going to take it to the lab and have a look at it. It might give us some clues.'

'Good idea. Right, I'm going to get my stuff together and make a move.'

'Okay, come and get me when you are ready, I'll clear up here,' said János.

Ruben went back to his room with his rucksack and collected all the pieces of equipment the Cube had constructed. He picked up the Cube and it morphed onto his wrist.

'XL-R, engage Safe-Mode and engage Body-Shield.'

'Safe-Mode and Body-Shield engaged,' replied XL-R.

'Confirm positional coordinates, Latitude North 47° 30' 35.3398" and Longitude East 19° 3' 2.1748" set. Teletransportation arrival time set at 18:30 Date set at Friday 17th August 2018.'

'XL-R, coordinates, time and date confirmed correct,' replied Ruben.

He put on his jacket and went down to Dad's office.

'So you're ready to go? Is your Body-Shield on? We don't want the same thing happening again, do we?' suggested János.

'Don't worry, Dad, it's on. Wish me luck.'

And with that, Ruben reconfigured the Cube into Solved-Mode-One, pressed the blue, green and white centre axis jewels, and at 10:15 he was gone.

■ ■ ■

TIME-JUMP BACKWARD
12:30 FRIDAY, 17TH AUGUST, 2018, BUDAPEST, HUNGARY
PAST

Budapest was alive and buzzing with energy as Ruben materialised in Honvéd Park for a second time. He quickly looked around to check nobody had seen him arrive this time. He was clear. He could hear the noise of people celebrating echoing around the city streets. The bars were full and everyone was partying.

He walked out of the park and headed towards the Parliament building. He decided to take the route along the side of the Danube. There were rows of street food stalls selling local traditional treats. Ruben suddenly felt hungry. The food stall menus listed such local specialities as, paprika-infused stuffed cabbage, ginger-flavoured sausages, various fresh breads and, much to his amusement, rooster testicle stew. Each stall seemed to be offering different types of traditional Magyar food and delicacies.

Naturally, there were loads of special beers and wines available, none of which Ruben had time to indulge in. He was on a mission and they would have to wait. The Danube was bustling with boats of all sizes, all elaborately decorated and most of them in full-on party mode. He stopped for a moment to take in the festive scene, just as a formation of agile stunt planes began to perform intricate routines overhead. The crowds cheered and whistled in appreciation of their daredevil acrobatics. He made his way round to the main entrance. Tonight was the concert to celebrate the birthday of St Stephen, Hungary's first king. As the queue snaked into the building, one of the pretty concert stewards caught his eye. It was Vikki the tour guide, again. As he got closer he decided to have a bit of fun.

'Hello. It's Vikki, isn't it? Very nice to see you again so soon.'

'Oh, hello, have we met before,' she asked.

'Yes, I did the Crown Jewels tour with you recently.'

'Oh, I think you are mistaken, I don't do that tour.'

'Do you have a twin sister?'

'No, I don't, how funny. Anyway, have you got your ticket?'

'Yes, here you are,' said a mischievous Ruben.

Vikki, the "not yet a tour guide", directed him to the main hall. He walked into the beautiful, cavernous hall and proceeded to find his seat. Scanning the rows and seat numbers, he soon found his and sat down. Up on the stage the musicians were starting to file in. Others were tuning up or running through little sections of the program to warm up. The hall was alive with an air of excitement and the gentle noise of people chatting. The concert was due to start at 19:00. Just then, he was politely asked to make way for someone to pass and sit next to him. He gave a friendly smile and the couple sat down. Soon the seat next to him on the other side was also taken.

The lights dimmed and the conductor walked on stage to a riotous applause. A blazing spotlight from the back dramatically picked him out. He bowed and directed the orchestra to stand and take a bow too. The lights came up and cast an atmospheric blue haze over the musicians. The conductor settled the orchestra and then using his baton, counted them in.

The gentle throbbing sound of the string section began to fill the hall. The pianist started to play in theatrical flourishes of notes, his hands dancing flamboyantly over the keys. As the melody developed Ruben could feel himself quite enjoying the sound of a big orchestra in full flight. He was quite surprised how loud it was. The piece was very dramatic, with a wide range of dynamics, moving through contrasting melodic motifs. The pianist was certainly giving it his all, with cascades of notes and scales pouring from his agile fingers.

In his haste to find his seat Ruben had forgotten to pick up a program for the evening's concert.

XL-R, what is this piece of music? he sent.

It is Béla *Bartók's Piano Concerto* number three in E major. It is a musical composition for piano and *orchestra. Bartók* composed the piece in 1945 during the final months of his life as a surprise birthday present for his second wife Ditta Pásztory-Bartók. *It consists of three movements. They are just coming to the end of the first movement, sent XL-R.*

E major, that's four sharps, F, G, C and D sharp. So that would be a C sharp minor blues then, as C sharp is the relative minor, sent Ruben.

Correct, sent XL-R.

Ruben was feeling quite pleased with his music theory knowledge. He wondered how he had got on in his music exam. His mind-doodling was disturbed by the orchestra coming to the climax of the first movement. Some of the audience applauded enthusiastically while others sat and silently tut-tutted at them, as it was bad form to clap at the end of a movement. It was only at the end of a piece when applause was deemed acceptable, but the crowd's enthusiasm was infectious. The conductor waited for silence once again and then carried on.

About three-quarters of an hour later there was an interval and the audience made their way to the bar for some refreshment. Ruben thought it was a good time to try an authentic Hungarian beer. He deserved it. He picked up his rucksack and as he followed the throng to the bar, he felt a gentle tap on his shoulder. He turned around to see Vikki the "not yet a tour guide" smiling at him.

'Hiya, how are you doing? Are you enjoying the concert? I wouldn't have thought it was your kind of thing. You look like you would be into grunge or something,' she cooed cheekily.

'Hi, err... yes, funnily enough, I do like a bit of grunge. My name's Ruben, by the way. Can I get you a drink?' he charmed.

'Yes, thank you. That would be nice.'

Ruben suddenly realised he could be getting himself into a complicated situation, so decided to be both flirty and vague at the same time. It came quite easily to him. They chatted for a while. His pleasant interlude over, he returned for the second half of the concert leaving Vikki at the bar slightly confused.

The concert began with Liszt's Hungarian Rhapsody Number Two, a beautifully melodic piece where the delicate sound of the flute weaved its way through the drama of the evocative musical light and shade. Ruben actually surprised himself when he recognized the main theme. His dad played it sometimes on a Sunday morning. Suddenly he felt achingly homesick. At the end of the piece, he decided to quickly Mind-Link Kat.

Hi Kat.

Oh, hi Ruben, how's it going?

I'm at the concert and was just thinking about you all.

Aww, that's nice. I can't stop, I am about to go into a job interview. Wish me luck.

Good luck, you'll be fine. See you later, love you. Say hi to Mum.

Just as he finished with Kat, XL-R interrupted.

The Body-Shield has been engaged too long and now power is down, sent XL-R.

In the excitement of the festivities, Ruben had left the shield engaged, somewhat draining the Cube's power.

I need to disengage the defence system and exit Safe-Mode for a short while, to recharge my power bank.

Okay, XL-R, understood.

Body-Shield and Safe-Mode disengaged.

Ruben suddenly felt a little uneasy, and vulnerable. The last part of the concert whizzed by and was surprisingly enjoyable considering there was no electric guitar in sight and no stage diving. It wasn't long before the final rapturous applause echoed around the hall. The conductor and the orchestra stood and took a bow and another and another, until finally they all filed off the stage, waving to the audience as they went.

Ruben waited for the couple on his left to get up. Suddenly he felt something poke him in his side. He quickly turned to see the man sitting next to him staring menacingly at him. He had a gun hidden under his jacket. His eyes were dead and cold and Ruben felt threatened.

'You will come with me now. Don't try to escape, or I will kill you where you sit,' he whispered.

Ruben bent down to pick up his rucksack, but it wasn't there. *Hell, where's my bag*, he thought. He quickly rummaged around under the seats. It definitely wasn't there. He felt a painful prod in his ribs again.

'Get going, now,' whispered the man.

Ruben duly got up and inched his way out of the row, while being directed by more painful prods to his ribs. They left the hall and went out into the corridor,

'Cooey, Ruben, Ruben, over here,' called Vikki, and came running over to him. The man pulled back slightly, to a safe distance and waited nonchalantly.

'Hiya, I have your bag. You left it in the bar,' she explained.

'Wow, thanks, that's fantastic.'

Just then the man moved forward, with the gun under his coat and dug it into Vikki's side. She yelped.

'Do not move pretty girl, or I will kill you,' he whispered in her ear.

She looked at Ruben; he nodded in agreement. The man would kill her. He quickly forced them across the corridor and through a doorway into a little side room. The door swung open again and another man came in then locked them inside. He shoved the two of them over to the other side of the room, against the wall, as his accomplice trained the gun on them.

'Have you got the Cube? Haha, of course you have. That's why you are here. Where are the jewels?' Tell me. He grabbed Ruben's arm and pushed up his sleeve. The Cube was there, its surface flashing with little lights.

'Yes you have it, give it to me. Where are the missing jewels?'

Vikki was now beyond scared. She was visibly petrified and was starting to whimper. Sensing her terror, one of the men took out a roll of tape, tore off a strip and put it over her mouth.

'Now, I suggest you start telling me where the jewels are located or I will have to start operating on your pretty friend.'

'You evil henchman types are always so predictable, always get the girl and dish out lame threats,' mocked Ruben feistily.

The man bent down and pushed up his trouser leg. The lower part of his leg was a shiny metallic dark blue. Ruben watched in disbelief as his assailant pushed a small side button in the leg, and a compartment clicked open. He took out a strange looking black satin tubular device. Meanwhile the other assailant kept the gun trained on the two captives.

'You might be interested to see what this little thing can do.'

The room they were being held hostage in was some kind of store room full of metal racking and labelled boxes. The man pointed the device at the rack, and suddenly an intense beam of light began to cut a tough metal strut. Small sparks spat out from the tip. Before it sliced right through he stopped, the beam switched off.

XL-R, are you recharged at all? sent Ruben.

I am at sixty two point nine six percent. I can't yet re-engage defence systems but will be able to engage in approximately five minutes and thirty-two seconds as the inductive feed in here is much more powerful.

'Tell me where the jewels are or your friend will regret it,' said the man with the gun.

'Which jewels do you mean?' said Ruben, stalling for time.

His accomplice with the cutting device was not amused. He grabbed Vikki's wrist and pinned her hand against the wall. She flinched in pain and looked at Ruben, tears welling up in her terrified eyes. Suddenly the cutting beam began burning its way through the wall towards her hand. Smoke and sparks began to fly. It got closer and closer. Vikki tried to wriggle away but she was no match for the man pinning her against the wall. The beam edged closer to her fingers.

'Do you expect me to talk,' quoted Ruben flippantly.

'No Mr Novak, I expect her to die,' came the brutal reply.

'Okay, okay, stop the beam. I will tell you where the jewels are. Just don't hurt her. Let her go and I will tell you,' pleaded Ruben.

'You are in no position to bargain with us,' came the blunt reply.

'Okay, but just let her go.'

'Not so funny now are you Mr Novak? TELL ME WHERE THEY ARE,' he yelled.

'Uh, okay, they are hidden in the handle of the royal sword.'

'Aha, so that is where they are,' laughed the gunman.

'Now give us the Cube.'

'No I can't.'

'Oh, is that right?' said the gunman, who then hit Vikki hard across the face and she crumpled to the floor.

Ruben was incensed, his blood boiled, he bolted forward lunging hard at the gunman, who dodged him and swung round hitting him squarely in the stomach. He fell holding his gut in pain.

'Not so fast, big guy. We aren't finished here yet,' taunted the gunman.

'Give us the Cube or today will be the day you are going to die too,' said the gunman. 'If you don't give it to us we will have to cut it off you.'

His accomplice began to fiddle with the black cutting device again. He walked up to Ruben and pressed the device against his chest. He suddenly felt an excruciating pain and looked down to see a small bead of blood start to seep through his shirt.

'You have five minutes to give us the Cube or you will die,' said the accomplice. 'Each drop of blood will take you closer to your death.'

XL-R, help me now, engage ballistics.

Ballistics can't be engaged. Three minutes and 15 seconds needed to fully charge.

Hell, that's cutting it a bit fine.

XL-R, what have they injected me with?

The substance is a toxin that gradually attacks your heart's SA node. It disrupts the electrical impulses sent to the top atriato causing them to contract. Eventually your heart will stop and your body functions will cease, sent XL-R.

XL-R, help me.

I will divert the toxins through different neural pathways to bypass the SA node. This way the disruption will be reduced, but I can't stop it.

Great, thanks.

Ruben felt his heart flutter, then the rhythm steadied again.

'How do you feel? You haven't got much time left. Give me the Cube,' snapped the gunman.

Instruct your assailants that you will give the Cube to them after they have reversed the toxin, I will arm the remote self-defence mechanism, sent XL-R.

Suddenly Ruben felt another flutter in his chest and for a split second blacked out.

'Okay I will give you the Cube if you reverse this poison.'

'At last,' said the gunman.

His assailant walked over to him and pressed the device against his chest again. There was a jolt and Ruben felt a surge of energy through his body.

Self-defence system is engaged, sent XL-R.

Ruben lifted his arm and pointed the Cube at the gunman. With his other hand he pressed a fake sequence of jewels.

The accomplice grabbed the Cube and wriggled it off Ruben's arm. The gunman came over and also put his hand on the Cube.

'We have it, and you will both die anyway,' laughed the gunman, then shot Vikki. Her body jolted on the floor.

XL-R, activate self-defence system NOW, sent Ruben.

Suddenly the Cube exploded into a blinding ball of white light. Both assailants froze on the spot and then began to shake violently, faster and faster. They became a blur, vaporising into a black cloud, then vanished.

XL-R, we need to help Vikki immediately.

Ruben configured the Cube into Solved-Mode-Two. He placed the blue segment on the wound and held it there. He then pressed the green centre axis jewel twice. The Cube began to pulse with a blue glow. Gently he peeled the tape from her lips. He felt another flutter in his chest, then everything went black. Moments later he was awake again and looked at the Cube. It was still glowing with a soothing blue light. Vikki shook her head, and slowly opened her eyes and peered around the room.

'Where am I? What just happened?' she asked.

'It's okay, we are in the Parliament building in a store room, for some reason,' whispered Ruben while gently holding her upright. 'You fainted in the corridor so I brought you in here to get some air. It's so busy this evening.'

She noticed the Cube device by her side flashing.

'What on earth is that thing?'

'Oh it's a little twisty puzzle thing I bought in one of the shops, it must have fallen out of my pocket when I bent down.'

Then he felt another flutter in his chest and toppled over onto the floor. He was motionless. Vikki looked at him in total confused disbelief. She panicked as she soon realised she was alone. She began shaking with fear and then heard a voice come from the Cube.

'Vikki, pick up this flashing object and put it on Ruben's chest in the middle of the breast bone, blue segment face down and hold it there. Press the top middle green button twice,' announced XL-R.

Momentarily confused where the voice was coming from she realised it was in fact emanating from the Cube "puzzle".

Still slightly dazed she picked up the Cube and held it on Ruben's chest and pressed the jewel twice, as directed. She waited and watched the Cube start to glow blue. The light pulsed and gradually faded into an orange hue, then slowly into a yellow glow. A few minutes later it cross-faded back into a blue light. Vikki looked at his face, looking for signs of life, then his eyelids flickered. She watched as his eyes began to slowly open until he was fully awake. He could make out Vikki's smiling face. She smiled back at him.

'You have just saved my life, thank you,' said Ruben.

'What is going on? Who are you? What is this thing? It's amazing. It talks and does weird stuff. How did it bring you back to life? Why did you collapse? I don't understand.' She paused for a moment. 'I seem to remember being in this room with you and two men, and, err, one of the men grabbed me and then I don't remember what happened,' said Vikki.

Ruben picked up the Cube and pressed five white jewels in an "L" pattern.

XL-R, perform a Memory-Wipe on Vikki from the moment she gave me the bag back, sent Ruben.

Memory-Wipe engaged, sent XL-R.

An intense yellow beam flashed across her face. He quickly slipped the Cube into his jacket pocket.

'How do you feel now? You fainted in the corridor, so I brought you in here to get away from the crowds,' explained Ruben.

271

'Oh, I'm okay, I feel a bit dazed, but all right. Thanks for looking after me. Did I give you your bag? You left it in the bar.'

'Yes, I have it here. Now let's get out of here. Unfortunately I have to go. I'm running late,' lied Ruben.

'Aren't you going to stay and watch the fireworks? They'll be starting soon.'

'No, I can't really. I have a train to catch. It's a long story,' said Ruben, and they left the room.

The building was starting to clear as everyone was heading outside to see the firework display.

'I'll say goodbye here. I need to go to the restroom, sorry, toilet. Have fun.' He gave her an affectionate kiss on the cheek. She smiled coyly and then made her way towards the exit, gave a little wave and was gone.

He stood there for a moment to gather his thoughts. He could hear the sound of fireworks going off outside,

XL-R, what is the current time here.

The time in Budapest is 21:09.

He took the Cube out of his pocket and pressed the four white corner jewels and put it back in his pocket.

XL-R, direct me to location one.

Turn round one hundred and eighty degrees and walk towards the third doorway on the right, sent XL-R.

He quickly headed towards the door. There were still quite a few people milling around, so no one was taking any notice of him. Once inside Ruben pressed the white centre axis jewel twice and the Cube morphed onto his wrist again.

Go down the steps, at the bottom turn left and go along until you reach a door on the right marked

"Biztonsági Rendszerek", which translates as *"Security Systems"*.

Ruben soon found the door and soon found it was locked too. He rolled up his sleeve to reveal the Cube, disengaged Safe-Mode and pressed the white centre axis jewel. The Cube morphed from his wrist into his hand. He looked at the latch mechanism. Next, he reconfigured the segments into Solved-Mode-Two, so the white and blue segments were complete. He pressed the three yellow diagonal jewels and pointed the centre yellow jewel at the latch. As he engaged the blue centre axis jewels a bright cutting beam emerged from the yellow jewel and fired into the lock. Ruben held it steady as it proceeded to break the security system.

Engaging lock bypass circuit. This will send a false monitor code to the master system masking forced entry, sent XL-R.

A few moments later, the lock gave a satisfying "clunk" and the door was released. He quickly went inside. The room was full of computer systems, with banks of little blinking LEDs flashing and flickering away in the half-light. Everything was being remotely monitored by two guards in the main control room.

XL-R, scan for main hypersonic data carrier wave and link to the main computer system.

He then pressed the seven blue jewels in an "H" pattern.

Whilst the Cube established a link Ruben got out his mini laptop computer and fired it up.

Hypersonic data carrier wave located and engaged with, reconfiguring firewall settings. Establishing extension interface, sent XL-R.

On the laptop screen came the Parliament building main security login page.

XL-R, break encryption and mask access with new rolling time ghost encryption code.

Ghost encryption code engaged.

XL-R, find security camera video footage file. We need to locate the cameras that cover the corridors we are going to use to get to the Central Hall.

A few seconds later the laptop screen displayed the file details. Ruben quickly clicked on one of the icons. It showed two views along one of the main corridors. He opened a couple more files to check what the footage showed and then skipped it until he found the timed video of the previous night. Within a few minutes he had located the video records of the previous night from the cameras on his planned route. He logged the file details. Next, he had a look at the security patrol details of the guards' movements, where they go, and at what times. Their route through the building was very carefully planned and the timings were very consistent across the previous few days. Ruben was quite pleased by that fact; it should make his task a little easier. The Central Hall had quite a clever security system in place but it was no real match for his dad's inventive problem-solving mind. He had quite quickly worked out a way of fooling the system, leaving Ruben free to get the jewels without setting the alarms off. He knew there was always the risk that some random event could cause them problems.

XL-R, find the system folder for the Central Hall optical security operational settings.

Optical system folder encryption decoded, located, bringing up on screen now.

Ruben opened the file. He studied the current status of the system. Over the next few minutes he created a new set of settings that when engaged would give him the chance to get close to the crown. All the pieces were falling into place nicely. The next bit was the tricky part, and he knew it.

XL-R, upload system updates.

Uploading files now.

File transfer completed, Ruben put his laptop back in his backpack and took out a pair of special head-up-display glasses that would help him to see in low light levels by following the scanning data from the Cube. Ruben pressed the centre white jewel to morph the Cube back onto his wrist.

XL-R, direct me to the Central Hall, sent Ruben.

Loading direction route map, sent XL-R.

A green map outline showing the planned route through the building appeared on the lens of his glasses. He put his back-pack on, quietly left the room and turned right. The corridor was only illuminated by a few low power lights. Slowly he edged his way along, the auto-scrolling map guiding him. At the end of the corridor were two doors. A quick look at the display showed the right one was the one he needed. It was locked. It had some kind of identity card reader on it.

XL-R, scan lock data feed. Locate recent ID card usage, then load cloned ID card details.

Accessing lock data file now, sent XL-R.

A few minutes later the lock triggered. He gently pulled the door open. Inside, a spiral staircase wound up to the next floor. Slowly he made his way upwards.

XL-R, prepare to upload camera video footage.

Camera number fifty-six video footage ready to upload.

The top door was also locked.

XL-R, scan lock data feed. Locate recent ID card usage, then load cloned ID card details.

XL-R accessing lock data file now.

Again, a few moments later the lock triggered but Ruben waited.

XL-R, scan for any nearby human thermal heat profiles.

Scanning for possible human thermal heat profiles. I have located one approximately forty-two point three seven six metres away, and getting closer.

Ruben took off his backpack and pulled out a little silver cube device, about the size of a grape. He pressed the five blue jewels in a "Z" pattern on the Cube.

XL-R, prime Assault-Cubie to level three, sent Ruben.

Assault-Cubie primed.

XL-R, lock Assault-Cubie on to thermal heat profile, and engage face recognition function.

Assault-Cubie locked on.

Ruben squeezed the door open and with the *Assault-Cubie* on his palm he set it off.

XL-R, engage Assault-Cubie.

Assault-Cubie engaged.

The little device lifted from his hand and whizzed out into the corridor. His head-up display glasses gave him a "Cubie-eye-view". Sure enough he could see a guard slowly coming along the passageway. He was armed with a semi-automatic machine gun. *Cripes, that looks a bit heavy, he thought.* The little drone flew along the passageway straight towards the guard. It scanned the guard's facial features, located the impact point and slammed hard into his forehead, knocking him unconscious. He would be out for quite a few hours. It then whizzed back to Ruben.

Nearby, on the left was a storage cupboard. Ruben opened the door and carefully dragged the stunned guard inside, hid the gun under some dust sheets and put the drone in his backpack.

XL-R, tap into main system power feed and prepare supply voltage spike, then cut to camera fifty-six archived video footage.

Creating system supply voltage spike and cutting to archive camera video recording, sent XL-R.

The remote control room would now see a small interference disruption to their video monitors, which would mask the switching over to the pre-recorded video feed from the camera, allowing Ruben to pass along the passage without being seen. He went out into the corridor and made his way towards the end of the passage and stopped at the corner.

XL-R, is it all clear?

Suddenly there was a loud "clunk" and a side door flew open. A slightly surprised guard grabbed Ruben by the back of his jacket and yanked him round. With a hard thump Ruben felt himself being winded and he doubled over in pain followed swiftly by another hard blow to the back of his head.

Increasing adrenaline functions to main muscle groups and augmenting powered delivery response by a factor of three, sent XL-R.

After a momentary pause Ruben got up and laid into the guard with a barrage of carefully aimed blows. The guard was no match for his skills. He tried to fight back but was soon lying, spark out, in a heap on the floor. Ruben opened the door and deposited the guard behind it. Slowly he edged his way closer to the Central Hall. At the corner of the corridor he stopped.

XL-R, prepare electricity supply spike and get ready to upload camera fifty-one footage. Scan for thermal heat profiles.

Spike engaged and footage uploaded. Scanning now. All clear to continue, sent XL-R.

Gingerly, Ruben made his way along the darkened passage. He knew time was running out as the guards would soon be missed. The head-up-display slowly guided him towards a door on the left. It was no surprise to find it was locked.

XL-R, scan lock data feed. Locate recent ID card usage, then load cloned ID card details.

Accessing lock data file now.

The lock triggered open. Ruben paused for a minute to allow XL-R time to scan the area. It was clear. He pulled open the door and quietly climbed the spiral stairs and he could see from his glasses that he was going up to the floor level of the Central Hall. At the top of the stairs there was another locked door.

XL-R, scan lock data feed, and scan immediate vicinity for guards.

Accessing lock data file and commencing area scan.

Ruben waited patiently as XL-R number-crunched again.

Lock scan complete and ready to unlock. Human thermal heat profile count is eight.

XL-R, prepare electricity spike and archived video footage of Central Hall to replace the live feed to the control room.

Preparing archived footage.

Slowly Ruben edged along the wall towards the Central Hall. Gradually the lights began to filter down the passage. Soon there would be no darkness to hide in. He edged as close as he dared to the outer hall corridor and stopped. He took out eight *Assault-Cubies*, and pressed the five blue jewels on the Cube again.

XL-R, set Assault-Cubies to level three and engage facial recognition system. Engage voltage spike in the control room and engage replacement archive video footage. Engage Assault-Cubies.

■　■　■

In the control room the monitors suddenly flickered and the two guards looked at one another.

'What is going on tonight? These monitors are acting up. Maybe the mains supply is faulty. It's probably all the bars that are open for the festival. Everyone is having fun except us,' mumbled the guard.

'I know, and we have to work, but I have a little surprise for you. I have got us a few beers for us to celebrate too. Here, have one,' replied the other guard. 'It will be our little secret. Nothing much will be happening tonight. Everyone is busy partying.' With that the two guards began to enjoy their beer, only keeping a cursory eye on the monitors.

■　■　■

The drones lifted from Ruben's palm and whizzed out into the corridor. He watched as the Assault-Cubies located the eight guards. They hurtled around the circular passage high up in the beautifully ornate ceiling. Each little Cubie positioned itself above a guard. Then in one synchronized motion, they flew down and slammed into the guards' foreheads. They all crumpled to the floor with a loud clatter. *Ooh, that is gonna hurt,* thought Ruben. With all the guards disabled, he quickly ran into the hall. The crown stood in its glass case in the centre of the hall, directly below the huge dome. Inside the case a red lazer beam was "criss-crossing" the crown. If it were moved an alarm system would be activated. Once again Ruben took a moment to wonder at the stunning beauty of the dome with its flower-like central detail. *Mum was right, I should study architecture at Uni'*, he thought. He walked over to the glass case, took off his backpack and pulled out a small padded mat. He then pressed seven blue jewels in an "H" pattern.

XL-R, scan locking mechanism, locate security system hypersonic data carrier wave and engage masking encryption data feed.

Scanning locking mechanism, locating security system hypersonic data carrier wave and engaging masking encryption data feed.

A few seconds later the glass case started to rise slowly up from its heavy marble base. The Cube had hacked into the jewel case security system and activated the release mechanism. The guards in the control room would be oblivious to what was going on as again, the camera feeds were no longer live. As the case cleared the top of the crown, Ruben slipped on some surgical gloves. Out of his backpack he took a small parabolic concave mirror, with a hole in the middle, and a small convex mirror mounted on a little tripod.

XL-R, prepare a mains voltage spike in the laser security system to last three seconds.

XL-R, engage spike now.

The red laser beam stopped momentarily. Ruben quickly placed the concave mirror over the laser and aligned the tripod mirror directly above it just as the beam started working again. The strands of light now bounced back and forth between the mirrors allowing the crown to be removed without triggering the alarm.

He carefully picked up the crown. It was heavier than he expected it to be. He slowly put it down on the mat. The four yellow stones twinkled under the dozens of little spot lamps dotted around the hall. From the side pouch of his backpack he took out a little leather wallet. He opened it out to reveal a selection of small precision tools.

On closer inspection, he could see that the jewels were crudely held into their mounts by small tabs of gold folded over their edges. Taking a small chisel-type tool Ruben began to gently fold the gold tabs back and prise the gems out one by one. A few minutes later he had removed all four.

He placed his finger on the white centre axis jewel, pressed it twice and the Cube slipped from his wrist into his hand. He then laid out the four yellow crown gems. He took the Cube, which was in Solved-Mode-Two and pressed five blue jewels in an "L" pattern. It began to pulse with a blue glow. He put it down on the mat and placed it in front of them. The Cube began to pulse with coloured lights then a yellow beam began arcing across the gems on the mat. Seconds later a second beam emerged from the Cube and a copy image began forming. Gradually three-dimensional clones of the jewels began to materialize, and a few minutes later the finished ones were fully formed on the mat.

XL-R, prepare to load yellow jewel cells, sent Ruben.

He pressed the yellow centre axis jewel four times.

Configuring system, connection sensors ready, scanning ready. Load yellow cells.

Ruben proceeded to gently push them into the yellow segment. Each click of engagement was verified by a yellow flash of light darting over the Cube's surface. When the fourth jewel was in place the Cube began to pulse with a soft yellow light, gradually getting faster and faster, then stopped.

Yellow cells are engaged. After system update, functionality will be at seventy point three per cent.

The yellow segment was now complete. Ruben started fitting the cloned jewels back into the crown. With all the gems in position he carefully folded the little gold tabs back into their original shape. *No one will ever know these are copies,* he thought. He placed the crown back on its red velvet pillow.

XL-R, spike security system, sent Ruben.

He quickly removed the mirror devices.

XL-R, re-seal the cabinet.

Engaging closing procedure, sent XL-R.

The heavy glass case began to slowly lower onto the base, finally coming to rest with a "clunk" as the locks reset. *Phew, that's a relief,* thought Ruben.

I am detecting three human thermal heat profiles getting nearer, sent XL-R.

XL-R, where are they coming from? sent a flustered Ruben.

They are approaching from the main staircase and heading in this direction.

He quickly delved into his backpack to find some assault drones only to find they were all gone.

Increasing adrenaline functions to main muscle groups, and augmenting powered delivery response by a factor of three, sent XL-R.

Just then Ruben caught a glimpse of a guard in the outer passage who had spotted one of his comrades lying on the floor. He crouched behind the glass case and watched. However he hadn't noticed another guard creeping up behind him. He felt a painful thud across his shoulder knocking him forward.

Slowly his eyes began to open, the bright room lights causing him to squint. Gradually the outline of two figures came into focus. In front of him sat two guards, one with a gun pointing at him.

'So, what were you doing by the Crown Jewels in the Central Hall tonight? Were you about to steal them? What is this funny looking cube thing?' asked the guard.

Ruben instinctively grabbed his wrist to find the Cube was not on it. He started to panic. *What would Dad do now?* he thought.

'Um, I am a history student and I am doing a project on the Hungarian royal family. I wanted to get some close-up pictures of the Crown Jewels without the crowds getting in the way, and I knew they would all be out watching the fireworks and having fun tonight,' explained Ruben, playing for time.

'Why were all the guards knocked out? How did you do that?'

'Hmmm, I thought it was a bit odd there were no guards about,' replied Ruben evasively.

'There is something odd going on here. Who are you? And why did you have tools and a computer with you? What is this strange cube thing?

'Oh, it's just a toy puzzle thing. It's like a brain teaser; you have to make all the coloured pieces the same in groups. It must have fallen out of my backpack. Let me show you, it's quite hard.'

The slightly inebriated guard tossed the Cube over to Ruben, who quickly spun the segments around in a blur of fingers.

'There, look, I have done three segments.'

The two guards peered at the Cube in amazement.

XL-R, set stun beam to level 5.

Stun beam set and ready.

Ruben pressed the centre red jewel twice and nothing happened. He panicked. *WHAT?* he thought.

Red jewel malfunction, sent XL-R.

He quickly pressed the red jewel again twice and this time a red beam shot from the Cube, then split in two and penetrated the two guards. They recoiled off their chairs and sprawled out on the floor unconscious. Before he had a chance to catch his breath the door suddenly swung open to reveal a tall man standing in the doorway holding a gun and that gun was pointing straight at Ruben.

'Put the Cube on the ground and go over and stand in the corner. Put your hands on your head,' he ordered menacingly.

Ruben did as he was told.

'Let me guess, are you one of Jutotzas' henchmen?' asked Ruben.

'You could say that. So you have the yellow jewels now I see.'

XL-R, arm self-defence system, sent Ruben.

Just then he noticed a small red dot tracking across the henchman's shoulder. There was a sudden loud crack as a bullet hit its mark. The man bolted forward, spun round and started firing wildly out through the doorway. In the confusion Ruben grabbed the Cube, pressed the white centre axis jewel twice and it morphed back on his wrist. He ducked down behind the desk as bullets began ricocheting around the room. Plasterwork exploded from the walls as the gunfire intensified. Ruben didn't like the way this was playing out. The henchman suddenly took another shot to the shoulder, making him drop his gun. He ran and crouched behind the desk with Ruben as bullets thudded into the wall, plaster and stonework splintering in clouds of dust. Ruben quickly pressed the blue, orange and white centre axis jewels.

XL-R, get me out of here, get me home, sent Ruben.

Initialising teletransportation protocols, confirmed XL-R.

The henchman quickly grabbed Ruben's leg. There was a blinding flash and at 23:30 the two men were gone.

■ ■ ■

15:15, TUESDAY, 22ND JULY, NOVAK RESIDENCE,
LOS ANGELES, USA
PRESENT DAY

In a split second the two men materialised back in Ruben's LA bedroom. It suddenly dawned on him that the henchman had hitched a ride through time too. Ruben grabbed him and pinned him to the floor. The man didn't struggle, he looked confused and stared hard at Ruben. Then he suddenly began to writhe around violently. He began kicking out with all his might, but Ruben had him under control. He started bucking wildly with fists flailing wildly around. Ruben dodged the blows but noticed the man's eyes were beginning to turn black. His skin was starting to change colour too. He kicked and struggled with all his might, but Ruben could sense he was getting weaker. Before long all his skin was turning black. Ruben looked up to see his dad standing in the doorway, his face as white as a sheet. He had heard the noise from downstairs. Ruben could feel the man's body starting to shrink as his efforts began to

285

fade. His eyes were now hollow and empty. His struggles subsided, he calmed, became still. The shadow of a man turned to dust and then vaporised into thin air, gone.

János ran over to Ruben and gave him a huge hug.

'Blimey, that was close.'

'Too right, I thought he was going to kick over my guitar,' laughed Ruben.

'That's not what I meant,' replied János, raising a slightly quizzical left eyebrow.

'This guy held onto my leg as I teletransported back here. I guess the time travel bit didn't agree with him.'

'I assume you got the jewels?' asked János.

'Yup, got them all. Here they are,' replied Ruben and showed his dad the Cube.

'Well I'm glad you are back in one piece. I can't figure out how Jutotzas' men seem to know where you go when you teletransport. Do they know where you are at this exact minute, here in the present.'

'Hmmm, it is weird. At least I am prepared for their appearance. They are seriously tough dudes.'

'I'm glad you can laugh about it. We have all been worried about you. I guess that's the way it is, parents always worry about their children, and the time travel part definitely doesn't help matters either. Anyway you are here now.'

'Where's Mum?'

'Well it's nearly half three so she's still at work with Kat. They'll be home later.'

'What have you been up to today Dad?'

'Oh I have been examining the bullet Mum found in your trouser pocket, a very interesting piece of kit.'

'In what way?' asked Ruben.

'Well, I managed to get it apart and found inside an incredible bit of circuitry. It appears to have some kind of propulsion unit that uses a micro atomic fission reaction to propel the bullet. Basically the atomic material contained inside is loaded with compressed nuclei that are made to subdivide releasing neutrons and, more importantly, energy to propel it through the air.'

'Blimey, that's amazing,' said a bamboozled Ruben.

'And what's more it flies very fast. I did a virtual model of the propulsion unit in the computer, which estimated its muzzle velocity to be over four times the speed of sound, about thirteen hundred metres per second. By comparison, a bullet from an AK-57 leaves the rifle at over six hundred and seventy metres per second. That's about double the speed of sound. Despite having a mass of about five grams it's got the same amount of energy as a brick dropped from a building thirty floors high. This device is twice as powerful and its muzzle velocity remains constant as the drag due to wind resistance is counteracted by the propulsion system. Also, the fission reaction would cause the bullet to vibrate, which would aid penetration, like a hammer drill. That's why it could penetrate your shield,' explained János.

'Thanks for the science lesson, Dad,' quipped Ruben.

'And, what's even more interesting is that when I did a 3D scan of it, the computer gave its actual physical mass to be about the size of a cucumber, about two hundred times bigger than what we see it to be. As far as I'm concerned, that is not possible. I have no idea how that can be done, but I will figure it out. It must be some kind of photon refraction process.'

'Uh, yes okay Dad, if you say so.'

'These guys have some amazing technology at their disposal, not unlike your Cube.'

'It sure seems that way. With the yellow jewels cells fitted the Cube should be more powerful too and the Body-Shield should be stronger.'

'XL-R, has your functionality improved,' asked Ruben.

'Functionality has improved by seven point four, zero, seven per cent and is currently at seventy point three per cent of full capability,' replied XL-R.

'I have a feeling there is some kind of link between where these jewels have ended up. If you think about it, the crown was fashioned during the reign of one of Grand Prince Zoltan's Great, Great, Great, Great Grandchildren. The blue jewels were in your Great Aunt's jewellery. Interesting, don't you think?' reasoned János.

'Hmm, yes makes sense. I wonder what the next adventure is going to be. I think I need a bit of a rest. I'd like to see if Frankie is about tomorrow and go and spend some time with her. Do you think that's okay, or am I being selfish?'

'No, you need to rest. These adventures are full on, so you need to be ready.'

'I will come back and do some preparation in the evening. I know we haven't got much time, but I am a bit whacked. I'll have an early night. Try to recharge my batteries. Shall we cook a curry for Mum and Kat later?'

'Yes, they'll like that. Maybe you can give the jewellery to them. I should be able to reassemble the necklace this afternoon, I guess,' János replied.

'That would be cool. Right, I'm going to have a quick shower, then play my guitar for a while – decompress, as it were. Then we'll do the curry.'

'Okay, let's hook up in a while. I'm glad you're back safe,' said János, and gave Ruben an affectionate kiss on his forehead. 'Practice those speed scale legato runs.'

Dad went down into his office and got back to work. His lab stuff was taking a back seat at the moment. He wanted to find a way of filtering the dust particles, but knew it may be a fruitless search. If he could slow down the effects in the body it could buy the world some valuable time. More time for Ruben to follow his destiny. He too felt the weight of the world on his shoulders. Their own self-imposed secrecy made his task so much harder. Dark forces were at work and he had the safety of his family to consider. The house's state-of-the-art security system should do that job, but for how long? Were Sarah and Kat safe at work? He couldn't possibly know the answer. He spent the next couple of hours running virtual tests on some of his ideas, while sporadically being interrupted by blasts of electric guitar coming from upstairs. *He's not playing that right*, thought János, and went upstairs to find Ruben sitting on his bed playing his dad's old salmon pink guitar.

'Show me how you're playing that third position run,' enquired János.

Ruben showed him, and made a pretty good stab at it.

'Hmm, try playing it like this using three fingers per string, then you can pick much faster, because if you pick down, up, down, you can hit the next string with the same down stroke. Watch.'

Ruben passed over the guitar and his dad showed him what he meant.

'Wow Dad, that's cool, here let me have a try.'

A few attempts later Ruben had got it.

'You can do that in all the modes, it's much faster, but practise slowly then gradually speed up. Use the metronome on your phone, and gradually increase the tempo.'

'But I can't hear it with my amp on.'

'Use your headphones and you will hear it then. The vibration goes through the bones in your skull so you should easily feel the click anyway. It's quite amazing how sound is transmitted. When the amp's speaker cone moves the air particles next to the cone vibrate and collide with other particles, so transmitting the sound vibration through the air. This is called wave compression and happens very, very quickly and this is what the ear uses to vibrate the bones in the inner ear, which sends the information to the brain. However, there is also another thing called bone conduction. It's similar, but the sounds travel through the skull to the temporal bone, which is situated around the base of the skull. The temporal bone transmits the vibrations to the basilar membrane in the inner ear. Inside there are tiny bundles of hair that vibrate at different frequencies and these detect the sounds and transmit the vibrations to the brain for decoding. Hold on a second,' János paused for a moment. 'I have just had an idea, I think. Maybe the way to solve this filtering problem is by using sound. Nearly everybody has a mobile phone and headphones. Hmmm.'

János had begun formulating an idea, a genius idea.

'Thanks for the science lesson, Dad. Always a pleasure. Sounds like an interesting concept. Was I disturbing you? sorry.'

'No, it's fine, I like to hear you play. We haven't had a jam together for a while.'

'Why don't you get your guitar and we can play some blues for a while as the house is empty,' said Ruben.

'Yes, I'd like that.'

With one eye on the clock, Ruben and his dad sat playing "the blues", enjoying each other's company in some rare "Father/Son Time".

Soon it was time to get dinner underway and they headed down to the kitchen. Ruben had a quick look in the fridge to see what there was.

'Do you fancy a beer Dad?'

'Yes, go on then, I'll have a bottle of "Wollop Export" please.'

'Good choice, me too. Right, you start on the curry and I'll do the Tarka Dahl.'

'What on earth is a Tarka Dahl,' asked János.

'Well it's like a Tikka Dahl, just a little 'otter.'

'Haha, very good, I like that one, very funny literary based joke Mr Williamson,' chuckled János smugly.

'Eh?' grunted Ruben ignorantly.

The next hour was spent making a chicken curry, a spinach and potato side dish and Ruben's comedy Tarka Dahl. He got the big saucepan and glugged in some olive oil and gently heated it up while chopping some onions, ginger, turmeric, red peppers and garlic. He threw all of the ingredients into the pan and fried them. He then chopped up some cauliflower and tomatoes, tossed them in and fried them for another minute.

'That smells good. Your mum should enjoy this,' said János.

'Hope so. Now all I have to do is stir in the water and lentils and leave to simmer for thirty-five minutes. Then Mum and Kat should walk through the door and be amazed at what we have made,' replied Ruben.

Once all the cooking was done Ruben put some plates in the oven to warm and also some naan breads to heat through. It wasn't long before they could hear the sound of mum's car pulling up into the garage. Right on cue Mum and Kat came into the kitchen.

'Wow, you boys have been busy. When did you get back Ruben darling?' asked Sarah, as she walked over to give him a hug and a kiss.

'Oh, a few hours ago. Dad and I have been doing some stuff.'

'You mean, he should have been working but you have been playing guitar together, more like.'

'No, I don't know "what" you mean, darling,' lied János unconvincingly.

Sarah was not fooled by their reactions and she gave Ján a peck on the cheek too. Kat gave her brother a lingering hug to welcome him safely back.

The evening passed slowly by as they all enjoyed each other's company and a few more cans of Wollop Export beer. Ruben was glad to be home and was looking forward to spending some time with Frankie tomorrow. The curry was a roaring success too.

EIGHT

THE QUEST FOR THE ORANGE "JEWELS OF FIRE"

PRESENT DAY

The Wednesday morning alarm went off with a gentle strumming harp sound. János flopped his hand out of bed and hit the snooze button. *Another ten minutes then I'll get up*, he thought. A snooze later he jumped out of bed as Sarah started to stir.

'Tea, darling?' asked a bouncy Ján.

Sarah nodded and he headed down to the kitchen. Two early cups of Darjeeling later and Ján was getting ready for work as Sarah caught up on the day's news.

He had soon ploughed his way through a vat of muesli and some peanut butter toast when, just as he was finishing his second slice both Sarah and Kat appeared.

'Gosh, you are up early this morning. How come?' asked Sarah.

'Well, I had a bit of a brainwave when I was with Ruben last night. We were talking about timing and tempo and nerdy guitar stuff when I had an idea to do with the particle filtration problem that has been bugging me.'

'Oh, I see, well that's good,' said Kat.

'Maybe, so I just want to get on with it. Are you off into the office with Mum today?' asked János.

'Yes, I am. It's fun working with Mum.'

'Aw, thanks darling. It's nice having you around the office too.'

'Well I think I am going to leave you two members of The Mutual Appreciation Society to have your breakfast and I'll head to work,' said János. 'I will be back later to help Ruben with his preparations for the next task, whatever that is.'

It was a bright morning and the sun was slowly rising over the mountains as János drove into the sprawling city. His urgency to try to find a solution was now more important than ever as the sky was clear meaning the particles were dispersing into the atmosphere. The journey up through the mountains whizzed by as his mind raced through various scientific scenarios and it wasn't long before he was pulling into the car park at S.P.A.C.E.

He passed through the security points and was soon in the lab. He hung up his jacket and put his case on his bench, then noticed that the three pencils on the tabletop were not in their regimented side-by-side formation of "B", "HB", "H". János' OCD had some uses. Someone had been at his desk; the vibration had shaken his pencils out of position. He logged into his computer and opened the Lab Surveillance file. Slowly he scrolled through the overnight night vision footage, until he saw a dim green spot of light. Quickly he rewound a few minutes back and changed camera angles. Then he saw it. On screen, in the dim moonlight, a shadowy figure materialised out of thin air, by the lab door. Over the next thirty-two point five minutes, the intruder methodically went through all the drawers and cupboards, searching for something. *What was he after,* he thought. Having seemingly not found anything the intruder just disappeared.

This added new complication unsettled János and he decided to rig up a simple light-activated trigger to log any such repeat performances and programmed the cameras with high-definition night vision capability. He sat at his workbench surrounded by circuit boards, wire, switches and a soldering iron and proceeded to wire together a simple piece of electronics to do the job.

There was a flash of light and János felt a strong arm clamp round his neck and another across his shoulders. Without hesitation, János grabbed the soldering arm and stabbed the searing hot tip into the arm around his throat. His assailant screamed in pain and momentarily relaxed his grip. János hit the panic button under his desk with his knee and jumped up out of his chair. The upward thrust of his head connected perfectly with the jaw of the attacker behind him sending him flying backwards into a filing cabinet. János turned and lunged at him, hitting him hard across the jaw knocking him sideways across a lab bench covered in delicate glassware. Shattered fragments sprayed across the floor. As the man in black clambered to his feet he pulled out a gun. János stopped in his tracks.

'Where is the Cube? Tell me or I will make you suffer like you have never suffered before. Sit in the chair with your hands behind your back.'

'Yes, that will make me suffer, this chair is quite soft,' replied a poker-faced János.

János slowly walked back to his desk and sat down as directed. The gunman approached him with the gun menacingly pointing at his chest. János noticed a shadow at the door. It sprung open and a security guard appeared at the doorway armed with a pistol.

'Put the gun down now,' shouted the guard.

The gunman spun round. There was a loud "crack" and he recoiled into the desk holding his bloodied shoulder and fired back at the guard. In the confusion János ran for cover, as bullets flew around the lab and shattered brickwork exploded from the walls. The guard returned his fire, a bullet hitting the gunman in the chest who screamed in pain and dropped to the floor. He began to kick and wriggle violently as his face contorted in pain. Faster and faster he struggled until he was just a blur of writhing limbs, then he exploded into a black cloud and vanished.

'What just happened?' asked the confused guard.

'Well, firstly you just saved my life, and secondly I'm not quite sure,' said János.

'Where did he go?'

'To hell I hope. Thanks, you really saved my neck, I owe you one,' János replied.

'No problem Mr Novak. I'm not sure what I am going to write in my report though,' replied the bewildered guard.

'Don't worry, I will deal with it. Thanks again.'

The guard left and János took a moment to gather his thoughts. The lab looked a mess with glass and broken apparatus strewn all over the floor. Thankfully, the main test equipment had escaped the gunfire, as had the computer system.

He sat at his desk and checked the data for the skin and blood test. A quick scan through the results showed that the cells were behaving in a strange way. Some of them had started to turn grey and were gently oscillating. The DNA change was starting to happen, the cells were beginning to fight one another, just as the Cube had predicted. János sat and thought for a moment, then jumped up with renewed vigour and started to clear the mess up. Armed with a broom and a dustpan and brush, he began to collect the glass fragments of test tubes and beakers that had been smashed until nearly two hours later the lab was looking tidy again, apart from some large craters in the walls. *A bit of filler and coat of paint, it'll look like new,* he thought.

János then proceeded to finish and install his electronic gizmo and then set up a little experiment. He went over to the fume chamber, unlocked the front cover and fitted a wide-angle magnifying lens to the optical feed connection to the electron microscope. He switched on the calibration smoke trace and watched as it made a path in front of the lens. Turning his attention to the monitor screen he set about adjusting the focus until the trace was crystal clear as the smoke particles whizzed across the screen. A quick fiddle with the spot lamps and he was happy. He went over to one of the store cupboards and rummaged around for a few minutes until he found what he needed. The aluminium case housed a White

Gaussian Tone Generator, a highly accurate piece of test equipment capable of producing frequencies over a vast range from sub-harmonic infra-bass through the bandwidth spectrum right up to pico-sonic.

■ ■ ■

Meanwhile, over in Santa Monica, an hour's drive from Altadena, Ruben and Frankie were lying on Venice Beach soaking up the late morning rays of the sun, wearing factor sixty sunscreen, of course. It seemed like ages since they had hung out together. *This is what summer holidays are made for, not racing through different time dimensions battling exploding henchmen at every twist and turn,* he thought, as he took a sip of his ice-cold ginger beer. He gave the Cube a reassuring pat. It was in Safe-Mode, so no one could see it on his wrist.

Frankie looked gorgeous in her red bikini and he couldn't wait to have a swim with her in the shimmering water.

'Come on let's have a dip, I need to cool down a bit,' said Ruben excitedly, grabbing Frankie's hand and gently coaxing her up from her towel.

They ran down the beach and plunged into the sea with a satisfying "kersploosh". The shoreline was crowded with everybody enjoying themselves with youngsters body boarding, toddlers splashing about and children just having fun in the surf. The beach was full of the sound of joy and laughter. Ruben and Frankie fooled about in the waves for a while, taking full advantage of their time together. She knew that Ruben would be away again very soon and he knew he couldn't tell Frankie the truth about his "other" life, but she was starting to ask him awkward questions. So far he had managed to bluff his way through her interrogations, but for how much longer?

As midday was fast approaching, they decided to try to find somewhere to have lunch and so they ran out of the water, dried themselves off, packed their bags and headed up the beach to find a little bar to relax in. It was a busy lunchtime, but as it was a weekday, it didn't take long to find somewhere in the shade to grab a bite to eat. They found a cool cafe overlooking the beach and sat down underneath a brightly coloured parasol. Ruben signalled to the waitress, who quickly came over to take their order.

They spent the lunchtime happily chatting together and decided that after lunch they would go back to the beach for a while longer and head back home just before the rush hour madness.

■　■　■

János had spent the rest of the morning setting up equipment around the fume chamber and had fabricated a rudimentary but clever test rig to try out his idea.

Inside the chamber were positioned two small loudspeakers either side of a clear acrylic tube, which were connected to two inputs on the tone generator so that a different frequency could be sent to each speaker if needed. One end of the tube was connected to the smoke trace nozzle. The air that had been contaminated with the black dust particles would be pumped through and then flow past the loudspeakers. Just in front of the speakers the electron microscope camera was positioned and focused to record the results. János loaded a canister of contaminated air into the flow trace pump and switched it on. On the monitor the flow of air was peppered with little black particles. He turned on the tone generator and gradually rotated the dial up through the frequency bands, starting at the low end. He kept an eye on the monitor as he slowly increased the frequency. He kept on going up the bands until he got into the sonic range and then something started to happen. As he very gradually stepped up the frequency, the black particles started to slow down. The pressure gauge remained constant meaning that the air was still flowing through the tube. Using micro adjustments János managed to make the particles almost come to a halt. *Interesting*, he thought. Next, he decided to set one loudspeaker so that it oscillated its frequency just above and then just below the constant frequency of the other speaker. Then he noticed that most of the particles were starting to oscillate themselves. He finely tuned the range of the oscillation while keeping one eye on the monitor and soon got the result he wanted. He estimated that about three quarters of the particles started to move backwards, away from the loudspeakers leaving the remainder to make it to the vent unaffected. *Excellent. That is quite a high success rate,* he thought.

János spent the next few hours fiddling with his test rig and making copious notes on his computer, logging all the results. The next stage was to try out his second hunch and see if that worked too. He removed the clear acrylic tube from the fume chamber and replaced it with the clear model skull from the lab skeleton model, held in firm with a few clamps on stands. He repositioned the speakers over the ears, like headphones. The smoke nozzle was directed about ten centimetres from the mouth, with the jaw pulled open. By moving the camera lens into the optimum position, he would get a good view of what was going to happen inside the mouth and nasal cavity. He turned on the contaminated airflow and watched the monitor. The black particles whizzed by, as normal. However, when he turned on the tone generator they stopped moving but only a very small number of the particles began to move back out of the mouth and nasal cavity and disperse around the skull. János was a little disappointed with the results, but figured that the mouth cavity was causing too much internal turbulence. It had still been a good few hours work and he was nearly done for the day with just one more quick modification to the test needed to give him the result he wanted, he hoped.

■ ■ ■

17:50, WEDNESDAY, 23RD JULY, NOVAK RESIDENCE, LOS ANGELES, USA
PRESENT DAY

The family was gradually reassembling in readiness for dinner and Kat and Sarah were first home. They were already getting the food on the go when Ruben burst through the door in full-on beach-hunk mode.

'Couldn't you have at least put a shirt on,' quipped Kat.

'Ooo, a saucer of milk for the Kat at table one please,' came Ruben's witty reply.

'Oh, haha,' laughed Kat overly sarcastically.

'Hello darling, did you have a nice day at the beach?' asked Sarah.

'Yes Mum, it was lovely; we had a really great time together. It has been a while since we just hung out.'

'You should have brought Frankie back. We haven't seen her for a while either,' replied Sarah.

'Maybe next time. I have got some stuff to do tonight. I need to prepare for the next quest. I can't believe I am actually saying those words, they sound ridiculous, even to me.'

'Well your dad will be home soon, so you can do that together after dinner.'

Right on cue, an ebullient János walked into the kitchen with a slightly smug grin on his face.

'You look very pleased with yourself. Have you won the lottery or found your old Sunburst Shergold Masquerader guitar on eBay, or something?' asked Sarah, planting a little kiss on his flushed cheeks. She knew him very well.

'No, but I'm still looking for it. Anyway, yes I am feeling quite chuffed with myself as it happens,' János.

' Oh Why?,' replied Sarah.

'Well I have been experimenting with sound at work in the lab and found out something quite amazing.'

'What's that, Dad?' chipped in Ruben.

'The black cloud that blotted out the Sun was made up of microscopically small particles which are carried along by the air particles we breathe in. Now the problem I wanted to solve was to find a way to filter out these harmful particles. Today I think I may have found a way to severely reduce the number that we inhale which should slow down the affect they have on our bodies.'

'That's great news Dad, but how did you do it?' ask Ruben.

'Well, the other night when I was talking to you about practising your guitar by using a metronome on your phone, using headphones, I had an idea. If you played specific frequencies through your headphones, it may be possible to conduct these sound vibrations through your skull bones. This would cause a pulsing sound wave in your head that would stop you inhaling a lot of the particles. So I tested it and it sort of worked. You see, the particles appear to have a resonant frequency, so if you find that frequency and put it out of phase by a certain amount the oscillation of the frequencies causes a sonic wave pattern that forces the particles in the opposite direction to the sound source. It is a bit like the waves on the shore pushing some of the pebbles back up the beach.'

'That's amazing Dad. You're a genius. How are you going to do that?'

'I think it could be done by using mobile phones and things like that. For example, if we set up a website, people could download the sound file and play it as much as possible. You can even hide the frequencies in music so you can broadcast it through radios, televisions, that sort of thing. I am going to get on to that tomorrow and try to contact the main broadcasters to see if I can get them on board as soon as possible. This is mega important as I think it will slow the effects down quite considerably, which will give us much needed time to get the Cube rebuilt.'

'Darling, you are so clever,' cooed Sarah. 'Now let's eat.'

Tonight they were having a Chinese takeaway, just for a change. They all tucked in as if they hadn't seen food before. After the dishwasher was loaded correctly and the kitchen cleared up, Kat and Sarah retired to the TV lounge to watch "The Real Housewives of Crouch End", a reality TV series set in a bohemian enclave on the outskirts of North London, England.

János and Ruben went upstairs to Ruben's room to do some preparation.

'Ok, let's see what the Cube has to say for itself. XL-R, which jewels do we need to locate next?' asked Ruben, putting the Cube on his desk.

'The next jewels you need to retrieve are the orange Jewels of Fire,' explained XL-R.

Over the next few hours Ruben and his dad used the Cube to plan how to get the jewels back. At just after 23:00 they decided they had formulated a good plan and so both went back downstairs to the TV lounge. Sarah and Kat were deep in conversation. Ruben gave them a goodnight kiss, then went off to bed leaving Dad to explain what lay ahead for Ruben tomorrow.

■　■　■

07:00, THURSDAY, 24TH JULY, NOVAK RESIDENCE,
LOS ANGELES, USA
PRESENT DAY

As always, the following morning seemed to come around far too quickly. Ruben struggled to open his eyes and it was only when Sarah came in with a cup of tea that he started to fully wake up. He turned on his TV. The news stations were awash with stories about the return of the sun. Various scientists could be heard explaining what they thought had happened, but none of them were close to the actual reason. Today's adventure should bring him that bit nearer to getting the Cube complete, and with it, the power to go into the future and save the Earth from disaster. However, he needed to have a good breakfast first. He could smell the aroma of sausages sizzling away downstairs, so quickly got up and joined the family in the kitchen, still in his PJs.

'As you have a busy day ahead I have made you a big breakfast to get you going,' said Sarah.

'Yum, smells good, Mum,' replied an enthusiastic Ruben.

'How can you eat those meat sausages. Don't you realise where they come from?' chipped in Kat.

'I know where they came from.' He paused for a second. 'The freezer.'

'Oh, haha. That's not what I meant, and you know it.'

'I think you must be the only Kat I know that is a vegetarian.'

'So, are you all ready? You know what you have to do?' asked János, trying to divert the conversation.

'Yes, sure thing, Dad. Don't worry, should be a piece of cake.'

'Let's hope so,' quipped János.

'What are you up to today, Dad?' asked Ruben.

'Hmm, well I am going to try and pull a few favours in and see if I can get this idea of mine off the ground. My concern is that I can't figure out how to pitch it to the media without causing mass hysteria. I need to think of some reason to get people to download the app or to get the broadcasters to go along with it. Tricky,' replied János.

Having successfully demolished his breakfast and a couple of pieces of peanut buttered toast Ruben got up from the table.

'Thanks for brekky Mum. I'll be down in a while to say goodbye.'

He put his plates in the dishwasher, correctly positioned, and went up to his room. He was going to travel light. After he had showered he dressed in the clothes the Cube had produced for him. He checked himself in the mirror. *Yeah, I look pretty cool*, he thought. He was wearing some heavy cotton dark tan trousers, a dark shirt and striped jumper with a casual double-breasted jacket. He wore heavy leather shoes. Over the chair was draped a thick navy blue overcoat, scarf and gloves. He then picked up the Cube from his bedside pod, pressed the white centre axis jewel and it morphed on to his wrist.

'XL-R, engage Body-Shield, level three,' directed Ruben.

'Body-Shield engaged. Confirming positional coordinates, Latitude North 47° 55' 8.99" and Longitude West −87° 38' 9.59" set. Teletransportation arrival time set at 09:30 Thursday, 14th February 1929.'

'XL-R, coordinates, time and date I confirmed are correct,' replied Ruben.

He went to the bathroom and slicked back his hair with some gel then put on his overcoat, scarf and gloves, finally topping off his ensemble with a rather groovy flat cap. With a quick look around his room he went down to the kitchen. He was greeted with the usual round of comments that ranged from the comical to the complimentary.

'Ok folks, it's time to go. Wish me luck.'

Ruben reconfigured the Cube to Solved-Mode-Three, pressed the blue, green and white centre axis jewel, and in a blue flash at 08:30 he was gone.

■ ■ ■

TIME-JUMP BACKWARD
09:30, THURSDAY, 14TH FEBRUARY, 1929, CHICAGO, USA
PAST

The snow was slowly falling as Ruben materialised in the narrow alley next to number 2118 North Clarke Street. It was a cold Thursday morning in the Lincoln Park area of North Chicago and the street was busy with people picking their way through the light snowfall. The huge tall tenement blocks towered over him. The road was drab, the buildings looked tired and Ruben could feel an underlying tension in the air as he mingled with the people on the street. They passed by with their heads down, trying to avoid catching his eye. As he walked up the road he saw a coffee shop called "Gino's" and went in to get a drink. He pushed open the door to hear a little bell announcing his arrival. It was warm inside and the gentle pleasant aroma of fresh coffee filled the air. There were a few people sat having breakfast. The stack of blueberry and maple syrup pancakes some of them were having looked delicious and Ruben, who was a bit partial to them himself, decided he would be able to manage a few too. *Time travel can really make you hungry,* he thought. He sat at a table by the window and waited to be served. Looking out across the street felt like watching a TV documentary. Over the road was the "S-M-C Cartage Co," which was a shipping and storage warehouse. It was a dull square brick building shoehorned in between two tall, equally dull residential blocks. It had a big name board with a dull awning over and a dull main doorway to the right. It was the architectural epitome of dull.

'Good morning, young man. What can I get you this cold morning?' asked the chirpy waitress.

'Oh hi, umm, can I have two pancakes and a coffee please.'

'Sure, no problem.'

She scribbled his order down on a little pad and went behind the bar and into the kitchen. Just then, he noticed two flashy cars pull up across the road.

XL-R, what are those cars? sent Ruben.

The red one is Franklin 153 Sport Touring and the pearl white one is a Packard Eight Dual Cowl Phaeton, replied XL-R.

Both cars were big and gleaming with lots of chrome, wire-spoked wheels, swooping fenders and looked totally out of place in the cheerless, depressing street. The doors opened and seven men in winter coats and hats got out and went quickly into the warehouse.

'Here are your pancakes and coffee. That'll be seventy-three cents please,' asked the waitress.

'Thanks, here's a Dollar, keep the change,' replied Ruben with his winning smile.

He took a sip of his coffee and made a start on the pancakes. There was a "ding" as the café door opened again and another customer came in and sat down opposite him, giving him an acknowledging nod. Ruben felt a shiver and became aware he felt slightly threatened. *The café isn't full, he could have sat anywhere*, he thought. As he looked out across the street again, he saw a Cadillac Sedan car drive by and pull in a little way up the road. He watched as two police officers in uniform got out accompanied by two other men in plain clothes. These two men were wearing long coats and had their hands in their pockets. *Interesting, should have worn gloves*, he thought. Two smartly dressed men then came into the café; one walked with a limp. They sat down in the booth next to Ruben, also by the window. The man put his walking cane in the umbrella holder at the end of the bench seat. They looked fidgety and nervous and were talking in hushed tones. Ruben was on his second pancake and feeling a bit full. The four men were now at the warehouse. The front door opened and they went inside.

Ruben looked at his watch; it was 10:29. Then suddenly there was an explosion of machine-gun fire coming from the warehouse. It seemed to go on for minutes then stopped momentarily, followed by some deafening shotgun blasts. Immediately the two smartly dressed men got up and quickly walked out of the coffee shop and up the street. Even the limping man ran, and he'd left his cane. The door of the warehouse opened and the two plain clothed men emerged with their hands up followed by the two armed policemen. They escorted them back to the police car, shoved them in the back and drove off at speed. The waitress came over and looked out of the window as a small crowd of people were starting to gather outside the warehouse building. She quickly went back behind the bar and picked up the telephone. Ruben could hear she was calling the police. A few minutes later the sound of police sirens could be heard approaching. The ever-growing crowd moved aside to let two police wagons pull up and stop outside the warehouse. Somehow, even the newspaper reporters were there. Cameras started to flash as the scene got ever more chaotic. Ruben decided it was time to go, so he surreptitiously took the cane from the holder and walked out into the street. Immediately a camera flash bulb went off in his face as he tried to push through the crowd and some policemen.

'Oi, watch it sonny, not so fast,' remarked the officer.

Ruben noticed that the stranger in the coffee shop was leaving. Ruben gradually forced his way through the crowd towards the alley across the street. It was time for him to also leave. He turned into the alleyway and felt an arm clamp round his neck and saw the glint of a cut-throat razor flash in front of his eyes.

'Give me your jack or I'll shiv yu,' demanded the man.

He wants your money or he will cut you with his knife, sent XL-R.

Yes thanks for that translation, I kind of guessed that's what he meant, sent Ruben.

Give me that fancy cane too, should be worth a clam or two.'

Ruben let go of the cane as the thug pinned him hard against the wall, the razor blade now pressed up close to his neck. He had a fear of razors ever since he was a boy. Once while playing in his dad's garage he found one in an old tool chest. He tried to open it and sliced the top of his finger really badly. He could still hear his screams as he ran to his mum. Suddenly he felt a felt a hard thud as his assailant slammed into him with blood exploding from his chest. He toppled backwards to reveal a tall man, the man from the cafe, pointing a very large, strange looking handgun at him.

'So, what do we have here? I would guess that your cane is important. You need this for the Cube, don't you?' came the menacing voice, as he leant down and picked up the walking stick.

'Umm, It has something engraved in the top. Ah, it says, "To Bugs, thanks for everything, István». Do you know who István is?› asked the henchman.

'Err, no, I don't. Should I?' replied Ruben.

'You should, he is your great grandad. He is a very important man.'

'How do you mean?'

'Well, let's put it this way. If he were to die, your father would never be born and so you would never be born. If you were to return to your own time dimension, you would be alone, your family would not exist.'

Just then out of the shadows appeared two men holding a third man, who had his head covered with a black bag. He was struggling and trying to break free, but he was no match for their muscle. They dragged him over and stood next to their leader who pulled the bag off. The man blinked as he adjusted to the light. He looked scared and confused. The leader spoke to him.

'Tell this boy your name,' he ordered.

'Err, my name is István.

'Your full name.'

'My name is István Novak,› he said, trembling.

Ruben shivered. As he looked at István he suddenly split into a vision of three images, one red, one yellow and one blue. They twitched and flickered then recombined into one solid focused image. Ruben shook his head and blinked a couple of times. The full significance of this meeting was starting to dawn on him.

'Who is this boy,' asked István.

'He is... you tell him boy,' ordered the leader.

'I am Ruben Novak, my dad was, well, is your grandson. I am your Great Grandson,' he stumbled.

'I haven't got a son. I don't understand, what is going on? Who are you all?'

With that the leader put the bag back on his head and the henchman on the left pulled out a pistol and pointed it at his head. Ruben tensed his jaw. *This is not good*, he thought.

'Give me the Cube or he will die.'

XL-R, when I give him the Cube Time-Freeze them all, exit Safe-Mode, sent Ruben.

Exiting Safe-Mode, preparing to disengage, beware massive power drain on fuel cells, sent XL-R.

He pulled back his sleeve and pressed the white centre axis jewel twice and the Cube appeared in his hand. The leader gave a chilling smile. Ruben slowly passed it to him. He looked at the little flashing lights in wonder.

'Finally, I have it.'

There was a deafening "crack, crack" and the hooded man fell to the ground.

'That was for Jutotzas,' sneered the leader.

XL-R, Time-Freeze.

Everything stopped, there was silence, no wind, no sound, nothing. Ruben quickly went over, picked up the Cube and re-engaged it on his wrist. He then went over to the man with a gun and moved his hand to realign his aim. *That should do it,* he thought, checking the imminent trajectory of the bullet. He then moved the arm of the leader, to realign his gun. Next he dragged the body out of the way, over to the wall.

XL-R, rewind time to just before the gun shots, then un— freeze, sent Ruben.

"Crack, crack" went the two guns and all three men crumpled to the ground like dominoes, then exploded into black dust and vanished. The hooded man began to wriggle on the floor. Ruben kneeled down and took off the bag. He stood up.

XL-R, record video, sent Ruben.

Recording, sent XL-R.

'Are you alright?' Ruben asked softly.

'I am alright thanks. What happened? Who are you? Do I know you? You look familiar,' he asked.

Ruben couldn't help notice how much he looked like his dad and him.

'No, I saw these three men jump you. They were about to rob you but I scared them off.'

'Oh... Is that Bugs' walking cane? I gave that to him a few years ago when I worked as a driver for him. I was coming to meet him about another job today. Why have you got it?'

'It's a long story. You'll read about it in the papers tomorrow, I'm sure,' chuckled Ruben. 'I would be going, if I were you. There are a lot of police around. If you have anything to do with Bugs Moran I would keep your mouth shut.'

'Oh, all right, I'll be off. Thanks for saving my life,' said the man in a slightly unsure, confused way.

Ruben watched as he ran out of the alley and disappeared into the crowd. Holding the cane tightly in his hand he pressed the blue, orange and white centre axis jewels, and at 11:05, in a blue flash he was gone.

■ ■ ■

10:05, THURSDAY, 24TH JULY, NOVAK RESIDENCE,
LOS ANGELES, USA
PRESENT DAY

Nano-seconds later he was back in his bedroom. The house was eerily quiet. Everyone was out, but then he heard a noise from downstairs. It sounded like it was coming from his dad's office. *Hmm, that's odd. Dad will be at work now,* he thought. The Cube was in Solved-Mode-Three so he pressed the four yellow corner jewels.

XL-R engage protective Body-Shield in C-Thru-Mode, sent Ruben.

313

Initialising protective Body-Shield in C-Thru-Mode, sent XL-R.

Ruben caught sight of himself suddenly vanish in the mirror. He slowly edged his way out on to the landing only to hear a tiresome creaky floorboard give his position away. He froze on the spot. Through the staircase spindles he could see his dad's office door below. It opened slowly and a man in black gingerly peered out just as Zooby ran across the landing.

'It was only a cat. Have you found anything yet?' asked the man and went back inside the room.

Slowly Ruben crept down the stairs. He wasn't sure what he was going to do, but he had to do something. He pressed five blue jewels in a "+" pattern on the Cube.

XL-R, give me Atomiser capability, sent Ruben.

Atomiser capability engaged, power reserves are low, sent XL-R.

Slowly he approached the office doorway. He could see the two intruders inside going through the contents of his dad's desk. Just then Zooby came running back along the landing and banged into Ruben's leg. He gave a loud miaow and leapt off straight into a nearby plant stand, sending it all crashing to the floor. The two men quickly turned round and bolted through the doorway slamming straight into an invisible Ruben. He fell heavily against the handrail and pivoted backwards over it. Luckily he managed to grab hold of a banister spindle and was left dangling precariously over the glass hallway table below.

'What just happened? I felt something knock into me just then,' queried one of the men.

'It was that stupid cat again.'

'No, it was much bigger than that.'

'He's here, that boy is here.'

'Where? I can't see him.'

'He's here all right, I can feel it.'

Both men then took out large pistols and started slowly scanning the landing and bedrooms for any signs of life, red lazer dots plotting the bullet impact points. Ruben's arms were now starting to ache. He wished he hadn't eaten as much for breakfast now. His mind raced. He was in a spot of bother and not sure what to do. He watched as the two men slowly walked downstairs and then he managed to haul himself back over the handrail. He slowly followed the intruders down into the hallway.

'There's no one here. Let's check the other bedrooms,' said one of the intruders as they headed back up the stairs towards Ruben.

Power cells compromised, C-Thru-Mode disengaged, sent XL-R.

Oh $#!t, thought Ruben, *an*d suddenly became very visible.

The two startled men couldn't believe their eyes

'See, I told you he was here.'

Without a moment's hesitation Ruben hit the man hard. He lost his balance and crashed into his accomplice. Both men barrel-rolled down the stairs in a blur of arms and legs. The men grappled for their guns and started firing wildly at Ruben and watched in amazement as the bullets hit his Body-Shield, stopped dead and dropped to the floor.

'Hmm, he's a tricky one, change to full combat power four,' ordered one of the men, and they started firing again.

Ruben didn't like the sound of that. Immediately a bullet hit the shield then started to drill into it. He watched in terror as the projectile bored into the edge of his arm. *Arr, that's going to hurt,* he thought as he braced himself for the imminent pain. *And... there it was. O-u-c-h,* he thought. He ducked quickly into Kat's bedroom, It was like a changing room massacre. *Typical,* he thought.

Body-Shield breached, power cells low. Atomiser capability low.

XL-R, lock on to thermal heat profiles.

Two thermal heat profiles located. Line of sight required for targeting, sent XL-R.

Engage remote optical scan.

Remote optical scan engaged, thermal heat profiles are approaching, sent XL-R.

The two men slowly moved along the landing, their guns panning around the area. Ruben took a deep breath then crouched down and rolled out onto the landing. Two blazing beams shot from the Cube and seared through the two intruders. There was a loud "crack" as one gun fired; Ruben felt a sharp pain in his right shoulder. He watched as the two men exploded into a black cloud and vanished as he fell to the floor grabbing his shoulder.

XL-R, Fully disengage Safe-Mode.

Safe-Mode disengaged, sent XL-R.

He pressed the white centre axis buttons and the Cube slipped from his wrist into his hand. He held the blue segment over the wound area and pressed firmly down on the skin, then he pressed the green centre axis jewel twice. A few seconds later the Cube issued more instructions.

Now lift the blue segment off the skin and keep it over the penetration wound area, focus the blue beam from the centre jewel, sent XL-R.

Ruben did as he was instructed and watched as the beam began to heal his wound. The excruciating pain seemed to last forever as the Cube repaired the damage to his shoulder.

XL-R, do you think you can mend the holes in the wall too? Dad won't be happy, he has only just finished decorating it.

I will attend to that shortly, sent XL-R.

A little while later Ruben gave his shoulder a reassuring rub. He felt better and the pain had eased considerably. He went up to his room, put the Cube on his desk, sat on his bed, grabbed his guitar and started to "noodle" away. His guitar always made him feel better. He could lose himself in his own imagination for a while and go into a state of calm, control and stadium rock euphoria. He could switch off from the real world for a little while. Suitably chilled, he decided to have a telepathic link with Kat.

Hi Kat, what are you doing? sent Ruben.

Hiya, I'm here with Mum. We're going through some 3D visuals trying out some different interior colourways.

Wow, get you, you'll be running the company next.

Maybe in a few years. Mum says 'Hi'. Is everything OK?

Yes, I'm fine. It went pretty well to plan. A few interesting things happened. I'll tell you all about it tonight, when Dad gets home. I'll call him now. See you both later. Love you, sent Ruben.

Love you, chorused Sarah and Kat.

Ruben grabbed his mobile and called his dad.

'Hi son,' came the cheery reply.

'I'm back, Dad. I have the cane. It was an interesting morning. You had better bring some filler home too.'

'Why, what for?'

'Err well there are a few marks on the wall you might want to attend to.'

'Oh really, tell me more.'

'I will when you get home. Where are you?'

'I'm actually at LA Media International. I am about to go into a meeting with their technical bods to discuss my idea.'

'Wow, cool, Dad. Knock 'em out.'

'I'll try. Better go, I'll see you later. Glad you're back.'

He put his phone on the bed and changed into his normal clothes. He liked his twenties outfit and carefully hung it in his wardrobe. The blood splattered overcoat was ruined, so he went down into the garage, put it in a carrier bag and threw it in the rubbish bin.. *Hmm,* he thought, pausing for a moment. He pulled the coat back out again, found a sharp pair of scissors from his dad's tool box and cut out a bloodied square of material then threw the bag back in the garbage and went back into the kitchen. He rummaged through the drawers to find some zip-lock bags and wrapped the sample up, placed it in the deep freezer clearly marked "SAMPLE-DO NOT EAT... and that means you, Kat".

Back in his room he picked up the walking cane and had a good close look at it. The handle was made from a nicely carved piece of dark black wood. *That looks like Ebony, like the fretboard on my old Valley Arts Custom Pro*, he thought. Set into the wood were the four gleaming orange jewels he needed. On the top was a silver disc with the engraved inscription. The bottom of the handle had two silver rings around it, with a silver collar connecting it to the shaft of the cane. *Dad won't have ever seen this. I think he'll be quite surprised. Hmm, I wonder,* he thought.

He jumped up off the bed and went over to his desk, flipped his laptop lid up and waited for it to boot up.

He began typing into the Google search bar. He clicked on "Images" and slowly scrolled down the pictures, and stopped. There it was, an old grainy black and white picture of the Chicago street where he had been earlier this morning. There was the huge crowd of people, the two police wagons, the warehouse and Ruben pushing through the crowd, next to a policeman. He blinked and looked again more closely at the old picture. He turned up the screen resolution. Sure enough, there he was in his flat cap and overcoat. He looked in stunned amazement at the picture, and then decided to print it out. *Cool,* he thought.

A few minutes later he went into his dad's office to get the picture. Zooby was sitting on his desk purring, so he decided to sit and have a chat with him for a while, as there was no-one else around. He also managed to while away the rest of the afternoon chatting to Frankie, catching up on his social media and trawling through YouTube for interesting guitar nonsense. Bliss.

At 18:30 precisely Ruben heard the sound of Mum's car pull up into the garage. He whizzed down into the kitchen to greet them.

'Hi Mum, hi Sis.'

'Hello darling, how are you? No stray bullets I hope,' joked Sarah, and walked over to kiss him.

Kat gave him a hug and playfully roughed his hair up.

'Yuk, what have you got in your hair?' she squealed.

'Oh, it's hair gel. I had to look the part,' Ruben explained.

'Couldn't you have had a shower?'

'S'pose so. Anyway, what's for dinner?'

'Cor, let me get through the door a minute. A coffee would be nice,' hinted Sarah. 'Thanks for asking.'

'Sure, no problem.'

Ruben set about putting some coffee on the go while Mum and Kat deposited their coats in the hallway closet.

'Ok, I thought we would have veggie burgers in buns with a side salad and special chips. How does that sound?' asked Mum

What's special about the chips?'

'They're special because Ruben is going to make them, aren't you darling?'

'Yes Mum.'

'Followed by some delicious blueberry pancakes.'

'Are you joking?'

'No, why?'

'Oh, no matter.'

'I thought you liked pancakes?'

'Err, well, I do, but you can have too many of them you know.'

'I don't get you.'

'Doesn't matter, that's fine.'

It wasn't long before János arrived home and once again they all sat down to eat and chat. János opened a bottle of red wine and charged everybody's glass.

'This looks lovely, honey,' remarked János. 'So how has your day been Kat darling?'

'I had an interesting day with Mum. I've been doing some visualisation work. Yeah, it was fun. Some nice guys there too,' giggled Kat.

'You're there to work, not eye up the staff, young lady,' said Sarah.

'Relax Mum, it doesn't hurt to window shop. You don't have to buy.'

'What about you honey, how was your day?' asked János.

'Oh, it was all right. We have this intern at the moment, who is a bit "flaky". Can't seem to keep her mind on her work. I might have to let her go,' replied Sarah while looking at Kat, with one perfectly manicured eyebrow raised quizzically.

'Okay, I get the point,' acknowledged Kat.

'And what about you Ruben? How did it go today?' asked János.

'Yes, interesting. You'll never guess who I ran into today Dad?'

'No, who?'

'Does the name "István" ring any bells?'

'Well yes. That was my grandad's name. Hang on a minute, don't tell me you met him?'

'Yup, sure did. He looked so much like you and me it was spooky. We can watch the video footage on the Cube later if you like.'

'Yes, that would be great, if not slightly spooky. We knew the family moved to America in the early nineteen hundreds. The family split up and Grandad moved to Chicago. He was a trained chauffeur. He worked for various people, some quite rich clients, by all accounts. He met Grandma when she worked as a maid in one of the big Chicago hotels. They were very young and had quite a tough life, not much money.'

'Well, it appears that one of the people your grandad also worked for was a Chicago gangster called George Moran, or "Bugs" as he was known. He gave him the cane as a gift, for some reason?'

'I do remember there was a rumour going around our family when I was young, that I heard my dad recount. It was something to do with my grandad; he had become involved in some dodgy dealings with the North Side Gang, a Chicago gangster organisation.

They specialised in running illegal booze and other "off-grid" stuff too, but they also made enemies, one of those was a now infamous gangster called Al Capone. Supposedly, Grandad was a good driver and did a getaway job for his boss. They were in a power struggle with Capone's gang and were involved in an ambush they'd set up, István managed to get them away, but he was badly injured and it ended in a bad crash. Instead of him going to hospital he was cared for privately so as not to alert the police and the other gang. His boss Bugs paid for his care. I guess the cane was a way to say thanks for saving his life.'

'Well, he was obviously off to do another job when I bumped into him,' quipped Ruben.

'That's amazing. There aren't many people that have met their own great grandad,' exclaimed Kat.

'Here, have a look at this picture, see if anyone looks familiar.'

Ruben then showed the old black and white picture of himself in Chicago he had found online. They looked in amazement as he recounted the scene as it unfolded. Sarah spotted him right away.

'Oh my word, look at that. It's Ruben. Look, he's by the policeman. Are you sure you haven't Photoshopped it?' asked Sarah.

'Nope, it is me all right. Trust me, I was there, straight off Google.'

The kitchen erupted into fits of laughter. It really was a great picture. The rest of the evening was spent watching some of the video footage from the Cube. It was much better than watching some half-baked Box Set on satellite TV. Ruben left out the end part but gave his dad a knowing wink. He would talk to him about it tomorrow.

'I am looking forward to the party on Sunday at Frankie's. Should be fun. Do you think Grandma will be able to come?' asked Ruben.

'Hmm, I don't think she'll be up to it. Why don't you and Frankie pop over and see her tomorrow, she'd like that,' suggested Sarah. 'Kat and I saw her on the way home yesterday. She's not great at the moment. She was a little puzzled to see us. They think she may have had another mini stroke. So be prepared.'

'Ok Mum, we will go and see her. She likes Frankie. She'll cheer Grandma up.'

It had been quite a day and Ruben eventually dragged himself up to bed, then spent another hour on the phone to Frankie. He so wanted to see her. He could easily teletransport over to her, but he couldn't let her know about the Cube, so decided to catch up with her tomorrow. He would sort out the Cube with his dad and talk to him about the coat sample too. He pressed the white centre axis jewel three times putting the Cube in Safe-Sleep-Mode to recharge and archive data, then he got ready for bed.

That night his dreams were alive with crazy adventures. They played for real in his mind and he found that he could actually alter the dreams as he slept. That was something he had never done before. He wondered what the next real adventure might be. He would find out soon enough.

■   ■   ■

The morning alarms all went off around the house in sequence as usual, with Ruben's being the last to chime. It was met with the usual groans and yawns. Sarah soon came in with a cup of tea.

'Morning, darling. Hope you slept well?'

'Errrg, yes okay, I s'pose,' came the unenthusiastic reply.

He flicked on the TV.

'Oh hi, Chynna. I haven't seen you for a while,' he said quietly. His favourite TV weather girl suddenly woke him up.

'So what shall we do when you finish doing the weather. He paused and waited for an imaginary answer then carried on his fantasy.

'Wow, that sounds great. I haven't been in a private jet to St Tropez. Sounds fabulous darling,' he continued.

The weather update ended and so did his little fantasy. About a quarter of an hour later he had showered and went down to the kitchen to get some breakfast. Sarah and Kat were just walking out the door, off to work while János was finishing his coffee and scanning the newspaper.

'Morning Ruben.'

'Hi Dad, can you help me with the cane so I can load the jewel cells this morning. Hopefully it will increase the power and reliability of the Cube. Some of the functionality still seems to get compromised. I had a couple of close scrapes yesterday. Actually, that reminds me. One of these henchman guys got shot and my coat got covered in blood. It was a bit of a shock but he vapourised as usual. However, I have kept a sample of his blood. I thought it might be useful to test it and see if anything unusual shows up. It might give us some more clues as to what we are dealing with.'

'That's a great idea. I think soon we are going to start hearing reports of contamination illness occurring.

It is only a matter of time before the particles we are inhaling will start to affect us. Our bodies will fight the infection in the usual way but it won't be able to keep up with damage being done and eventually the immune system will become overloaded and cease to function effectively.'

'How did it go with the media boffins yesterday?'

'Umm, not great if I'm honest. Transmitting the frequencies required to achieve the filtering effect are way out of the range commercial transmitters are able to work at. Theoretically they agreed it would be possible to hide the frequencies in transmissions but the network is just not set up to do it right now. Basically it means it is all up to us – well, you, I guess – but what I have done is link the frequency range to our domestic sound system so it is now running all the time. You won't be aware of it. I have written a simple app that will embed the frequency range into your mobile phones too. I have told Mum and Kat to use their mobile headphones as much as possible, or plug them into their work music system. I think we are going to need as much time as possible.'

'Blimey, Dad, you have been busy.'

'I have. Come on, let me get some breakfast then let's get the Cube sorted.'

Ruben ate his muesli as quickly as it was possible to eat ready mix cement, then put a crumpet in the toaster to have with some of János' Marmite spread. A while ago his dad was doing the shopping with his mum and saw it in the International Aisle. Ruben loved it, but Mum and Kat hated it with a passion.

The toaster catapulted the crumpet onto the counter. He picked it up, applied the butter and Marmite, came back over to the table and sat down.

'No, no, no. How many times have I told you? Let the crumpet cool down so the butter doesn't melt, then apply the Marmite. That is the proper way to have it,' exclaimed János.

'Oh Dad, I haven't got time to wait for toast to cool down. I've got the world to save.'

'Good point, well put. Come on, let's get this Cube fixed.'

After he had chomped through his crumpet Ruben ran upstairs to get the Cube and the cane. They both then went out into the garage. János picked up the cane and had a close look at the orange jewels. They were each held in place by four little silver claws. From his vast tool box he got a flat needle file. He went over to his grinding wheel and turned it on. It whirred into life. He put on his safety specs and carefully ground the file into a little, sharp chisel-end, shooting sparks into the air. Happy it was shaped to his exact specification he went back over to the bench. Carefully he peeled the little silver claws back allowing the jewel cells to fall freely away. A couple of minutes later all the gleaming jewels were lying on the bench. Ruben picked up the Cube and started to manipulate the segments into Solved-Mode-Three and pressed the green centre axis jewel twice. It began to pulse with a yellow glow. He put it down on the bench and placed it in front of the four jewels. He then pressed the yellow centre axis jewel. The Cube started to glow with coloured lights, then a yellow beam began arcing across the jewels on the bench. Seconds later a second beam emerged from the Cube and a copy image began forming. Gradually three-dimensional clones of the orange jewels began to materialise, and a few minutes later the finished jewels were fully formed on the bench.

XL-R, prepare to load four remaining orange jewel cells.

Configuring system, connection sensors ready, scanning ready. Load orange cells.

Ruben proceeded to press the centre axis orange jewel cell four times, followed by gently pushing the four jewel cells into the orange segment. Each click of engagement was verified by an orange flash of light darting over the Cube's surface. When the fourth jewel was in place the Cube began to pulse with a soft orange light, gradually getting faster and faster, then stopped.

Orange cells are engaged.

The orange segment was now complete. János started fitting the cloned jewels back into the cane. With all the jewels in position he carefully folded the little silver tabs back into their original shape.

'There we are, Grandad's cane. I can't believe it's here. What a treasure,' marveled János.

'XL-R, what is your functionality level now?' enquired Ruben.

'I have approximately eighty-eight point eight recurring per cent functional capability now.'

'Gosh, why approximately?' asked Ruben.

'My system is still loading so I have estimated it for you. More functionality will be added as the system updates,' replied XL-R.

'Hmm, XL-R, are you sure you aren't made by Apple?'

János nodded in agreement.

'Anyway, I'm glad we have got that done. So Dad, do you want to talk about the blood sample I got?'

'Yes, so what happened?' asked János.

'Well, it got a bit dicey at one point. I got cornered by one of Jutotzas' creeps again, and he had two accomplices. We were in the alleyway where I teletransported to, and these two guys had your grandad. He had a black bag over his head. I had to use the Cube to stop them and I managed to free your grandad, but some bullets were fired in the aftermath and I got sprayed with blood. It was pretty scary stuff. Anyway, when I arrived back I cut out a section of the fabric and wrapped it up and put it in the freezer.'

'That was good thinking. However, I am not sure if I am the right guy to check this out. I think I will call my old pal Doctor Jefferies at the LA Medical Research University. He specialises in blood disorders and has done a lot of research into DNA coding, genetics and brain functions. He would know what to look for. Actually, it was him who figured out how it was possible for you and Kat to be genetically identical twins but not the same sex. We have quite a history of twins in our family. The stuff I have done is really quite basic compared to what he can do. I will take the sample to work today and give him a call, see if I can get him over and explain what is going on. I won't tell him about the Cube but I'll show him what I have done so far.'

'That sounds good. How do you know him?'

'We were at university together. Like me, he played in a band and we kept bumping into each other at gigs. He was an awesome bass player and eventually I got him to join my band. I haven't seen him for ages so it'll be nice to catch up with him again.'

'Cool.'

'I'll find the freezer box and pack it with ice and take it to work today.'

'I am going to see Frankie and then go and see Grandma for a little while. It's a nice day so we can take her out into the garden, have a cup of tea and a chat.'

'Ah, yes, she'll like that. Okay, you get the sample and I'll get the box sorted.'

With the sample safely packed in ice János headed off to the lab whilst Ruben drove over to Frankie's place. As he approached her house he could see loads of vans parked up with people scurrying in and out of the main entrance. He got out of his car and caught sight of Frankie by the front door. He ran up the path and swept her off her feet. He wrapped his arms around her and nuzzled affectionately into her neck. Her gentle perfume and flowing hair totally enveloped him. He loved her so much and wanted to hold her forever. She turned and kissed him.

'Good morning handsome, how are you today,' she cooed softly.

'Better for seeing you. What's going on?'

'Oh, it's all the arrangements for the party on Sunday. It's going to be great. There's going to be a big marquee, a hot DJ and loads of food and drink. They are decorating the whole garden. It's going to look amazing. Mum has also invited a few of her celebrity friends. It should be fun. I can't wait. So what are we going to do today?'

'I thought it would be nice to go and see my grandma for a little while, then go mountain biking up in the hills. Grab some lunch and just hang out for a while,' suggested Ruben.

'Yes, okay. Come inside for a minute. I'll get my stuff ready. My bike is in the side garage.'

They went into the house and were greeted by Mrs Rosenberg.

'Hello, nice to see you Ruben.'

'Hi, Mrs Rosenberg.'

'Please call me Robyn. Mrs Rosenberg sounds so formal.'

'Yes, sorry, I have got so used to calling you that. I will try.'

'Good, anyway, Frankie has been getting under my feet this morning. I hope you are going to take her out for a while so I can get on. There's so much to get organised,' she joked.

'Thanks Mum,' replied Frankie with mock indignation.

'We are going to see my grandma for a while, then go cycling up in the hills,' chipped in Ruben.

'That sounds fun. Don't come back too early. Haha...'

Frankie ran upstairs and Ruben went back outside, got Frankie's bike out of the garage and strapped it on to his car's bike rack. Frankie soon joined him outside with her backpack and helmet. They jumped into the car and headed towards the hills. Ruben's grandma lived in a lovely little retirement development on the edge of the San Gabriel Mountains, on Monterosa Drive.

She had always been quite an independent woman, but since the passing of her husband Richárd, a few years ago, her dementia had become more apparent. Grandad had been her memory and had kept their lives running smoothly and filled in for the things she had forgotten. Now, a few strokes later her mind wasn't as sharp as it once was. She had resisted the invitations to go and live with János and his family. Having wardens in the retirement development was at least some peace of mind for János at the moment.

The car pulled into Monterosa Drive and headed towards the entrance to the development. It was a warm, sunny morning and the sky was a clear blue, not a cloud in sight. They drove into the little car park then went into the foyer and over to the visitor area. Ruben spoke to the lady in charge.

'Good morning. We have come to visit Mrs Paulina Novak in number seven.'

'Oh hello, it's Ruben isn't it? What a lovely, unusual name. Okay, can you both sign in please? You know where to go, don't you?'

'Yes, we're fine, thank you.'

They signed the visitor book and walked through the foyer area out into the garden. The ten little bungalows surrounded the central garden area. A gardener was attending to the shrubs in the manicured flower beds. In the centre was a pretty little pagoda with chairs underneath. There were a few residents enjoying the sun having their morning coffees. It looked idyllic in every way.

'I can see why Grandma likes it here. She gets so well looked after, like in an expensive hotel.'

'Yes, it is lovely here,' replied Frankie. 'Oh look, there she is, over by the little summer house.'

They followed the winding paved path over to her. She saw them coming and gave a little wave. Ruben bent down and gave her an affectionate kiss on the cheek, followed by Frankie.

'Hi Gran, how are you today?' he asked.

'I am fine thank you my darling grandson. And who is this rather pretty girl you have brought with you?'

'Oh Gran, it's Frankie,' replied a slightly puzzled Ruben.

'Oh yes, yes of course, how silly of me. Hello Frankie my dear. It's so lovely to see you. Can I get you both a drink? It's already really quite hot out here.'

'Hello Mrs Novak, you are looking very well today. How are you feeling?' enquired Frankie.

'Oh, I'm okay. Some days are better than others, you know how it is. Shall we go in and get some drinks? Maybe you can push me and we can catch up on why my grandson hasn't "popped the question yet",' she chuckled.

'Grandma, don't be a stirrer, all in good time,' said Ruben jokingly. 'I will have an orange juice if I may, thanks.'

Frankie took the brakes off the wheelchair and slowly pushed Grandma over to her bungalow. They went into the kitchen and made the drinks as Ruben sat in a deck chair on the grass checking his social media.

'I am glad you have come to see me. I have a little present I want to give you. Wait here a moment. I will be right back.' She slowly wheeled herself down the little hallway and turned into her bedroom. A few minutes later she trundled back into the kitchen.

'Here we are. Now look at this. I want you to have it.'

In her hand she held a little red leather-covered jewellery case. She clicked the lid open to reveal a beautifully intricate bracelet studded with jewels and pearls, held together with a fine mesh of gold wire.

'This was my mother's favourite piece. She loved it. I want you to have it. I think you will be in our family for a very long time. I certainly hope so, judging by what my grandson has told me,'

'Oh Mrs Novak, surely it should be Ruben's Mum who has this?' queried Frankie.

'No, she has her own special pieces. I want you to have this. I have recently had it repaired especially for you. One of the red jewels kept falling out. We had a guest antiques dealer come in to do valuations for us, his name was Dan, I think. Nice young man, very tall. Anyway, he said he could fix it for me.'

'Oh, I see, Katarina's boyfriend is also called Dan. Perhaps he is moonlighting as an antiques dealer,' and she laughed. 'Gosh, I don't know what to say. It looks beautiful. Thank you, thank you so much. I will treasure this forever. I was hoping you would be able to come to our party on Sunday.'

'No, I don't think so this time, my dear. I am not as light on my feet as I used to be. You youngsters have fun. Maybe you can wear the bracelet at the party as a special surprise for Ruben. It is rather stunning, don't you think?'

'Oh yes, it's so, so lovely. I have just the dress to wear to show it off too,' replied an excited Frankie.

'Come on let us go back into the garden. Our little secret.'

Frankie maneuvered the wheelchair out of the bungalow and back across to Ruben as Grandma balanced the tray on her lap.

They all sat chatting for a while, enjoying catching up with one another. Soon the little bell could be heard ringing from the restaurant area alerting the residents that it was lunchtime.

'Will you stay for lunch?'

'No, I don't think we will this time, Gran, if you don't mind. We are going to do a bit of mountain biking on the trail just around the corner. We will grab some lunch a bit later up at one of the cabins. Come on, we'll push you to the restaurant if you like?'

'Thank you my darling. It has been so lovely to see you both. Enjoy your party, um, er, er, Frankie,' said Grandma hesitantly.

'We will, Mrs Novak. We'll see you soon. Enjoy your lunch.'

'Thank you, my dear, I'm sure I will. I do believe

it's soup and salmon salad today if my memory's right. Anyway, it will be nice whatever it is, I'm sure. See you soon. Lots of love.'

Frankie and Ruben kissed her goodbye, went out to the parking lot and got in the car.

'Your grandma is so sweet, so elegant. I hope I look like her when I'm her age. She is amazing,' said Frankie.

'She is, but her memory isn't as good as it was. Since Grandad passed away she has been getting more forgetful, it has become more obvious now she has to think for herself.'

'Yes I noticed she didn't know who I was to start with, then wasn't sure of my name when we said goodbye, I guess it's only going to get worse,' reasoned Frankie with a heavy sigh.

They turned left into East Loma Alta Drive and drove a little way along to the Sam Merrill Trailhead car park on the corner. The gravel gave a loud crunch as they parked up. Ruben quickly unstrapped the bikes while Frankie fastened up the rucksacks. There was a gentle breeze coming along the side of the mountain, perfect biking weather. They put their helmets and packs on, locked the car and set off up the trail.

■ ■ ■

Meanwhile, up in the San Gabriel Mountains János was already hard at work. The sample had been deposited in the freezer and he was on the phone to Doctor Jefferies. After a quick catch-up they got down to business and he agreed to come over straight away to the lab. As the university was on its summer recess Doctor Jefferies was much more flexible in his work schedule and he immediately understood the urgency of the situation. About half an hour later János had his concentration disturbed by the deafening sound of a huge Harley-Davidson motorbike pulling up into the parking area. He quickly got up and went to meet the Doctor at the entrance. The two friends gave each other a big "man hug".

'Wow Eddie, it's been way too long dude. Still playing those arpeggiated hammer-ons?' asked Doctor Jefferies in a hilarious, over the top, American accent.

When the two friends played together they gave each other stupid musician nicknames. János was "Eddie Van Rental", and Doctor Jefferies was "Thunder Mcloud".

János reciprocated. 'Yo Thunder, you old slapper. How's the king thumbster? Still spanking the plank?'

'Yup, sure thing, it's all good. Who would have thought we would end up trying to save the world?' replied Doctor Jefferies.

They headed for the lab, as they both chuckled at their own brand of nonsense. János made some coffee and they sat and talked through the problem. He described the basic experiments he had done and showed him the data he had collected. It soon became apparent to the Doctor that this was indeed a very unusual problem.

'Hmm, so the DNA information being stored in the cell's nuclei are being altered. If the DNA codes are damaged then the cells will malform,' pondered the Doctor.

'Exactly, so the body will start to reject its own cells. Then we have had it.'

'Yup, what we need to find is a way of neutralising the nano-particles so they can't attack the DNA strands. Hell, that's not going to be easy. You told me you had some kind of special blood sample you wanted me to take a look at.'

'Yes, hang on a sec' I will get it from the fridge and I'll mount it on a slide. I haven't even had a chance to look at it myself yet. I think Earth's magnetosphere has been damaged by these charged nano-particles, which has allowed them to break through into our inner stratosphere. It might be that polarity of these particles is important, it might be something to look into,' pondered János.

A few minutes later he loaded a section of the sample into the electron microscope and the blurred image came up on the monitor. János pulled it into focus. He located a suitable blood cell to study. They looked at one another.

'What the heck? What is that? Where is this sample from?' asked the Doctor.

'Umm, I don't quite know how to explain this to you,' stumbled János.

'Well try. This is not like anything I have ever seen before.'

'No, it is odd, very odd.'

'The DNA strands seem to be covered with some extra kinds of atomic particles.'

The Doctor himself couldn't even believe what he was saying.

'That's not possible. That can't be done, can it?' asked János.

'Well it obviously can be done. Where did you get this?'

'Hmm, well it is hard to explain, suffice to say it is very weird,' said János avoiding the real answer.

The Doctor then manipulated the microscope around the sample a bit more.

'It looks like it has deteriorated a bit in places. It would be interesting to see how it degrades. It might give us some clues to its structure. Compounds tend to decay in different ways depending on their chemical makeup. Presumably you have a sub-atomic spectrum analyser here?'

'Err yes, we have got one of those,' replied János.

'Okay, good. Decay is a bit like geological erosion. The weak substances fall away quickest. The more resilient ones take longer. How much of this sample is there? Can you get a fresh sample? That is what we really need. We could then experiment with ways to make it decay. This could take us a while to crack and I'm guessing we don't have much time do we?' asked the Doctor.

János took a deep breath, then let out a heavy sigh.

'Ok, there is something I haven't told you, which you will not believe, but trust me, you need to believe me.'

Over the course of the next half hour János told the Doctor the whole unbelievable story, Cube and all.

■　■　■

Up in the mountains Frankie and Ruben were powering their way up the trail. The cool breeze fanning the trees was keeping them energised. The track was rough and punishing but the thought of the high-speed descent kept them motivated. They eventually made it to the top of the trail where the view over the city was spectacular and the sky was peppered with cotton wool clouds. They took off their backpacks and stood transfixed.

'I love this view. We're so lucky. Come on, let's go and eat our lunch over on one of the tables. It was a weekday so it wasn't too busy. In fact it looked like mostly students who had ventured up the trail today.

They sat down and spread their little picnic out on the bench.

'Oi, Ruben, over here,' came a loud voice.

Ruben spun round and saw his school pal Howard sitting nearby.

'Hey, Howard man, come on over here,'

Howard collected up his things and sauntered over and sat down.

'Hi Frankie. How are you guys?' coughed Howard.

'Yeah, we're good. You sound a bit rough.'

'I know,' he croaked. 'I seem to have developed this cold overnight.' He coughed again.

'That's not good. It's not contagious is it?' joked Ruben.

'No, man. I shouldn't think so. It feels like my asthma has got worse today.' He cleared his throat. 'Maybe it's all the crap we keep pumping into the atmosphere. That black cloud that covered the city probably has something to do with it. I bet that was just a huge cloud of pollution and the government are just giving us "BS" to keep us quiet.

'Yeah could be, who knows?'

'What are you cats doing up here anyway?'

'Well the same as you I would guess. Just getting out of the city,' said Ruben.

They sat and chatted for a while then decided it was time to head on back down.

'Nice to see you guys. I'll say goodbye, I'm not going down just yet,' coughed Howard as he got up and left them to continue their day.

'Blimey his cough was bad wasn't it?' asked Ruben.

'Yes, come on. Let's go.'

Having finished their snack they packed their rucksacks and unlocked their bikes. They peddled over to the track and set off down the mountain. The descent followed a twisting route through the trees and over the rocks and stones. As their confidence grew so did the speed they were doing. Carefully twitching the brakes and navigating the quickest line through the boulders they were soon hurtling along. The trees were a green blur as they whizzed down the trail in clouds of dust. Frankie screamed with a mixture of fear and delight. The back wheels spat out dust and stones as they skidded through the corners. Faster and faster they went. Up front, Ruben could see a jump opportunity approaching quickly. He lifted off the saddle and braced himself for the jump. He hit the ramp square on and sailed up into the air, altering his balance ready for impact.

'Yee-hi,' yelled Ruben.

He landed in a cloud of dirt and skidded round to watch Frankie.

He waited for a moment and then Frankie appeared from the trees. She was hammering along too and lined herself up for the ramp and hit it hard. The shock wave went up through the front forks, through the headset and along the handlebars. She lost her grip as she took off and wrestled with the bike trying to get it under control. With a colossal crunch she hit the dusty ground, stones spraying everywhere. The front wheel buckled sideways and she ploughed into a hefty boulder catapulting her over the handlebars and straight towards a huge tree trunk. She flew through the air like a discarded rag doll. Ruben watched helplessly as she smashed head-on into the tree. She fell to the ground entangled in the bike. Ruben jumped off his and ran over to her. He carefully removed the bike. She was covered in blood, motionless. He started to panic.

XL-R, check Frankie for body functions and life signs, he sent.

Deep life signs are fading. Body functionality will terminate in thirty-three point four seven of your Earth seconds.

Quickly Ruben pressed the white centre axis jewel twice and the Cube morphed on to his hand. Immediately he configured it into Solved-Mode-Four.

XL-R, prepare for full body re-animation.

Preparing now. Place the orange segment face down on her chest near the blood pumping muscle, sent XL-R.

He did as instructed and pressed the white, red and yellow centre axis jewels and gently let go of Frankie's hand.

There is a functionality problem with the red jewel, press it again, sent XL-R.

He tried it again and waited.

He could feel his own heart racing now as he watched her. The Cube began to pulse with a faint orange glow. He breathed a sigh of relief. Slowly it got quicker and quicker. Then suddenly an orange beam shot from the centre of the Cube and began forming a glowing cocoon around her body. Ruben was transfixed by the spectacle. She lay motionless. Her beautiful face, splattered with blood, started to clear. The cocoon began to turn a deeper, more intense shade of orange. Slowly her body became engulfed in an orange cloud.

XL-R, what is happening?

I am restoring all deep body functions to an earlier time and analysing all brain and memory pathways. It should take another four minutes and twenty-two point three seven of your Earth seconds to complete.

XL-R, can I hold her hand?

Yes, that is permissible.

The time seemed to last forever as he watched. Then he felt movement as her hand tightened around his. He squeezed it back. She squeezed again. Slowly the orange cocoon of light began to fade and there she was. Her beautiful blue eyes opened and she looked up at him. Ruben quickly moved the Cube and re-engaged it on his wrist. He gently helped her to sit up. They embraced and kissed. She was alive, but a little confused.

XL-R, thank you for saving her life, sent Ruben.

It was my pleasure to serve you.

'Come on Frankie. Let's get back to the car, but let's take it easy, eh?' suggested Ruben. 'That was quite a tumble you took. You were out cold for a little while.'

'Oh, was I? I feel a bit odd.'

Ruben looked at Frankie's bike. It was a bit mashed. The front wheel was like a banana. He quickly removed it and leant it against a boulder and carefully tried to bend it back into some semblance of circularity whilst adjusting the spokes. He then repositioned the handle bars. They both got back on their bikes and took it more slowly as Frankie's front wheel was still off-centre, but just about rideable.

■ ■ ■

Doctor Jefferies was still in a state of shock having listened to János's fantastical story. However, he could see that in reality it was a perfect explanation for what was transpiring. János' experiments were very instrumental in convincing him to take it seriously.

'There are some experiments we can do on this sample to get us started but what we will need, as soon as possible, is a fresh sample of this blood type to test,' said the Doctor.

'Okay, well the only way we are going to get some is for Ruben to get it on his next time-travel jaunt. He will no doubt be doing the next one as soon as possible. He is out today with his girlfriend. These time-travel trips really take it out of him, so he needs a bit of time to recharge his batteries.'

'I'm not surprised. We will need to prepare some kind of sample collection unit for him.'

'I have some special vacuum-powered syringe units that have a nitrogen-filled protective casing which will keep it fresh,' replied János.

'That sounds ideal. Right, what we should do first is set up a new sample and let it decay naturally. By plotting the decay characteristics we should be able to compare them to a database I have. This will tell us, hopefully, what type of substances we are dealing with. What we need are a couple of low-power lasers. If we focus these on specific decay points within a grid pattern we will be able to triangulate the exact decay process and be able to reproduce it in three dimensions in a virtual test using the computer,' explained the Doctor. 'Then, when we have the actual sample we should be able to focus our tests more specifically.'

'Yes, that makes sense. We can do that. I just need to rummage through my cupboards and find all the stuff. I know where most of it is. Let's get started.'

They spent the rest of the afternoon finding the equipment needed and setting it all up. As more and more pieces of equipment were added to the test rig, the sea of connecting cables covered most of the floor of the lab. It was a hard day's work but productive and everything was now ready for testing the new fresh samples. It was now, once again, up to Ruben.

■ ■ ■

The rest of the descent was much more sedate, but still enjoyable as the chance to enjoy the panoramic views more than compensated for the lack of velocity. Soon they arrived back at the car park and loaded the bikes back on to the rack.

'If I take you home now we should miss the rush hour. I have a lot to do tonight. I hope you are feeling better now after your "flight".'

'Yes, I seem to have escaped without a mark. Just lucky I guess? Anyway, it's been a lovely day. Thanks,'

Frankie gave him a hug and a big kiss. He didn't want to let her go, so he didn't.

'Wowwee, what's that for?' she asked.

'Oh, I just realised how much I love you.'

'Aww, that's nice. I love you too. C'mon, take me home you old softie,' she cooed.

They jumped in the car and headed over to Frankie's house. As they approached the city the traffic was already starting to build up, but they made good time and soon he was pulling up outside. There were still lots of vans parked up and people milling about in and out of the house.

'Blimey, it's still full on here isn't it? It is going to be one heck of a party by the looks of it.'

'Yes it is. Mum and Dad don't do things by half. It is a shame your Grandma can't make it,' said Frankie.

'I know, she would have loved it. Oh well. Look, I'm gonna shoot off. If I don't see you before, obviously I'll see you for the party. Call me, we'll talk.'

'Okay "International Man of Mystery",' mocked Frankie, kissing him goodbye.

Ruben unloaded Frankie's wreck of a bike, put it in the side garage next to the bins, then jumped in his car.

With a loud "VROOM" he whizzed off. *Right I need to prepare for my next trip*, he thought, as he headed for home. He clicked on the car hi-fi and found a local rock station to help while away the time. About half an hour later he was pulling up into the garage at home. It was too early for any of his family to be home, so he went straight up to his room. He disengaged the Cube and placed it on his desk.

'So XL-R, what is my next mission?' asked Ruben.

'For you next adventure you will travel back in time, to the city of San Francisco,' replied XL-R.

'Great, I love San Francisco. What's the plan?'

Ruben spent the next couple of hours listening to the Cube. He knew it was going to be a tough trip. As dinner time was approaching he heard voices downstairs in the kitchen. He pressed the centre white axis jewel and the Cube morphed back on to his wrist, so he went down to say hello. In the kitchen he found Mum and Kat laden down with bags.

'Hiya, gosh, what have you been buying, Rodeo Drive?' quipped Ruben.

'Oh, a few bits and pieces, we decided to hit the shops after work,' explained Sarah. 'How was your day with Frankie?'

'Yeah, we had a nice time with Grandma. I see what you mean about her memory. She was a little vague at times, but we sat and had tea and a nice chat. It was nice.'

'Ah, I'm glad you spent some time with her. I'm sure she loved seeing you both,' said Sarah.

'She couldn't remember Frankie's name.'

'Hmm, sadly that isn't going to get better. We have to make the most of our time with her while we can and there will come a day when she won't know who we are anymore,' said Sarah. 'It is such a cruel disease, she is gradually fading away, we are losing her.'

Ruben put the coffee pot on and they started to make dinner together, ready for when János walked in later. Ruben was assigned the job of slicing and dicing. They were going to have a nice fresh green salad with Thai spicy fishcakes and new potatoes. He picked up the chopping knife and brandished it like a ninja warrior letting out a huge comic book hero battle cry."

'Ruben, be careful with that axe Eugene, it's sharper than your dad's wit. How about pouring that coffee?' hinted Sarah sternly.

'Okay Mum, nice Floyd reference too' replied a scolded Ruben.

He went over to the coffee pot.

Beware, high explosive in nearby vicinity, sent XL-R.

He stopped dead in his tracks.

XL-R, where?

Approximately eighty-seven point four, one three of your Earth centimetres away from you, directly ahead. An object made from chrome plated brass cradling a glass substance formed into a cylindrical receptacle. I think you call it a "Cafetiere"? sent XL-R.

The plunger was up ready to push down.

It will explode in approximately fifteen point one three of your Earth seconds, sent XL-R. Disengage me and place me next to the object, with my orange segment facing it, and press the centre, white and yellow jewel cells as quickly as possible.

Ruben whizzed the segments around, disengaged the Cube, manipulated it into Solved-Mode-Four and placed it quickly next to the coffee pot. He pressed the white and yellow centre axis jewels and stood back.

What's going on, Ruben? What are you doing?' asked Sarah.

It's ok, Mum, we have a bit of a problem with the coffee pot.

'What do you mean?'

An orange beam of intense light blasted from the Cube and completely encased the pot in a translucent orange shell.

Two point one three of you Earth seconds to detonation, sent XL-R

'Move back Mum, quickly. Come with me.'

They both ran into the hall and watched. There was an almighty explosion sound and the Cube shuddered as the orange shell absorbed the detonation. The shell turned bright red then faded back to orange.

Detonation has been absorbed and dispersed. It is now safe, sent XL-R

The orange shell then vaporised. The pot was gone.

'What just happened?' asked Sarah.

Hmm, hard to explain, but I think the Cube just saved us from some really bad coffee,' joked Ruben.

'Oh well, that's lucky. Let's open some wine instead then,' said a slightly befuddled Sarah.

Just then, Kat came running back downstairs into the kitchen.

'What on earth was that noise?'

'Don't worry darling, that was your dad's old car backfiring,' she winked at Ruben.

'Blimey, he needs to get that sorted.'

With almost perfect timing, János' spluttering V12 truck could be heard pulling up into the garage. Sarah dished up dinner as Kat poured the wine. Conversation darted back and forth across the table as they all caught up on each other's day.

Once again after dinner it was time for János and Ruben to go over the plans for the next adventure; time was in short supply. Armed with a couple of instant coffees they retired to Ruben's room. János decided to run a quick security check on the house alarm system. He increased the sensors' sensitivity as he didn't want any more intruders. He also adjusted the panic alarm settings. He was worried by the latest event but it spurred him on to get Ruben ready for his next time-travel mission. In the back of his mind he realised that these time travellers were after them and his security hadn't been designed to cope with multi-time dimensional beings. He knew he may have to move Sarah and Kat out to a secret location, to keep them safe. For now he would turn his attention to Ruben.

Down in the television lounge Sarah and Kat had immersed themselves in a "chick flick" and were happy chatting and finishing off the wine. As the evening drew to a close János and Ruben reappeared to say their goodnights and everyone made their way to bed. Ruben knew he had a busy day ahead.

NINE

THE QUEST FOR THE GREEN "JEWELS OF THE EARTH"

PRESENT DAY

Whilst Ruben slept the Cube did an auto Mind-Link data transfer to him in preparation for the coming day. János had scrutinised the details to make sure he was satisfied Ruben would be as safe as possible. He knew the added complication of obtaining a blood sample from one of the henchmen, who would doubtless show up again at some inopportune moment, was an interference they could do without. This was going to be a Saturday unlike any one he had encountered before. Weekends were usually a relaxed affair in "Novak Towers" with quite a lot of snoozing in bed, a leisurely late breakfast and lots of chilling out, but not this Saturday; everyone was working.

The alarm went off at 09:00 precisely, Ruben hit mute and clicked on the TV, quickly turning the volume down so as not to wake everyone. He had the familiar feeling of butterflies in his stomach. The next quest was a dicey one and he knew it. Suddenly there was a quiet knock on his door and János walked in with a cup of tea for him.

'Morning, son. I hope you slept well.'

'Hi, Dad. Yes, not too bad. You didn't have to get up to make me a tea. I was going to head off and let you guys sleep in, but thanks anyway.'

'Oh your mum's awake anyway. She was tossing and turning all night. It was like sleeping with a whale, the way she was thrashing about. Anyway, I'll go and make you some breakfast; you get yourself ready,' said János, and went down to the kitchen.

Ruben took a few sips of tea then threw back the duvet and picked up the Cube.

XL-R, confirm teletransportation co-ordinates and arrival time details, sent Ruben.

The exact mapping co-ordinates are; Latitude North 37° 24' 32.492" and Longitude East 122° 24' 39.434". Your proposed arrival time is 13:00 on Tuesday, April 17, 1906. Weather conditions will be unseasonably warm and clear, at about eighty degrees Fahrenheit, and windy. All your travel equipment is ready. Your Mind-Implant has been successful. Added functionality means we can materialise anywhere without causing a disturbance or alarm, sent XL-R.

How is that possible?

Before we materialise at the given point in time I send forward an exact ghost copy of you that is one point three recurring nano-seconds in front of the real you. Anyone who happens to see this will see this image flicker, but the image won't lodge in the conscious part of their brain's memory, so that when you appear one point three recurring nano-seconds later the brain will assume it has seen you before, and so it will assume you have always been there, sent XL-R.

It sounds like what we call "Déjà Vu", when we think we have seen something before.

Yes, exactly, sent XL-R.

Ruben noticed his clothes were lying over the back of his chair, but decided to have his breakfast in his PJs for a change. He went downstairs to find János in the process of dishing up breakfast. He looked at the mountain of food on his plate.

'Blimey Dad, that's a lot. How am I going to eat all that?'

'It's only a cooked breakfast. I thought you might like it as a treat.'

'Wow, okay, I'll give it a go. Thanks.'

They both sat at the table and started to tuck in.

'I am going to have to be very careful on this trip. The timing will be critical if I am to succeed,' said Ruben, 'but I have it all worked out. If something goes wrong I'll "hop" back.'

Eventually Ruben's plate was clear.

'Why don't you take Mum and Kat a cup of tea up and then you can say goodbye too,' suggested János.

Ruben agreed and made two cups of tea, put them on a little tray and went up to his mum and dad's room. The door was slightly ajar, he could see she was stirring so he quietly tiptoed over to the edge of her bed and sat down.

'Morning, my darling. How are you this morning? Are you all set?' asked Sarah.

'Yes, Mum, all ready. Here's your tea,' and he placed it on the bedside pod. They had a little cuddle and Sarah kissed him goodbye.

'See you later, darling. Be careful,' whispered Sarah.

'I will,' and he blew her a kiss as he left to go and see Kat.

'Her door was shut so he gave a gentle tap.

'Hi sis. Are you awake?'

'No,' came the reply.

He flung open the door and boldly marched in.

'Okay, who have you got in here? Where's he hiding?'

He put the cup of tea down then dramatically threw open one of the wardrobe doors, looked behind the blinds and under the bed.

'C'mon, where is he?'

'Oh Ruben, you are so funny. Stupid, but funny,' she laughed.

'I wanted to see you before I went.'

'Ah, thanks bruv. How sweet.'

They had a little hug.

'Now you know where I am if you need me, don't you?' she said.

Ruben smiled and left Kat to enjoy her morning cup of tea and went to his room to get dressed. He had a quick shower then dried his hair. He was going to wear it slicked back, so he proceeded to squeeze out a generous bubble of styling hair gel "gloop" onto his palm. Carefully he massaged it through his hair until he had the desired look. He put on his white starched collar shirt. This was finished off with a thin white tie. The waistcoat was snug and made from a heavy fabric. Matching trousers and jacket were loose and comfortable, completing his ensemble. His stylish shoes were a light brown-and-white pair of "wingtips". For a second he looked at himself in the mirror and thought he looked quite smart. His shoulder bag was packed so he picked up the Cube and pressed the white centre axis jewel and it morphed onto his wrist.

XL-R engage Safe-Mode, sent Ruben.

Safe-Mode fully engaged.

He went across to Kat's room and poked his head round the door and said goodbye. Next he went down to say goodbye to his mum then finally he went into the kitchen.

'Hi Dad, I'm off now.'

'Are you sure you have everything?'

'Yes I have double-checked. Don't worry.'

They gave each other a hug, then Ruben stood back and had a quick glance at the clock. It was 10:30. He placed his fingers on the Cube, spun the segments into Solved-Mode-Four, then pressed the blue, green and white centre axis jewels. There was a sudden flare of light and he was gone.

■　■　■

TIME-JUMP BACKWARD

13:00, TUESDAY, 17TH APRIL, 1906, SAN FRANCISCO, USA

PAST

Across the road in front of him stood the white stone edifice that was the Fairmont Hotel. The huge, impressive entrance was flanked by classic stone pillars and heavily ribbed massive stonework. Intricate railings lined the edge of the balcony topped off by a display of flagpoles with flags of countries of the world blowing in the breeze. It was quite warm, but it was definitely windy. He stood and took it all in, enjoying the pleasant sound of horses' hooves, which gave the scene an enchanting air of period splendour as the carriages bobbled along the street. It felt odd seeing just a few cars whizzing around. It was mainly horses doing the work of the day. He looked left along Mason Street right down to the bay, to Fisherman's Wharf.

Ruben had been to San Francisco a few years ago with Mum, Dad and Kat, and had really enjoyed being there. He could see the Island of Alcatraz out in the bay, but the Golden Gate bridge was missing; it hadn't been built yet so presently it was the ferries sailing from Fisherman's Wharf that took people across the bay to Marin County. The Novaks had driven across the bridge to Muir Woods near Sausalito to walk amongst the huge Redwood trees. Ruben remembered how awesome they were.

As he looked left he could hear a rumbling sound getting louder and he waited to watch a tram trundle past with people hanging off every corner as the little bell sounded its arrival at the tram stop on the corner. It was lunchtime and the streets were quite busy with people going about their day.

Ruben wasn't hungry as he had just had one of János' mega breakfasts but he could do with a drink, so decided to cross the street and go into the Hotel to see if he could have a coffee and a little snack. He waited for a few horse-drawn carriages to rattle by and strolled over the road into the hotel foyer. Having whirled through the huge rotating doors he found himself dwarfed by the gigantic, sumptuous foyer. The walls and ceiling were painted in a light cream colour with extravagant gold leaf detailing around the massive marble columns. Ornate ceiling panels were picked out in gold too, the whole entrance was one of pure opulence. Delicate plants and ferns sprang from the huge pots dotted around the seating areas. To the right was an archway through to more of the hotel while straight ahead was a huge double zigzag staircase that went to the next level. A section of the foyer was roped off with big dust sheets covering the floor and ladders everywhere with decorators and tradesmen working away. The hotel was new and was in the final stages of completion, but it still looked magnificent. Ruben could remember bits of it from his previous visit. He remembered his mum going into raptures about "how it was the first hotel to be built using reinforced concrete". *Just as well,* he thought.

He quickly scanned the seats and saw a nice comfy leather chair and table so he sauntered over and sat down. Before he had a chance to make himself comfortable he was aware of somebody hovering by his side.

'Good day, sir. Can I be of assistance?' asked the smartly dressed hotel porter.

'Oh, err, yes could I possibly have a cup of coffee and a light snack please?' asked Ruben, in his poshest voice.

'Certainly, sir. I will bring you our lunchtime choices.'

A few moments later he returned with the menu and hovered again. Ruben quickly scanned the list of delicious treats available and decided to go for a Spanish omelette with his coffee. The porter took his order and headed for the kitchens. Ruben noticed a newspaper on the table and picked it up. It was a San Francisco publication entitled "The Call". The headline read:

"Brilliant Assemblage Crowds Grand Opera House". The front cover had a centre spread of black and white pictures of cast members and an ink line drawing of the stage set. On quick inspection the article was about a new production of the opera "The Queen Of Sheba", with tag lines such as; "It's grandeur never equalled before", and "Miss Walker plays the regal part splendidly". The review was quite odd as it seemed to centre on what the audience were wearing and doing. He chuckled at the line:"Detectives mingled with the gaping crowds that surrounded the theatre doors and persons of suspicious character were speedily and noiselessly removed beyond the temptation afforded them by the dazzling jewel show."*What the heck is that all about? Sounds more like a Foo Fighters gig to me,* thought Ruben. He continued to thumb through the paper and came across an advert for the "Kimball Piano". The advert read: Emma Eames says of the Kimball Piano, "I wish to give the Kimball Piano unstinted praise, both as an instrument and as an accompaniment for the voice". *Huh, I'd rather have an old Roland Juno 106 synth,* he thought. Another old advert that he found amusing was:"Dr Lyon's Perfect Tooth Powder", which finished with the strapline: "Convenient For Tourists". All in all it was a pretty standard kind of local paper and covered sport, jobs, things for sale, politics and local crime. Just then the porter reappeared at the table.

'Hello, sir, I have your lunch order.'

'Great, thanks. I wonder if you could possibly help me. I am going to the party that Miss Gish is throwing tonight and I want to send her some flowers with a little mysterious note attached. Do you know who I could contact to arrange my little surprise this afternoon?' asked Ruben.

'Well, sir, yes I do. The gentleman you need to speak to is Mr Hernandez, the hotel's events manager. He is in charge of all social functions here. I will go and see if he is available.'

'Thank you, that would be most helpful.'

The waiter put the plate, cutlery and coffee on the table and left Ruben to enjoy his snack. He wasn't really very hungry but needed an excuse to stay in the lobby to observe the comings and goings of the staff. He proceeded to slowly nibble his omelette as he people-watched. About ten minutes later Ruben noticed a tall, smart man heading his way.

'Good afternoon, sir, I am Mr Hernandez and I believe you require my assistance with a little matter concerning the delivery of some flowers to the suite of our guest Miss Gish?'

'Hello, Mr Hernandez. I am Ruben Novak. Yes, that is correct. I wish to surprise her. I have flown in especially from my home in Los Angeles to be here.'

'I believe I can help you with that. Where are the flowers?'

'Hmm, well I need to go and buy some. Can you recommend a nearby shop by any chance?' asked Ruben.

I can indeed, sir. The hotel uses a little shop further down Mason Street on the right, on the corner of Jackson Street. You can't miss it. It is called "San Francisco Flowers". They are very helpful in there. I am sure they will be able to oblige.'

'Perfect, I will go down after my snack and see what bouquet they can make for me and bring it back to you if that is all right?'

'Certainly, sir. It would be my pleasure. Enjoy your lunch.'

The porter walked over to the front desk to talk to a colleague. The coffee and omelette were soon dispatched, Ruben settled his bill and went for a stroll down Mason Street towards the wharfs on the edge of the bay.

■　■　■

János was hard at work in his lab adjusting the test equipment set-up when his intercom phone rang. It was the reception desk informing him that his friend Doctor Jefferies was in the foyer. He put down his screwdriver and went to meet him. The doctor had brought some equipment with him, so János helped carry a few of the metal storage cases back to the lab.

'So how is it going?' asked the doctor.

'Fine, I have calibrated the electron microscope and started to focus the lasers. However, I need to be able to see the monitor and adjust them at the same time to set the micro adjustment bias, so we could start by finishing that first. Did you bring the three-dimensional virtual modeller?' asked János.

'Yup, sure did. I also brought a photon analyser. That will measure the energy given off as the substance degrades, which should help us to identify its possible chemical and atomic structure more accurately. A handy piece of kit.'

When they were happy it was ready to test, János collected another small sample of the bloodied coat, placed it on a slide and put it into the electron microscope. Slowly he focused the device on the sample.

357

'Ok let's do it,' announced János triumphantly and started the test equipment running.

'Right, let's have a coffee,' he continued.

He went to the kitchen area and proceeded to make the drinks.

'So, doc, how long do you think we need to run this test for?'

'Umm, I think we should run it for a couple of hours, then reset it all and do the same test again on another sample. That way we can be reasonably sure that the results are consistent. This test will give us some kind of idea what possible substances we could be dealing with. When we get the fresh sample we will be able to be far more accurate in our investigation. Usually when a substance first starts to decay it gives off tracer elements. These are very important in the identification process too.'

'Sounds like a good plan. Why don't we go and get an early lunch and leave it running. C'mon, we can go to the refectory – most of the food is edible,' he joked.

■　■　■

TIME-JUMP BACKWARD
02:36, TUESDAY, 17TH APRIL, 1906, SAN FRANCISCO, USA
PAST

The wind was whistling up Mason Street as Ruben finally found the little flower shop. He crossed the street and went in. The florist was crammed full of gorgeous blooms, all standing proudly in little metal vases. Just then a young girl appeared from behind the colourful displays.

'Good afternoon, sir, how can I help you?' she enquired cheerily.

For a brief moment he felt himself staring at her a little too long. A pretty girl always turned him into a bit of a bumbling wreck.

'Err, umm, I need some flowers,' he stumbled.

'Well, that's lucky, because that is what we sell, in our flower shop,' she giggled.

'Err, yes of course it is. Anyway, I'd like a big bouquet for a special friend of mine. Lots of white lilies and some Gypsophila maybe?'

'Yes, that would be a nice combination, with some soft green foliage to help frame the little flowers too, perhaps?' explained the girl.

Ruben took a seat and watched the girl prepare all the flowers. She carefully selected the choicest blooms and artistically gathered them into a beautiful display and bound the stems together with some white ribbon all wrapped in some pretty white and silver paper.

'There, how does that look?' she asked.

'That looks absolutely perfect. Thank you so much.'

'Are they for a special lady?'

'You could say that,' he replied coyly.

'That will be one dollar and sixty cents please, sir.'

'Thank you, this should cover it. Please keep the change.'

'Why, thank you, sir. Perhaps we should cover the top of the flowers as well, seeing as the wind is a bit blowy today.'

She carefully covered the flowers with some clear cellophane and Ruben headed back to the hotel. He strolled into the grand foyer and approached the front desk where the porter greeted him with a polite 'Good afternoon, sir, how can I help you?'

'Good afternoon, I had a meeting with Mr Hernandez a little while ago concerning some party arrangements here this evening. I wonder if I could have a quick word with him. He is expecting me,' explained Ruben.

'Yes, of course. And your name is?'

'It's Mr Novak.'

'Right, wait here just a moment and I will see if he is free.'

A few minutes later the porter appeared with Mr Hernandez.

'Good afternoon Mr Novak, I see you have the bouquet. Perhaps you would like to come to my office.'

Ruben then followed him back to his room and they sat down.

'So you have the flowers. Was there something else you wanted me to do for you in the way of some surprise you mentioned earlier?'

'Well yes, I wonder if I could ask you for a sheet of paper and an envelope. I would like to attach a little mysterious message to go with the flowers.'

'Yes, of course,' replied Mr Hernandez, and looked through his desk drawer to find a pen and paper. Whilst his attention was distracted, Ruben disengaged Safe-Mode. Quickly he configured the Cube into Safe-Mode-Four and pressed five orange jewels in an "X" pattern.

XL-R, prepare for absorption processing, partition brain storage, sent Ruben.

Absorption processing ready to engage. Power drain will be heavy, sent XL-R.

Mr Hernandez handed the paper to Ruben who quickly grabbed his hand. He immediately froze; he couldn't move. He looked at Ruben in complete terror and could feel his eyes burning deep into him. Ruben reached over with his other Cube-clad arm and put his hand on the man's head. There was a blinding flash of orange light as time stopped. Ruben could sense the manager's stream of unconsciousness and memory data being loaded into his partitioned brain storage. Slowly he felt Mr Hernandez was weakening. Carefully he let him sink to the floor, his eyes closed. Ruben quickly locked the office door.

Configuring settings for absorption process to be completed, sent XL-R.

Ruben pressed the orange centre axis jewel and put his hand over the manager's heart, waited and closed his eyes. Gradually the two bodies morphed together. A few minutes later Ruben, the events manager, opened his eyes. He got up and sat at the desk. He felt strange being two inches taller and heavier. He was glad this was only going to be a temporary body alteration. Picking up the pen he wrote a cryptic message on the paper, sealed it in the envelope and carefully poked it into the side of the bouquet.

He unlocked the door and carrying the bouquet, he caught sight of his reflection in the window. *Blimey, I look old,* he thought. He walked towards the lobby area where the lifts were. He selected floor five and waited as the lift smoothly delivered him there. The doors whooshed open, he turned left and walked towards room number 121 at the end of the hall. He gave a polite tap on the door. It was opened by Miss Gish. She was obviously getting ready for the party as she was in her long, silk dressing gown with her hair wrapped in a big white towel.

'Hello Marcus. Gosh, are those for me? Oh you shouldn't have,' she cooed, with a little giggle.

'No, no, Miss Gish, these are from an admirer who has asked me to deliver them to you.'

'Oh, how exciting, how mysterious. You are naughty.'

'I think there is a little message too. Shall I arrange them for you? They would look nice in a brightly coloured vase.'

'Yes, that would be lovely of you. I do have a beautiful green glass vase, as it happens.'

'Yes, that would look perfect.'

'Come in and I'll find it for you.'

Inside, the suite of rooms was already being prepared for the party and there were several other members of staff busy arranging furniture and getting the drinks organised. A member of staff approached Ruben.

'Excuse me Mr Hernandez, where would you prefer the glasses to be stored?'

'I think they will be best kept in the bay window area, near the drinks trolleys,' replied Ruben as he felt a cold shiver suddenly shoot up his spine.

I am sensing a malevolent force at work. I can't pinpoint it yet, sent XL-R.

Miss Gish soon returned with the green vase.

'This is a very special vase, it was given to me by a very dear friend of mine many years ago. Let's put the flowers by the door on the little cabinet there, underneath the picture, so when my guests arrive later they will all see them.'

'Perfect, yes they will look absolutely fabulous there,' stated Ruben.

Heck, I'm glad I don't talk like this normally, he thought.

The green vase had six dangly glass jewels hanging from the lip of the top edge. The glass was heavily engraved with an intricate diamond shaped pattern that sparkled in the light. Ruben carefully transferred the flowers into the vase and went to get some water to fill it up.

XL-R, scan the green vase, are they the jewels we are looking for? sent Ruben.

Scanning vase now, sent XL-R.

Ruben paused for a moment and looked out over the San Francisco Bay. The water was looking a bit rough and he could see the distant waves breaking with white froth on the Alcatraz rocks.

The jewel cells are not in the vase, but they are close by. They are within a one point three, seven metre radius, sent XL-R.

Ruben was puzzled. He quickly looked around the room. He couldn't see anything nearby that fitted the bill.

'Will you be working at the party this evening Marcus? Err, hello Marcus?' asked Miss Gish.

'Oh sorry, I was miles away. What was that you said?'

'I was just asking if you were going to be helping me at the party this evening?'

'Yes, yes of course. I know it is a special occasion, so I will be on hand all evening to make sure it all runs smoothly. We are expecting the first guests to arrive at about eight o'clock, so my staff will be on hand to welcome them and offer canapés.'

'Gosh, you have got it all planned, how lovely. Now I need to get dressed as time is pressing on and you know how long it takes us girls to get ready,' said Miss Gish.

Too right, Frankie's a nightmare to get ready, she needs two weeks advance notice, he thought.

'I will carry on with the preparations, if that is all right?'

'Yes, I will be out of your way anyway. How exciting,' she giggled and floated off into her en-suite bedroom.

The room was looking very festive and all the arrangements were coming together nicely. Ruben gave the staff a few more helpful pointers and then left them to it for a while and headed back down to the kitchens. It was just after 16:30 and there was still a lot of work to be done. Ruben felt he was running on a kind of autopilot program, as he seemed to know what to do without even thinking about it.

■　■　■

Sarah placed a cup of tea down on Kat's desk.

'How's it going, Kat darling? How's it look?'

'I am struggling a bit with the rear elevation. There seems to be discrepancy over the height of the rear windows and the surrounding trees. Something is wrong somewhere.'

'Have you checked the surveyor's report?' asked Sarah.

'Yes, twice. It seems fine, but the windows will have no view on this elevation, which is not what we want is it?'

'No, I think I will send one of the guys out to check the measurements. It might mean we have to raise the height of the base as those trees are protected, plus the neighbours below will not agree to them being removed. We can push for them to be pruned, that's all. However, that won't solve this problem. It might mean we have to redesign that balcony area. I am glad you spotted that now before we got the contractors underway. Well done darling,' congratulated Sarah.

Kat was really enjoying working with her mum. She was picking up lots of useful experience, plus she was earning quite good money too.

■　■　■

Meanwhile, several miles away, across the city, János was busy in the lab with the doctor. The first sample had been under test for two hours and all the data had been collected. It was now possible to run the scanning information through the 3D modeller, enabling the computer programme to take the information and build a virtual model of the sample and animate how it degraded. It would show the sub-atomic activity occurring within the sample so that the degradation signature of the substance could be cross-referenced against a huge database of substances to see if there was a match or a partial match. Using the computer it would also be possible to watch a virtual replay of the sample decomposing. It might give them some clues. However, before they could start to analyse the results they would need to test another sample under the exact same conditions. The doctor double-checked the settings on the equipment and the thermostatic temperature modules were calibrated for stability and accuracy. When they were happy everything was ready János loaded the second blood sample into the electron microscope, locked the fume chamber and with a theatrical flourish flicked the switch to start the test. He took a bow.

'You're not on stage now,' laughed the doctor. They spent the next couple of hours working on the first virtual test results trying to narrow down possible groups of substances that could be useful when they had harvested a "fresh" sample. That was up to Ruben to sort out.

■   ■   ■

TIME-JUMP BACKWARD
17:35, TUESDAY, 17ᵀᴴ APRIL, 1906, SAN FRANCISCO, USA
PAST

The room was coming together perfectly now. It was looking very pretty with more flowers strategically placed around the room. The drinks and glasses were now all in position and there were extra cases of champagne stored in the third bedroom, along with more spare drinks. It was going to be a very special evening. The room had been cleaned from top to bottom so every surface and object were gleaming; it looked immaculate.

Ruben went over to one of the staff.

'Kyle, what time are the musicians arriving this afternoon?'

'They will be here at six o'clock, Mr Hernandez.'

'Excellent, that is excellent news. It will give them some time to set up their instruments,' enthused Ruben.

Why do people talk like that? he thought. He took a quick glance at his watch. It was 17:45 and the musicians would be arriving soon, so Ruben walked over to the corner of the room where the piano was and had a quick look around to make sure there was enough space for the trio to play. He shifted a few pieces of furniture over to the side of the room a little and then stood back to survey the area. Just then the apartment door chimes rang out. One of the nearby staff quickly went to open it. In the doorway stood three guys. *They must be the band,* thought Ruben and went over to greet them.

'Good evening gentlemen, you must be "The Marin Men"?'

'Yes, and you must be Mr Hernandez. It is good to finally meet you.' They shook hands.

I am sensing a malevolent force again. I can't pinpoint it exactly yet, sent XL-R.

'I am Johnny, Johnny Beaufoy. We have spoken. This is Fludey, our drummer and Mr P. Webb, our guitarist. Where would you like us to set up?'

'Yes, good to meet you gentlemen. I hope you chaps had a good journey here.'

'Yes, it was fine thank you,' replied Johnny.

'I suggest you set up over by the piano. I have cleared you some space.'

The band brought in their instruments and began unpacking them. Ruben was naturally intrigued to see what gear they had. The drummer had a nice simple drum kit and a couple of cymbals. The guitar player had two cases with his name proudly displayed on the side. Ruben couldn't help himself; he had to go over and take a look.

'Good evening, Mr P. Webb. I assume you are the guitarist then?' asked Ruben.

'I am tonight, sometimes I play double bass, nice to meet you.'

He opened one of his guitar cases.

'Wow...is that a Gibson L1 Archtop?' he asked. The Ruben partition of his brain had now fully kicked back in.

'It sure is. You know your guitars. There aren't many of these beauties out there yet. I was lucky. My uncle works for The Gibson Mandolin-Guitar Manufacturing Company Limited. He got me one. He sent it all the way from Michigan. It's a peach.'

'Oh yes, I have read about them in Guitarist Magazine,' explained Ruben.

'I didn't know there was such a magazine,' muttered a confused Mr P. Webb.

Ruben suddenly realised that of course there wasn't. It wouldn't be published for another eighty years or so. He had read his dad's old copies in the garage.

'It looks really nice. I love the dark spruce top. Is it an ebony board?

'Ummm. I believe so. Do you play?' enquired Mr P. Webb.

'Yes. A little.'

'Here, have a go.' Mr P. Webb handed Ruben the guitar. Suddenly he felt a surge of power run up his arm.

Heavy static charge of 2678.098 volts transferred to right limb due to charge polarity inconsistency, sent XL-R

'Wow... this is very nice,' continued Ruben,

He then proceeded to play his favourite blues licks at quite some considerable speed, throwing in a few tapping licks for good measure, much to Mr P. Webb's amazement.

Just then, a member of staff came over.

'Gosh, Mr Hernandez, I didn't know you played the guitar.'

'Oh, haha... I just play a few tunes from time to time, nothing much really,' he chuckled.

'Oh you are too modest. You are very good. Where did you learn that stuff with your fingers hitting the fretboard?' asked Mr P. Webb.

'I learnt it from a Dutch guy I saw play a few years ago, and just "kinda" worked out what he was doing.'

'That's amazing. What guitar do you play?'

'Actually I have a Gibson too, funnily enough,' replied Ruben proudly.

'I tell you what. I have two guitars with me. Why don't you play with us on a number or two? We do a few twelve-bar blues numbers when we have run out of other stuff to play; you could sit in on those.'

'Maybe later. That would be fun. Unfortunately I have to work now. Let me know if you need anything.

I will organise some food and drinks for you too. Your room is all ready for later, probably a lot later. They nodded and began to tune up and get ready. As he made his way to the door XL-R suddenly sprung into life.

My sensors are picking up location data for the jewels. They are approximately one point two, seven, five metres away, sent XL-R.

'Excuse me, Mr Hernandez, where would you like us to position the hot plates for the buffet food later?' asked one of the staff.

'Umm, errr, umm, ah yes, put them over on the two white occasional tables over there,' he stumbled, pointing to the ornate chair in the corner.

Ruben decided to have a further look for the jewels. There was no apparent sign of them anywhere. They were not part of the vase. *Where are they?* he thought, in confused desperation. Time was running out. He had a brainwave. *Perhaps the room next door could hold a clue,* he thought. He went out into the corridor and knocked on the neighbouring door. It was opened by a tall, elegant gentleman with a little black dog at his heels.

'Good evening, Mr Paige, hello little Bonzo. Please excuse this unexpected interruption. I believe you will be coming to the party in a short while. I wonder if I could possibly ask you the very smallest of favours?'

'Of course, Mr Hernandez. How can I help?'

'Unfortunately, we have a slight electrical problem in the suite next to yours. There is a wall lamp that isn't working properly. I have changed the bulb and checked the wiring as best I can, but I wondered if you had noticed any problems with your lights?'

XL-R, start a scan of the area now, sent Ruben.
Scanning now.

'I don't think we have. Let us check it now.'

369

Mr Paige flicked the switch and the light came on.

'No problem here.'

'Hmmmm, that's a bit of a mystery. Oh well, we'll just have to make do then, won't we? Sorry to have disturbed you. Look forward to seeing you later,' said Ruben.

'Do you by any chance have a jazz band playing at the party? I think I just heard some music,' asked Mr Paige.

'Indeed we do. Why?'

'Oh, nothing really. I used to play a bit of guitar in a little skiffle group years ago and our neighbours would complain about the noise whenever I practiced...great days.'

'Oh you should enjoy yourself tonight. They are a nice group of young men. Well, see you later.'

Ruben went back out into the corridor.

XL-R, what did the scanning show up? he sent.

Scanning results were very similar to before.

Ruben scratched his greasy hair, as he pondered the conundrum and immediately wished he hadn't. He took out his handkerchief and wiped the gel off. *Yuk,* he thought. He decided it would be a good idea to check how the food preparations were progressing, so he jumped in the lift and pushed the "B" button. The lift doors soon opened at the basement and he walked briskly to the kitchens.

They were a bustling hive of noisy activity. This was a busy time, as the restaurants were now filling up with residents and guests wanting their dinner. Porters were rushing about delivering the meals as the chefs barked their orders to the frantic staff. Ruben cornered one of the chefs.

'So Chef Romsley, how is the buffet coming along?'

'It's @#$£¥€ done, now &#&@ off and leave me alone, can't you see I'm busy?'

'A little abrupt and unnecessary don't you think Mr Romsley?' said Ruben and walked over to the awaiting buffet. Everything seemed in order, so he directed the porters to start taking the food trays to Miss Gish's suite. It was getting close to 20:00 and the first guests would be arriving soon.

He went to the lift and back up to the party room to make a final check. He was slightly taken aback when Miss Gish herself opened the door.

'Hello Marcus, I am ready.'

Blimey, wow, she's stunning, he thought.

'Gosh, you look absolutely fabulous, Miss Gish'.

'I hope guests start arriving soon. I am quite excited.'

'So am I in a strange way,' replied Ruben cheekily.

'Oh Marcus.'

The porters filed in with all the food and proceeded to lay it out. The hot plates were already lit and gently warming the delicious dishes. As the clock chimed 20:00 the first group of guests arrived. Miss Gish greeted them all in her over-exuberant, jazz-hands manner and made them all feel welcome. On cue the trio started to play and filled the room with some easy-listening jazz standards. Over the course of the next hour there was a continuous stream of guests arriving and soon the room was comfortably full. The food was being served and the champagne was flowing. Ruben looked around, happy that the party was running smoothly to plan and the trio was the icing on the cake. He was pleased the piano had been tuned too as Johnny's hands darted over the keyboard playing the jazzy melodies everyone seemed to know.

Ruben was the perfect maître d' but soon realised that working had made him quite hungry, so he walked over to the buffet and plated up a selection of nibbles. He gave Johnny and the boys a knowing nod. He stood and gazed out of the window. Over the bay the weather was getting considerably windier and the sea looked rough and choppy.

As the evening wore on Ruben could feel the nerves building. His stomach was starting to feel unsettled too. He decided he would calm his tummy by putting some more food in it. The party was still in full swing as the clock struck 03:00, early on Wednesday morning.

Two hours and twelve minutes remaining, sent XL-R.

Oh blimey, sent a suddenly flustered Ruben.

The trio had had a few breaks but were still going strong. Mr P .Webb gave Ruben the nod. It was time for him to have a play with them. He made his way over to the band and Mr P. Webb handed him a guitar. The guitarist introduced "Mr Hernandez" to the remaining guests, who clapped appreciatively. With a one, two, three, four count-in they launched into a blues jam that seemed to ramble on forever. Mr Paige was enjoying it. Ruben used the opportunity to show off in his own inimitable style and was happy with what he played. He graciously left the trio to the rapturous approval of the well-oiled party-goers and mingled with the remaining guests for a little while. Taking a well earned break Ruben grabbed a little glass of wine, went over to one of the big bay windows and sat looking out over the city. He wondered what was going on back home. He Mind-Linked to Kat.

Hi Kat, it's me. What are you up to? sent Ruben.

Oh, hi Ruben, I am at Dan's place. His folks are out

so we are snuggled up on the couch just coming to the end of a film we're watching, sent Kat.

Which one?

It's "The Ludicrously Fast and The Really Furious Twenty-Four". Usual car crash, bang, wallop, girls in unnecessarily tight shorts type stuff. How's San Francisco? It must be a bit weird seeing it again in a different time. Do you remember any of it?

Yes, bits of it.

Make sure you keep track of the time, bruv.

I will. I will. I tell you what is weird and that is being a man in my late fifties. I know how Dad feels now.

How do you mean?

Ha...I'll explain when I get back.

Are you excited about the party at Frankie's tomorrow night? sent Kat.

Sort of. I am a bit partied out at the moment but I am sure I'll be fine.

Dan is coming too. It should be fun.

Should be. Well I had better go. I can see someone is looking for me. Tell Mum and Dad I am okay. See you soon, love you.

Miss Gish was signaling to Ruben to come over.

'I say Marcus, darling, have we got any more "champers"? I need a top-up.'

'Of course, Miss Gish. Leave it to me.'

'Oh call me "Vilmer" darling. We are old friends, are we not?'

'We are indeed. I will go and organise some more drinks immediately.'

The party had thinned out but the room was still quite full and careering full-speed towards 04:00. Ruben decided to organise some fresh coffee for the friends that were staying at the hotel and instructed a porter to go to the kitchen and organise a drinks trolley. The trio eventually ground to a halt as they finally exhausted their vast repertoire. Suddenly the room took on a mellower, gentle hubbub of hushed conversations as the party wound down.

One hour and twelve minutes remaining, sent XL-R.

■ ■ ■

01:31, SUNDAY 27ᵀᴴ JULY, NOVAK RESIDENCE,
LOS ANGELES, USA
PRESENT DAY

János and Sarah were sat relaxing in the TV lounge. They both had had a hard day and their glasses of wine were helping to ease the tensions. János looked at his watch.

'Blimey it's nearly 01:35. Time for bed I think. Not long now. I hope Ruben has got himself ready. This is a big one and he can't afford to get this wrong.'

'I am sure he has it all under control. I think you under-estimate him sometimes,' said Sarah.

'Maybe, remember how long it took him to learn his Times Tables? Haha ,I suppose we just worry as parents. It doesn't seem to get easier as they get older, does it?'

'I know, it gets harder...One day, when they have children perhaps they'll understand. Talking of which, it seems Kat is quite into Dan.'

'Yes, it certainly seems so. I am not totally convinced by him,' queried János.

'How do you mean?' enquired Sarah.

'Oh, I'm not sure. It's just a feeling. Interestingly, Ruben has some reservations about him too.'

'It's probably some male thing. He seems nice to me,' said Sarah.

'That's probably a female thing.'

Suddenly a news item on the T.V. grabbed János' attention. They both listened.

Reports were coming in from around the globe of cases of people being admitted into hospitals with severe breathing disorders. János had noted these reports were getting more regular as the days passed. He knew why now. The lab tests had narrowed down the possible substance types that could hold the key to figuring out the way to combat the virus. It was crucial for Ruben to get a fresh sample. He wondered how these time-travelling demons would manifest themselves to their son this time, as they invariably would. The Cube was now stronger than before. It had increased functionality, so he would be safer now, hoped János. They had prepared all the details; it was now up to Ruben to make it happen.

'Do you think he will want to go to the party at Frankie's?'

'Yes, I expect so. He loves a good party,' said Sarah.

■　■　■

The coffees were going down well and gradually the last faithful few said their goodnights and retired to their rooms.

Twenty-nine of your Earth minutes remaining, sent XL-R.

Ruben and Miss Gish showed the last two remaining guests out, looked at one another and sat down.

'Well Marcus, darling, that went swimmingly. Thank you so, so much for your efforts. You are a star,' she said, feeling slightly tipsy.

'No Miss Gish, it is your name up in lights in Hollywood. I think you'll find you're the star,' replied Ruben smoothly.

They laughed. She came over and sat on the couch next to him.

'Marcus darling, will you have a nightcap with me? Those flowers you gave me were lovely, you naughty man,' she slurred, and edged a bit closer. *Uh oh, this could be awkward,* thought Ruben.

'Err, yes I am glad you liked them. That vase they are in is lovely too.'

'Well let me tell you a little secret,' she slurred. 'That is a copy of a *very* special vase I have.'

'A copy?' interrupted Ruben.

'Err, yes, hic, as I said, many years ago a lovely gentleman friend I was in love with gave it to me. He told me to keep it safe, as one day in the future a special man would come and ask for it. That special day is today, hence the party, and I realised earlier that you are *the* special man. I can feel it. You are not Marcus are you? hic. You look like him, but you aren't him?'

Ruben was totally flabbergasted by her admission.

'No, Miss Gish you are right, I'm not Marcus,' he paused.

'My real name is Ruben Novak.'

'The gentleman I mentioned earlier was, in fact, my husband. He was Elek Novak. So how are you related to him?' she asked.

'I'm sorry, but really I haven't got time to explain. It's complicated. I am a distant relative, a very distant relative. Forgive me. Please can you get me the vase?' asked Ruben. 'Is it green with six hanging jewels?'

'Yes it is indeed. I will get it for you.'

Twenty of your Earth minutes and counting, sent XL-R.

She quickly got up and went over to the door by the flowers. She moved the blooms onto the nearby coffee table and took the painting down to reveal a wall safe. She spun the dial back and forth and then with a flick of the handle the heavy door swung open. She took out the vase and brought it over to Ruben. He held it near the secreted Cube.

XL-R, scan the vase.

Scanning, collecting data, yes, these are the jewels.

Engage Body-Shield, power level four immediately.

Initialising Body-Shield, sent XL-R.

'Forgive me, Vilmer, but I need to take these jewels.'

'I understand, I think. Elek had a little book, which he also showed me. I don't know where that is. It didn't really make sense to me then, but it somehow does now.'

'I'm glad.'

He carefully unthreaded them, put them in his zipped pocket and placed the vase on the floor. He looked at his watch.

Suddenly the front door exploded into splinters of wood. Johnny stood in the doorway. Clenched in his fist was a large futuristic handgun and behind him stood the other two men from the trio. Mr P. Webster looked particularly menacing now in the half-light. The two accomplices rushed forward and grabbed

Vilmer, pulled her from the couch and dragged her in front of the giant fireplace. She screamed with all her might. One of the henchmen tightened his grip around her neck. She froze in fear, silent, her eyes locked on Ruben. He noticed that in the reflection in the mirror he could see little blue lights flashing in the back of the henchmen's heads. *So that might explain why the Cube doesn't pick up any pure life-sign traces. They must be some kind of biomechanical machines,* he thought.

'So, you know why we're here don't you?' asked Johnny.

'Yes, and you also know I can't give the Cube.'

'I thought you might say that. I suppose I now have to persuade you.'

Two of your Earth minutes and counting, sent XL-R.

Ruben surreptitiously fumbled his fingers over the coded markings on the Cube until he found the blue centre axis jewel, then pressed five blue jewels in an "X" pattern.

XL-R, arm full ballistics capability, sent Ruben.

Ballistics armed.

Johnny walked arrogantly into the room.

'So Ruben, where are the jewel cells? this time.'

He looked at Ruben and noticed the green jeweled vase on the table. He walked over to it and picked it up, and threw the flowers across the room.

'I would guess this is what you came for? By the way, I am loving the new "you". A definite improvement, haha,' laughed Johnny.

Ruben's mind was now racing. *What's my next move?* he thought. The petrified look in Vilmer's eyes told him he had to do something quick.

Thirty of your Earth seconds remaining, sent XL-R.

XL-R, lock on to the three non-human life sign traces, sent Ruben.

Ruben pulled his sleeve back to reveal the Cube.

'Is this what you want?' he asked. 'Well you can have it.'

Ruben pressed the centre blue jewel again as he pointed his arm at Vilmer's two captors.

Targets locked on, sent XL-R.

A dense beam of blue light shot from the Cube and seared into the two men. They crumpled to the floor, then vapourised into a black cloud, and vanished. Vilmer looked around in shocked disbelief and fainted.

Ruben swung his arm round.

05:12,Zero time reached, sent XL-R.

Suddenly there was a massive earth tremor and the whole building shook violently.

Ruben quickly fired again and lost his balance as another tremor hit. The beam scythed across the room hitting the picture by the door reflecting off the glass and hitting Johnny in the chest. He blasted backwards into the corridor wall and crumpled to the ground. Ruben watched and waited. Much to his surprise Johnny stirred; he opened his eyes and got up. *Heck, that's not supposed to happen*, thought Ruben. Before he knew it, Johnny charged at him and head-butted him into the wall, sending the picture crashing to the ground, shattering the glass into razor-sharp fragments. Ruben clasped his hands together and thumped down hard on his back. He groaned. He jabbed his knee up into his face, sending him flailing over the little table into a heap on the couch.

XL-R, what happened? sent Ruben.

It appears the reflected beam has changed its dynamic polarity and so has increased the power capability of the non-human life form.

Oh @$/#, thought Ruben. "C-R-U-N-C-H"... He felt his jaw crack as a fist connected with it. He spun round and crashed into a glass cabinet. There was another massive tremor; ornaments and shelves came crashing down. He stumbled. *Wow, that hurt,* thought Ruben. Before he could get himself together he felt two powerful hands grip his throat and start squeezing. He felt powerless.

XL-R, increase muscle power, level 7, sent Ruben.

He swung his arms upwards under Johnny's arms and broke his grip immediately head-butting him with so much force that he lifted off the ground and flew over the piano, crashed through the door and out onto the balcony into a motionless heap. Ruben ran after him. The wind was now blowing a gale and he looked around to see nearby buildings starting to crumble. Another tremor hit and the tenement building opposite started to crack and move violently. The balcony shook also and Ruben held the rail tightly. As he watched, the building crashed to the ground in a gigantic plume of dust. People were shouting and running into the streets. The roads were starting to move and split. A night tram coming up Mason Street suddenly jumped its rails and began skidding uncontrollably down the hill. Screams were coming from all directions. Ruben couldn't believe his eyes. He scanned the bay area and could see the outline change as more buildings began to fall. Little specks of flames began to show in the distance fanned by the winds whistling up the streets. A perfect storm. Ruben looked at the building he was hanging off and quickly clambered back. He felt a hand clamp around his ankle causing him to stumble. Both men clawed their way back inside. Johnny wrestled himself on top of Ruben, slamming his arm down on his throat, and produced a sharp blade.

'I will have the Cube,' he shouted menacingly.

He thrust the blade down onto Ruben's arm. The Body-Shield repelled the blade as he sawed away maniacally.

XL-R, Time-Freeze, now.

Suddenly there was stillness, silence and calm. Ruben shoved his assailant off him and got up. *Phew, that was close,* he thought. He went over to Vilmer and carefully picked her up, moved her into the bedroom and gently pushed her under the huge metal-framed bed. He quickly got some blankets and covered her.

XL-R, confirm the time-line for Vilmer.

Miss Vilmer Gish died on 8th February, 1941 at the age of eighty-one in Los Angeles, California.

XL-R, confirm time-line for Marcus Hernandez.

Mr Marcus Hernandez died on 18th April 1906, aged forty seven in San Francisco, California.

He rifled through Vilmer's desk and found some of her headed notepaper and a pen. He wrote her a quick note and gently placed it in her hand. She would read it when she awoke. Ruben went back into the lounge area. The twisted body of Johnny was by the door, frozen in time. He knelt down beside the body. From his jacket pocket he produced a small vacuum syringe unit. He located a vein in Johnny's arm and began to withdraw a blood specimen. A few seconds later a "bleep" signified the sample had been extracted successfully. Ruben put the unit in his jacket pocket and paused for a moment. He looked around and went onto the balcony again. He couldn't believe the devastation.

XL-R, disengage Time-Freeze.

The mayhem resumed; buildings continued to crumble. Down below a small shop exploded into flames. Johnny clambered up off the floor and ran at Ruben with his glinting blade. He ploughed into him and they both toppled over the balcony and hurtled to the ground slamming into the pavement in a cloud of dust. Both men stood up and looked at each other. Johnny moved quickly forward brandishing the knife and lunged at Ruben, who expertly dodged him. He spun round and did a high karate kick, which knocked him to the ground again. Ruben moved back just as another tremor violently shook the street. The nearby building began to move violently and started to crack apart, the windows exploding out into the street. Ruben instinctively covered his head as huge shards of glass rained down on them both. He watched as Johnny was sliced to pieces by the falling glass. He slumped to the ground in a bloodied heap then suddenly exploded into a black cloud of dust and was gone. Ruben quickly ran back into the hotel. The foyer was shaking; a huge chandelier broke loose from its rose and smashed to the ground. He dodged it and ran into Marcus' office and closed the door. He reconfigured Solved-Mode-Four. and pressed seven orange jewels in an "H" pattern.

Initiating separation now, sent XL-R.

Suddenly the Cube emitted a glowing light that surrounded Ruben. Slowly the silhouette of two figures began to form in the blue light. The light then vanished leaving Marcus and Ruben in the room. Marcus was in a daze, confused and anxious.

'Are you okay Mr Hernandez? I think we are in the middle of an earthquake,' stated Ruben calmly.

Before he could even answer, Marcus ran from the

office and out into the streets and disappeared in a cloud of rubble and dust.

XL-R, get me out of here. Take me home, sent Ruben.

He pressed the blue, orange and white centre axis jewels.

Initialising teletransportation protocols, sent XL-R.

It was 05:51 and with a blinding blue flash he was gone.

TEN

THE QUEST FOR THE RED "JEWELS OF LOVE"

03:21, SUNDAY, 27TH JULY, NOVAK RESIDENCE, LOS ANGELES, USA

PRESENT DAY

He looked at his bedside clock. It was really early in the morning and the house was silent. The silver moonlight was casting shadows in his room. He was glad to be back home. He quietly opened his bedroom door and tiptoed downstairs to the kitchen and was surprised to see his mum at the sink filling a glass of water.

'Hi Mum.'

'Gosh, hello my darling. How are you, everything okay?'

'Yes I am fine. It was a bit of a close one, again.'

'I am just getting some water. I couldn't relax, thinking about you, I guess,' said Sarah.

'You don't need to worry about me. Did you and Dad have some wine last night by any chance?'

'Yes we did, hence the water.'

'I blame the parents myself,' joked Ruben.

'Oh haha, anyway, I'm back off to bed. We can catch up in the morning. Now go and get some sleep darling.'

'Ok Mum, love you.'

Ruben took the syringe device out of his pocket and slipped it in a sealable bag marked "Sample" and put it in the freezer. He then went back to his room. Out of his zipped pocket he took the six green jewels and laid them in the drawer by his bed. He would sort that in the morning with his dad. He put on his PJs and jumped into bed, pressed the white centre axis jewel three times and disengaged the Cube into Safe-Sleep-Mode to do updates and recharge. He then snuggled under the duvet and in a matter of minutes was fast asleep.

As he slept the Cube started to pulse with a soft blue light. It tracked across the room and stopped on Ruben's forehead. It started to phase in and out gently until it had locked on to his body's pulse frequency. The time portal was now open.

Ruben, this is Overlord Ebucski-Bur. You have done well. The Cube is nearly at one again. When you have completed the final quest you will be ready to take on the ultimate challenge. As you know by now there are Time-Warriors out there trying to take the Cube. You must never let them have it. The history of your world would be changed forever. It would cease to be. You are the chosen one. I am growing weak, our world is dying. The war has ravaged us to the point of extinction. Our resistance has been crushed. A few of us remain. The army we are at war with and are trying to escape from have all but obliterated our world now. They have almost destroyed our communications system, have decrypted our escape plans and will be heading to Earth, your Earth, to finish what we unfortunately started. Will you ever forgive us? Vast intergalactic motherships are almost ready to leave for your planet. Remember, when the Cube is complete it will have extraordinary powers. You will be able to go into the future and save your world. Time-Warriors will follow you to the future. They follow the ripples in time you leave in your wake. Be careful.

The blue light faded. The Cube was still but kept on working on updates and data-harvesting through its time portal.

Ruben shuffled in his bed and turned over. It would soon be a new day. He slept until he was woken by his phone flashing. It was Frankie calling.

'Morning, honey,' she said softly, sensing he wasn't quite awake. 'How was your trip?'

'Oh, yeah, it was okay. I managed to get what I needed,' he said vaguely.

'Are you looking forward to Mum and Dad's party tonight? It is going to be fun. I've missed you.'

'I've missed you too. I'll call you in a while when I am more awake. I need a coffee then I'll be fine. Love you,' he whispered and put the phone down.

It dawned on him he had another night of partying ahead, but at least he would be in his own body. He snoozed for a while, listening to the gentle sounds of the house percolating up to his room. His mum and dad were definitely awake. Sundays were usually a chill-out day. All he had to do was sort out the Cube with Dad, then the rest of the day was a blank canvas. He would go over to Frankie's later.

Having wasted some time on EgoGram, catching up on his friend's exciting fantasy lives, he dived into the shower to "de-gunk" himself. Once dressed, he sauntered downstairs to find Mum and Dad in the garden room reading the papers with the TV rattling away in the corner, unloved.

'Good morning again, Sleepyhead,' said Sarah affectionately.

His hair was indeed all over the place. With a quick flick of his well-trained fingers through his hair he was Ruben again.

'Hiya. Where's Kat?'

'She is at Dan's. I guess we will see her at Frankie's later no doubt,' pondered Sarah.

'Yes, I expect so. I'm going to get some breakfast.'

He disappeared into the kitchen and put a couple of pieces of bread in the toaster and poured out a bowl of "Super Whizzo Choccy Chunky Chimps", drowning them all mercilessly in cold oat milk. Ruben had a sophisticated palate and liked the idea of chocolate chimps jumping around in a chocolate-filled hot tub whilst being attacked by the huge spoon monster. With breakfast finished he took his coffee into the garden room and sat down.

'So Dad, what has been going on here then?' he asked.

'Well I went to work and started the tests with my old pal Doctor Jefferies,' said János.

'Oh the guy with the amazing thumb?'

'Yes. Did you get the blood sample for us?'

'I sure did. It was a bit of a close one, though. It all pretty much went to plan, apart from the fact I couldn't initially find the jewels and I didn't know which nutter was going to have a go. On the plus side, I did get to play a lovely Gibson L1 Archtop guitar though.

'So you did get the jewels, presumably?'

'Yes, the Cube told me they were in the apartment; I just couldn't find them. It turned out they were in a hidden safe. Vilmer gave them to me, no problem. She was sort of expecting me.'

'How do you mean?' asked János.

'Well, her husband gave them to her and told her that one day a special man would visit her and ask for the green jewels. She was expecting me on the very day I teletransported back in time. Her husband was called Elek Novak?'

'Aha yes, he was your great, great grandad and he married Vilmer, but she kept her stage name. She was quite a star in her day and actually worked in Hollywood for a short while. She lived up in the L.A. hills somewhere, many years ago, probably not far from here. Anyway, so you got the jewels. What else?'

'I got a few more bruises, nearly got my arm cut off, got thrown off a fourth floor balcony and just avoided being sliced to ribbons by falling glass. All in a day's work for a young superhero,' he laughed.

Mum looked visibly shocked by his revelations.

'It's okay Mum, the Cube looked after me. I told you, no need to worry.'

'That's all right for you to say. Wait until you're a parent,' said Sarah.

'I'll tell you what was interesting and that was being your age, Dad. Seeing yourself as old was a bit scary. I looked at everybody in the room and I really felt like a young man trapped in an old body,' said Ruben.

'Shall I tell you what is scarier than that? I feel like a young man in an old body now at my age. I remember being your age like it was yesterday. I look at you and see a bit of me staring back. So don't wish your life away,' said János, in full on Dad-Mode.

'I won't, Dad. So, what else has been happening while I have been away?'

Well, the news coverage about the cloud fall-out has been much more frequent, that's for sure. From what I can gather there are reports coming from around the world that more and more cases of breathing difficulties are popping up. These seem to roughly correlate with the higher atmosphere detonations that occurred. The areas near the first detonation have filed reports first, and so on. So we have a little time before L.A. succumbs. I guess we should install these jewels right away.'

'Okay Dad, I'll go and fetch them.'

A few minutes later Ruben returned with the Cube and spread the jewel cells on the table.

'XL-R, prepare to load remaining six green jewel cells,' ordered Ruben.

He then configured the Cube in Solved-Mode-Four and pressed the green centre jewel six times.

'XL-R, prepare to load the six remaining green jewel cells.'

Mum watched with eager anticipation as the Cube began to pulse with green light.

'Configuring system, connection sensors ready, scanning ready. Load green cells,' replied XL-R.

Ruben proceeded to gently install the jewel cells in the green segment. Each click of engagement was verified by a green flash of light darting over the Cube's surface. When the sixth jewel was finally in place the Cube began to pulse with a soft green light that gradually speeded up, then stopped.

'Green cells are engaged, installation completed. Now running system check and configuration protocols. This may take some time,' announced XL-R.

It did. Meanwhile Ruben, his mum and dad talked about the impending party. As usual, Sarah could not decide what she would wear. János thought he would make an effort and wear a suit. Ruben thought he might wear his twenties box jacket suit; he was pretty certain it didn't have any bullet holes in it.

Suddenly the idle banter was interrupted by a bright flash emitted from the Cube.

'System configured. Running at eighty-eight point eight recurring percent functionality,' announced XL-R.

'Now the Cube has been updated I could show you some video footage from Vilmer's party. It's not every day you get to see your great, great grandma in a movie,' said Ruben as he pressed the orange, blue and yellow centre axis jewels.

'XL-R, project video footage from Miss Gish's party.'

'Video footage playing from 20:00,' replied XL-R.

The three-dimensional holographic projection focused in the middle of the room. As Ruben moved around the party his mum and dad got a chance to see the guests. When Vilmer appeared Ruben froze the footage. They sat in silence dumbfounded by what they were witnessing.

'She was quite a lady, by the looks of it,' remarked János.

'Yes, very elegant, and a little tipsy too, I would say,' said Sarah.

Ruben let the video file run on. When he went up to the window the view across the bay was eerily different. The streets were quite clear. As the video ran on, János suddenly saw something he wanted to see again.

'Ruben run it back. Is that you in the mirror? What are you wearing?'

'Uh, a new, sorry, old body. I was the hotel's events manager.'

'You look hilarious,' laughed Sarah.

'That was when I was trying to find the jewels.'

A few scenes later the musicians arrived.

'Oh, this is the bit you were interested in, no doubt,' suggested János.

'Yes, sort of. There, look, there is the Gibson I told you about.'

'Wow, looks lovely. That would be worth a fortune now,' said János.

'Hmm, I wonder?' said Ruben after a short thinking pause.

'XL-R, locate three-dimensional scanning info. Search for the guitar I played,' instructed Ruben and then pressed the two blue jewels in an ":" configuration.

'Guitar scanning information located,' replied XL-R.

'XL-R produce an exact replica.'

Ruben placed the Cube on the floor and pressed five blue jewels in an "L" pattern.

'Replication initiated,' said XL-R.

Slowly the translucent image of the guitar began to form. The image built and gradually became a solid form, until a few minutes later, there lying on the floor was a perfect replica Gibson L1.

Ruben picked it up.

'Here you are, Dad, a little present for you.'

János took hold of it. The pure joy written across his face said it all.

'Thanks, son. How wonderful. Gosh it sounds great,' said a smiling János, as he strummed a big open G chord.

'Don't I get a present?' asked Mum, jokingly.

'Sorry Mum. It only just occurred to me the Cube might be able to do that. Actually I do have something for you.'

He went and whispered in János' ear, he promptly jumped up and went to his office. A few minutes of rummaging later he returned with a little box and gave it to Sarah.

'This is from Ruben. I have been mending it. Take a look.'

Sarah opened it. The jewelled necklace from the plane crash looked resplendent, cradled in its velvet-lined case.

'Ooh, how wonderful,' she cooed.

'That was Ruben's great aunty Jayne's,' explained János. 'It is very, very old. We also have something for Kat, if and when she turns up.'

'There, now everyone has a present. Those guys in the trio were real bad dudes. Johnny, the piano player was ferocious. Anyway, I got the sample from him, so it will be interesting to see what you find out.'

'Yes, I will get on it first thing Monday,' said János.

Ruben skipped through the rest of the video up to the point when Johnny turned bad.

'That was quite a night by the looks of it. Gosh... the destruction was beyond belief,' remarked Sarah. 'So what are you up to this morning, Ruben?'

'Do you know what, I think I might go and snooze for a bit. I still feel whacked.' He got up and wandered back to his room and flopped onto the bed.

'Poor lad, he looks shattered.'

'Hardly surprising, given what he has been through these last few days,' replied Sarah. 'It will be nice for him to take it easy today, then he might feel refreshed for the party later.'

After János and Sarah had cleared up the breakfast things they headed into the garden to do a spot of tidying up and pruning of the bushes by the deck. It also gave János a chance to whiz around on his crazy mower. It really didn't need to be as fast as it was or have a V8 Chevy eco-fuel engine driving it, but hey, he was having fun. Zooby shot off and hid behind the sofa as soon as he fired the thing up. They pootled around in the garden until lunchtime, when Kat finally turned up.

They all sat and had a casual lunch together; soup, warm crusty bread and fresh fruit and yogurt. Kat spent the rest of the afternoon catching up with Ruben and his recent exploits. He managed a bit of guitar playing, reacquainting himself with the finer points of the "thrash metal" genre. Mid-afternoon, Frankie called to see what time he was coming over.

'Hiya, It'll be about four-ish. Is that alright?'

'Yes that's fine. Can't wait to see you. I have a little surprise for you too,' teased Frankie.

'Ooh, sounds interesting. What do you want me to wear to the party?'

'I don't mind. Something smart though, please. "Mwaah",' and she blew him a kiss goodbye.

As time was getting on, he grabbed his sports bag and neatly packed his suit, shoes, a change of clothes, his lucky pants and his overnight wash bag. Happy he had everything, he picked up the Cube and put it in Safe-Mode, pressed the white centre axis jewel and it morphed onto his wrist. He took his denim jacket out of the wardrobe, went downstairs and into the garden. His mum and dad were taking an afternoon tea break and Zooby was lying on his back, paws up, taking in some sunrays.

'Right, I'm off to Frankie's. I'll see you later. Don't forget the present for Mr and Mrs Rosenberg,' said Ruben.

'Oh, thanks for reminding me. What would I do without you? I had completely forgotten about it. Have you got your phone,' said Sarah mockingly.

'Er, um, I'm not sure.'

He checked his pockets and finally found it in his jacket top pocket.

'Touché... OK darling, see you there,' chuckled Sarah, point made.

'I will probably stay at Frankie's tonight.'

'We assumed you would.'

'Rosanna, unlock garden garage door,' instructed Ruben. He went inside and got in his old Mustang. Rosanna opened the main garage door and he reversed it down onto the road, shifted into "Drive" and drove round the corner of Rubio Vista Road, down Pleasantridge Drive and into the city. There wasn't much Sunday traffic, so he made swift progress and pulled up outside Frankie's just after four o'clock.

Frankie was on hand to meet him at the door and enveloped him in a long, lingering kiss.

'I've missed you,' she whispered.

'I've missed you too,' he replied.

She took his hand and led him into the kitchen. Mr and Mrs Rosenberg were out on the deck.

'Hello Mr and Mrs Rosenberg.'

Hello Ruben. I think you can call us Kyle and Robyn now. You're almost family. Anyway, how are you today?' asked Robyn.

'I'm fine, thank you.'

'Would you both like some iced tea?' enquired Kyle.

'That would be lovely, thanks. The garden looks fantastic, by the way, with all the lights and stuff. It looks like you'll have perfect weather too tonight. You have been busy,' said Ruben.

'I am embarrassed to say it, but I haven't really done much; it has been Robyn who has brought it all together. People should be arriving at about eight o'clock,' explained Mr Rosenberg.

Ruben and Frankie spent a little while in the garden chatting with her mum and dad, then made their polite exit and disappeared up to Frankie's room.

'I really like Ruben. He is such a nice young man,' said Robyn.

'He is. He could be your son-in-law soon by the looks of it,' suggested Kyle.

It was nearing 19:30 and Frankie had finally decided what she would wear. Ruben, now feeling shattered again, lay amongst the discarded items tossed aside by Frankie. She stood in front of the mirror and gave herself a last look over. The simple, immaculately fitted, flowery, knee-length summer dress suited her perfectly.

'You look fantastic Frankie, come here.'

She went back over to the bed for another long lingering kiss.

'Come on Ruben, you had better get ready, people will be arriving soon.'

'Okay, yes, I will. I'll be down in a while.'

Frankie left him to get himself together and as he lay amongst her rejected clothes the intoxicating smell of her perfume sent him drifting off into a warm, shallow snooze.

Downstairs, everything was set. The smartly dressed party waiters were all ready. It was showtime and soon cavalcades of expensive vehicles began arriving at the house. Each guest was warmly greeted with a glass of champagne and ushered into the garden. Discreet security guards mingled with the guests. The brightly coloured marquee on the left of the lawn housed more drinks and nibbley food. Groups of elegant tables and chairs were dotted around the garden with crystal vases full of spectacular flowers as a centrepiece for each table. At the end of the garden was a dance floor complete with a DJ who was just sorting his playlist, coloured lights, a big sound system and a huge disco ball to help the nightclub vibe. Strings of party lights festooned the trees and were draped between them all over the garden. Around the fencing soft glowing lights cast shadows of the plants. It wasn't long before the lawn was a hive of buzzing conversation and huddled groups of friends catching up and enjoying the evening. The 80s music selection was soon in full flow and once the drink had dissolved a few inhibitions, the dance floor began to weave its magic spell and draw in the closet disco dancers for a cheeky boogie. To the right, near the summer house, the Rosenbergs sat chatting with the Novaks.

'Thank you for the wonderful painting. How fantastic. It's a real statement piece. Can't wait to put it up, I think it will look great on the first landing area,' said Robyn.

'We're so glad you like it. Art is so subjective,' replied Sarah.

'Indeed, and after you have been married thirty years you have most things, but art isn't one of them,' said Kyle. 'Thanks, it's lovely.'

Their children were the next obvious topic of conversation as Frankie joined them and sat down.

'Gosh, you look gorgeous Frankie. I love your dress, and what a delightful bracelet,' said Sarah.

'Thanks, you look lovely too. I am glad you like the bracelet; I wanted to show it off. I have a little confession to make. You know we went to see Grandma Novak on Friday, well, she told me she had a special present for me so we went into her apartment and she got the bracelet and gave it to me, there and then. She told me it was a family treasure so I said I couldn't accept it, but she insisted. So here it is. I love it. I wish she could have come this evening.'

'Yes, she probably would have really enjoyed herself. I did try to persuade her, but she just said she would ruin our evening,' explained Sarah.

'It can be difficult sometimes with parties. We ummed and ahhed about whether we should have young children at the party or not and decided against it as out garden isn't particularly child-friendly now. Also, we wanted our friends to enjoy the evening with us on this occasion without having to keep an eye on their children. Most of them understood our reasoning just this once. Our children are grown up now. I am glad Frankie is here. I wish...' Robyn was interrupted.

'...Josh was here, by any chance?'

Robyn spun round to see her son knelt down by her chair. He threw his arms around her neck and planted a big kiss on her cheek.

'Josh, what are you doing here? I thought you were in Dubai.'

'Well I was and now I'm here to celebrate your and Dad's special anniversary,' explained Josh.

Frankie and her dad started laughing.

'You knew about this, didn't you? How long have you known? You rotters,' chuckled Robyn.

'So, Mum, it was a little touch-and-go that I would be able to make it, but here I am,' said Josh.

They had another cuddle and then Josh got up and went to find himself a drink.

'What a lovely surprise having my Josh back home – for a while, I hope. I see Kat is with her new man. How is that going?' asked Robyn.

'They seem to be getting on very well. Dan is very nice, very polite and all that, but he can be a bit intense sometimes,' said Sarah.

Elsewhere the party atmosphere was in full swing. The dance floor was slowly filling up.

■ ■ ■

I have picked up some non-human thermal heat profiles.

in the immediate vicinity. My sensors tell me there are sixteen different life thermal profiles nearby. They match the similar traces I have already recorded, sent XL-R.

It took a moment for XL-R's announcement to actually penetrate Ruben's sleepy brain and for him to realise its major significance. He shot up from the bed.

XL-R, where are these life forms? sent Ruben.

They are within one hundred metres of my current position. I am experiencing some issues with my scanning sensors. There is a high frequency signal shadowing my scanning sensors. It is being corrupted by phase reversal data. I will continue to run diagnostics to alleviate the fault, sent XL-R.

Oh $&@! That means they are here. Don't they ever give up? he thought. He jumped off the bed and put on his trainers. He quickly configured the Cube into Solved-Mode-Five and pressed five blue jewels in an "X" pattern.

XL-R, engage Body-Shield and ballistics on power level ten.

Systems engaged. My sensors are picking up other conflicting impulses. There appears to be a ring of low power devices around us, and in close range. My sensors are struggling to get exact data. At this level power consumption will be considerable. I suggest power level of seven so I can continue diagnostics. I will engage.

With the Cube in Safe-Mode on his wrist he went over to the window. He could only see a part of the garden, so went out on to the landing to see if he could get a fuller view. He found a better vantage point. Everything in the garden looked normal, but he thought Johnny was normal until he saw the tiny blue lights flashing in the back of his skull. Where were these Time-Warriors hiding? Who were they?

He started to panic. The full enormity of the situation was just becoming clear. *All my friends and family are here,* he thought. He stood and looked out over the garden, his mind racing through possible permutations and none of them were good. He could feel his palms getting sweaty and suddenly catching sight of Frankie made his heart jump.

Outside in the garden the relentless disco music stopped and the DJ handed the microphone over to Mrs Rosenberg, who stood holding her husband's hand. Frankie and Josh joined them. Frankie was looking around trying to spot Ruben; she wanted to hold *his* hand.

'Good evening to you all. We are so happy that all our dear family and friends could join us here tonight for our little party to celebrate our thirtieth wedding anniversary. I won't bore you all with a long speech, I'll leave that to Kyle, haha... but we just wanted to tell you all how special you are to us and how we cherish your friendship and love. We are truly blessed to have you in our lives.'

'No long speech from me, Robyn has said it all perfectly, but I did just want to wish you all a lovely evening and thanks again for making this a special day for us.'

Josh then took the microphone.

'Frankie and I want to tell our Mum and Dad how much we love them and thank them for being the greatest parents in the world. Please raise your glasses to "Robyn and Kyle", our mum and dad and your friends,' he announced.

Applause, whistles and cheers rang out across the garden and into the evening sky as the Rosenbergs took a tongue-in– cheek bow.

'Now I'll hand you back to DJ Sam-U-L,' announced Josh.

The speakers came alive as the disco lights began to flash to the beat. XL-R sprung into life again.

I am detecting the presence of the red jewel cells. They are very close. I will continue to scan.

It was now obvious to Ruben that the final set of cells was somewhere nearby, at the party. It all suddenly made sense. He was at the party, the Cube was with him, the jewels and, no doubt, a bunch of unsavoury Time-Warriors he would have to dispatch, were at the party too. However, he couldn't yet work out where the henchmen were. Maybe they would reveal themselves. He just didn't know and it made him nervous.

He looked out onto the garden, feverishly searching for clues that might give him a warning as to how the evening was going to play out, but he couldn't see anything untoward.

Suddenly there was a loud gunshot. The music stopped and Ruben looked over to the dance floor to see Dan wielding a huge hi-tech handgun and holding the microphone. *I knew there was something odd about him, not boyfriend material,* thought Ruben. The DJ lay on the floor, a motionless heap with a trickle of blood snaking down the side of his head. People started screaming as a ring of bright red beams from the ground lights began encircling the whole garden in a glowing wall of light, arching over the house and completely sealing it in a red glow. There was a loud clattering of trays and glasses as the waiters all produced handguns and aimed them on the startled guests. They fell silent with terror.

'Okay people, listen up. You were gathered here for one reason, but I am here for another. The party is over, the fun stops now,' announced Dan menacingly.

The security guards broke cover too and pulled out their weapons, immediately training them on the armed waiters. Before they could fire, a rapid volley of shots echoed out across the garden as the guards fell like dominoes. The garden was silent again.

'That's better. Now I have got your attention. Don't any of you think of playing the hero. You will die,' threatened Dan.

Kat looked on in horror as she watched her boyfriend take fearsome control of the situation. The red beams of the force field pulsed with a low, malevolent rumble in the background.

I am experiencing considerable disruption to my operating system, sent XL-R.

Great! thought Ruben. He wasn't quite sure what to do. He hadn't had time to prepare for this encounter. His whole family were right in the thick of it and he knew there had been something about Dan that he wasn't sure of. Now he knew what it was: he was a murdering time-travelling psychopath. He also knew what he was after.

'So, ladies and gentleman, this is where it gets interesting. I have come here for one reason and that is to take back something that is rightfully mine.'

'Oh good grief, I know where this is heading. I had a horrible feeling this day might come – and where is Ruben?' János whispered to Sarah. Dan continued with his maniacal rant.

'Yes, János, you are correct. You thought this day would come and it has. What the rest of you don't know is why it has come. Well, let me explain. Many hundreds of years ago my family was split in two. Twin brothers were made to turn against each other by their father, who favoured one over the other. One brother was given a kingdom and immense powers and riches, the other was banished to the wilderness to struggle in poverty.'

'Hmm, not exactly accurate. Time seems to have distorted the truth a little,' whispered János again, still wondering where Ruben was.

'Those two brothers began their own bloodlines. The two bloodlines are here tonight,' continued Dan.

'Here it comes,' whispered János.

'The rich powerful bloodline ends with the Novak family sitting over there, and one person in particular – Ruben,' explained Dan.

He paused.

'The not-so-rich-and-powerful bloodline is where I come from. I am here to change all that and rewrite history. I need to see Ruben here, now, or I will exact my revenge and the world will come to know my name,' threatened Dan.

'That is if there is a world left after all this,' whispered János to Sarah. Suddenly the sound of guns erupted from the house as some security guards took deadly aim and opened fire. The guests dived for cover as the Time-Warriors returned their fire. Bullets whistle over their heads, but the Warriors' firepower was too accurate and within minutes the battle was over. The motionless bodies littered the decking. The emotional cost of witnessing such merciless slaughter was too much for some; they buried themselves in the arms of their partners unable to understand the horror being played out in front of them.

Hi Kat. It's me, I am here. Don't worry, I am watching what is going on from up near Frankie's room. I am trying to figure out what to do. Carefully let Dad know I am here. Dan hasn't turned out to be the best boyfriend choice you made? he sent.

I know, I feel so guilty, sent Kat. This is my fault.

It isn't, sis, don't worry.

The garden stayed in hushed silence as they waited for Dan's next move. He spoke.

'So what I want now is for Ruben to show himself to me or things could get messy. Ruben, WHERE ARE YOU?' he shouted into the microphone. 'Oh yes, I forgot to say, the drinks you have all been sipping on so elegantly this evening have had a few extra substances added which will mean in about thirty minutes you will all be, literally under the table, DEAD, so, Ruben, I suggest you get here NOW.'

The guests' state of panic suddenly notched up a few levels as the terrifying implications of his words sunk in. Dan clicked his fingers and pointed to the house. Immediately six of his Time-Warriors ran into the building. Inside, Ruben quickly configured the Cube to Solved-Mode-Five and pressed the four yellow corner jewels.

XL-R, engage C-Thru-Mode, sent Ruben.

My system is compromised, it is being jammed and C-Thru-Mode is currently unstable. Engaged.

Ruben flickered into invisibility just as he saw the men run in through the garden doors brandishing their weapons. They quickly fanned out into the rooms looking for him and a few minutes later they regrouped, went up the stairs to the next level and again started to search the rooms.

XL-R, lock on to the six non-human thermal heat profiles. Engage ballistics.

Ruben edged out on to the landing just as the six men began coming up the stairs. He took aim and fired. The first two fell as the blue beam blasted through them. Suddenly Ruben came into view. They shot at him. With lightning reflexes he dodged the bullets and rolled across the landing into a bedroom doorway. The Time-Warriors blasted again at the flickering image. Shards of plaster and brick exploded from the walls as bullets ricocheted around him. Ruben took aim and picked off another Warrior, who exploded into a black cloud, then vaporised. He flashed into invisibility again and took aim and two beams blasted into the Time-Warriors, who vaporised.

XL-R, change ballistics to Stun-Mode, level 4.

Level 4 engaged.

Ruben took aim and pressed the centre axis blue jewel. The beam hit its mark. The sixth Warrior slumped into a heap on the stairs. Quickly he ran down and dragged the body up into a bedroom.

Meanwhile, outside in the garden the guests were silent. The gunfire had scared them, they were paralysed with fear and the clock was ticking.

'Ah, here he is,' announced Dan. 'What kept you?'

Ruben appeared on the deck accompanied by a Time-Warrior holding a gun to his head. The guests gasped in disbelief. Slowly he was brought out into the garden and led over to Dan.

'Hello, old friend. It's taken a while but here we are, finally.'

'Huh, you're no friend of mine,' sneered Ruben.

'You know why I am here?'

'To try the canapés?' Ruben replied mockingly.

'Very funny. See if you find this amusing.'

He clicked his fingers and pointed to the Rosenbergs' table. Immediately one of his Warriors accomplices walked over and roughly grabbed Frankie. Kyle stood up and tried to fend him off. A swift swipe across the face sent him sprawling across the grass. He got up. The Warrior swung his gun round at him. Frankie was then delivered to Dan. Ruben tried to lunge at Dan, but the gun at his head made him withdraw and wait.

'So, Ruben, we are nearly at the end of this very long road we have been travelling. Here at last is the journey's end. Show me the Cube,' commanded Dan.

Ruben rolled back his sleeve to reveal it in all its glory.

'Arh, there it is. So all we have to do is complete it.'

He grabbed Frankie's wrist.

'Here is the final part of the puzzle. The red jewels we need are hidden in this delightful bracelet on your delightful girlfriend's wrist.'

Frankie winced as Dan undid the clasp and the bracelet fell into his hand.

'So, Ruben, now all you need to do is fit them to the Cube for me.'

'Why should I?' he taunted.

Dan lifted his gun to Frankie's head. She started to whimper.

'That's why.'

'Okay, okay, I get the picture.'

Ruben morphed the Cube from his wrist and placed it on the table. He then took Frankie's bracelet and put it on the table next to it.

'I need a small penknife or a screwdriver,' requested Ruben.

'Okay, no funny stuff or this gun might just go off. Mr Rosenberg, perhaps you can help?'

Kyle went into the house and returned with a small multi-tool. Using a screwdriver blade he proceeded to liberate the six jewels from their mounts.

XL-R, prepare to load six remaining red jewel cells, sent Ruben.

Configuring system, connection sensors ready, scanning ready. Load red cells, sent XL_R.

Ruben then proceeded to gently push the six jewel cells into the red segment. Each click of engagement was verified by a flash of light darting over the Cube's surface. When the sixth jewel was in place the Cube began to pulse with a soft red light, gradually getting faster and faster, then stopped.

'Red cells engaged,' announced XL-R

One of the jewels is not functioning properly, system running at ninety-eight point one, four percent, sent XL-R.

'So what happens now?' asked Dan.

'Wait and see,' replied Ruben, wondering what the problem was.

XL-R, configure new system settings, sent Ruben.

They waited whilst the Cube flashed with all different colours flickering over its surface. It then stopped and glowed with a soft green hue. The guests were transfixed by the unfolding situation.

I am ready, however, the systems are not running at full capability, all jewel cells are fully engaged, sent XL-R.

Okay, wait for the signal, sent Ruben.

'Right, now you have to give it to me, so reprogram it, or tell it, whatever it takes to make it mine. Do it now or Frankie won't see her next birthday,' said Dan menacingly.

'Okay, I get it, I get it.' replied a shaky Ruben.

XL-R, prepare to configure temporary ghost settings, sent Ruben.

'Cube, prepare to alter settings for new host. When I place you on your new master's arm, reconfigure all settings,' ordered Ruben.

He picked up the Cube and held it next to Dan's arm. He spun the segments around, then held down the two centre axis white and green jewels. The guests watched in disbelief as it morphed on to Dan's wrist.

'Right, in a moment the Cube will contact you telepathically and then it will start to configure itself to lock into your full body brain functions. This will take a few minutes then it will be yours,' explained Ruben.

Dan waited for contact.

'Great, finally it will be mine. Which means it doesn't need you and I don't want you spoiling my plans,' mocked Dan.

Without a moment's hesitation, he lifted his gun and shot Ruben. His body crumpled to the floor.

Frankie screamed with all her might. It cut the night in two and the horrified guest became restless and agitated. The henchmen fired a few shots into the sky to focus their attention a bit more. At the Novak table János was holding Kat and Sarah in his arms trying to be strong and failing miserably.

'Well, that's him out of the way. Let's see what this thing can do,' smirked Dan.

XL-R, Time-Freeze, one hundred meter radius from here.

The whole garden immediately became completely and utterly motionless. The Time-Warrior next to Ruben's lifeless body then went over to Dan and manipulated the Cube's segments, pressed the centre axis white and green jewels twice this time and the Cube morphed into his hand. He bent down and placed the orange segment over Ruben's head wound area and pressed firmly down on the skin. A few moments later the Time-Warrior pressed the red, yellow and white centre axis jewels and an orange beam formed a cocoon over his body, which filled with an amber mist. Slowly the wound in Ruben's head started to heal as an orange beam tracked over the surface. The blood began to fade as the repair took place. A few minutes later, it was as if nothing had happened and the orange cocoon dissolved into the warm night air.

The Warrior then manipulated the Cube's segments into Solved-Mode-Six and pressed the white centre axis jewel upon which it morphed back on to the body of Ruben. He pressed the seven orange jewels in an "H" pattern, placed his hand on Ruben's forehead and closed his eyes.

XL-R, engage separation, sent Ruben.

Separation engaged, sent XL-R.

Suddenly the Warrior's arm began to twitch as the vast amount of power was funneled back out through him. His body began to shake more violently. Ruben's body moved, he arched his back and let out a deafening scream that echoed around the stillness of the garden. His body started to twitch and shake uncontrollably as the power coursed back into his body. A few minutes later the Warrior fell to the ground, drained of life. Ruben shook his head a few times and stood up.

XL-R, separation is complete, thanks, sent Ruben.

My pleasure, master, sent XL-R.

XL-R, have you updated your sense of humour now?

I believe that is a distinct possibility.

Right, well, we have things to do. Let us sort this mess out first, sent Ruben.

XL-R, rewind the time fragment to the point where the bullet from Dan's gun is about ten centimeters from where my body was standing and freeze it there. Suddenly the time fragment began to slowly scroll backwards to the appropriate point.

XL-R, this is spooky, sent Ruben.

He went over to Dan and awkwardly shuffled his motionless body over to stand in front of the bullet he fired that was hanging in the air. He then had a look at the Time-Warrior's hand gun.

XL-R, scan this weapon. Can we modify or alter it to obliterate all of Dan's men in one go?

Scanning. They have a biomechanical feedback circuit that is directly linked to Dan's core brain functions. If I can tap into their processing networks and break their deep level encryption I should be able to make them do whatever we want. This may take me a few minutes, sent XL-R.

It did.

I have broken the deep level encryption, so now can access the core brain functions. Also, all of the Time-Warriors are linked to a central command system, which is Dan. I can set up an automatic termination response in the system so that when Dan ceases to be, so will the rest of them. Shall I proceed?

Yes, proceed. Let's get this over with. On my word.

Ruben then tenderly picked up Frankie and moved her back over to the Rosenbergs' table.

Okay, XL-R, run time fragment.

There was a loud "BANG" and Dan fell to the ground. Suddenly he exploded into a black cloud. One by one, each Warrior detonated then vapourised too. The guests watched in stunned amazement as all the Time-Warriors disappeared before their very eyes and the force field around the garden vanished.

XL-R, prepare to Mind-Wipe all human time-shifted memory storage and event threads from this position on the time-line.

Ruben reconfigured the Cube into Solved-Mode-Six and then pressed the five white jewels in the shape of an "L". An intense yellow beam radiated out across the garden.

All time-shifted memory storage threads erased, sent XL-R.

As the last particles of the black clouds disappeared the guests resumed the party atmosphere totally oblivious to what had just occurred. Frankie ran into Ruben's arms.

'Where have you been? I was about to come and get you. You missed Mum and Dad's speech,' said Frankie.

'No, I saw it from the landing window.'

'Let's go and have a dance. Hold on, where's the DJ?' asked a confused Frankie.

'Oh, I think he had to leave urgently. Said something about him becoming a father or something like that. Anyway I'll do it if you like, you can help me.' Ruben took the microphone.

'Our DJ seems to have vanished into thin air so I hope you don't mind if I fill in for him. Let's get some groovy eighties stuff back on,' announced DJ Ruben.

The mood lightened and was greeted with cheers of approval. He took to the decks like a duck to water and Frankie was impressed.

'Where did you learn to DJ like that?' asked Frankie.

'A friend of mine showed me how to do it,' he lied.

The dance floor began to fill again and the evening carried on as if nothing had happened. Ruben had a quick scan of the DJs song choice on his laptop, set up a new playlist, then hit the dance floor. To say Ruben couldn't dance was an understatement, but he loved trying and Frankie thought he looked cute as he blundered around. After a few high-energy disco tracks he thought he would take a breather and sat down with his mum and dad.

'Nice moves. You sure know how to throw the shapes on the dance floor, my boy,' quipped János.

'Thanks.'

'Well what just happened, or should I say, didn't happen? I can't seem to remember much after the speeches,' said János.

'No, me neither,' agreed Sarah.

'What happened to Dan? I can't find him anywhere,' asked Kat.

'Hmm, let me try to explain. Well, Kat I am sorry to say this, but Dan was not who or what you thought he was. His real full name, it appears, was Danálmos, cutting a very long story short, he has history with our family and when the time is right I will explain. You know I have been quite busy the last few days trying to rebuild the Cube, well, I think he was behind all the troubles I have had along the way. I haven't figured it all out yet and now is not the time to go through it.'

'But hold on a minute. Dan has been with me at various times when you have been away,' Kat pointed out.

'Hmmm, I guess it is possible that he may have been able to hack our telepathic links in some way. Who knows?' pondered Ruben.

'Anyway, when we are home I will tell you all more about it. Suffice to say, I am not sure if we'll see him again. Sorry,' continued Ruben. He leant over and gave Kat a brotherly hug. Sarah looked concerned.

'It's alright Mum, we'll talk about it later. Now I want to do some more dancing,' reassured Ruben.

The party went on through the evening with the main topic of conversation being about what did or didn't happen at the party. As it approached midnight the guests began to leave and say their goodbyes until it was just the Novaks and the Rosenbergs left sitting round a table cosily chatting. It had almost been a perfect evening apart from the brief interruption by a homicidal, time-travelling, maniac, hell bent on revenge. Luckily no one would remember that part.

'What a lovely evening. I hope you enjoyed yourselves too,' said János.

'Oh we did, we did. Robyn and I are very lucky. I think I must have drunk a bit too much, there seems to be a whole part of the evening that I don't really remember. Weird. Oh well. Thanks again for the lovely picture, I can't wait to put it up.'

'What Kyle won't tell you is that he always puts the hook in the wrong place and has to re-measure it and drill it again, usually two or three times,' chuckled Robyn.

'Thanks, darling,' said Kyle.

'Haha, my dear old dad always said, measure twice, cut once,' added János.

'Anyway,' interjected Ruben, trying to pull the attention back his way. 'Frankie and I have a little announcement of our own to make, and this seems like a good time to do it, as we don't get together as families that often.'

'Oh my word, how exciting,' said Robyn.

Ruben took hold of Frankie's hand.

'Mr and Mrs Rosenberg, I ask for your blessing to get engaged to your beautiful daughter. I want to spend the rest of my life with her. I know we are still young, but we want to get married in the next couple of years. Right now is not the best time for us, but we want to show our commitment to one another.

Frankie nuzzled into Ruben's neck.

'Gosh, how fabulous. Yes of course, we welcome you into our family with open arms,' said Robyn as Kyle nodded.

'Well, my dear son. You are growing up so quickly. Your mum, Kat and I are so happy for you both and we welcome Frankie into the Novak family with all our love too,' continued Sarah. János nodded in agreement.

'Champagne I think is in order,' announced Kyle and he jumped up and ran into the kitchen to find a suitable bottle. Armed with a tray of eight charged glasses he returned to the buzzing table, handed everyone a glass and made a toast.

'To Frankie and Ruben, and the joining of the Novaks and the Rosenbergs. Cheers.'

'Cheers,' rang out into the still night air.

'Frankie and Ruben looked at each other. Their smiles said it all. The two families spent the next hour

413

cementing their union until it was time for the Novaks to leave, minus Ruben.

János knew Monday was important for him to press on with his research.

As the Novaks headed for home the Rosenbergs headed for the drinks cabinet. They didn't want their evening to end just yet. More champagne flowed as did the rum and cokes. It finally got to just after one o'clock and Frankie decided it was time for bed, so grabbed Ruben's hand, kissed her mum, dad and Josh goodnight and went upstairs with him.

They lay in each other's arms and gradually drifted off to sleep as XL-R began to glow and flicker.

I will be doing a system update whilst you sleep and will transfer new control data by subconscious Mind-Link. Thank you and goodnight, sent XL-R.

■　■　■

Ruben cursed his phone for waking him up early. Frankie cursed Ruben for not turning his phone off. They soon snuggled into each other's arm and had a little romantic snooze. They could hear the noises of the house coming to life as a new work day got underway. Reluctantly, Ruben told Frankie he would have to go, as he had a busy day ahead. He was going to the lab with Dad.

That's okay, I can spend some time with Josh as I haven't seen him for a couple of months. It will be nice to spend some time with him before he goes back to Dubai.

'Come on, let's go down and get some breakfast, I expect Mum and Dad are there. Mum has an important board meeting today, so she will be raring to go. Dad probably less so, judging by how many glasses of champagne he had. He is so funny when has had a few,' said Frankie.

In the kitchen Mum and Dad *were* there, but engrossed in a TV news item, eating toast on autopilot. Sensing it would not be a good time for idle chat Frankie poured themselves some coffee and sat down.

'Morning, you two. We are just watching this rather depressing news item. It's nearly over,' said Robyn.

By the time they had buttered their toast, normal breakfast business was resumed.

'Sorry about that. It was an article about the growing numbers of people being affected by this so-called pollution smog we had. The thing is, it appears that people are starting to die from it, by the looks of it. The boffins now think it is some kind of cosmic dust that has penetrated through the ozone layer at the North and South Poles. Apparently, the layer has holes there because of the cold. Sounds like nonsense to me. What does your dad think Ruben?' asked Kyle.

'Huh, he thinks that is not what is happening. He has some other bonkers theory he is investigating.'

'These cases of lung problems are very worrying. The reports suggest they are spreading across the world. What lies ahead for us all? I wish I had a crystal ball,' said Kyle.

'Yes, that would be interesting. It might be a bit scary too. Do we really want to know what the future holds?' replied Ruben, the sound of his own words echoing around inside his head.

Suddenly the glowing euphoria from last night vanished. He felt a sense of urgency welling up inside. He panicked.

'That reminds me. I have to see Dad in the lab this morning so I had better get a move on.'

As soon as breakfast was finished Frankie and Ruben went upstairs again.

'You were a bit odd at breakfast this morning. It seemed like you suddenly rushed to finish and went silent. What's wrong? Is it me? Don't you want to get engaged or something?' asked Frankie tentatively.

'No it's not that. I am really happy we are engaged. As I said, I want to spend the rest of my life with you. I want to be with you forever. I want to die in your arms.'

A small tear trickled from his eye.

'Blimey, wow, that's a bit deep. What's suddenly brought all this on, my darling?' asked Frankie.

She went over to give him a cuddle and sat on the bed with him and locked her arms around him, and kissed him on the cheek. She could taste the salt of his tears. She had never seen him like this before and she was worried, very worried.

'What is it, Ruben? What is troubling you? Talk to me,' she pleaded.

Ruben's sobbing came deep from within his very soul. It was a momentary release from the stress of knowing what possibly lay ahead. He had so much buzzing around inside his head. The pain was too much and finally it found a little way out through his tears. He dried his eyes and slowly calmed down.

Frankie held him tight and looked into his red, puffy eyes.

'So what's troubling you? You were fine until a little while ago.'

Ruben slowly regained a little composure. He sighed, then paused for a moment.

'It's a long story, but I think I have to tell you.'

ELEVEN

TIME IS RUNNING OUT

PRESENT DAY

'I hope Ruben hasn't forgotten I need him at the lab today. I have rung his mobile a few times, but it clicks straight to answerphone. I expect he had a late night too and not much sleep either,' said János.

'Shall I see if I can get through to him?' asked Kat.

'Yes, why not?'

A few minutes later Kat gave up too.

'He's not allowing me to Mind-Link him for some reason.'

'Okay, not to worry. I will try him from the car on the way to work.'

János kissed Sarah and Kat goodbye and went out to his truck. He climbed in the cab.

'Rosanna, tell me a joke,' requested János.

'Two fish in a tank... one says to the other, "How do you drive this thing?"'

'Hmmm... Rosanna, put on LA Talk Radio,' instructed János.

'Talk Radio is playing for you now.'

The assembled studio guests were discussing the growing epidemic spreading across the globe. János listened with interest as he navigated his way to work. He was now acutely aware that time was definitely not on his side. The experiments were very complex and very slow. Sifting through the results was like trying to find a needle in a haystack. They had more tests to run on the Time-Warrior body fluid sample Ruben had procured, but it was throwing up some strange results, which they were finding hard to interpret. That in itself was giving them a clue as to where to concentrate their tests, but nothing was happening quickly and János and Dr Jefferies were finding it intensely frustrating.

He arrived at the S.P.A.C.E. main gate and security check done, drove into his parking place by the lab. Much to his surprise he noticed Ruben's old Mustang already parked. He went to the lab and, sure enough, his son was sat at his dad's desk nonchalantly spinning a pen on his fingers. As Dad walked in he jumped up and gave him a hug.

'Hi Ruben, how are you this morning?'

'Oh, okay, I guess.'

'You don't sound very sure.'

'No, I have had a bit of a strange morning.'

'How do you mean?'

'Well, I was sat with Mr and Mrs Rosenberg and

we were talking about the health epidemic that is spreading across the world and I think I had a bit of a breakdown. I just...' He paused. 'I just couldn't handle the emotion of it all.'

Again, little tears began to well up in his eyes.

'What if I fail, Dad? What if I...?'

'Come here,' said János.

He could feel Dad's strong arms envelop him, the force of his dad's love instantly made him feel better..

'You are our very special boy. You have been given a tremendous gift and you will not fail. I will be with you every step of the way. I will always be with you. Don't worry,' reassured János.

'But... what if... if I?'

'We will get through this together. Now, come on, dry your eyes. Dr Jefferies will be here shortly and we have work to do. So the Cube is fully functional now, I assume?' asked János.

'Yes, well, sort of. I was running a bit late at Frankie's so I thought I would give it a try this morning. I think you'll find that you have forgotten your house keys.'

'What!'

He checked his pockets just as his mobile phone rang.

'Hello darling, what's up? Oh, I left them by the door... Oh, it's okay, Ruben's here. I think he has been here for a while. I'll explain later. Love you,' said János.

'I got here by using the Cube. As you were a bit late I decided to have a fiddle with it, so I went into the future a little to see what would happen. When you came into the lab and put your car keys in your jacket pocket you realised that you had forgotten your house keys. You then phoned Mum who told you that you had left them by the door. I then returned to the present but a couple of minutes earlier to watch it play out again,' explained Ruben.

'Oh, I see, so that's how you knew. So what *actually* happened at the party that none of us can now remember?' asked János.

'Oh yes, of course, I forgot. I did a Mind-Wipe on you all. Wait, I will show you.'

He pressed the white centre axis jewel twice and the Cube morphed onto his hand. He then pressed the centre axis orange, blue and yellow jewels.

'XL-R, access the video file of the Mind-Wipe section from last night's party,' instructed Ruben.

'Accessing file now.'

He put the Cube on the table as a three-dimensional holographic projection began playing in the lab. János quickly turned the security cameras off.

'Oops, we don't want people seeing this, do we?' said János.

They both watched the playback. After the video file had finished they looked at one another.

'Blimey, that was smart thinking, changing places with one of the Time-Warriors. I wouldn't have thought of that,' admitted János.

'It was the only way I could think of to get close to our "friend" Danálmos and be at the centre of the action.'

'I have been thinking about what happened at the party on the way over. The tests we are doing are going really slowly and we are not making much progress. There is just so much to do. I think we will get there, but I just don't know how long it is going to take. There is also the chance we won't find the answer.

We know that people are going to start dying from this and it has already started. We need some pointers to get this solved quickly. That is where the Cube comes in. If you could go into the future and get the answers we need, we could save a lot of people from dying.'

'Yes I agree, but how do we do it?' asked Ruben.

'My feeling is that we are the most likely people to find a solution as I think we are probably the only ones that have a sample of the original cloud, plus we have the blood sample you got from one of the Time-Warriors. No one else will have that. It must give us a head start to finding the answer.'

'True. However, what if we got a sample from the original alien being that came to this planet as well? If you remember, their plan was to eradicate all human life on Earth and then repopulate it, so that suggests that this cloud particle stuff would not affect them. If we could analyse that sample, any possible differences almost certainly would give us the answer we need, would it not?' asked Ruben.

'Hmm, that's a good point. Could we do that?'

'I don't see why not. Also, we may be able to find out what actually killed the alien. That could be very useful too. Imagine if they actually make it to our planet,' continued Ruben.

'We don't want any more of those "pesky" aliens turning up on our doorsteps again, do we?' stated János.

'Too blimmin' right.'

'So, if you can go back in time, get the samples and return to the present, we can root it in the present and start a new timeline event from that point. Then, you should be able to follow that timeline into the future and see what happens. We will hopefully solve the problem like you *solved* the Cube. If we do, you should be able to bring the answers back, which we can add to the present event timeline so compressing our research into almost no time at all. I am hoping that if you go into the future this timeline will not be embedded in our future, as it hasn't yet existed in the present time dimension, hence the future is flexible, as we know. And, I wish there was another word for timeline! We need to invent one. I'll think on it.'

'Yes, exactly what I was about to say,' said Ruben, being somewhat economical with the truth.

'And remember, we can't alter any events in the past as it disrupts the timeline,' continued János.

'Right, so we need to check what data the Cube can access about that event.'

'XL-R, what data do you have about the alien that brought you to Earth?' asked Ruben.

'Searching data banks now. I have exact event times and position coordinates,' replied XL-R.

'That's a start. We need to get a body fluid sample from the alien before it absorbed into the human host. Is that possible?'

'Due to the previous damage sustained and certain file corruption, I cannot synthesize the fluid.'

'XL-R, can we get a new specimen?'

'Yes, it will be possible. Now I have almost full functionality I will be able to travel much further back in time. I will search for an event on the timeline we can utilise for that purpose. Calculating.'

'Perfect. XL-R, could we get a fluid specimen from the alien after absorption too?'

'Yes, that will also be possible. I will search for an event on the timeline that satisfies both objectives. Calculating.'

'Great, if we get both samples we should be able to find the differences between them and discover what made the alien resistive to the cloud, because they created it, and, what actually killed the alien after absorption,' reasoned János.

'I suggest you take a blood sample from the alien shortly before death also. This will more accurately tell you what it died of,' announced XL-R.

'Yes that's a good idea XL-R,' said Ruben.

'There we are then. That's what you have to do. Two quick trips back in time to get the fluids. We have an alien absorption specimen already, so we need the near-death one and the pure alien fluid. Do you feel up to going now, today?' asked János.

'Heck, I hadn't really given this bit much thought yet. I don't see why not. I have the Cube, which is functioning well. What could go wrong? We have all the data we need. I have had a shower. I just need a couple of vacuum syringes and a cup of coffee.'

'Yes my lordship, your wish is my command.'

'Thanks Dad, haha.'

Dad duly went and made a couple of cups of coffee and they sat and talked through the next stage. Theoretically, he didn't need to take much with him. He packed the vacuum syringes in his rucksack. The Cube was all set with the time and position data. Ruben finished his coffee and put on his jacket and rucksack. He gave his dad a hug.

'Good luck Ruben, see you in a little while.'

'Okay, Dad.'

Ruben pushed his sleeve back. He spun the segments round into Solved-Mode-Six.

'XL-R, confirm teletransportation details,' instructed Ruben.

'The position coordinates are 74°44'20.2" North, 17°46'48.2" East, on the banks of the Danube near Győr. Time and date are Monday, 9th May, 898 A.D. I have changed the transmission encryption so my functionality is not compromised by my duplication on the earlier timeline,' replied XL-R.

'Details confirmed.'

He placed his fingers on the blue, green and white centre axis jewels and pressed them. There was a bright flash and at 10:35 he was gone.

■ ■ ■

Ruben quickly looked around. He was in a lush forest. It was a warm day and a gentle breeze was rustling through the branches. The sky was bright and clear.

Nearby he could hear the sound of a horse "neighing". Carefully Ruben picked his way through the undergrowth until he came to the edge of a clearing. Under the trees was a lovely, colourful travellers' caravan and the horse he had heard, nibbling on the lush grass. It was parked on the bank of a wide, sparkling river that twisted and turned into the distance. It was a perfect picture of tranquillity. He glanced at the name written in rainbow colours on the side of the roof. "Antoine Jean de L'Avoitier-The Mystical Magician", it read. He was in the right place and hopefully, at the right time. On cue, he heard a "whooshing" sound coming from his left. He crouched down and waited.

The sound gradually became more focused and nearer. He saw a huge image begin to take shape. The form became denser until it was completely defined. This was the right time. He looked on in utter amazement as the huge alien stood, clad in a dark metallic white Exosuit, in amongst the trees. Little coloured lights flashed across its multi-panelled surface. It was a formidable sight. Ruben could feel his nerves starting to build up.

The alien being is most vulnerable when it commits to the absorption transition process. It will need to disengage the Exosuit. We will be able to get the fluid sample when that happens, which will be in two point five seven of your Earth minutes, sent XL-R.

Okay, great.

Suddenly the huge alien swung round and looked straight through Ruben. He froze on the spot.

XL-R, can it see me? sent Ruben.

No, I took the precaution of putting your body shield in C-Thru-Mode. However, it may sense something nearby. I would have been able to detect a presence at this point in the timeline. I was running an early operating system. My current processing updates have improved my functionality. I will increase the power of the proximity sensor jamming transmission, sent XL-R.

The huge alien continued to scan the area then turned away, looking at the caravan by the lake, and started to walk towards it. Ruben watched. As he approached the horse, tied up nearby, he stopped. It turned its head and the sight of the massive alien caused it to kick wildly and started to "neigh" noisily, expressing its state of panic. Suddenly the alien's Exosuit vanished, leaving the towering giant standing in all his powerful glory. *Holy $#!?*, thought Ruben. As the alien moved closer to the caravan Ruben could see a man sitting by the river. He had caught a fish and was pulling it in, and struggling to hold the line. It was a big one, trying to thrash its way away from the bank.

XL-R, when shall we do the timeline event?

My functionality is still being compromised by the proximity of my other self. We will need to get as close as possible. I will need to divert power from the C-Thru-Mode also. That will allow me to do phase reversal on its protection system sensors. However, you will then become visible to it, explained XL-R nonchalantly.

WHAT? Oh great!

The alien edged closer. The fish finally succumbed to the inevitable and was soon swinging in the air into the hands of its jubilant capturer. He held it aloft for a moment, then bludgeoned it to a merciless death with a stick and a prayer to his God. Dinner would soon be cooking over an open fire.

In all his excitement he had failed to notice the alien and Ruben approaching him from behind until a loud cracking sound startled him and made him turn round. His eyes gazed up in terror at the huge alien. He was rooted to the spot. He could not move. He could not run, even though every muscle of his being was telling him to. It got closer, shadowed by Ruben. The alien bent down and touched the man's head.

XL-R, engage Time-Freeze now.

Time stopped. Ruben took off his rucksack and pulled out a vacuum syringe device. He paused to look at the amazing alien being. It was a spectacular demon, half creature, half machine. Ruben was well aware of what it was capable of. He looked up at its face. Suddenly he saw some little blue lights flash on its head. $#!?, thought Ruben, again.

XL-R, is the alien aware we are here? sent Ruben.

Yes. The alien's timeline runs at a much faster rate than Earth in this dimension, so it will still be processing data, but at a much slower rate, not visible to you. I can see it moving, sent XL-R.

We had better get a move on then.

XL-R guided his hand to the optimum puncture point, just below the base of the skull, at the back. Without a moment's hesitation the needle was plunged into the alien. The vacuum syringe quickly filled with brownish red fluid. He could feel the gentle vibration of the cold alien moving a microscopic amount. A few seconds later the sample phial was full. He withdrew the needle and put the syringe in his rucksack. Quickly he re-configured the Cube into Solved-Mode-Six and put his fingers on the blue, orange and white centre axis jewels and pressed in sequence.

XL-R, okay we're done, get us out of here, back to the lab. Disengage Time-Freeze.

There was a flash of blue light and he was gone.

■　■　■

11:05, MONDAY, 28ᵀᴴ JULY, THE LAB, LOS ANGELES, USA
PRESENT DAY

Dad was in the lab still sat at his desk when Ruben re-materialised.

'Gosh, that was quick. I assume everything went to plan?' asked János.

'Yup, perfect,' replied a confident Ruben. 'Wow, that alien dude was huge. He would have made a great basketball player.'

'Oh really?'

427

'Yes, it was a massive bio-mechanical creature. He was about to do an absorption on this traveller guy when we did a Time-Freeze, like at the party. Funny thing was the Cube told me it was still moving, but incredibly slowly. I could feel it when I put the syringe in. Weird. Here's the first fluid sample.'

'Hmm, that's an odd colour. It has glittery stuff in it too. Now that *is* weird,' queried János.

He carefully put the syringe device on his desk.

'So are you going to do the next jaunt now?'

'Err, yes, might as well. I have the other syringe. Let's do it... after I have reduced my mass! Haha.'

A few minutes later he returned from the Rest Room.

'XL-R, confirm new position coordinates and time and date information.'

'I can confirm position coordinates; Latitude, North 47° 41' 3.012", Longitude, East 17° 38' 3.984", the castle at Győr, and the time and date information: 05:32, 9th May, 898 A.D are correct. Ready to proceed.'

'Okay Dad, I'm off. See you in a while. Don't wait up,' joked Ruben.

With the Cube in Solved-Mode-Six he pressed the blue, green and white centre axis jewels. In a blue flash he was gone, *again*.

■   ■   ■

TIME-JUMP BACKWARD
17:32, THURSDAY, 19TH MAY, 898 A.D. GYŐR CASTLE, 120KM
WEST OF BUDA(PEST
PAST

Antoine was lying in bed when suddenly a bright blue flash in the room woke him from his shallow slumber.

XL-R, engage Time-Freeze now, sent Ruben.

Suddenly there was complete stillness.

Ruben walked over to the bed. He gently turned Antoine's head to the side on the pillow. It felt quite cold to touch. He took the vacuum syringe out of his rucksack and, being guided by XL-R, he inserted the needle. Again, he felt the alien's body gently pulsing. As soon as the phial was full, he withdrew the needle. He looked around the opulent, warm stone room, with a little fire crackling away in the fireplace. Ruben thought it was cosy, but would not be his first choice for bedroom décor.

Okay XL-R, let's go, disengage Time-Freeze.

He pressed the blue, orange and white centre axis jewels, there was a bright blue flash and at 05:37 he was gone.

■ ■ ■

11:10, MONDAY, 28TH JULY, THE LAB, LOS ANGELES, USA
PRESENT DAY

Back in the lab, János was still working at his desk, planning the next series of tests when Ruben re-materialised.

'Hi Dad. Not started work yet? Blimey, I've been whizzing round all over the place.'

'Hello Mr Time Traveller,' said János. 'Good journey? Not too much traffic?' joked János.

'Yes, there was a bit of congestion around 1943. Turns out there was some mad man on the loose, rampaging around Europe. Apart from that, not a lot else,' parried Ruben.

'Haha... very good. I don't know who you get your "wittiness" from.'

429

'The milkman,' replied Ruben, drolly.

'Ha... anyway, enough of this idle hereditary-based comedic banter. Did you get the sample?'

'Sure did. He didn't have much time left by the looks of him. Anyway, yes here it is.'

Ruben gave his Dad the second sample, and he labelled it and put it in the storage fridge.

'So Dad, what have you been doing?'

'Well, thinking mostly. I have been wondering if the Cube could help us with our research. After all, it was originally

built by these alien types. Surely it has some idea what we should be looking for,' said János.

'XL-R, can you help us with our experiments?' asked Ruben.

'Yes I am able to assist you. However, large sections of the nano-technology used in the planet's defence system was not embedded into my operating system just in case I fell into the hands of our enemies,' explained XL-R.

'So we have the second sample, which means our fluid specimens are now established as a real event on this timeline. They exist here in the present. So what you have to do now are some jaunts into the future, on this timeline and find the point where we, hopefully, find the solution to this problem,' said János.

'Yes okay, that sort of makes sense. So how far should I go into the future?'

'Hmm, gosh... um... why not try three days and see where we are at? Obviously I will start working on the samples immediately. Dr Jefferies should be here at lunchtime today. I will explain to him what we are attempting to do. Do you want to head off now?'

'Why not? No time like the present'

He went and sat at one of the other tables. He quickly pressed the white centre axis jewel twice and the Cube morphed onto his hand. He placed it on the desk.

XL-R, set co-ordinates for current location. Set time for three days from now, sent Ruben.

Co-ordinates and time and date set. Ready for teletransportation, sent XL-R.

Dad watched as he configured the Cube into Solved-Mode-Six, pressed the white centre axis jewel and re-morphed the Cube back onto his wrist. He placed his fingers on the blue, yellow and white centre axis jewels, and at 11:20 he was gone, again.

■ ■ ■

TIME-JUMP FORWARD
11:20, THURSDAY, 31ST JULY, THE LAB, LOS ANGELES, USA
FUTURE

János and Dr Jefferies were working on the fluid samples when Ruben re-materialised in the lab. The flash of blue light made them both stop what they were doing and turn round.

'Hi Dad, Doctor Jefferies. How's it going?'

'Hmm, not great. We have tried loads of comparison tests but, as yet, have not really made any progress. We have figured out that the pure alien body fluid does have a lot of similarities to human blood, but there are also a lot of elements that we haven't come across before. It is as if their fluid is also used as a form of lubrication for the mechanical components. It's a bit like a car engine, it needs oil, and as it warms up the effect of friction between surfaces reduces and so the engine parts work more efficiently,' explained János.

'Actually Dad, there is something I noticed that struck me as a bit odd. When I took the fluid sample from the alien, it felt really cold and when I took the fluid from the absorbed alien it felt cold too, but not as cold.'

'That's interesting, we should investigate that.'

'So, shall I go forward a bit further?'

'Why not go another three days and check on us then,' suggested János.

Ruben placed his fingers on the blue, yellow, and white centre axis jewels, and in a blue flash, was gone.

'That sure is some party trick your son can do. Imagine what you could do with that,' said Doctor Jefferies.

'Yes, you could save the world from dying for one thing,' replied János.

'A good point well put. Let's get on with it then.'

They continued with their work. They ran test after test on the samples. What they found was that the pure alien body fluid was completely unaffected by introducing the cloud particles. It did not attack the cells at all. If anything, it helped "feed" the cell nucleus, making it marginally stronger, whereas, on human blood it began destroying the nucleus and its DNA strands. They decided to run a series of virtual simulation tests to see how possible body internal heat affected the fluid samples. What they eventually found was that if the temperature of the human blood sample was lowered to below the normal reading of 37 degrees Celsius(98.6 degrees Fahrenheit) the nucleus destruction slowed right down, almost to nothing. The cloud particles seemed to remain inactive. This was interesting, but János found it hard to imagine a way to use this information in a practical way. Over the next couple of days János and the Doctor worked on trying to fathom out what was going on at a cellular level. There was obviously something in the alien fluid that was controlling the cellular running temperature. The frustration at the lack of progress was starting to show. János was getting short-tempered and irritable.

■　■　■

TIME-JUMP FORWARD
11:55, SUNDAY, 3RD AUGUST, THE LAB, LOS ANGELES, USA
FUTURE

It was late morning of the third day, and János and the Doctor were having a coffee break when a bright blue flash signalled Ruben's reappearance.

'Hi guys,' he cheerily greeted them. 'How's it going?'

Dad piped up.

'Slowly, we seem to be going round in circles. Cellular operation temperature seems to be important. We just can't find the chemical mechanism that seems to control it.'

'Yes, there is something being masked that we are missing. If the cells are being altered then we should be able to find the trigger," continued Doctor Jefferies.

'XL-R, can you help?' asked Ruben.

'Let me connect to your network.'

Ruben disengaged the Cube then configured Solved-Mode-Six and pressed seven blue jewels in an "H" pattern.

'Connecting. Analysing data. My results are as follows: the body temperature results are interesting but not important overall to the degenerative condition of the DNA double helix chain structure. The problem lies in the DNA chain itself. The double helix pitch has been altered, meaning that the DNA information is being disrupted by having the data pathways stretched by the attached particle atoms and so causing that information to be corrupted. If the double helix can have the extra cloud particle atoms removed it would return to its optimum shape and regenerate and repair itself,' said XL-R.

'How do we do that?' asked Ruben.

'Scanning data banks for your answer. No solution found as yet on information provided.'

'You're on your own, Dad, for the moment. I think I should go forward a couple more days, right now.'

'OK,' replied János.

Ruben configured new settings on the Cube and in a blue flash was gone, once again.

■ ■ ■

TIME-JUMP FORWARD
13:10, TUESDAY, 5TH AUGUST, THE LAB, LOS ANGELES, USA
FUTURE

Moments later he re-materialised in the lab. It was still and deserted. Confused, he sat at his dad's desk and glanced up at his wipe board. It had a message written on it. "Ruben, I am at the USC Verdugo Hospital. Bring a couple of vacuum syringes. Your mum has been taken ill, Kat is here too. She will give you the details. Love Dad x"

He Mind-Linked to Kat

Hi Kat it's me, what's up with Mum? he sent.

Hi Ruben. It's not good. Since you have been away Mum has become ill with a lung problem. It seems the whole world is reporting mounting cases of this lung condition. Dad has told us what is going on. You need to come quickly. We're at 1812 Verdugo Boulevard, Glendale, CA 91208. She is now in the East Wing, Ward 5, room 2.

Ok, the Cube will load communication location data and I will be with you in a moment.

He had a quick look round the lab to check the equipment was off and safe, picked up the two vacuum syringes then prepared to Time-Jump. Ruben re-spun the segments into Solved-Mode-Six, pressed the yellow, green and white centre axis jewels and at 13:12 there was a bright blue flash and he was gone.

■   ■   ■

LOCATION-JUMP
13:12, TUESDAY, 5ᵀᴴ AUGUST, THE USC VERDUGO HOSPITAL, LOS ANGELES, USA
FUTURE

Ruben suddenly appeared in the hospital room. Mum was sitting up in bed, wired up to all manner of equipment, with tubes coming out all over the place. Ruben was shocked by the sight of his mum. He had never seen her ill. To him she was indestructible; this clearly proved to him she wasn't. He felt his eyes watering. Kat gave him a hug. Mum, sensing his distress, carefully removed her ventilator mask.

'Hello, my darling. Don't worry, your dad has me wired up to one of his crazy contraptions, so I should be fine. How are you? I have missed you these last few days. The house has been so quiet with no "guitar-based rock" coming from your room, I've had to just contend with

Dad listening to Toto' she chuckled. 'We saw Frankie a couple of days ago. She is really missing you too.'

'I have missed you all. It feels very odd, this "time-hopping" into the future lark is very strange. What's going on, Dad?'

'Well, your mum has the onset of the lung condition we have been studying so I have hooked her up to the vibration device I was experimenting with. It has definitely slowed down the effects of the particle inhalation,' explained Dad. 'Have you got the syringes? In the rush I forgot them.'

'Yes, here they are.'

János proceeded to clean Sarah's skin and then gently held the syringe in place. The phial quickly filled with blood. He put a small plaster on the wound and held it in place for a moment.

'Right we can test that and see what is going on for real now,' said János. 'Let's go and get some coffees. Kat, stay here with your mum please.'

János and Ruben headed for the cafeteria.

'So Dad, what's up?'

János paused for a moment and sighed.

'Umm, a couple of days ago your mum was coughing a bit and complaining of a tight chest, just like one of her asthma attacks. However it got worse quite quickly so I knew it was the particles from the cloud. She is aware that it isn't asthma, she knows it is not good, but she is putting a brave face on it.'

'Dad, is she going to die?'

'If we don't find the answer quick, then yes I think she will.'

They both went silent and looked at one another, János' words echoing around their heads.

'We sure need to come up with the answer soon. I am

going to head back to the lab for a few hours and do some tests on your mum's blood sample. I will get a sample from Kat also. I suggest you take another trip forward another couple of days and I will see you in the lab.'

'Ok Dad. Tell Mum I will see her soon.'

They waited for the corridor to clear. Ruben put his hand on the Cube, pressed the blue, yellow, and white centre axis jewels, then in a blue flash was gone.

■ ■ ■

TIME-JUMP FORWARD
13:32, THURSDAY, 7TH AUGUST, THE LAB, LOS ANGELES, USA
FUTURE

Ruben re-materialised in the lab and the atmosphere was subdued.

'Hi guys.'

'Hello Ruben,' said János.

'Hi Ruben, you must be really clocking up some free "Air Miles",' chipped in Doctor Jefferies, trying to lighten the heavy mood.

'What's up Dad? Is it Mum? How is she?'

'Not good I'm afraid, and *I am afraid*. I know we are going to lose her. I can't imagine my life without her,'

His dad's vulnerability was painfully plain to see.

'I am expecting a call any minute from the hospital, but I have to work, I have to find the answer, I have to,' he said, tearfully.

Ruben gave his dad a hug, a hug that said "I love you" from the depths of his heart. It was a very hard pill to swallow, seeing his father cry. He too was only human.

'Your dad is struggling, but we have made progress. It appears you, your dad and sister have a different blood type to your Mum,' said Doctor Jefferies. 'The early tests your father did were slightly misleading in as much as they masked the deeper problem. We now know the DNA double helix in the cell nucleus is attacked. This is done by the cloud particle atoms sticking onto the double helix between the DNA molecules, deforming the pitch of the double helix and corrupting data transfer. It is a bit like threading too many beads onto a necklace and making the shape distort and not hang in a regular, smooth curve,' explained the doctor.

'Oh, I see. So we have to remove these atoms?'

'Yes, and the way we do that is like how your father tried earlier, by using sound, incredibly high-frequency sound, up around the 24th fret. Haha, no I am joking. You've seen the experiment where an opera singer shatters a wine glass? Well, it is like that. We need to find the exact frequency that causes the cloud atoms to resonate and break their bond with the DNA double helix. The tests your dad did to reduce the number of particles inhaled was definitely a major step in the right direction. Even if he couldn't convince the communications giants it was worth a try,' explained the doctor.

János had calmed down a bit now, had dried his eyes and was listening intently.

At 13:36 the phone rang. János went white as a sheet. He gingerly picked it up and answered it. He listened, motionless, then put the phone down. He looked at Ruben, the tears welling up in his eyes.

'What is it, Dad? Who was that?'

'She's gone. She's gone, my Sarah. I never even said goodbye. I should have been there. She's gone, what am I going to do?' he spluttered and put his head in his hands.

Ruben knew what the news was, and for a moment he felt a deep, aching empty feeling inside. He felt helpless. He went over and held his dad close. He now needed to be the strong one, take control, make it right again.

'Dad, I am going back in time a little to see Mum and tell her we will see her again, tell her we love her. I must do this on my own as I can't take you back with me. If we alter the past on this timeline we will invoke a "Temporal Paradox". You can't meet yourself,' explained Ruben.

'That's right. I know that. We'll set up a "Causal Loop". So you have been listening to me,' János half joked. 'Go, go now, I will be okay, just a bit overwhelmed right now. I will be all right here with the doctor. We have work to do.'

'I'll look after your dad. Go and see your mum and put her mind at rest, said the doctor.

Ruben nodded and configured the Cube, he pressed the blue yellow and white centre axis jewels, there was a blue flash and he was gone.

■　■　■

TIME-JUMP BACKWARD
13:34, THURSDAY, 7TH AUGUST, THE USC VERDUGO
HOSPITAL, LOS ANGELES, USA
FUTURE

In the hospital room Kat sat at her mum's bedside. She tenderly held her hand. Mum was awake, her eyes peeking out from above her ventilator mask.

'Hi Mum, hi Sis. I have just left Dad to see you. He told me to tell you that he loves you with all his heart and that you will be together again soon. He wished he could be here, but he can't, it's complicated.'

439

He put his hands round Kat and Mum's hands, and squeezed them gently. They were at one together. Sarah slowly closed her eyes.

'Love you, Mum,' sobbed Ruben.

He looked at Kat, tears streaming down her face.

'I know this is hard for you. It is for all of us. When we find the answer you will not remember any of this, as it won't have happened, and won't happen, this day will be a long way off. Trust me, I will make this right. You need to be strong for Dad too. There are just the three of us now, we have to support one another, don't stop believing. We are on a crazy journey that we have to travel before we can go back and be together as a family again,' explained Ruben.

A nurse poked her head around the door.

'It is time to leave your mum in our hands now. If you are ready we will take care of her from here. Go to the ward reception, they will help you there. I'm so sorry for your loss,' whispered the nurse.

Kat and Ruben gave their mum one last look then left the room. He held Kat's hand and they slowly walked down the corridor.

'Kat, Dad and Doctor Jefferies are really close to cracking this conundrum. We will do it, we will beat this thing. It is only a matter of time, and to quote Mr Jagger-"Time is on our side, yes it is", and we will be able to stop Mum and all these thousands of people dying. Remember, we *will* be together, as a family, again.'

'Oh Ruben, if this is what it feels like when someone you love dies, I don't ever want to feel this again,' sobbed Kat.

'Death is part of our lives. You know we will have to go through it and find a place in our hearts where those memories of our loved ones are safe with us, where we can cherish them for the rest of *our* lives. Mum is with us, she will always be with us. Now go and make plans and be strong. I love you Kat. I will see you very soon.'

She had never seen her brother like this, so strong and determined. He pressed the blue, green, and white centre axis jewels and in a blue flash was gone.

■ ■ ■

TIME-JUMP FORWARD

13:38, THURSDAY, 7ᵀᴴ AUGUST, THE LAB, LOS ANGELES, USA

FUTURE

'Hi guys,' said Ruben. 'All done Dad, all good. Kat is okay, confused, but okay. We said our goodbyes. Mum understood why you weren't there. She knows.'

'Thanks Ruben, I feel strange. I don't want to go home to an empty house tonight,' said János.

'Sure, I understand, I do, neither do I. So come on, let's get this show on the road. Let's rock this thing. So as I understand it, we need to find the exact resonant frequency that causes the cloud atoms to break away from the DNA double helix inside the cell nucleus, yes?'

'XL-R, can you help?' asked Ruben.

He morphed the Cube onto the desk, and pressed seven blue jewels in an "H" pattern.

'Searching for the lab computer hypersonic data carrier wave. Found, breaking encryption again. Clever scrolling fractal encryption system Mr Novak. I'm impressed. Connection complete,' replied XL-R.

'XL-R, access blood sample test in the electron microscope and find the resonant frequency of the cloud atoms,' instructed Ruben.

'Test sample accessed. Frequency test underway.'

The minutes passed.

'I have concluded my tests. The frequency required for resonance to occur is 160.23GHz (Gigahertz).'

'Ah, damn it, of course. That's the peak frequency for "spectral radiance" to occur,' announced János excitedly.

'What?' said Ruben.

'Oh it's... I can't believe I missed that. It's to do with the origin of the universe. Cosmic microwave background electromagnetic radiation is a remnant from an early stage of the universe's creation. It is sometimes called "relic radiation". It is the faint cosmic background radiation filling all space that is an important source of data on the early universe. It is the oldest electromagnetic radiation in the universe. It is almost conclusive proof of the "Big Bang" theory of creation, that's all,' said János triumphantly.

'Well, not confusing at all, I am glad we finally nailed that, then,' replied Ruben sarcastically.

'So let's quickly test Sarah's blood again. I'll prepare the sample. János, you reset the microscope and set up the tone generator again. Let's try this magic frequency and see what happens in real time. Ruben, you make us all some coffees,' instructed the doctor.'

'Yes Sir, coffee, Sir, coming right up, Sir,' joked General Ruben.

It took about half an hour for the new test rig to be arranged. Eventually the blood sample was set up and the special scanning transmission electron microscope was in position, focused, and set at 850,000x magnification. Slowly the particle sample was introduced into the cell. They sat in silence and watched the monitor. The fluids immediately began swirling around the double helix structure. As expected, the cloud atoms quickly began sticking to the structure. They watched. Soon the double helix was completely smothered with extra atoms and its structure twisted and distorted. The next stage of the test was to bombard the cell with very high-frequency sound waves. János turned on the tone generator, programmed in 160.23GHz, and set the test running. They all sat and watched the monitor.

Suddenly the double helix on the screen began to shake, slowly to start with, then more quickly. The cloud atoms started to detach from the double helix structure. János cheered. It had worked. Gradually all the atoms fell away and were left floating around in the cellular "gloop".

'What happens if we turn off the sound generator? I am hoping they don't reattach. I would guess once the bond has been broken it won't be repairable,' said János.

He turned the machine off and watched the monitor. The displaced atoms remained floating around the edge of the nucleus and didn't reattach, but started to shrink.

'Great. That is fantastic. So what we must try now is introducing another contaminated cell to the test, but not use the sound generator, and see what happens,' explained János.

A few minutes later a newly prepared sample of Sarah's contaminated blood was taken from the lab fridge and introduced into the testing dish. János refocused the electron microscope and they all watched the monitor again. As the two nuclei became closer the detached cloud atoms began seeping through the wall of one nucleus and penetrating the other. The second double helix structure started to release its cloud particle atoms too. János panned the camera lens over the whole sample. A chain reaction had started and all the cell nuclei were shedding their infecting atoms. As they watched the detach particle atoms began breaking up all over the sample. A chain reaction had triggered a complete destruction of the cloud particle atoms. Soon the blood was totally clear of them. János looked at the monitor in total disbelief. He looked at the others. They were speechless. It was 03:35 p.m. and time was pressing on.

'I think we are on to something here,' said Doctor Jefferies.

'Indeed, we need to test this on a living, contaminated person,' said János.

'I know this is a bit weird, but we could test Mum. We know she was infected. I could go back in time two days, to Tuesday morning, before she went to hospital, and bring her back here to the lab where we could test her,' explained Ruben.

'Would that work?' asked János.

'Yes, it would definitely work. Remember I brought one of those demon chaps back with me. The Cube will sort it.'

'Oh yes, you did. I remember the wall damage. What do we need to do?' asked János.

'Well... first we probably need to get some ready mix surface filler and... oh, sorry you mean... um, I will go get Mum whilst you and the doctor organise a bed and prepare the equipment. How long do you need?' asked Ruben, realising his misunderstanding.

'Give us an hour, that should be enough. Don't tell your mum, her future won't happen if we get this right.'

Ruben set the Cube with the new coordinates and timings. He reconfigured it into Solved-Mode-Six and pressed the blue, green and white centre axis jewels. At 15:37 in a blue flash, he was gone.

■ ■ ■

'Hi Mum.'

'Gosh, hello darling. You made me jump.'

Sarah was in her office, poring over some design drawings.

'What are you doing here?'

'Huh, it is a long story and utterly unbelievable as well. Suffice to say, I need to take you on a little trip to see Dad in the future.'

'How exciting. What's the matter? I have to say, my asthma is getting worse today.'

'Well, nothing at the moment but we need to do some tests on you. Dad and the doctor think they have found the possible answer to the cloud particle thing and we need to run some observation tests on you. Mine, Kat's and Dad's blood is slightly different, for some reason, and we can't trust anybody else right now,' he explained.

'Oh I see. Luckily your Dad told me to keep an overnight bag with me. Your dad is so clever.'

'Yup, he sure is. Must be where I get it from,' Ruben chuckled.

Sarah went into the design studio and told Kat she was "just nipping out for a while" as she was feeling a bit odd and needed some fresh air. She surreptitiously pushed a scribbled note into her hand, which told the real reason she was going.

She then went back into her office where Ruben was

445

waiting. He had reconfigured the Cube and was ready to go.

'Ok, now don't be afraid. Grab your bag and slip this teletransportation ring on your finger. Hold on to me tightly. Ready?'

He placed his fingers on the Cube and pressed the blue, yellow and white centre axis jewels in sequence. At 11:19 there was a bright blue flash and they were gone.

■　■　■

TIME-JUMP FORWARD

14:38, THURSDAY, 7ᵀᴴ AUGUST, THE LAB, LOS ANGELES, USA

FUTURE

The lab exploded into light, signalling their arrival.

'Hello you two. Good trip?' asked János.

'Yes, amazing. So what's up, Ján my darling?' asked Sarah.

János gave Sarah a kiss and tenderly took hold of her hand.

'What's the matter, darling? I know that face. That's your "I have just had some bad news" face,' continued Sarah.

'No, no, everything is okay. We just need to run some tests on you. All you need to do is sit and let Ruben look after your every whim,' explained János, before introducing the doctor.

'Gosh, that *will* be a treat, albeit a rare one.'

'So darling, I am sure you remember my old friend Doctor Jefferies? He has been helping me work on my experiments and we have made a major breakthrough, which is why you are here,' explained János.

'Doctor Jefferies, what a lovely surprise to see you, it has been quite a while, doesn't time fly when you are trying to bring up identical twins?' chuckled Sarah.

Doctor Jefferies leant forward and tenderly took her hand and planted a kiss on it.

'How lovely to see you Sarah, it *has* been a while and you haven't changed a bit... unlike János, haha,' replied the doctor.

János then outlined to Sarah what they intended to do. She didn't really like the idea of being a human pincushion, but knew from János' tone it was vitally important she helped them. The test equipment was wheeled into position as Sarah sat propped up on the bed. She winced a few times as various tubes were attached to her. Ruben hooked up the Cube to the lab's computer system hypersonic data carrier wave, so it could monitor Sarah's body functions. It was not long before all the equipment was in position and ready.

'I can give you a real-time direct feed to the monitor if I link the Cube,' said Ruben.

He morphed the Cube into his hand and configured it into Solved-Mode-Six. He pressed five yellow jewels in the shape of a "+".

'Now the Cube is running at full capability, after it updated its system, it can now do some pretty clever stuff. We can use it to scan Mum, a bit like ultrasound, but much more powerful. It can collect data at a much higher magnification than your pre-historic microscope.'

He picked up the Cube and gently placed it on his mum's stomach. Immediately a huge, high-resolution image came up on the monitor.

'XL-R, increase magnification up to 600,000x,' instructed Ruben.

Suddenly the monitor showed a picture of blood cells swirling around.

'Okay, Ruben, move the Cube over to your mum's left lung area,' directed the doctor.

The picture flashed and a new image came up on the screen.

'Right, increase magnification to 850,000x,' continued János.

'XL-R, increase magnification to 850,000x,' instructed Ruben.

The monitor showed a detailed view of a cell nucleus and the double helix structure. As expected the strands were clogging up with cloud particle atoms.

'Right okay, now Ruben, move the Cube gently over Mum's heart area. Great, okay. Now move it to various other positions nearby.'

Each new location produced a similar picture. It looked as if all the cells were being systematically attacked.

'How am I?' asked Sarah. 'I can't see the monitor.'

'Err, everything looks fine, darling,' said János.

'You only use the word "fine" when things aren't okay. So what is *really* going on inside me?'

'Umm, well, you are showing signs of infection. Not bad, but there is definitely infection present.'

'So not asthma then? What else are you not telling me? Is it getting worse, spreading, or whatever it does?'

'Err, yes, it will get worse if we don't treat it now. So keep your fingers crossed. Ruben, can the Cube induce the frequency directly into Mum?'

'XL-R, can you produce the frequency of 160.23GHz whilst in this mode, so we can monitor it live, in real time?' asked Ruben.

'Yes, I can produce the required frequency. Ready.'

'XL-R, transmit the frequency now, instructed Ruben.

'Transmission commencing,' confirmed XL-R.

They watched the monitor again. A few seconds later the cloud atoms began to vibrate and then gradually detach from the DNA helix structure. There was a huge collective sigh of relief in the room.

'I am hoping that is a good sign?' asked Sarah.

'Yes, it is. Okay, Ruben, turn off the sound generation and move the Cube to some other positions nearby and see if the detaching process is spreading,' said János.

He changed the Cube settings and began to track it over Sarah's body. The monitor confirmed that the detaching process was underway. The atoms were gradually transmitting their coding through her body, effectively causing the cloud atoms to self-detach and die.

'Great, that seems to be working perfectly. Well, Doctor Jefferies, old bean, I knew this was more than a feeling. Ladies and Gentlemen, I think we have lift off, all systems go,' beamed János with a cheer.

'Well done, you guys. Now, how do we implement this on a worldwide scale?' asked Ruben, bringing them crashing down to reality again.

The room suddenly went noticeably quiet.

'I would love a coffee, darling, thanks for asking' piped up Sarah.

'Er, good idea, I will make us all one,' said Ruben.

János and the doctor sat in thoughtful silence mulling over the next problem they faced.

'So now we have to reproduce this effect on a global scale. Didn't you say you approached a network broadcasting company a while back?' asked the doctor.

'I did. They weren't interested at the time, so I put together my own simple system for the house. I'm not sure how useful it has been.'

'We need someone with power and connections in the right places,' suggested the doctor.

'Erm... yes... Hold on a minute, I think I know just the man. A few days ago I had some dealings with the military. It was them who helped get us a high-altitude cloud sample. We went up in a top-secret military fighter jet to about seventy thousand feet, right on the edge of space, and scooped up a huge cloud sample. I also happen to know they have a network of orbiting military satellites. I bet they could be "tweaked" to broadcast the "magic frequency". Probably do that without breaking a sweat,' said János, 'so Ruben, you must travel back in time to the point when I met General A.Whitehall. I am sure the military stuff they have in the upper atmosphere can do what we need it to. The capabilities of these systems are top secret; only a few people know what they are capable of.'

'Wasn't I with Frankie that day?' asked Ruben.

'Yes, you were. You will have to go back to a point on the event timeline before you see Frankie. That won't be a problem as the future scenarios won't have been embedded in the timeline yet, so there will be no paradox,' explained János.

'Right, yes, of course.'

'So I will go to the appointment, as arranged on the Saturday, 19th July at 14.00. Then at some point you can appear in the General's office, which should convince him to take us seriously, very seriously indeed. We will work out a way I can send you a message, so you know when to appear?' said János.

'Yup, agreed. If seeing the Cube doesn't convince him, nothing will,' replied Ruben.

'I am sorry to interrupt this "meeting of great minds", but can someone explain to me what is exactly going on here?' asked Sarah.

'Sorry darling, got a bit carried away. I think we have solved the lung problem but we now need some help from the military to, hopefully, make it happen on a global scale.'

'How does the monitoring of Mum look?' asked János.

'XL-R, how is the experiment progressing?' relayed Ruben.

'The results show that the body being scanned is now 87.56% clear of hostile cellular activity. Progression is self-generating as predicted. The patient will make a full recovery over the next fifty-seven point three recurring, of your Earth minutes,' announced XL-R.

'I'm glad to hear that,' quipped Sarah.

'So am I. That means if we can get this sorted we can save a huge number of people very quickly. Let's get you unhooked from all this equipment,' said János.

A few minutes later Sarah was free of wires and tubes and sitting by the desk.

'So yes, I will go back in time and you go to this meeting as planned and I will join you. I'll make sure XL-R has all the relevant data files we'll need.'

'XL-R, confirm experiment data files are all complete.'

Ruben quickly reconfigured the Cube and it morphed back onto his wrist.

'Checking now. Data files complete,' replied XL-R.

'Right Dad' I'm off. Doctor Jefferies, Mum, I will see you all very soon.'

'Hold on one second Ruben,' interrupted the doctor. 'You are going nowhere.'

Suddenly there was a sickening bone-breaking sound. Ruben, Sarah and János looked at the doctor in open-jawed disbelief as his body began to split open from the centre of his skull. Blinding shafts of intense green light began to shoot out from the gaps. The body continued to split and fragmented as the light increased. They shielded their eyes from the blinding brightness.

XL-R, engage Exosuit, sent Ruben, in a panic.

Within seconds Ruben was encapsulated in his body armour. Sarah and János couldn't believe their eyes. As the doctor's shattered body continued to fracture wide open, the shadowy silhouette of a figure began to form, surrounded by a dense green glow. The body shell began to crumble to the floor as the huge alien "being" stretched up to its full, imposing height. They watched in terror as the awesome presence took shape. Suddenly the green light was extinguished to reveal a towering chrome-and white-bodied biomechanical alien "being" standing in front of them all.

Oh $#!?eroony, that's the alien dude from by the lake that I took the fluid sample from. So that's how he regenerated here somehow, thought Ruben.

The room was silent as the fearsome presence stood watching menacingly for their next move. Suddenly there was a deafening booming sound as the alien spoke. Its voice was like nothing they had heard before

'You will all die. Your planet will be wiped clean of all air-breathing life as planned. I cannot allow you to live and alter the course of our future. Lord Ebucski-Bur and his army are all but defeated. We have taken control of their escape vessels. Our fleet will soon be in your earth's Orbit. This planet will be ours, and you will perish in our cleansing. Prepare to meet your gods.'

'Uh, excuse me, "Mr Alien Sir". You seem to have overlooked one thing... ME,' announced Ruben proudly.

He lifted his arm and a bright red beam of light blasted across the room and seared into the alien. It crashed backwards, smashing equipment as it absorbed the full force of the beam. Sarah and János quickly dived for cover behind a huge metal storage cabinet. The alien rose to its feet and charged at Ruben, ramming him hard into the wall. The building shook violently. They locked arms and wrestled, limbs flailing as they thrashed across the floor. Glass and debris rained down on them. Ruben managed to break free from the alien's clutches and with an almighty thump landed a skull-crunching blow to its head. The alien pivoted backwards hurtling through test equipment, completely obliterating it. Ruben ran over and grabbed the alien by the throat and locked onto it with vice-like force. It struggled and strained and then with a massive surge of pent-up energy pushed hard on Ruben thrusting him up against the wall. The plasterwork began to crack and crumble as the wall started to bow and split. Fractured joints radiated out across the wall as the force increased. Suddenly it gave way and Ruben fell through the shattered bricks and plummeted onto the roof of a parked vehicle below, crushing it. *That's blown his no-claims bonus then,* thought Ruben as he looked up to see the alien flying towards him. He braced himself for the impact. The Exosuit absorbed the shock and he immediately forced the alien to roll off onto another vehicle crushing it. Ruben got up and fired a beam. The alien faltered, stumbling backwards over another parked car that crumpled and creaked as it smashed onto it. *Ooh, that's gonna hurt*, thought Ruben again. Suddenly out of the checkpoint security building three armed guards appeared. Ruben shouted to them. They aimed their weapons at the alien and let off a volley of rapid gunfire. The bullets ricocheted off the alien's armour. They fired again. Nothing. The distraction gave Ruben the chance to reconfigure the Cube to Solved-Mode-Six. He placed his fingers on the centre line of three green jewels and pressed them. Suddenly eight green Nano-Cubies shot out from the Cube and flew over the dazed alien. Before it was aware what was happening the miniature hi-tech spheres created a web of light beams that completely encapsulated it. The alien was trapped. It kicked and thrashed but couldn't break free.

XL-R, start compression, sent Ruben.

Compression initiated.

The Nano-Cubies began to draw in closer, tightening their strands of light. Slowly the beams got shorter. The contained alien couldn't resist the crushing effect. The network pulled tighter and tighter. It screamed out. They closed in, tighter and tighter. It shrieked. They drew closer until they became one. There was a bright green flash and they were all gone.

Ruben sat down and gave a huge sigh of relief. He looked up to see his dad peering out through the hole in the lab wall.

XL-R, disengage Exosuit.

Exosuit disengaged.

'I'm all right Dad. I'll be right up.'

He looked around the building to see faces pressed up against the windows. What had they just witnessed? Ruben pressed five white jewels in the shape of an "L".

XL-R, Mind-Wipe all recent event witnesses, sent Ruben.

Engaging Mind-Wipe, sent XL-R.

A bright blue flash radiated from the Cube. Ruben quickly ran back upstairs to the lab.

'What on earth happened here? All the equipment is destroyed and there is a huge hole in the wall. How am I going to explain that?' asked János.

'Hmm, how about a gigantic mice infestation? No, no, I am joking, it's a bit of a long story. Basically, we had a visitation from one of our alien friends. He didn't want us to stop the disease spreading. I think it had regenerated from the alien fluid sample I took, then it must have absorbed into Doctor Jefferies to track what we were doing. Anyway, we had a bit of a scuffle, hence the damage, and, err, I think he fell on your truck,'

'WHAT,' exclaimed János.

Sure enough, a quick glance out of the "gigantic mouse" hole confirmed that his truck had indeed taken a very serious side impact.

'Don't worry Dad, I'm sure that will buff out. You won't notice it, it's just a scratch,' joked Ruben.

Dad raised one eyebrow and frowned.

'Yeah, right, you might get a serious side impact young man if you're not careful,' replied an annoyed János.

Sarah laughed. János didn't. There was a silent moment.

'So we need to sort out the time I arrive at the General's office. I think we should plant a nano-transmitter into your watch, then you can send me a covert signal when to teletransport in,' said Ruben.

'Sounds like a plan.'

'Great. Right, I am going to make a move. See you shortly at home. Love you.'

Ruben reconfigured the Cube to Solved-Mode-Six and pressed the blue, green and white centre axis points, and in a bright blue flash was gone.

TWELVE

WHAT THE FUTURE HOLDS

EARLY MORNING, SATURDAY, 19ᵀᴴ JULY, NOVAK
RESIDENCE, LOS ANGELES, USA

NEW PRESENT DAY

Ruben re-materialised in his bedroom seconds before his dad walked through the door. They spent some time with the Cube sorting out his next jaunt and organising how the afternoon with the General would now play out. Once Ruben had explained what had happened in the future János quickly got his head around it and they set to work. The meeting was arranged as before and János took Kat to Dan's place before going to the rendezvous.

■ ■ ■

It was 16.32, János glanced at his watch as it bleeped, aware he was due to pick Kat up.

'Have you got to be somewhere? or can I get you a drink, Mr Novak, while we wait? Coffee? or something stronger?' asked the General.

'No, a coffee would be fine, without sugar or milk please, thanks. I was just keeping an eye on the time; I have to pick up my daughter in a while. Oh, and please call me János. Mr Novak is so formal. It's what my students call me. I do a bit of part-time lecturing up at the UCLA on Bio-Mechanical Quantum Physics. Actually not that far from here.'

'Okay, János it is then, no problem. And you can call me General Whitehall,' he chuckled.

The General then tapped on his computer keyboard.

Suddenly there was a blinding flash and Ruben appeared in the room.

'What the...! Who the hell are you? Where the hell!' exclaimed the General, unable to finish his expletives.

'General Whitehall, please let me introduce you to my son Ruben,' stumbled a slightly surprised János.

'Where on God's Earth did he come from?' asked the General.

'Please let me explain,' continued János.

The General was visibly shaken by what he had just witnessed.

'It is hard to explain, but I hope my son's spectacular arrival will convince you to listen to what we have to say.'

'Hmm, I am listening.'

Suddenly there was a knock at the door and a soldier walked in carrying a tray of coffees.

'Oh, I am sorry, General, I didn't realise you had *two* guests,' he said.

'No neither did I,' quipped the General. 'Can I offer you anything Ruben? It must have been quite a journey?'

'Oh, just some water would be fine. Thanks.'

The soldier deposited the drinks then left to get a glass of water.

'So where were we?' asked the General, still shaken.

János took a deep breath.

'Well, I know this is going to sound totally unbelievable, but I think my son has come back from the future to ask for your help.'

'Go on.'

'Well, as you know the black cloud that descended on Earth blotted out the sun. So we started running tests on the cloud samples we have just collected, and, I'm guessing, my son went into the future to see what we found.'

'I can't believe I am actually going to ask this, but here goes. How did he travel to the future?' asked the General.

'Ruben, show the General.'

Ruben rolled back his sleeve.

XL-R, disengage Safe-Mode, sent Ruben.

Safe-Mode disengaged, sent XL-R.

The Cube became visible on his wrist.

He then quickly twisted the Cube segments into Solved-Mode-Six, pressed the white centre axis jewel twice and it morphed onto his hand.

The General could not believe his eyes. The multi-coloured Cube was flashing, with blinking jewels all over its surface.

'Wow, how did you do that? What is it?' asked the General.

'This is the Cube. It is a very special device, which has amazing powers, and one of those powers is that it can manipulate time, as you have seen,' explained Ruben.

'Where did you get it? Who made it?' asked the General.

'That is a very good question,' continued János 'Basically, this "thing" and a little book I have, has been in my family for hundreds of years and passed down through the generations. This amazing object must have puzzled all my forefathers but nobody ever actually figured it out. Anyway, the book predicted these days of darkness, and so I gave it to Ruben as instructed by the book. He immediately took the puzzling object and solved it. However, back in the mists of time it was damaged and it took us a little time to rebuild it. As it got repaired, it became more powerful. It has some truly awesome features,' enthused János.

'Can I have a look at it?' asked the General.

'No, not really, sorry General. It is encoded to me and only I can operate it,' explained Ruben.

'Oh, I see... So why are you here?'

'Well, I travelled into the future to see if Dad had worked out what the cloud was made of and what its purpose was. After only a few days thousands of people were falling ill and a few had died. It was happening right in front of me.'

'I see, go on.'

'It turned out that the cloud's purpose was to spread a genetic disease that would kill all human and air breathing life on Earth.'

'Jeez. We have already started testing the cloud particles and our research was heading in that direction

460

too. Interesting, I was intrigued by your call earlier,' exclaimed the General.

'So it turned out Dad and a friend of his, a leading geneticist, found a way to reverse the damage the particles were doing on the cell DNA structure. They discovered a way to neutralise the effects of the particles. That is why we are here. Let me show you.'

Ruben pressed the orange, blue and yellow centre axis jewels and placed the Cube on the edge of the General's desk.

XL-R, play video highlights from recent time-shifted scenarios, sent Ruben.

Suddenly a bright red beam began to arc across the room as a three-dimensional holographic projection pulled into focus. The General watched as the Cube replayed footage of the tests being done by János and the Doctor. He was transfixed by what he saw. About five minutes later the free picture show was over.

'Wow, that is a mighty impressive bit of kit you have there. I know a lot of governments who would like one of those things,' said the General.

'I bet, but it isn't for sale,' said Ruben sternly.

'Everything has its price young man, and I mean everything!' replied the General.

'Maybe, but not the Cube. I have been entrusted with it to save the world, it is priceless.'

'Which brings us back to the question of what exactly do you want from me?' asked the General.

'We know you have a ring of satellites and other top-secret stuff orbiting the planet. What we need are for those satellites to transmit a special frequency sound wave across the planet,' continued János. 'What we found when we did our tests was that there was a specific resonant frequency which caused the invading particle

461

atoms to break their bonds with the DNA strands.'

'Interesting,' acknowledged the General.

'Our tests proved it was totally possible to halt and reverse the damage. If we don't do something fast this cloud will kill us all, make no mistake. The clock is ticking. Once the bonds are broken they trigger a chain reaction through the body causing all the bonds to break. If we do this now, it will mean that the cellular destruction can be repaired. If we waste time it may be irreversible,' explained János.

'I see. Well yes, you are right. We do have some hi-tech stuff orbiting our little planet capable of doing that and a lot more besides. At some point I would still like to know how "you" know that too?' replied the General.

'All in good time, General. Is it possible we can organise this now?' asked János.

'I will have to speak with my advisors and the President, of course. That takes time.'

'Err... which we don't have,' interjected Ruben.

'I appreciate that, gentlemen. I will have to make some calls,' said the General.

There was a knock on the door and in walked the soldier again with a glass of water for Ruben.

'Ah, Lieutenant Chapman, can you take our guests to Hospitality Room One and keep them fed and watered. This is going to take some time,' instructed the General.

'Yes Sir. Come this way, gentlemen please.'

The soldier took János and Ruben down the corridor to Room One and made them comfortable.

■　■　■

17:10, SATURDAY, 19TH JULY, SECRET MILITARY FACILITY.
LOS ANGELES AIRPORT, USA

462

'Good afternoon Madam President, apologies for disturbing your holiday, but we have a situation,' stated the General.

'So General Whitehall, what is this problem?' asked the President.

'I need clearance to access the Global Defence System Satellites, Ma'am.'

'Tell me more. This must be serious. Is it to do with the testing you have been doing?'

The General proceeded to explain what he knew to the President in as much detail as he could and they discussed the way forward.

'Okay, leave it to me. I will keep you informed. Goodbye,'

The General quickly headed to Room One.

'So, gentlemen, it seems the President of the USA respectfully requests your presence as soon as possible.'

'Wow, great. Where?' asked Ruben.

'The family are currently on a short vacation with friends at their ranch.'

'I see, but where is it?' enquired Ruben.

'That is classified information,' replied the General briskly.

'Okay, so how do we get there then?' asked Ruben.

'We use your Cube device. Is that possible?' asked the General.

'Yes it is. It would certainly save time, but I will need the exact positional coordinates of where we are going, to set the Cube,' explained Ruben.

'Ah, right, yes I see, I can get you those. What else?' asked the General.

'Nothing really. You will have to trust me. Give me a moment.'

XL-R prepare to teletransport two additional people, Dad and General Whitehall, sent Ruben.

The Cube then produced two teletransportion rings from a slot in its case.

My sensors are picking up a strange life form very nearby, sent XL-R.

XL-R, How near?

Within a two point seven eight metre radius from here, sent XL-R.

Ruben quickly looked around the room. There was only himself, Dad and the General.

'General, is it possible you could give us a few minutes on our own, I just want to have a quick chat with my dad.'

'Sure, no problem. I will go and get the coordinates we need.'

While they were alone, Ruben instructed the Cube to Mind-Link with his dad and fill him in with what had happened in the future on their timeline strand.

The General returned ten minutes later and handed a sheet of paper to Ruben, who proceeded to program the data into the Cube.

'Okay, to time travel with me I have to link you to the Cube. So to do that you need to put these teletransportation rings on,' explained Ruben, handing out two polished metal ring devices.

The General and János slipped them on.

'Right, now we are ready,' announced Ruben.

'Yes,' they both replied.

'XL-R, prepare to teletransport us to the set location coordinates,' instructed Ruben.

'Ready for teletransportation,' replied XL-R.

Ruben reconfigured the Cube into Solved-Mode-Six, pressed the yellow, green and white centre axis jewels, and in a blue flash they were all gone.

Moments later they materialised in a clearing in a dense forest, next to a beautiful lake shimmering in the half-light. The silhouetted backdrop of mountains were capped with grey clouds, backlit by an endless expanse of dark blue sky. Nestled in the corner of the idyllic scene was a picture book log cabin, cradled by towering trees that pierced the sky.

'Wow, gee, that was a-w-e-s-o-m-e,' exclaimed the General.

'Glad you liked it, Sir. Sorry the cabin service was a bit lacking,' quipped Ruben.

'Yes, where were my complimentary nuts?' continued János.

'Between your complimentary legs, I expect,' Ruben fired back.

'Haha, next time I want an upgrade,' continued János.

'I suppose you'd want to go up on the flight deck and meet the Captain too?' replied Ruben smartly.

The comedy banter was interrupted by a tall man dressed in black and wearing dark shades, carrying a submachine gun.

'Aha, Lieutenant Wallis. You have been expecting us, no doubt?' said the General.

'Yes, Sir, but not yet,' he replied, a little confused.

'Yes, we got a very fast flight,' added Ruben.

'Come this way, gentleman,' beckoned the Lieutenant.

The secret service agent proceeded to take them towards the cabin. Ruben could not help but notice a lot of men dotted around the floodlit cabin area, all equipped with earpieces and guns. Understandably, there was a lot of firepower guarding the President. As they approached the cabin, the sound of children playing by the lake slowly drifted towards them. It was a warm evening and the water still looked an inviting place to cool off and relax, even in the half-light. Unfortunately they were there to save the World. The agent knocked on the cabin door. The veranda light clicked on, and the door opened to reveal the President standing in the hallway.

'Good afternoon, Madam President. Please let me introduce Mr János Novak and his son, Ruben,' said the General.

'Good evening to you, General Whitehall, Mr Novak, Master Novak. Welcome to our home from home.'

'It's an honour to meet you, Madam President,' replied János nervously.

'Yes, it's really cool to meet you,' added Ruben casually.

After they had all shaken hands, the President led them into the lounge area. The huge picture window gave them a panoramic view of the lake and the distant mountains.

'Wow, what a beautiful place you have here, Madam President. I can see why you would want to get out of the city,' said János.

'Yes, it is lovely here. It is odd being dark all day. Anyway, perhaps we can drop the formalities here; please call me Opira.'

'Yes, Ma'am.'

'From what I understand from General Whitehall, you have some amazing information with regards to this strange atmospheric condition we are experiencing today. It has been an odd couple of days, to say the least.'

'Yes Ma'am. From our research we have found that the black cloud high in the atmosphere is as a result of a cluster of spore bombs that have been detonated high in the stratosphere. We know the particles fall to Earth and we inhale them. These particles then attack our cell DNA at an atomic level. If we don't act fast all life on Earth will perish,' explained János dramatically.

'I see. The General said you knew all this because you had seen the future.'

'Yes, I know it sounds crazy, but it is true. Ruben, show Opira your gadget,' said János.

'Would you like to know if you win the next Presidential election Ma'am?' ask Ruben.

'Oh yes, that is tempting, but no, no thank you, how about the State Lottery next month?' she replied jokingly.

Ruben rolled back his sleeve to reveal the Cube.

'Gosh, how fantastic. What is it? what can it do?'

'Let me show you, Ma'am,' said Ruben, with just a touch of excitement in his voice.

Ruben proceeded to disappear and reappear in various points in the room.

'That is obviously just a party trick, but the Cube has awesome capabilities,' he said.

Suddenly Ruben was clad in his Exosuit. The President was amazed. Then in a flash the Exosuit vanished.

'We could sure do with some of those for our guys,' chipped in the General.

'That is pretty impressive stuff, I have to say. So I understand that you need to use our upper atmosphere defence satellites?' asked the President.

'Yes, we sure do. From our research we found a resonant frequency that destroys the bonds of the invading atoms at a cellular level. They break away from the DNA stands and dissolve, starting a chain reaction through the entire body. This allows the cell nuclei to repair themselves, so quickly reversing the deadly infection. The satellites would, I hope, allow us to cover the whole planet with this frequency transmission very quickly,' explained János.

'Well, General, can we do that?' asked the President.

'Yes Ma'am. I believe we can. Our technical people say it is possible, so we could, potentially, get it up and running very quickly.'

Suddenly there was a sound of gunfire very close by.

'What's going on?' exclaimed the alarmed President.

Just at that moment two secret service agents burst into the room.

'Madam President, there has been a breach in security. We need to get you all to the bunker. The children are being brought here. We have no further intelligence information at the moment. We are in contact with Octagon HQ,' said one of the agents.

The secret service men led them through the plush cabin to a special doorway in a back bedroom. One of the agents punched in a security code and the door opened to reveal a heavy metal shutter. The President pressed her hand on the scanner and with a loud "clunk" it slowly swung open.

They went inside and down a gently descending passageway, which led to some more doors that opened leading through into a small corridor. Eventually they found themselves sitting in another comfortable lounge area. Hearing the new arrivals, the children ran in to hug their mother. She took them into a side room.

I won't be long. Gentlemen, make yourselves at home,' she said, calmly.

János noticed a set of security monitors over by the desk in the corner and nudged Ruben.

Excuse me for a moment, gentlemen. Make yourselves comfy – we may be a while,' said the General as he left the room, guarded by the two agents.

■ ■ ■

Outside, the once-discreet agents were now "armed to the teeth," and were taking cover from the shadowy figures hiding in the half-light. A red beam then cut through the darkness, panning across in a small arc. There was a loud, eerie high-pitch whistling sound, a tree splintered and the agent hiding behind it was blown to pieces. Immediately, rapid machine gun fire could be heard as the agents retaliated. They watched the monitors. More agents began fanning out through the woods, wearing night vision glasses. There was sporadic gunfire as more beams appeared through the half-light accompanied by the explosive disintegration of more agents. The malevolent shadows slowly began closing in on the cabin. Two agents retreated and crouched behind a black 4x4 truck. Immediately red beams began arcing over its surface. Flames began to ignite as the beams sliced through the metal bodywork. Bursts of machine gun fire radiated out from behind the truck, spraying bullets frantically into the darkness. Suddenly there was a massive explosion as the truck was blown to pieces, engulfed in a fireball. Flames shot into the sky as red-hot metal fragments rained down. Then from nowhere, two blinding spotlights appeared from the sky, as the throbbing sound of a helicopter grew louder.

It began to hover lower, the rotor downdraft bending the trees into submission. The spotlights darted about, trying to locate the attacking force. The agents took aim, their night vision glasses showing nothing more than vague silhouettes of the enemy moving about in the shadows. The helicopter hung in the air, the on-board machine gun poised for action. A green beam hit the helicopter and immediately the agents aimed their fire at the other end of the beam. There was an ear-splitting cacophony of bullets slicing through the air. The beam went out and the shadow fell to the ground. Then a fan of intense green beams emerged from the darkness. The agents dived for cover. All the beams locked onto the helicopter and began carving it up. The fuel tank was hit and exploded sending the crippled helicopter into a descending tailspin. It plummeted from the sky crashing into the trees, the wildly spinning rotor hacking the branches into a cloud of splinters. A carpet of flames shot from the wreck as it ploughed into the ground. A nearby agent found himself suddenly engulfed in fire. He quickly ran into the lake to extinguish himself. Volley after volley of machine gun fire ripped into the darkness. The shadows scurried about in the dark, their beams gradually picking off agents one by one.

János and Ruben watched as the carnage grew. The agents were no match for whatever was cutting them down. The green beams of death gradually advanced towards the cabin mercilessly slaughtering anything in their way. The cabin floodlights revealed the deadly truth. They were a group of four heavily armed men, dressed in black.

A door opened and in walked the President. Behind her was an agent with a machine gun and, finally, the

General. The group was led from the bunker back into the main cabin lounge area.

'Sit down,' ordered the General.

The agent ushered them over to the sofas.

'General Whitehall, what is the meaning of this? What is going on here?' asked the President, indignantly.

'Well, Madam President, I said we had a "situation". However, the situation has changed considerably,' explained the General. 'Madam President, it isn't you we are interested in. Sorry to disappoint you.'

'Explain, General.'

'Let me show you.'

Suddenly the cabin door opened and in walked four large, heavily armed "beings", clad in hi-tech body-armour.

!@#$, thought Ruben. *That's not good.*

János looked at Ruben.

'I'd like you to meet some friends of mine,' quipped the General.

The fearsome beings stood still with their weapons trained on Ruben and János.

'Unfortunately your escape helicopter met with a *slight* accident, Madam President. I expect you heard the unfortunate noise? So you really have no option but to listen to me now. As I said, you are not our prize; we are after something far more valuable. Young Master Ruben, perhaps you can show us again the amazing device you have hidden on your person,' ordered the General.

Ruben, begrudgingly, revealed the Cube to the General and everyone in the room.

'Why should I give it to you?' asked Ruben.

'Well, I will tell you why you will give it to me. Let me keep it simple. I have been tracking you for quite some time. Since your father has been investigating the comet cluster we have been watching you. Then when he came to see me about our top-secret aircraft I realised that our Global Defence System had been compromised by something, or someone. So we decided to see what you were up to. From our surveillance reports it became obvious that your device had amazing military potential. However, it also became apparent other people had the same thoughts, even though it was impossible to properly find out who they were.'

'So you want the Cube for military purposes?' asked Ruben.

'Initially, yes, but then we saw the time-travel potential and it moved to a much higher level of importance.'

'Why was I not notified about what you were doing General?'

'Well, Ma'am, as our investigations evolved we found that there was another group of people after the Cube also.'

The General pointed to the four fearsome guards.

'Seeing the potential of the situation "I" engineered a meeting with them and worked out a plan for me to join them and command their army,' continued the General.

'Oh it's "I" now is it, General?' interrupted the President.

The General quickly pulled out a gun and shot the secret service agent holding the machine gun.

'Yes it is "I"...'

The agent fell in a crumpled heap on the floor. There were gasps of disbelief.

'So listen up, people. Here is what is going to happen. I will...'

I am sensing a time line multi-dimensional disturbance. There is a near field power surge building up, sent XL-R.

The General stopped mid-sentence and started to shake, his body began to violently convulse. His face contorted into torturous, pained lines. Muscles bulged from his neck as his eyes began to turn red. They watched in horror as a silhouette of another figure began to form next to him. Slowly the additional image grew in intensity and definition. The features of a man were soon clearly defined. The room was silent as the transformation continued. Moments later a fully formed man stood next to the General. The man calmly placed his hand on the forehead of the General, who dropped to the floor, dead.

'Who or what are *you*?' asked the President.

'I am Enzó, son of the "Great" Jutotzas, and that General was delusional. János and Ruben will know the significance of my name?'

János nodded. 'Yes, I believe he owns a chain of pizza restaurants on the west coast.'

'I am glad you have a sense of humour. You're going to need it.'

'Yes of course I know who you are. You are the end of the bloodline descended from the evil, murderous traitor who killed his own brother, or at least thought he did,' taunted János.

'Yes, so I am here to finally get what is mine. I will have the Cube and I will go back in time and rule my forefather's kingdom. I will go down in the pages of history as a great leader, a great warrior, and be rich beyond my dreams, and my dreams *will* come true. It will be my bloodline that continues into the future. I will be revered and worshiped as a god.'

'*You're* the delusional one,' interrupted János.

There was a brief silence and then Jutotzas spoke.

'What do you mean, "At least, thought he did"?'

'Aha, I wondered if you had spotted that. Zoltán didn't die, he nearly did but he didn't. At the moment you are at the end of your bloodline. What would you think if I told you my middle name was Zoltán? Guess where my bloodline comes from? However, I am not the end of our bloodline, I have a son, Ruben Novak. Guess what?' said János, leaving the question hanging in the air.

'Excellent, so our forefathers were brothers.'

'Yup.'

'So we can finish this now, once and for all time. Here is what is going to happen. Your *son* is going to give me the Cube and reconfigure it for me. He will then fit this final red jewel into it. My little insurance policy.'

At this point Enzó proudly showed Ruben the ring on his finger with the gleaming red jewel mounted in the centre.

'Oh, so that's why the Cube has been glitching. One of the jewels must be compromised,' Ruben whispered to his dad.

'Once I have the Cube, the puzzle will be solved,' said Enzó triumphantly.

'Why should I give it to you?' asked Ruben.

'If you take a look over to the door you will see my four heavily armed Time-Warrior friends, who will kill everyone in this bunker, unless you do as I say, NOW.'

'You're an insane monster,' exclaimed the President. 'You'll never get away with this.'

'Thank you Ma'am, and, yes I will. Ruben, I suggest you bring me the Cube.'

'I don't have much choice, do I?'

'In a word, NO.'

Ruben reluctantly rolled up his sleeve to reveal the Cube. One of the Time-Warriors trained their weapon on Ruben.

'If you try anything clever my friends will vapourise everyone in this room. Women and children first.'

Ruben spun the segments quickly round into Solved-Mode-Six. He then put his fingers on the centre white jewel and pressed. The Cube morphed onto his hand.

'BRING IT TO ME,' demanded Enzó loudly.

Ruben calmly walked over to him. Enzó gave him the ring. Ruben put the Cube on the table and then, using his trusty pocket multi-tool, gently prised the jewel from the ring's mount and put it on the table as well.

XL-R, release the defective jewel cell, he sent.

The Cube's red segment began to flash, then one of the corner jewels faded and "clicked" up. Ruben took that jewel out and put it on the table too but clumsily knocked over a silver candelabra. His nerves were getting the better of him. He fumbled about on the table and stood it upright again.

'Getting nervous are we?' said Enzó sarcastically.

Ruben took the jewel and slotted it into the Cube. The red jewels began to flash in sequence, faster and faster, stopped, then flashed once.

Okay, it is done. Now, will your four friends be travelling with you?' quipped Ruben .

'No, they will stay here until we are done. They are also part of my insurance policy. If you trick me they will kill you all.'

'Understood. Right, I will fit the Cube on your arm. It will then contact you telepathically and configure its settings to be commanded by you,' explained Ruben.

Xl-R, prepare to configure new "ghost" settings and engage four Nano-Cubies, sent Ruben.

Ruben picked up the Cube and configured it to Solved-Mode-Four. He pressed the centre axis white and yellow jewels and it morphed onto Enzó's arm. The President watched in silence as the scene unfolded.

'Right, in a few moments the Cube will give you instructions. Do as it says.'

'Ruben, you can't let him have it. He will change history, who knows what will happen,' pleaded János, over-acting a little.

'What can I do?' asked Ruben.

Enzó was silent as he concentrated on the Cube. There were four flashes of yellow light as four silver Nano-Cubie spheres shot from the Cube. One hovered over each Time-Warrior and bathed them each, in a cocoon of yellow light. They were motionless. Enzó smiled knowingly. *@#$$, this doesn't look good,* thought János.

XL-R, Time-Freeze this room now, sent Ruben.

Suddenly time stopped. Enzó's smile was frozen. He looked at János and the President. They were living statues. Ruben went over to János, who winked and started to move. He then went over to the President and touched her on the forehead. She instantly came "alive".

'Okay, Madam President and Dad, we need to get out of here quick. Let's go to the bunker. Can you lead the way, Ma'am?' asked Ruben.

She led the men back through the cabin to the special doorway in the back bedroom. She punched in a security code and the door opened to reveal a heavy metal shutter. The President pressed her hand on the

476

print reader and with a loud "clunk" it slowly swung open. They went into a corridor and another set of doors. Again, the President put her palm on the reader and the door opened to reveal an armed guard. Without hesitation, János hit him hard, sending him reeling backwards across the floor, out cold.

'He was one of my men,' exclaimed the President.

'Oops, so was the other guy and look what happened to him,' said János, as he bent down and picked up the gun.

He dragged him in and bound his hands together with his belt. The President went to get her children. They squealed with delight as she picked them up for a hug. After they had calmed down she quickly got them some food and left them to watch the television while she rejoined the others.

'So, what happens now,' she asked.

'Well Ma'am, if you watch the monitors you will see,' replied Ruben.

The inhabitants of the cabin lounge were still motionless, trapped in a moment of frozen time.

XL-R, disengage Time-Freeze, sent Ruben.

Time-Freeze disengaged, sent XL-R.

Immediately, Enzó and the four Time-Warriors looked around the room. The others had just vanished. He looked at the Cube on his wrist and spun the segments around into a new configuration. Suddenly there was an almighty explosion and a blinding flash as he vapourised. They could feel the vibration from the safety of the bunker. They continued to watch the monitors. The four Time-Warriors had taken the full impact of the blast that had floored them. Slowly they all got up, still shrouded in a yellow glow. Before they could figure out what had just happened there was another loud explosion and the first Nano-Cubie detonated, vapourising one of the Time-Warriors into oblivion. Then there were another three deafening blasts as all the others were totally and utterly obliterated.

'And that, as they say, is the end of that,' quipped Ruben.

The room was silent.

'Err, what about your Cube device?' asked the President, tentatively.

'Dad, roll up your sleeve.'

János pulled back his cuff to reveal the Cube.

'The one Enzó had was just a non-functioning copy I made before we got here, while the General was busy. I knew there was something odd about the General, so I took precautions.

'I used the Cube to rig the whole situation,' explained Ruben.

'But what about the final red jewel you put in the copy?' asked Dad.

'Ah, I'm quite chuffed about that. You saw I put the dodgy jewel and the one Enzó had on the table. Well, when I deliberately knocked the candelabra over I switched the jewels and palmed the real one,'

Ruben opened his hand to reveal the jewel.

'The quickness of the hand deceives the eye,' he chuckled, to rapturous applause from the very small, but appreciative audience.

'Brilliant, quite brilliant,' congratulated János.

'Indeed, very clever,' added the President. 'You are quite a special young man.'

'Thank you Ma'am. So I don't think we will be hearing from those guys again. Now we have to sort out this satellite business. How do we go about that, Ma'am?' asked Ruben.

'Okay, firstly I will need to brief Octagon HQ on what has happened here, then we will sort out the use of the Global Defence System. I have an operations room here in the bunker. Make yourselves at home, as much as you can. There is food and drink etcetera in the kitchen. Help yourselves and I will be back shortly.'

Just then the secret service agent stumbled into the room..

'Hey, I am really sorry I walloped you so hard. I thought you were one of them,' said János.

'Huh, that's okay. All part of the job, I guess. It was my partner who was the double-crossing one, not me,' explained the agent. 'Perhaps you could undo your belt from my wrists now.'

'Yes, of course. Can I get you a drink or something as a peace offering?' asked János.

'No, I'll be fine after a rest. Thank you,'

'Ah, Agent Rickenbacker, I hear you have been lying down on the job. How's your head? Glad you could join us,' chuckled the President, as she returned to the room with her two children. They gingerly hid behind their mother as she proudly introduced them to János and Ruben.

'Now please excuse me for just a moment. I need to get them some drinks and settled, then we can get on. Agent Rickenbacker, would you mind coming with me? Thanks,' said the President.

Ruben went to the kitchen and made some coffees.

'So, hopefully, Madam President should be able to sort the next bit quite quickly given what she now knows,' said János.

'Indeed, we have all the data stored in the Cube. I should fit that last red cell while we have the time.'

XL-R disengage from temporary host, sent Ruben.
Disengaging temporary host, sent XL-R.

The Cube appeared in Ruben's hands and he reconfigured into Solved-Mode-Six, and placed it on the table.

XL-R, prepare to eject malfunctioning jewel and accept replacement.

The Cube began to flash the red jewels then the middle one went out. With a gentle "click" the jewel was ejected. Ruben replaced it with the one Enzó had.

Reconfiguring system. Installing new update. Confirming new operating bias coding. Waiting. New system fully configured. All systems are running at maximum functional capability, sent XL-R.

'Good, right, the Cube is now running at 100 per cent functionality,' announced Ruben.

He pressed the white centre axis jewel and the Cube morphed back onto his wrist

'Finally, it is done,' said János, with a sigh of relief.

'Well done Ruben, amazing achievement.'

A few minutes later the President returned to the room.

'Right, gentlemen, shall we get on. If you care to follow me we can get started.'

Ruben and János went with her into another side room. It was packed with monitors and associated hardware, and lots of little LEDs flashing and blinking.

'Wow, this looks like a mini mission control,' enthused Ruben.

'Yes, I suppose it does, and I suppose it is' she replied.

'What is that big red button for?' asked Ruben, pointing to a large control panel.

'Oh, nothing really. We won't be using that today or, hopefully, ever,' she replied. 'Right, let me access our Global Defence System.' The President lent over to the facial recognition scanner and waited for the beam to move over the surface of her features. Two circular beams then concentrated on her eyes and scanned them, then the rest of the face was mapped. The computer screen proceeded to flash up the Global Defence System logo. The President entered a long octadecimal password to complete her login. She quickly navigated through to the satellite section.

'Right, I need all the data concerning the frequency of the transmission,' requested the President.

'Sure, no problem. I will link the Cube to your mainframe and it will transfer all the data,' replied Ruben.

'That won't be possible as the system encryption will stop it.'

'With all due respect, Ma'am, by the time I finish this sentence the Cube will have broken your encryption,' said Ruben.

Immediately the computer monitor flashed up a new message: "Data download complete".

'Oh I see what you mean,' conceded the President.' That really is an amazing piece of equipment you have there, and rather worrying for us.'

She spent the next few minutes tapping away on the keyboard as screens of data flashed by.

'Okay, we're done. The Global Defence System should be transmitting on the programmed frequency within ten to fifteen minutes. We will get a notification when it begins. So let us get a drink to celebrate.'

'Fantastic, I think we may have averted a global tragedy,' said János.

'What you and Ruben have done is nothing short of unbelievable. I think I can probably speak for the whole world, when I say "thank you". This could make you famous.'

'Thank you, Madam President. I think we would prefer to keep this just between you and us, if you don't mind,' said Ruben.

'Understood. Of course, that is a very wise decision. I think there could be a lot of people who would be interested in your Cube device, and not necessarily for the right reasons, as we have seen.'

'Yes, a lot of those people would try to use it for their own ends.'

'Well, I guess we are done here. So I think we will make a move back home. I expect this place is going to need a major rebuild. I am sorry about the mess, but I don't think there was any way round it,' said Ruben trying to apologise.

'No, don't worry. It can be rebuilt again.'

'So we will be monitoring the cloud and the health implications, and will be in touch very soon. Here is my card,' said János.

He had written a little cryptic note for the President explaining that the satellites must keep transmitting until "we" are sure there is no danger to health, and all infection is eradicated completely once the cloud has descended and days get back to normal. This would help explain who he was, just in case she forgot.

'Oh, thanks. I will put this in my Contacts right away. I don't want to lose your number. I am sure we will be in touch in the near future.' She read the note.

Ruben quickly went to the cloakroom and hid an auto self-destruct, Nano-Mind-Wipe Cubie that would erase all knowledge of the Cube. He returned to the room.

'Well, Madam President, we must be off now. We will be in touch,' said János.

They all shook hands and said their goodbyes.

XL-R, set Nano-Mind-Wipe Cubie for this area after we have teletransported to current timeline home location, sent Ruben.

He manipulated the Cube's segments into Solved-Mode-Six and pressed the yellow, green and white centre axis jewels. It was 22:37 and in a blue flash they were both gone.

■ ■ ■

LOCATION-JUMP
22:37 SATURDAY, 19TH JULY, NOVAK RESIDENCE, LOS ANGELES, USA
PRESENT DAY

Ruben and János appeared in the TV lounge to find Kat watching the Vintage Sci-Fi channel.

'Dad, quick, move out of the way. I'm trying to watch "Star Trek-The Next Generation". Spock and Kirk have just beamed down to the planet,' said Kat.

The delicious irony of the situation was not lost on Ruben and his dad.

'Gosh I know how they feel, let's have a look at your ears Dad,' quipped Ruben, as they both dutifully stepped aside.

'It's so good to be home,' said János.

Just then Sarah walked in.

'Hello you two. I was wondering where you were.'

She gave János an affectionate hug and a tender kiss. She wrapped her arms around Ruben and kissed his cheek. Kat got up and joined the family hug. It was a moment to treasure.

'It has been quite a busy few days. I am so glad we found the solution to the cloud particle problem. It was such an honour to meet the President,' said János.

'Wow, you met the President? repeated Kat, in disbelief.

'Yup, we sure did. It's a long story. I'll tell you all about it, at some point, but suffice to say, she really helped us,' continued Ruben.

'You have been amazing Ruben. We are all so proud of you,' said Sarah.

'Thanks. Dad helped me a lot and your love gave me the strength I needed to do this,' said Ruben.

He rolled back his sleeve to reveal the Cube.

'And, we should all thank the Cube. Without it we would have failed, big time. At least tomorrow I can relax as I don't have to go to Miami now. I can see Frankie.'

They all laughed. The rest of the evening was spent in quality family time, a family that would soon be growing, watching the hit UK soap opera "The Real Housewives Of Crouch End" on Channel5H1T. Ruben was looking forward to the party at Frankie's house a week on Sunday. It was going to be a memorable evening. After a celebratory nightcap they all went to bed.

Ruben opened the door to his bedroom and saw the welcoming sight of his Salmon Pink 1962 Fender Stratocaster guitar. He grabbed it from the stand and peeled off a few legato cascades of meaningless twaddle, then popped it back on the stand. He was home. He pressed the white centre axis jewel and the Cube morphed onto his hand. He placed it on his bedside pod. He went into the bathroom and turned on the shower music system. As the steam began to rise he stepped into the cubicle to wash away the stress of the day.

Suddenly the orange, blue and yellow centre axis jewels on the Cube began to flash as the segments whizzed around into a new configuration. A blue holographic beam began projecting a faint, ghostly image into the room. It began to speak intermittently as the crackling signal drifted in and out.

'Ruben, can you hear m-? It's Ov--lord —--ki-Bur. Are you th---?, can —-- hear me?' said the broken up transmission. 'Our ar-y ha- —een defe---d and the pl--et —--stroyed. I ha-- stowed aw-y on one of o-r own, hij--ked, —-cape ships w--- a few of m- —ellow re---ance fight---. —e are hea--ng to your planet, are y-u p----red. I —-ed to —--ak wi-- —o- ur---y. —--------------.'

The transmission ended and the holographic projection faded. A while later, a sparklingly clean Ruben walked into the bedroom. He happened to glance at the Cube. *That's an unusual configuration*, he thought, just as Katarina walked into his room.

'Ruben I have just had the strangest telepathic message, did you get it too?'

THE END... is just the beginning

ACKNOWLEDGEMENTS

Having spent the last few years nurturing the idea of writing a young adult action novel with the Rubik's Cube™ centre stage the time came to actually write it and there were some special people who made it possible. I could not have written a page of it without the unerring support of my darling Dee, my toy inventing widow, guitar playing widow and now book widow. She has kept everything in our family moving while I buried myself in yet another project, this time in the lives of an entirely different, but strangely familiar family. *All my love Dee xx*

We all draw inspiration from those around us, and for that I thank our special son, Sam. He has provided the soundtrack for this book, supplying the beats upstairs that have kept me on the rhythm of writing. He was always going to be my Ruben. *Love you xx*

Thanks to by brother Mike and his family, Dad looking down on us, miss you every day, and my dear Mum, for being the best Mum in the world, and for inspiring parts of the story too. *Love you all xx*

I would also like to thank my dear friend Martin, who has always been hovering on my shoulder and providing much needed laughs and unusual open-tunings. Many thanks to Sheila Nforno, Hayley Woodward and the Rubik's team at Spin Master Limited, for believing in me and my crazy idea, to Jamie Brownhill for turning my scribble into his fantastic cover artwork, to Phil Webb for checking my attempts at graphic design and to Sue Rylance for casting her expert eye over my manuscript and associated material.

I would also like to thank my friends (purely by coincidence) Vince Legg, John Gardonyi, Mark Chase, Chris Hare, Martin Keatman (again), Paul Martin, Kevin Jefferies, John Beaufoy, Phil Webb, Alan Flude (miss you matey), Craig Huxley, Richard Carter, Steve Mills, Richard Crowe and John Fry (wherever you are?) for filling my life with music. Hi to all my other friends who have dotted themselves around the world, and all my Seven Towns toy design chums.

Finally I would like to thank Ernő Rubik for inventing such an amazing, world famous, mind-boggling puzzle. The signed cube he gave me a while ago, still sits proudly on my desk.

For all things book related:
rubennovak.com
christopherbeach.co.uk

ABOUT THE AUTHOR

Toys have always been part of my life, from the joys of Lego, to playing out my wildest fantasies through the exploits of my team of Action Man figures. One of life's pivotal moments happened on a wet Cornish Sunday in 1979. Having spent many weeks idly fiddling with a Rubik's Cube™, on this special day I was suddenly aware that in my hands was a solved cube. Wow, amazing.

As I grew up my 'boys toys' morphed into musical instruments, but that original affection for my playthings stayed with me mentally and physically, stored in my loft. A few years later and I found myself actually making and designing them for many of the major games companies across the world. I also have managed to bring some of my own designs to market: The Rubik's Safe Cube, Dinky Inks, Fantasy Flowers, Secret Treats, The Golden Coin Maker and Thumb Warriors.

To this day I continue to work in the toy industry, inventing, designing and producing highly detailed prototype models. It is an ongoing challenge to solve design problems and find solutions to bring ideas to life.

My love of toys is as strong as ever and the challenge of writing an adventure story about the most famous puzzle in the world was one I couldn't resist.